Meanjin

Meanjin *Anthology*

First Published 1940

MELBOURNE
UNIVERSITY
PRESS

MELBOURNE UNIVERSITY PRESS
An imprint of Melbourne University Publishing Limited
187 Grattan Street, Carlton, Victoria 3053, Australia
mup-info@unimelb.edu.au
www.mup.com.au

First published 2012
Text © individual pieces remains with individual contributors, 2012
Design and typography © Melbourne University Publishing Limited, 2012

Cover design by Jenny Grigg
Typeset by Sonya Murphy, Typeskill
Printed by Griffin Press, South Australia

National Library of Australia Cataloguing-in-Publication entry

Meanjin anthology / edited by Sally Heath ... [et al.]

9780522861556 (pbk.)
9780522861563 (ebook)

Anthologies.
Australian poetry.
Australian literature.

Other Authors/Contributors: Heath, Sally.

A820.8

THE UNIVERSITY OF
MELBOURNE

Australian Government

Australia Council
for the Arts

CONTENTS

CONTENTS

CONTENTS

Foreword

Gerald Murnane

This piece of writing might well be called 'Return of *Meanjin*' or '*Meanjin* strikes back'. Exactly fifty years have passed since I first struggled to compose something fit for *Meanjin*, and here I am, going at the task again and finding it hardly less trouble. Moreover, nearly twenty years have passed since I decided not to renew my subscription to *Meanjin*. I had taken early retirement from my position as a teacher of fiction writing in a university. During my sixteen years as a teacher, I had subscribed to *Meanjin* and every other Australian magazine publishing fiction. I needed to advise the best of my students where they might send the best of their writing. Sometimes my advice proved sound—not a few of my students achieved what I had never achieved and had an unsolicited contribution published in *Meanjin*. In the early 1990s, however, I not only gave up teaching fiction—I gave up writing and reading the stuff for the time being and followed other interests. Three years ago, I even left Melbourne, where I had lived continuously for sixty years. Of course, I had not forgotten *Meanjin* but here, in a stone cottage near Little Desert, and with no computer or mobile phone, I would have supposed that *Meanjin* had forgotten me. Not at all. Near me on the floor is a pile of back copies sent to me yesterday by the editor after I had been persuaded to do this piece of writing. I spent most of today looking through them, surprised at how interested I was after all these years and pondering the question, why has *Meanjin* flourished for so long?

Meanjin and I are almost exact contemporaries. I was born just a few kilometres north of the present *Meanjin* office in the year before *Meanjin* was born in Brisbane. Each of us had had a few narrow squeaks over the years but each seems in excellent health today, although the younger of us will surely outlive the older. I did not enrol at university until my mid-twenties, and so my early mental map of Melbourne had as its literary centre Cheshire's Bookshop, which a few readers might remember as being situated below street level in Little Collins Street, just West of Elizabeth Street. Fittingly, I found one day in Cheshire's the first copy of *Meanjin* that I had yet seen. I found there also—and bought and took home and pored over—other little magazines, so to call them, but *Meanjin* seemed superior, even to my unpractised gaze. I was interested mostly in the published poetry, for I thought of myself at that time as a poet.

For several years in the early 1960s I sent batches of poems to *Meanjin* and other magazines. At that time, I knew no one who read or wrote poetry, let alone assessed it or published it, and so the few comments that came back with my rejected poems seemed messages in bottles from unknown lands. I got a sardonic comment from James McAuley, a pompous put-down from Max Harris, and a tentative message of encouragement from Clem Christesen, the founding editor of *Meanjin*. Clem's few words not only confirmed my belief in *Meanjin's* superiority but caused me to perceive a sort of welcoming aura about the magazine. Even so, I was probably less naive than the young man I seem to remember. Clem's brief annotation contained only generalities and no reference to any of my poems, and I surely felt, while I re-read his well-meant words, what I would feel time and time again in later years: that most literary criticism is of no interest or use to a writer.

Fast-forward, as they say, a quarter of a century … In late 1989 I was fiction consultant for *Meanjin* and one of a team compiling *The Temperament of Generations*, a book meant to celebrate the fiftieth anniversary of the magazine. As part of my work, I spent hours looking through the *Meanjin* archive in the Baillieu Library at the University of Melbourne. I learned how humble had been the origins of the magazine. I learned that the first issue had something of a vanity publication about it— the editor's own poems were prominent among the contents. (Several early issues also had poems or prose by the editor.) During my years as a teacher of writing, I had seen many a small magazine launched in rather more promising circumstances than attended the birth of *Meanjin*. Many of those magazines had failed after a year or two, and yet poor, skinny *Meanjin* soon began to thrive. Leafing through the archive, I was astonished by the swift development of not only the magazine but also its editor. To judge from the earliest editorials, Clem Christesen had never lacked for confidence, but as *Meanjin* developed from a collection of poetry and short fiction into a prestigious journal of ideas its editor managed to deal assuredly with all manner of academics and experts and to earn the respect of most.

While I looked through the archive, I was more interested in the fiction and the poetry than in the social and political material. I had seen in early issues a number of short stories and poems that I considered unworthy of publication, but I was satisfied by the bulk of the literary contents and I would have liked to read in some form or another the editor's explaining what he looked for in fiction and poetry: how he distinguished between good and inferior writing. The nearest I found was a passage in which he dwelt on the word *quality*. He was defending himself against the suggestion that he was influenced by political bias when selecting items for publication. He insisted that he looked only for *quality*. The word had a fine sound to it, but Christesen's waving it like a magic sword helped me not at all to learn what he was thinking and feeling when he decided which of two poems or short stories would fill the last available space in his magazine.

Before I began this piece of writing, there occurred to me a notion persuasive enough to satisfy me and yet vague enough to be safe from disproof. While I was making notes, I supposed I was preparing to write for a magazine that never was but might have been and ought yet to be: a Holy Grail of magazines; a better-than-ever-yet *Meanjin*. Now, as I compose these sentences, I indulge my fancy further. I feel the ghostly presence of notable writers from earlier issues of *Meanjin* demanding my best from me and warning me against mediocrity or worse. I would like to think these imaginings of mine would make sense to Clem Christesen and later editors of the magazine he founded. I would like to think that he and they were trying continually to put together my conjectured *Meanjin* of *Meanjin*s; that he and they felt themselves often so crowded around by so many talented and passionate writers, scholars, thinkers, and would-be reformers that they, the editors, found their judgment being screwed to a higher pitch and so excelled themselves.

I met Clem Christesen only once. He had been retired from the magazine for fifteen years but the then-editor, Jenny Lee, took me to meet him at his home in Eltham—I forget why. It was a strange afternoon. Clem stayed behind closed doors in his study for several hours while Jenny and I were entertained by his charming wife, Nina. Just before we left, Jenny and I were separately shown into Clem's study, there to be presented with a signed copy of a published collection of his prose and poetry. I myself had had five books of fiction published at the time but as I approached his room I overheard Clem asking Nina to tell him again what my name was. Whenever I recall our brief meeting, I think of a comment made by someone after visiting the elderly Thomas Hardy. 'He was no longer a novelist; he had been delivered of his novels.' Clem Christesen had been delivered of *Meanjin*. After thirty and more years of strenuous editing, he had gone back to what he had been before: a minor writer on the margins of the literary world. But the ideal *Meanjin* that had exercised him for half his lifetime still existed and still exists today. Perhaps its nearest embodiment is the book in your hands.

1940s

Battle (1942)

Vance Palmer

The next few months may decide not only whether we are to survive as a nation, but whether we deserve to survive. As yet none of our achievements prove it, at any rate in the sight of the outer world. We have no monuments to speak of, no dreams in stone, no Guernicas, no sacred places. We could vanish and leave singularly few signs that, for some generations, there had lived a people who had made a homeland of this Australian earth. A homeland? To how many people was it primarily that? How many penetrated the soil with their love and imagination? We have had no peasant population to cling passionately to their few acres, throw down tenacious roots, and weave a natural poetry into their lives by invoking the little gods of creek and mountain. The land has been something to exploit, to tear out a living from and then sell at a profit. Our settlements have always had a fugitive look, with their tin roofs and rubbish heaps. Even our towns ... the main street cluttered with shops, the million-dollar town hall, the droves of men and women intent on nothing but buying or selling, the suburban retreats of rich drapers! Very little to show the presence of a people with a common purpose or a rich sense of life.

If Australia had no more character than could be seen on its surface, it would be annihilated as surely and swiftly as those colonial outposts white men built for their commercial profit in the East— pretentious facades of stucco that looked imposing as long as the wind kept from blowing. But there is an Australia of the spirit, submerged and not very articulate, that is quite different from these bubbles of old-world imperialism. Born of the lean loins of the country itself, of the dreams of men who came here to form a new society, of hard conflicts in many fields, it has developed a toughness all its own. Sardonic, idealist, tongue-tied perhaps, it is the Australia of all who truly belong here. When you are away, it takes a human image, an image that emerges, brown and steady-eyed from the background of dun cliffs, treed bushlands, and tawny plains. More than a generation ago, it found voice in the writings of Lawson, O'Dowd, Bedford, and Tom Collins: it has become even more aware of itself since. And it has something to contribute to the world. Not emphatically in the arts as yet, but in arenas of action, and in ideas for the creation of that egalitarian democracy that will have to be the basis of all civilised societies in the future.

This is the Australia we are called upon to save. Not merely the mills and mines, and the higgledy-piggledy towns that have grown up along the coast: not the assets we hold or the debts we owe. For even if we were conquered by the Japanese, some sort of normal life would still go on. You cannot wipe out a nation of seven million people, or turn them all into wood-and-water joeys. Sheep would continue to be bred, wheat raised; there would be work for the shopkeeper, the clerk, the baker, the butcher. Not everyone could be employed pulling Japanese gentlemen about in rickshaws.

Some sort of comfort might even be achieved by the average man under Japanese dominance; but if anyone believes life would be worth living under the terms offered, he is not worth saving. There is no hope for him unless a breath of the heroic will around him stirs him to come out of the body of this death. Undoubtedly we have a share of the decadent elements that have proved a deadly weakness in other countries—whisperers, fainthearts, near-fascists, people who have grown rotten through easy living; and these are often people who have had power in the past and now feel it falling away from them. We will survive according to our swiftness in pushing them into the background and liberating the people of will, purpose, and intensity; those who are at one with Australia's spirit and are capable of moulding the future.

I believe we will survive; that what is significant in us will survive; that we will come out of this struggle battered, stripped to the bone,

but spiritually sounder than we went in, surer of our essential charac-
ter, adults in a wider world than the one we lived in hitherto. These
are great, tragic days. Let us accept them stoically, and make every
yard of Australian earth a battle station.

Letter to Tom Collins: Mateship (1943)

Manning Clark

Geelong Grammar School Victoria

Dear Tom,

I feel embarrassed in addressing you by your Christian name—in this your centenary year; nor does your hatred of pretentiousness, your enthusiasm for intimacy put me at my ease. Australian writers have become more polite, more formal since your departure from human society; the drawing-room has replaced the drover's hut. I don't think you would like us if you came back to earth. We wince at the behaviour you approved of. Perhaps it is 'matey' or 'friendly-like' to call you Tom, to use the vernacular to communicate our experiences to you. You and Lawson almost canonised the word 'mate.' 'Mateyness,' I believe, made life bearable for you; it was your metaphysical comforter. A true mate was a 'dinkum Aussie,' a real pal. Please don't think that I disapprove of your sentiments, that I am ridiculing the ideal which warmed your heart. The French were the inspiration for all men of good will when they were the apostles of 'fraternité.' But … yes, you should see what has happened to your ideal 'Dad and Dave,' 'having a good time,' and then the sneer of the upper 1000 at the vulgarity of things Australian. This hurts us, Tom, and I believe it would hurt you. So I ask you: what are we to do about Dad and Dave, about this ideal of yours which embarrasses the elite and sustains the vulgar? You see there is a rift in our society—the elite flee to the garret, to the polite drawing-room, to Europe, while the people ape the mate ideal, being bonzer sorts! I am not asking you to feel penitent, to take back what you said. I am addressing you because I believe you tried to do some-thing worth while—to interpret Australian life.

6

I said you and Lawson gave us the ideal of being 'mates,' that it was your comforter. But I wonder whether either of you had the courage to say what you really felt about Australian life. Perhaps you were horrified, even terrified and thought that things would not be quite so bad with a mate, that if men huddled together, if they were as endearing to each other as little children they would repress the awful spectacle you saw. Yes, Tom, in Australia we are all afraid; and you and Lawson had a great chance to explain why, because by your time the excitement of the discovery was over: man had uncovered the woman he was to live with (queer, Tom, how expectancy distorts a judgment). Yet you do not seem to have noticed the queer relationship between man and earth in Australia: how he treated her as a harlot, frenziedly raped her for her wealth—wool, gold, wheat; no wonder his conscience was uneasy, no wonder he was restless. The monuments he erected, the houses he gave his fellow men, the entertainments he provided—vulgar, meretricious, pretentious. It was beginning even in your time. Yes, and the swaggering, and the sensitivity to criticism— this was the behaviour of guilty men. Yet you did not see how ill we were, nor how profound our despair was to become.

Even if life with the drovers was exciting, if their company warmed your heart, and made you feel glad, I still cannot understand how you repressed the painful sensations left by our countryside. It hurt Lawson—despair with it is always seeping through his mind. You may remember this passage from his story: '... Plains like dead seas ... scrub indescribably dismal—everything damp, dark and unspeakably dreary.'

Perhaps man's environment is always hostile; perhaps his works are always vile. But we cannot live by that faith. We spew it out. The queer thing is that we are tortured by doubt. Civilised life with us is artificial. It is a shock to see houses, churches, even towns in Australia. And because we are aware of a gulf between the acquired idea of what life could be, and what our environment insidiously suggests—was sun-bathing popular in your time, Tom?—we behave like guilty though we were concealing some crime. So we must ask

7

the dreadful question: do we belong here? I do not mean to imply that the country belongs to the aborigines, or that our sense of guilt Children, as is due to the crime our ancestors committed against those strange members of human society. In that we are disinterested. The emotions roused on that score are 'salon' emotions—not conducive to action! What I am saying is that this myth of 'mateyness' which you preached to your generation is just not enough: we want, curse us, the something more. I know that we have only vulgarised the ideal of the Europeans who believed that affection would bind men together when the old comforters were removed. And perhaps it is only over-refinement or squeamishness which makes us jib at being 'mates'; or perhaps it is the peculiar environment which rouses these cursed doubts in our minds, and makes us only half believers. Do we need a prophet to preach a new myth, or a sage to convince us that it is better to accept things as they are, better to forget the something more? If the dead stand by and help, we need you now. Tom, because the unhappy want us to confess our failure, to embrace the old faith. When we see Dad and Dave we feel angry with you and Lawson. When we contemplate the alternative we are thankful for you and your ideal. I wonder what we will do.

Yours ever,
MANNING CLARK

The Man who Bowled Victor Trumper (1945)

Dal Stivens

Ever hear how I bowled Victor Trumper for a duck? he asked.

—No, I said.

—He was a beautiful bat, he said. He had wrists like steel and he moved like a panther. The ball sped from his bat as though fired by a cannon.

The three of us were sitting on the verandah of the pub at Yerranderie in the Burragorang Valley in the late afternoon. The sun fell full on the fourteen hundred foot sandstone cliff behind us but the rest of the valley was already dark. A road ran past the pub and the wheeltracks were eighteen inches deep in the hard summer-baked road.

—There was a batsman for you, he said.

He was a big fat man with a chin like a cucumber. He had worked in the silver mines at Yerranderie. The last had closed in 1928 and for a time he had worked in the coalmines further up the valley and then had retired on a pension and a half an inch of good lung left.

—Dust in my lungs, he said. All my own fault. The money was good. Do you know, if I tried to run a hundred yards I'd drop dead.

The second man was another retired miner but he had all his lungs. He had a hooked nose and had lost the forefinger and thumb of his right hand.

Before they became miners, they said, they had tried their hand at many jobs in the bush.

—Ever hear how I fought Les Darcy? the big fat man asked.

—No, I said.

—He was the best fighter we have ever had in Australia. He was poetry in action. He had a left that moved like quicksilver.

—He was a great fighter, I said.

—He was like a Greek god, said the fat man reverently.

We sat watching the sun go down. Just before it dipped down beside the mountain it got larger and we could look straight at it. In no time it had gone.

—Ever hear how I got Vic. Trumper?

—No, I said. Where did it happen?

—It was in a match up at Bourke. Tibby Cotter was in the same team. There was a man for you. His fastest ball was like a thunder-bolt. He was a bowler and a half.

—Yes, I said.

—You could hardly see the ball after it left his hand. They put two lots of matting down when he came to Bourke so he wouldn't kill anyone.

—I never saw him, I said, but my father says he was very fast.

—Fast! says the fat man. He was so fast you never knew anything until you heard your wicket crash. In Bourke he split seven stumps and we had to borrow the school kids' set.

It got cold and we went into the bar and ordered three rums, which we drank with milk. The miner who had all his lungs said:

—I saw Tibby Cotter at the Sydney Cricket Ground and the Englishmen were scared of him.

—He was like a tiger as he bounded up to bowl, said the big fat man.

—He had even Ranji bluffed, said the other miner. Indians have special eyesight, but it wasn't enough to play Tibby.

We all drank together and ordered again. It was my shout.

—Ever hear about the time I fought Les Darcy? the big fat man asked me.

—No, I said.

—There wasn't a man in his weight to touch him, said the miner who had all his lungs. When he moved his arm you could see the muscles ripple across his back.

—When he hit them you could hear the crack in the back row of the Stadium, said the fat man.

—They poisoned him in America, said the other miner.

—Never gave him a chance, said the fat man.

—Poisoned him like a dog, said the other.

—It was the only way they could beat him, said the fat man. There wasn't a man at his weight that could live in the same ring as Les Darcy.

The barmaid filled our glasses up again and we drank a silent toast. Two men came in. One was carrying a hurricane lantern. The fat man said the two men always came in this night for a drink and that the tall man in the raincoat was the caretaker at one of the derelict mines.

—Ever hear about the kelpie bitch I had once? said the fat man. She was as intelligent and wide-awake as you are. She almost talked. It was when I was droving.

The fat miner paid this time.

—There isn't a dog in the bush to touch a kelpie for brains, said the miner with the hooked nose and the fingers short.

—Kelpies can do almost anything but talk, said the fat man.

—Yes, I said. I have never had one but I have heard my father talk of one that was wonderful for working sheep.

—All kelpies are beautiful to watch working sheep but the best was a little bitch I had at Bourke, said the fat man. Ever hear how I bowled Victor Trumper for a duck?

—No, I said. But what about this kelpie?

—I could have got forty quid for her any time for the asking, said the fat miner. I could talk about her all day. Ever hear about the time I forgot the milk for her pups? Sold each of the pups later for a tenner.

—You can always get a tenner for a good kelpie pup, said the miner who had all his lungs.

—What happened when you forgot the pups' milk? I said.

—It was in the bucket, the fat miner said, and the pups couldn't reach it. I went into the kitchen and the bitch was dipping her tail

11

in the milk bucket and then lowering it to the pups. You can believe that or not, as you like.

—I believe you, I said.

—I don't, said the other miner.

—What, you don't believe me! cried the fat miner, turning to the other. Don't you believe I bowled Victor Trumper for a duck? Don't you believe I fought Les Darcy? Don't you believe a kelpie could do that?

—I believe you bowled Vic. Trumper for a duck, said the other. I believe you fought Les Darcy. I believe a kelpie would do that.

The fat miner said: You had me worried for a minute. I thought you didn't believe I had a kelpie like that.

—That's it, said the miner who had all his lungs. I don't believe you had a kelpie like that.

—You tell me who had a kelpie like that if I didn't, the fat miner said.

—I'll tell you, said the miner with the hooked nose. You never had a kelpie like that, but I did. You've heard me talk about that little bitch many times.

They started getting mad with each other then so I said:

—How did you get Vic. Trumper for a duck?

—There was a batsman for you, said the fat man. He used a bat like a sword and he danced down the wicket like a panther.

Dust (1945)

Judith Wright

This sick dust, spiralling with the wind,
is harsh as grief's taste in our mouths
and has eclipsed the small sun.
The remnant earth turns evil,
the steel-shocked land has turned against the plough
and runs with wind all day; and all night
sighs in our sleep against the windowpane.

Wind was kinder once, carrying cloud
like a waterbag on his shoulder; sun was kinder,
hardening the good wheat brown as a strong man.
Earth was kinder, suffering fire and plough,
breeding the unaccustomed harvest.
Leaning in our doorway together
watching the birdcloud shadows,
the fleetwing windshadows travel our clean wheat
we thought ourselves rich already.
We counted the beautiful money
and gave it in our hearts to the child asleep,
who must never break his body
against the plough and the stubborn rock and tree.

But the wind rises; but the earth rises,
running like an evil river; but the sun grows small,
and when we turn to each other, our eyes are dust
and our words dust.
Dust has overtaken our dreams that were
wider and richer than wheat under the sun,

and war's eroding gale scatters our sons
with a million other grains of dust.
O sighing at the blistered door, darkening the evening star,
the dust accuses. Our dream was the wrong dream,
our strength was the wrong strength.
Weary as we are, we must make a new choice,
a choice more difficult than resignation,
more urgent than our desire of rest at the end of the day.
We must prepare the land for a difficult sowing,
a long and hazardous growth of a strange bread,
that our sons' sons may harvest and be fed.

1950s

The Cultural Cringe (1950)

Arthur Phillips

The Australian Broadcasting Commission has a Sunday programme, designed to cajole a mild Sabbatarian bestirment of the wits, called 'Incognito'. Paired musical performances are broadcast, one by an Australian, one by an overseas executant, but with the names and nationalities withheld until the end of the programme. The listener is supposed to guess which is the Australian and which the alien performer. The idea is that quite often he guesses wrong or gives it up because, strange to say, the local lad proves to be no worse than the foreigner. This unexpected discovery is intended to inspire a nice glow of patriotic satisfaction.

I am not jeering at the A.B.C. for its quaint idea. The programme's designer has rightly diagnosed a disease of the Australian mind and is applying a sensible curative treatment. The dismaying circumstance is that such a treatment should be necessary, or even possible; that in any nation, there should be an assumption that the domestic cultural product will be worse than the imported article.

The devil of it is that the assumption will often be correct. The numbers are against us, and an inevitable quantitative inferiority easily looks like a qualitative weakness, under the most favourable circumstances—and our circumstances are not favourable. We cannot shelter from invidious comparisons behind the barrier of a separate language; we have no long-established or interestingly different cultural tradition to give security and distinction to its interpreters; and the centrifugal pull of the great cultural metropolises works against us. Above our writers—and other artists—looms the intimidating mass of Anglo-Saxon culture. Such a situation almost inevitably produces the characteristic Australian Cultural Cringe— appearing either as the Cringe Direct, or as the Cringe Inverted, in the attitude of the Blatant Blatherskite, the God's-Own-Country and I'm-a-better man-than-you-are Australian Bore.

The Cringe mainly appears in an inability to escape needless comparisons. The Australian reader, more or less consciously, hedges and hesitates, asking himself 'Yes, but what would a cultivated Englishman think of this?' No writer can communicate confidently to a reader with the 'Yes, but' habit; and this particular demand is curiously crippling to critical judgment. Confronted by Furphy, we grow uncertain. We fail to recognise the extraordinarily original structure of his novel because we are wondering whether perhaps an Englishman might not find it too complex and self-conscious. No one worries about the structural deficiencies of *Moby Dick*. We do not fully savour the meaty individualism of Furphy's style because we are wondering whether perhaps his egotistic verbosity is not too Australianly crude; but we accept the egotistic verbosity of Borrow as part of his quality.

But the dangers of the comparative approach go deeper than this. The Australian writer normally frames his communication for the Australian reader. He assumes certain mutual preknowledge, a responsiveness to certain symbols, even the ability to hear the cadence of a phrase in the right way. Once the reader's mind begins to be nagged by the thought of how an Englishman might feel about this, he loses the fine edge of his Australian responsiveness. It is absurd to feel apologetic towards *Such Is Life*, or *Coonardoo* or *Melbourne Odes* because they would not seem quite right to an English reader; it is part of their distinctive virtue that no Englishman can fully understand them.

I once read a criticism which began from the question 'What would a French classicist think of *Macbeth*?' The analysis was discerningly conducted and had a certain paradoxical interest; but it could not escape an effect of comic irrelevance.

A second effect of the Cringe has been the estrangement of the Australian Intellectual. Australian life, let us agree, has an atmosphere of often dismaying crudity. I do not know if our cultural crust is proportionately any thinner than that of other Anglo-Saxon communities; but to the intellectual it seems thinner because, in a small community, there is not enough of it to provide for the individual a protective insulation. Hence, even more than most intellectuals, he feels a sense of exposure. This is made much worse by the intrusion of that deadly habit of English comparisons. There is a certain type of Australian intellectual who is forever sidling up to the cultivated Englishman, insinuating: 'I, of course, am not like these other crude Australians; I understand how you must feel about them; I should be spiritually more at home in Oxford or Bloomsbury.'

It is not the critical attitude of the intellectual that is harmful; that could be a healthy, even creative, influence, if the criticism were felt to come from within, if the critic had a sense of identification with his subject, if his irritation came from a sense of shared shame rather than a disdainful separation. It is his refusal to participate, the arch of his indifferent eyebrows, which exerts the chilling and stultifying influence.

Thinking of this type of Australian Intellectual, I am a little uneasy about my phrase 'Cultural Cringe'; it is so much the kind of missile which he delights to toss at the Australian mob. I hope I have made it clear that my use of the phrase is not essentially unsympathetic, and that I regard the denaturalised Intellectual as the Cringe's unhappiest victim. If any of the breed use my phrase for his own contemptuous purposes, my curse be upon him. May crudely-Dinkum Aussies spit in his beer, and gremlins split his ever to be preciously agglutinated infinitives.

The Australian writer is affected by the Cringe because it mists the responsiveness of his audience, and because its influence on the intellectual deprives the writer of a sympathetically critical atmosphere. Nor can he entirely escape its direct impact. There is a significant phrase in Henry Handel Richardson's *Myself When Young*. When she found herself stuck in a passage of Richard Mahony which would not come right, she remarked to her husband, 'How did I ever dare to write *Maurice Guest*—a poor little colonial like me?' Our sympathies go out to her—pathetic victim of the Cringe. For observe that the Henry Handel Richardson who had written *Maurice Guest* was not the raw girl encompassed by the limitations of the Kilmore Post Office and a Philistine mother. She had already behind her the years in Munich and a day-to-day communion with a husband steeped in the European literary tradition. Her cultural experience was probably richer than that of such contemporary novelists as Wells or Bennett. It was primarily the simple damnation of being an Australian which made her feel limited. Justified, you may think, by the tone of Australian life, with its isolation and excessively material emphasis? Examine the evidence fairly and closely, and I think you will agree that Henry Handel Richardson's Australian background was a shade richer in cultural influence than the dingy shop-cum stuffy Housekeeper's Room-cum sordid Grammar School which incubated Wells, or than the Five Towns of the eighteen-eighties.

By both temperament and circumstance, Henry Handel Richardson was peculiarly susceptible to the influence of the Cringe; but no Australian writer, unless he is dangerously insensitive, can wholly escape it; he may fight it down or disguise it with a veneer of truculence, but it must weaken his confidence and nag at his integrity.

It is not so much our limitations of size, youth and isolation which create the problem as the derivativeness of our culture; and it takes more difficult forms than the Cringe. The writer is particularly affected by our colonial situation because of the nature of his medium. The painter is in some measure bound by the traditional evolution of his art, the musician must consider the particular combinations of sound which the contemporary civilised ear can accept; but ultimately paint is always paint, a piano everywhere a piano. Language has no such ultimate physical existence; it is in its essence merely what generations of usage have made it. The three symbols m-a-n create the image of a male human being only because venerable English tradition has so decreed. The Australian writer cannot cease to be English even if he wants to. The nightingale does not sing under Australian skies; but he still sings in the literate Australian mind. It may thus become the symbol which runs naturally to the tip of the writer's pen; but he dare not use it because it has no organic relation with the Australian life he is interpreting.

The Jindyworobaks are entirely reasonable when they protest against the alien symbolisms used by O'Dowd, Brennan or McCrae; but the difficulty is not simply solved. A Jindyworobak writer uses the image 'galah-breasted dawn'. The picture is both fresh and accurate, and has a sense of immediacy because it comes direct from the writer's environment; and yet somehow it doesn't quite come off. The trouble is that we—unhappy Cringers—are too aware of the processes in its creation. We can feel the writer thinking: 'No, I mustn't use one of the images which English language tradition is insinuating into my mind; I must have something Australian: ah, yes—' What the phrase has gained in immediacy, it has lost in spontaneity. You have some measure of the complexity of the problem of a colonial culture when you reflect that the last sentence I have written is not so nonsensical as it sounds.

I should not, of course, suggest that the Australian image can never be spontaneously achieved; one need not go beyond Stewart's *Ned Kelly* to disprove such an assumption. On the other hand, the distracting influence of the English tradition is not restricted to merely linguistic difficulties. It confronts the least cringing Australian writer at half-a-dozen points.

What is the cure for our disease? There is no short-cut to the gradual processes of national growth—which are already beginning to have their effect. The most important development of the last twenty years in Australian writing has been the progress made in the art of being unself-consciously ourselves. If I have thought this article worth writing, it is because I believe that progress will quicken when we articulately recognise two facts: that the Cringe is a worse enemy to our cultural development than our isolation, and that the opposite of the Cringe is not the Strut, but a relaxed erectness of carriage.

Lena (1952)

John Morrison

Half-past three, and the usual note of irritation has crept into Lena's voice.

—Tins, Joe!

Without getting from my knees, I reach backwards, seize a couple of buckets, and push them through under the drooping eaves of the vines. Before I can release them they are grabbed and pulled violently away from me. Between the top leaves, and only fifteen inches away, I get a glimpse of a freckled little face, keen eyes leaping from bunch to bunch of the clustering grapes, always a split second in front of the darting fingers and slashing knife. I hear the thump of tumbling fruit, and get up wearily. No use trying to feed her with tins as we go—she's too quick, too experienced, too enthusiastic. Or is it just that I'm too old and too slow?

Empty tins are thrown only into alternate rows, leaving the other rows clear for the passing of the tractor that takes away the gathered fruit. Right from the start of picking it has fallen to me, no doubt as gentleman's privilege, to work that side of the vines where the empties are. As Lena and I make equal division of the day's earnings, I try to keep up with her, but every now and then forget to keep her supplied with tins.

—You should let me know before you cut right out, Lena, I say gently as I push the first ones through just ahead of her.

She doesn't answer, which means that she's lost patience with me. I, too, am irritated, irritated by this tally-anxiety that seizes her every day about this time. But I remind myself that at tea to-night, with the day's work over, she will forget everything, wait on me as though a devoted daughter, chatter brightly about the circus we're all going to in Redcliffs, ask me if I have anything for the wash to-morrow.

So I go about twenty yards down the row, pushing through a couple of tins every few feet, and say nothing until I get back.

It is a relief to bend my aching legs again, to press my knees into the warm red earth, to get my head out of the sun and stare into the cool recesses of the vine eaves. Off the first bunch of grapes I pull a handful, stuff them into my mouth, swallow the juice, and spit out the residue. While I was away Lena has conscientiously picked right through to my side, leaving only one or two clusters she can't reach, so that in only a few minutes I'm up with her again. I can't see her, but the violence with which she is banging the buckets tells me that she is still sulking.

—Angry with me? I ask.

No answer. I wait a few seconds, then bang a bucket myself just to let her see that I, too, can be provoked.

—You never have much to say this time of day, do you? I venture.

—You can't talk and work.

—You can in the mornings. You were telling me all about your dad before lunch.

—That's why we're behind. We only got two hundred and ten buckets this morning.

—Only? Isn't that good?

—We should have got two hundred and fifty. We'll be going flat out to get four hundred and fifty to-day.

—Do we have to get four hundred and fifty?

—Yes, she says very emphatically.

To that I give no reply. Everything I could say has already been said, more than once. I can, at the moment, think of no new lead in an argument which has become wearisome. To Lena, piecework is the road to riches—'the harder you work, the more you get.' She's too young to know anything of the days when armies of unemployed converged on the irrigation belt to struggle for a chance to pick grapes at 5s. a hundred tins. We're due for a visit from a union organiser; I keep wondering what she'll do when he asks her to take a ticket.

I'm working on, not saying a word, but she takes my silence as a sign of weakness, and presses the attack herself:

—It's all right for you. I need the money.

—We all need money, Lena.

—You'll get plenty when you get back to the wharves. And get it easier, too, I bet.

—Sometimes. It depends on what the cargo is. But we never get paid by the ton!

—Wharfies wouldn't work, anyway.

Hitting below the belt. She must be quite upset to say a thing like that. I let it go, though, because it would be a preposterous thing to fall out with her. We're both Australians, but in a way that has nothing to do with geography I know that we come from different countries. She's a big loveable child, inherently forthright and generous, and usually quite merry, but her philosophy is a bit frightening to a man brought up on the waterfront of a great city. She comes from a poor little grazing property deep in the mallee scrub over the New South Wales border. One of a family of eleven. Forty-six weeks in the year she works sheep, helps to bring up nine younger brothers and sisters. The six weeks' grape-picking is the annual light of her drab little life: money of her own, appetising food, the companionship of other people's sons and daughters; above all the fabulous Saturday morning shopping excursions into Mildura. After the picture of home that she painted for me this morning I can understand all this, but I'd give something to open her innocent young eyes to the world I know. Her conception of fighting for one's rights extends no further than keeping a wary eye on the number of filled tins.

'You've got to watch these Blockies,' she tells me knowingly every day. It would never occur to her that there are robbers higher up, that hard-working Bill McSeveney may also not be getting what he deserves. That is why at night-time here, looking out through the fly-wired window of the men's hut, I'm conscious of a darkness deeper than the heavy shadows that lie between the long drying-racks and over the garden of the sleeping house.

And it seems to me that this obsession of Lena with piecework is where the darkness begins. There was the twilight of it just a minute ago when she passed that unpleasant remark about wharfies.

We pick on in silence for perhaps fifteen minutes.

I'd always imagined there was a fair amount of noise associated with grape-picking. Perhaps there is on some blocks. On this one it is always quiet. The rows are unusually long, and between the visits of the tractor to replenish the supply of empty tins and take away the full ones, we hear nothing except the occasional voices of the two boys picking several rows away, and the carolling of magpies in the belars along the road. The sun is beginning to go down at last, but it's been a particularly hot day—110 degrees in the shade at noon—and I'll be glad when five o'clock comes, whatever the tally. That is always the best part of the day, when we trudge up to the house and throw ourselves on to the cool thick buffalo grass under the jacarandas, and Bill the boss cuts up a big sugar-melon and passes around pink juicy slices that we can hardly span with our jaws. It would be better still, though, if they would talk of something else then besides the day's work. Smoky, the house cat, usually joins us, and I can never contemplate his great lazy blue hide without reflecting:

'Oh, you wise old brute! Even as I went out to work this morning you were lying in the coolest spot under the water-tank and every hour of the day you've followed the shifting shadows. While I ... '

The hum of the approaching tractor gives promise of some relief, and as the crash of falling buckets sounds far off down the row I say to Lena:

—Here they come. How many have we got?

—If you were a good union man you'd be counting them yourself.

True, no doubt, but coming from Lena it's quite meaningless. She just doesn't know what a trade union is. Instinctively I cast a glance up the row to see if our long-expected visitor, the Rep., is coming.

—Aren't you going to tell me the tally?

—All I know is we're behind. We only had three hundred and thirty at smokoh, and this is the shortest run.

—That patch of mildew kept us back early in the afternoon.

—It wasn't that.

—Was it through my not keeping you up in buckets?

She doesn't answer that. Whether she knows it or not, she's angry with me not for what I do or don't do, but for the things I say. I work hard, but I've said some harsh things about piecework, ridiculed her persistent argument that 'the only way to get money is to work for it.' It would be a good world indeed if that were true. She knows I don't approve of competing with the boys for big tallies, but she can't see that nevertheless, out of principle, I must try to keep up with her because I get half of our combined earnings.

The tractor pulls up, and I crawl through to Lena's side and go for the water-bag hanging from the canopy. The grimy faces of Bill the boss, and Peter the rackman, smile down at me. They call me 'Sponge-guts' because of the vast amount of water I drink without getting pains.

—How's your mate, Joe? asks Peter.

—She's got the sulks again. She thinks I'm sitting up on her.

Bill, in the driving-seat, gives Lena a friendly wink. Naturally … they're his grapes. He's a good employer, even as employers go these days, but I'd be interested to see his form if pickers were easier to get. He and his wife think the world of Lena. She's an expert picker, but she's also a nice change in the home of a couple who've raised three sons and no daughters.

He's eyeing her now with all the detached benevolence of a bachelor uncle.

—Get your five hundred today, kid?

She steals a cautious sidelong glance at me, pouts, and shakes her head. She makes a charming picture of bush youth, standing stiff and straight in the narrow space between the tractor wheel and the vines. She wears old canvas shoes, a pair of jodhpurs several sizes too big for her, a man's work-shirt with the sleeves cut off, and a limp-brimmed sun-bonnet that throws a shadow over half of her cherubic face. The fingers of the hand nearest me fidget ceaselessly with the keen knife.

Usually she's full of talk, particularly with Bill, but at the moment she only wants to work. And she can't even kneel down with the tractor standing where it is. Her restless eyes leap from me to Peter, and from Peter to Bill.

—Come on, she says, load up. We've got over a hundred buckets to pick yet.

—All right, boss! Bill engages the clutch, and as the tractor moves on I swing the first bucketful up to Peter.

Slowly we move along the row. Sixty full buckets, about 20 lb. of fruit to the bucket—'fill 'em up to water-level!' They get heavy towards the end; one has to work fast to keep up with even the snail-crawl of the tractor. I come back to Lena sweating afresh, and blowing a bit.

She hears me, and without stopping, or looking at me, demands peremptorily:

—How many?

—Sixty on the load, and twenty-five left.

—That makes three hundred and ninety. We've got fifty minutes to get sixty more.

—Who says so?

—I do.

—Suppose we don't get them?

—We've got to get them.

It's on again, but before the usual evening dispute can get properly started a man I haven't seen before ducks through from the next row and confronts me. I give him good-day. Lena takes a long curious look at him, then goes on working. Middle-aged, and wearing a blue suit with an open-necked sports-shirt, he carries a couple of small books in one hand, and in the other a handkerchief with which he wipes his moist forehead. He'd have made a better first impression if he'd kept those books in his pocket a few minutes longer.

—Sorry I've been so long getting around, he says affably. I'm the Union Rep., A.W.U.

—I'm glad to see you.

We've been picking for four weeks here, and the A.W.U. is the wealthiest union in Australia. Something of what I'm thinking must show in my face, for his manner becomes a trifle apologetic.

—I've been flat out like a lizard since eight o'clock this morning. My God, it's hot, ain't it? How're you for tickets here?

He just can't get to the point soon enough,

—I've seen the boys through there; they're all right.

—I've been waiting for you, I tell him, bringing out a ten shilling note.

He opens one of the little books, takes a pencil from his breast pocket.

—Good on you, mate! How about the girl?

—I'm one of the family, replies Lena, with a promptness that shows not only that she has been listening, but that she has been well schooled. Bill has no time for trade unions.

The organiser gives me a conspiratorial smile, which I don't return.

—You could still join if you wanted to, girlie.

Lena doesn't answer that. She hasn't stopped picking for an instant. She's already a few feet away along the row, slashing and bucket-banging in a way that tells both of us not to be too long about it.

I watch him write in the date.

—I wish they'd all come in as quick as you, he says in a lowered voice. You've got no idea the song some of the bastards make about it. I can give you a full ticket if you like? Cost you thirty bob.

My gorge rises. What does he think he's selling? This great Union wasn't built by men like him.

—No thanks—just a season ticket. I'm already in a union. You don't cover me in my usual job.

—Okay. What are you in?

He begins to write. Just making conversation, he doesn't really care,

—Waterside Workers' Federation.

And for the life of me I can't keep a note of superiority out of my voice. I get the very devil of a kick out of it.

He goes on writing, without looking at me, but I can fairly see the guard coming up.

—That's a pretty good union. You'd make better money on the wharf than up here, wouldn't you?

—Yes. We're well organised.

A deliberate challenge, but he pretends not to see it.

— Up here for a bit of a change?

—I was crook. I had to get out of Melbourne for a few weeks. A man has to keep working, though.

I wouldn't tell him even that much, only I don't want him to think I came here for the 'big money.' 17s. 6d. a hundred tins!—and fill 'em up to water level ...

I'm tempted to ask him if he's been to the next block, where the pickers are working all hours and living like animals, but he's too easy to read. He isn't an organiser; he's a collector. If he were doing his job he would talk to Lena, as I've talked to her. I watch him tramp away through the dust quite pleased with himself—he's got my ten shillings. He didn't ask me if I am getting the prescribed wages, where I sleep at night, what hours I work, or what the food is like here.

It's a relief to get back to Lena. At least she's honest. She'd fight all right if she thought anybody was trying to put something over her. She just doesn't understand, that's all.

For minutes after I catch up with her we work without speaking. She's picking furiously, savagely, and by and by I find that I, too, am clapping on the pace. I've seen it elsewhere, the instinct to do one's bit, to keep up with one's mate. Piecework isn't an incentive; it's a device. But there's something else fermenting in me. A longing to please her, to win her respect, to get her to listen to me, to chase out of her eager young head some of the lies and nonsense that have been stuffed into it. Only last night I put in a hectic hour at the dining-table trying to explain to her—and others—that it isn't wharfies and railwaymen who gum up the works of the man on the land. Not wharfies and railwaymen ...

The falling bunches go plump-plump into the buckets. I know that she, too, is thinking. She wants to say something. Every time I catch sight of her bobbing head through the leaves I observe that she is peeping, as though trying to gauge what kind of humour I'm in.

By and by it comes, a non-committal uncompromising little voice that nevertheless sends a thrill through me:

—Joe.

—Hullo there.

—What is a trade union, anyway?

Lena, Lena, where am I to begin …?

Australian Literature and the Universities (1954)

A.D. Hope

About five years ago the Fellowship of Australian Writers (Melbourne section) invited me to talk to them on this subject and in the discussion which followed there occurred some polite but trenchant criticism of the Australian universities for their neglect of our national literature. My talk had been a defence of the attitude of at least one of our universities but I was compelled to admit the force of what many of my critics had to urge.

It was pointed out that our literature is approaching its second century and, while it has produced few outstanding writers, it has already a respectable and growing body of writing to show. And yet of the eight teaching universities in the country not one has so far established a course in Australian Literature. While there are literatures which it is important for any university to study, it is the peculiar right and the duty of each country to establish and to foster the study of its own writers.

The second point was that the study of literature depends on a number of ancillary studies, historical, biographical and bibliographical, which can only be carried out by expert research workers and this sort of research it is the proper function of universities to maintain. They spoke of the material for these studies still uncollected and unassessed and of the scholars of the future who would deplore our neglect. As they talked I remembered how a year or two before, after a lecture on Charles Harpur, one of my students had told me that she was a descendant of the poet and that only a few months earlier her mother had put a whole trunk-full of Harpur's papers under the laundry copper thinking that there was no longer any interest in keeping them. I was compelled to admit that our universities were at fault.

Why then have they neglected Australian literature? I think it is not hard to see why. In the first place modern literature has only just come to have a recognised place in the English courses of universities. Until recently their attitude was that noted by Henry Handel Richardson of her schooldays:

… We had learned a fair amount of Milton, Wordsworth, Gray, Cowper and so on; *but Tennyson was not yet accounted a classic*, and stray scraps were all I knew of him. (The italics are mine).

Australian literature in fact shared this general feeling in the past that nineteenth and twentieth century literature were too modern for university studies, which ought to be reserved for the established classics. However this attitude has been out-moded for a good many years now, so that it will hardly account for the fact that Australian literature is still a neglected subject in university studies. Yet modern English literature has found a place there. A more important reason perhaps is a vague feeling that Australian literature is not good enough or that it is not well enough established as a separate branch of literature, or again, that there is not yet enough of it to justify its having a course to itself. And although it may be infuriating to some partisans of Australian literature, I believe that these feelings are substantial and just. To argue against them is I think the wrong sort of argument and the right sort of argument is to show that, even if these contentions are true, there are other good reasons for universities to establish such courses. The pass course in English in our universities is usually one of three years. Some universities have honours courses of four years. But the plain fact is that English literature can only be covered in this time with the greatest difficulty. To give a considerable part of this time to the study of Australian literature would mean that neither could be properly dealt with. On the other hand to establish separate and independent courses in Australian literature is a luxury that none of our universities, always desperately short of money, has so far been able to afford.

To see the reason why, in spite of its justice, this argument ought not to be accepted, I think we need to ask ourselves what sorts of justification there are for establishing a subject of study at a university. There are three sorts of answer: educational, intellectual and utilitarian.

In the first place certain university studies have the function of helping to maintain and promote a cultural tradition. Their aim is, in part at least, educative, and their method is to foster critical understanding and to civilise the imagination. For this the study of English literature is of prime importance. And if we have to choose what shall go into such a course, we are right to choose the best we can get. It would, I think, be hard to argue that Australian literature has anything comparable to offer. It is not a matter of arguing whether Goldsmith is inferior to Henry Handel Richardson, or Lovelace to Shaw Neilson. It is the more general argument that the great English writers cannot without loss be replaced by even the best of our Australian writers and that if we are to study great writers we ought to study them in their natural context of the lesser writers of their periods. To find a place for Australian literature within the present English courses is a disservice to both. And I am not sure that the present practice of most universities, the compromise by which, not Australian literature, but a few Australian books are included in the English course has anything to be said for it at all. It may be argued that the body of literature is one body and I think that this is so. But the man who graduates with B.A., honours, in English literature has had an opportunity of knowing that body in all its range and beauty: the man who graduates with B.A., honours (Aust. Lit.), would be like a doctor setting out to practise medicine after having dissected the left knee and the liver.

Yet even if we admit this, there is an argument for the study of Australian literature as a separate subject. In the maintenance of the cultural tradition the study of English literature may have claims immensely superior to those of Australian literature. But it would be foolish to ignore the fact that our native literature has something important to contribute in the very fact that it is native: that the civilisation, the way of life and the problems of this country are our own problems and that it is through literature that a civilisation expresses itself, through literature its values and its tendencies become conscious and its creative force becomes eloquent and evident. Even if it were argued that the cultural tradition of Australia is not yet a very important one, it is still true that it is very important for Australians to consider it. However, I shall be prepared to maintain that the cultural tradition of Australia already has considerable importance and that quite apart from this there is a growing body of Australian writing which is well worth studying in itself. I would certainly not suggest that the only reason for studying Australian literature is for its historical interest and the light that is throws on local problems.

But universities exist for another purpose than the education of individuals. They exist primarily for the promotion of studies, for the advancement of knowledge in particular fields. As their name suggests, they exist in theory at least for the promotion of studies in all the fields of knowledge. No single university can do more than dream of this, but for each there will be subjects which have special claims not likely to be felt so strongly in other universities. And one of these claims is indisputable: the claim of the national literature to be a subject of study in the universities of the home country. It is not only the natural and obvious place for such studies but it is the natural and obvious duty of the home universities to initiate such studies so that they may take their due part in the idea of the *universitas*, the universal body of knowledge which nowadays can be covered not by any single university institution but by the general body of universities in the world. From this point of view it is not a question of whether Australian universities can afford to establish courses in the study of Australian literature but whether they can afford not to do so if they are to carry out their functions. If literature is recognised as one of their proper fields of study, the universities as a whole should study literature as a whole wherever it exists and Australian universities have the right and the duty to see that the literature of their own country does not form a gap in the general body of studies.

The third reason for the establishing of a university course is technical and practical: the provision of the community with experts in the arts and sciences. Even if the study of literature is not a means, it depends, as I have said, on certain technical and expert studies, bibliographical, historical and so on, without which it cannot do its work effectively. And this forms another reason for the establishment of courses in Australian literature. If you are to have the study of literature in itself, you must have these ancillary studies as well.

From these considerations I would draw certain conclusions. In the first place it is high time that we had courses in Australian literature in our universities, that universities themselves and the sources from which they draw their funds should be prepared to budget for this. In the second place these courses should not form a part of, or an addendum to, existing courses in English literature but should be independent and separate courses of study. In the third place, because our native literature is a minor one among the literatures of the world, because it is limited in range and has hardly any writers of first rank, and because it is a branch of English literature in general, its study should not be simply an alternative to the study of English literature. It should, I believe, he undertaken only by students who have already undergone or who are undergoing training in one of the major world literatures, preferably that of England. With such ideas in mind Canberra University College is at present experimenting in the establishment, for the first time in this country, of a complete course in Australian literature. The present course has been designed on historical lines and we hope that it will develop and in time help to encourage the establishment of studies in other places.

The Tomb of Heracles (1954)

James McAuley

A dry tree with an empty honeycomb
Stands as a broken column by the tomb:
The classic anguish of a rigid fate,
The loveless will, superb and desolate.

This is the end of stoic pride and state:
Blind light, dry rock, a tree that does not bear.

Look, cranes still know their path through empty air;
For them their world is neither soon nor late;
But ours is eaten hollow with despair.

Apocalypse in Springtime (1955)

Lex Banning

So I was in the city on this day:
and suddenly a darkness
came upon the city like night,
and it was night;
and all around me, and on either hand,
both above and below me,
there was—so it seemed—a dissolving
and a passing away.

And I listened with my ears, and heard
a great rushing
as the winds of the world left the earth,
and then there was silence,
and no sound, neither the roar of the city,
nor the voices of people,
nor the singing of birds, nor the crying
of any animal;
for the world that was audible had vanished
and passed away.

And I stretched forth both my hands,
but could touch nothing,
neither the buildings, nor the passers-by,
neither could I feel
the pavement underneath my feet,
nor the parts of my body;
for the world that was tangible had vanished
and passed away.

And I looked around and about me,
and could see nothing,
neither the heavens, nor the sea, nor the earth,
nor the waters under it;
for the world that was visible had vanished
and passed away.

In my nostrils there was a fleeting
fume of corruption,
and on my tongue a dying taste
of putrefaction,
and then these departed, and there was nothing;
for the world that was scent,
and the world that was savour had vanished
and passed away.

And all around me, and on either hand,
both above and below me,
there was nothing, and before me and behind;
for all of the fivefold
worlds of the world had vanished
and passed away.

And all my possessions of pride
had been taken from me,
and the wealth of my esteem stricken,
and the crown of my kingdom,
and all my human glory,
and I had nothing, and I was nothing;
for all things sensible had vanished
and passed away.

And I was alone in nothing,
and stood at the bar
of nothing, was accused by nothing,
and defended by nothing,
and nothing deliberated judgment
against me.

And the arbitrament of the judgment
was revealed to me.

Then the nothing faded into nothing,
and that into nothing,
and I was alone in a darkness like night,
but it was not night;
then the darkness faded into darkness,
and that into darkness,
and there was no light—but only
emptiness,
and a voice in the void lamenting
and dying away.

Last Look (1959)

A.D. Hope

His mind, as he was going out of it,
Looked emptier, shabbier than it used to be:
A secret look to which he had no key,
Something misplaced, something that did not fit.

Windows without their curtains seemed to stare
Inward—but surely once they had looked out.
Someone had moved the furniture about
And changed the photographs: the frames were there,

But idiot faces never seen before
Leered back at him. He knew there should have been
A carpet on the boards, not these obscene
Clusters of toadstools sprouting through the floor.

Yet Arabella's portrait on the wall
Followed him just as usual with its eyes.
Was it reproach or pleading, or surprise,
Or love perhaps, or something of them all?

Watching her lips, he saw them part; could just
Catch the thin sibilance of her concern:
'O Richard, Richard, why would you not learn
I was the only soul that you could trust?'

Carefully, carefully, seeming not to know,
He added this remembrance to his store.
Conscience, in uniform beside the door,
Coughed and remarked that it was time to go.

High time indeed! He heard their tramping feet.
To have stayed even so long, he knew, was rash.
The mob was in the house. He heard the crash
Of furniture hurled down into the street.

'This way!' The warder said: 'You must be quick.
You will be safe with us … ' He turned to go
And saw too late the gaping void below.
Someone behind him laughed. A brutal kick

Caught him below the shoulders and he fell
Quite slowly, clutching at the passing air,
And plunged towards the source of his despair
Down the smooth funnel of that endless well.

1960s

Bog and Candle (1960)

Robert D. Fitzgerald

1

At the end of life paralysis or those creeping teeth,
the crab at lung or liver or the rat in the brain,
and flesh become limp rag, and sense tap of a cane—
if you would pray, brother, pray for a clean death.

For when the work you chip from age-hard earth must pause,
faced with the dark, unfinished, where day gave love and jest,
day and that earth in you shall pit you to their test
of struggle in old bog against the tug of claws.

2

What need had such a one for light at the night's rim?
Yet in the air of evening till the medley of sound—
children and birds and traffic—settled in the profound
meditation of earth, it was the blind man's whim

to set at his wide window the warm gift of flame
and put a match to wick for sight not like his own—
for his blank eyes could pierce that darkness all have known,
the thought: 'What use the light, or to play out the game?'

and could disperse also the fog of that queer code
which exalts pain as evidence of some aim or end
finer than strength it tortures, so sees pain as friend—
good in itself and guiding to great ultimate good!

Then he would touch the walls of the cold place where he sat
but know the world as wider, since here, beside his hand,
this flame could reach out, out, did touch but understand …
Life in a man's body perhaps rayed out like that.

So it is body's business and its inborn doom
past will, past hope, past reason and all courage of heart,
still to resist among the roof-beams ripped apart
the putting-out of the candle in the blind man's room.

Arrows (1960)

Mary Gilmore

I.

Why gibe
That woman is a woman?
As man
She, too, is human;
So human
That, since time began,
She gives her son
What makes him man.

II.

Since from the boundless
To the limited life came,
Prayer is the cry of man
For oneness with the Infinite
Again.

III.

Save that by memory
Man's reason lives,
For all we see or do,
Lives are but sieves.
If memory went
What would remain?
Only the scattered chaff
Without the grain.

IV.

Not life but memory makes man.
Life leaves no mark on time;
But memory has given us words.
Words are the steps by which we climb.

A Case (1961)

Gwen Harwood

Uprights undid her: spires and trees.
One night she lived a vital dream.
By water and by land she came
delayed by manifold stupidities
into a wicked, feasting town.
Her Samson mind cracked pillars down
and left no trees, no upright towers.
By righteousness endowed with powers

extravagant beyond belief
she resurrected from the gutter
the President of Dogs, whose utter
gratitude made words of barks: 'O Chief
Lover of Cleanliness, no more,
I swear, shall dogs befoul your door
or copulate in public places.'
She resurrected girls whose faces

purified of alizarin shame
were safely quarantined from sex;
charms against men hung from their necks
to the division she would never name.
All sweet, all clean this level town.
A phallus rose, she whipped it down.
Day broke.
            Erect, the bawdy spires
poked in red clouds' immodest fires.

She bathed. She munched her food chopped raw.
Blackstrap molasses charged her power.
'Shadowy Redeemer, come this hour!
Help me enforce thy horizontal law,
and scourge the crude obscenities of
dogs and girls and posturing trees.'

She met him in a crowded street,
Tore off her clothes, and kissed his feet.

At My Grandmother's (1961)

David Malouf

An afternoon, late summer, in a room
Shuttered against the bright, envenomed leaves;
An under-water world, where time, like water,
Was held in the wide arms of a gilded clock,
And my grandmother, turning in the still sargasso
Of memory, wound out her griefs and held
A small boy prisoner to weeds and corals,
While summer leaked its daylight through his head.

I feared that room, the parrot screeching soundless
In its dome of glass, the faded butterflies
Like jewels pinned against a sable cloak,
And my grandmother winding out the skeins I held
Like trickling time, between my outstretched arms;

Feared most of all the stiff, bejewelled fingers
Pinned at her throat, or moving on grey wings
From word to word; and feared her voice that called
Down from their gilded frames the ghosts of children
Who played at hoop and ball, whose spindrift faces
(The drowned might wear such smiles) looked out across
The wreck and debris of the years, to where
A small boy sat, as they once sat, and held
In the wide ache of his arms, all time, like water,
And watched the old grey hands wind out his blood.

Being Kind to Titina (1962)

Patrick White

First mother went away. Then it was our father, twitching from under our feet the rugs, which formed, he said, a valuable collection. We were alone for a little then. Not really alone, of course, for there was Fräulein Hoffman, and Mademoiselle Leblanc, and Kyria Smaragda our housekeeper, and Eurydice the cook, and the two maids from Lesbos. The house was full of the whispering of women, and all of us felt melancholy.

Then it was explained to us by Mademoiselle Leblanc that she and Fräulein Hoffman had gone out and sent a telegram to Smyrna, and soon the aunts would arrive in Egypt. Soon they did: there was our Aunt Ourania, who was less stern than she seemed to be, and Aunt Thalia—she was the artistic one—nobody, said Fräulein Hoffman, could sing the German *Lieder* with such *Gefühl*.

Soon the house began to live again. There were always people on the stairs. There was a coming and going, and music, in the old house at Schutz. That year my eldest sister Phrosso thought she was in love with an Italian athlete, and my brother Aleko decided he would become a film star. The girls from Lesbos hung out of the upper windows after the dishes had been stacked, and tried to reach the dates which were ripening on the palms. Sometimes there was the sound of dates plopping in the damp garden below. The garden was never so cool and damp as when they brought us back from the beach. The gate creaked, as the governesses let us in through the sand-coloured wall, into the dark-green thicket of leaves.

My eldest sister Phrosso said it was awful, awful—mouldy Alexandria—if only they would let her wear high heels, or take us to Europe, if only she could have a passionate love affair; otherwise, she was going to burst. But it did not occur to me that our life was by any means insufferable. Though I was different. I was the sensible one, said the aunts; Dionysios is a steady boy. Sometimes I felt this bitterly, but I could not alter, and almost always I derived an immense pleasure from the continuous activity of the house: my second sister Agni writing essays at the oval table; the two little ones giving way to tempers; the maids explaining dreams in the attics; and at evening our Aunt Thalia playing the piano in the big *salon* with the gilded mirrors—her interpretation of Schumann was not equalled by that of Frau Klara herself, Fräulein Hoffman said, not that she had been there. Our aunt was very satisfied. She crossed her wrists more than ever. She sang *une petite chanson spirituelle de votre Duparc* to please Mademoiselle Leblanc, who sat and smiled above her darning-egg. I believe we were at our happiest in the evenings of those days. Though somebody might open a door, threatening to dash the light from the candles on our aunt's piano, the flames soon recovered their shape. Silences were silenter. In those days, it was not uncommon to hear the sound of a camel, treading past, through the dust. There was the smell of camel on the evening air.

Oh yes, we were at our happiest. If my sister Phrosso said it was all awful, awful, it was because she had caught sight of the Italian athlete at the beach, and life had become painful for her.

That year the Stavrides came to live in the house almost opposite.

'Do you know,' I informed Aunt Ourania, 'these Stavrides are from Smyrna? Eurydice heard it from their cook.'

'Yes, I know,' our aunt replied rather gravely. 'But I do not care for little boys, *Dionysi mou*, to spend so much time in the kitchen.'

It hurt me when our aunt spoke like this, because more than any of us I was hers. But I always pretended not to have heard.

'Did you know them?' I had to ask. 'These Stavrides, Aunt Ourania?'

'I cannot say I did not *know* them,' Aunt Ourania now replied. 'Oh, yes,' she said, 'I *knew* them.'

It seemed to me that Aunt Ourania was looking her sternest, but as always on such a transformation, she began to fiddle with my tunic, to stroke my hair.

'Then, shall we know them, too, Aunt Ourania? There is one child,' Eurydice says. 'A little girl. Titina.'

But our Aunt Ourania grew sterner still.

'I have not decided,' she said at last, 'how far we shall commit ourselves. The Stavrides,' she said, clearing her throat, 'are not altogether desirable.'

'How?' I asked.

'Well,' she said, 'it is difficult to put.'

She went on stroking the short stubble of my cropped hair.

'Kyria Stavridi, you see, was the daughter of a chemist. They even lived above her father's shop. It is not that I have anything against Kyria Stavridi,' she thought to add. 'For all I know, she may be an excellent person by different standards. But we must draw the line. Somewhere. Today.'

Then my Aunt Ourania looked away. She was herself such a very good person. She read Goethe every morning, for a quarter of an hour, before her coffee. She kept the Lenten fasts. Very soon after her arrival, she had ordered the hair to be shorn from the heads of all us boys. We were to wear the tunics of ordinary working-class children, because, she said, it was wrong to flaunt ourselves, to pretend we were any different. She herself wore her hair like a man, and gave away her money in secret.

'Still,' my Aunt Ourania said, 'there is no reason why you children should not be kind to Titina Stavridi, even if her parents are undesirable.'

Her eyes had moistened, because she was so tender.

'You, Dionysi,' she said, 'you are the kindest. You must be particularly kind to poor Titina.'

For the present, however, nothing further happened.

Our life continued. After the departure of our parents, you could not say anything momentous took place. There were always the minor events, and visits. Our Aunt Calliope, the professor, came from Paris. She made us compose essays, and breathe deep. My brother Aleko wrote for a course on hypnotism; Phrosso forgot her athlete, and began to notice a Rumanian; my second sister Agni won her prize for

algebra; and the little ones, Myrto and Paul, each started a money-box.
With so many unimportant, yet necessary things taking place all the
time, it did not occur to me to refer again to the Stavrides. Or perhaps
it did cross my mind, and I made no mention of them, because our
Aunt Ourania would not have wished it. So the days continued more
or less unbroken: the sun working at the street wall; the sea-water salt-
ing our skins; the leaves of the ficus sweating in the damp evenings of
the old house at Schutz.

When, suddenly, on a Tuesday afternoon, there was Kyria Stavridi
herself sitting in Aunt Ourania's favourite chair beside the big
window in the *salon*.

'Which one are you, then?' Kyria Stavridi called, showing an awful
lot of gold.

'I am the middle one,' I replied. 'I am Dionysios.'

In ordinary circumstances I would have gone away, but now I was
fascinated by all that gold.

'Ah,' Kyria Stavridi said, and smiled, 'often it is the middle ones on
whom the responsibilities fall.'

It made her somewhat mysterious. She was dressed, besides, in
black, and gave the impression, even at a distance of several feet, of
being enclosed in a film of steam.

I did not answer Kyria Stavridi, because I did not know what to
say, and because I had noticed she was not alone.

'This is my little girl, Titina,' Kyria Stavridi said. 'Will you be kind
to her?'

'Oh,' I said. 'Yes.'

Looking at the unknown child.

Titina Stavridi was standing at her mother's elbow. All in frills. All
in white. Wherever she was not stuck with pink satin bows. Now
she smiled, out of her oblong face. Some of the teeth appeared to be
missing from Titina's smile. She had that banana-coloured skin, those
rather pale, large freckles, the paler skin round the edges of the hair,
which suggested to me, I don't know why, that Titina Stavridi might
be a child who had long continued to wet the bed.

Just then my Aunt Ourania came into the room, to which our maid Aphrodite had called her. She put on her man's voice, and said:

'Well, Kyria Stavridi, who would have expected to see you in Alexandria!'

Holding out her hand from a distance.

Kyria Stavridi, who had got to her feet, began to steam more than ever. She was exceptionally broad in her behind. Kyria Stavridi was bent almost double as she touched my aunt's fingers.

'Ah, Mademoiselle Ourania, such a pleasure!' Kyria Stavridi was bringing it out by the yard. 'To renew acquaintance! And Mademoiselle Thalia? So distinguished!'

Aunt Ourania, I could see, did not know how to reply.

'My sister,' she said, finally, 'cannot come down. She is suffering from a headache.'

And Kyria Stavridi could not sympathise enough. Her breath came out in short, agonised rushes.

After that, they spoke about people, which was always boring.

'Dionysi,' my aunt said, during a pause, 'why don't you take Titina into the garden? Here there is really nothing for children.'

But I did not move. And my aunt did not bother again.

As for Titina Stavridi, she might have been a statue, but an ugly one. Her legs seemed so very thick and lifeless. All those bows. And frilly pants. By moving closer I could see she had a kind of little pock-mark on the side of her lumpy, freckled nose, and her eyes were a shamefully stupid blue.

'My husband,' Kyria Stavridi was saying, 'my husband, too,' she murmured, 'does not enjoy the best of health.'

'Yes,' said my Aunt Ourania, 'I remember.'

Which somehow made her visitor sad.

Then all the others were pushing and rushing, even Phrosso and Aleko, the two eldest, all entering to see this Kyria Stavridi from Smyrna, and her ugly child. Everybody was introduced.

'Then I hope we shall be friends,' Kyria Stavridi suggested, more to us children, because it was obvious even to me that her hopes of our aunts were not very high. 'Dionysios,' said Kyria Stavridi, 'will be, I feel, Titina's little friend. He has promised me, in fact. They must be the same age, besides.'

This made my sister Agni laugh, and Aleko gave me a pinch from behind. But my little brother Paul, who was never in two minds about anything, went straight up to Titina, and undid one of her satin bows. For a moment I thought Titina Stavridi would begin to cry. But she did not. She smiled and smiled. And was still smiling when her mother, who had said all the necessary things, presently led her out.

Then we were all laughing and shouting.

'So that was Kyria Stavridi!' my sister Phrosso shouted. 'Did you notice the gap between her front teeth?'

'And the bows on her dreadful Titina!' Agni remarked. 'You could dress a bride in all that satin!'

'Do we have to know such very vulgar people?' asked my brother Aleko.

Then our Aunt Ourania replied:

'You are the one who is vulgar, Aleko.'

And slapped him in the face.

'Aleko, you will go to your room.'

This might have shocked us more, Aleko the eldest, already so strong, if Myrto—she was the quiet one who noticed things—had not begun to point and shriek.

'Look! Look!' Myrto shouted. 'Titina Stavridi has done it on the floor!'

There, in fact, beside the best chair, was Titina's pool. As if she had been an untrained dog.

At once everyone was pushing to see.

'Such a big girl!' Aunt Ourania sighed.

She rang for Aphrodite, who called to the Arab, who brought a pail.

After that I began to suspect everybody in our house had forgotten the Stavrides. Certainly the two girls from Lesbos had seen the Kyrios Stavridis singing and stumbling at the end of the street. He had put his foot through his straw hat. But nothing was done about Titina, until one hot evening as I searched the garden with a candle, looking for insects for a collection I was about to make, Aunt Ourania called me and said:

'Tomorrow we must do something about Titina. You, Dionysi, shall fetch her.'

Several of the others groaned, and our Aunt Thalia, who was playing Schumann in her loveliest dress, of embroidered purple, hunched her shoulders.

'Oh!' I cried. 'I?'

But I knew, and my aunt confirmed, it could not have been otherwise. It was I who must be the steadiest, the kindest. Even Kyria Stavridi had said that responsibilities often fell to the middle ones.

On the following afternoon I fetched Titina. We did not speak. But Kyria Stavridi kissed me, and left a wet patch on my cheek.

We were going to the beach, on that, as on almost any other afternoon.

'Oh!' moaned my sister Phrosso. 'The old beach! It is so boring!'

And gave Titina a hard pinch.

'What, Titina,' asked Agni, 'is that?'

For Titina was wearing a blue bead.

'That is to keep away the Eye,' said Titina.

'The Eye!'

How they shouted.

'Like an Arab!' cried Myrto.

And we began to chant: 'Titina, Titina, Arapina ...' but softly, almost under our breath, in case Mademoiselle should hear.

So Titina came to the beach, on that and other afternoons. Once we took off her pants, and beat her bottom with an empty bottle we found floating in the sea. Then, as always, Titina only smiled, rather watery certainly. We ducked her, and she came up breathless, blinking the sea out of those very stupid, deep blue eyes. When it was wet, her freckly skin shone like a fish's.

'Disgusting!' Phrosso decided, and went away to read a magazine.

You could not torture Titina for long; it became too uninteresting.

But Titina stuck. She stuck to me. It was as if Titina had been told. And once in the garden of our house at Schutz, after showing her my collection of insects, I became desperate. I took Titina's blue bead, and stuck it up her left nostril.

'Titina,' I cried, 'the holes of your nose are so big I'd expect to see your brain—if you had any,' I shouted, 'inside.'

But Titina Stavridi only smiled, and sneezed the bead into her hand.

In my desperation I continued to shout pure nonsense.

Until my Aunt Thalia came out.

'Wretched, wretched children!' she called. 'And you! Dionysi!'

During the heat of the afternoon my aunt would recline in a quiet room, nibbling a raw carrot, and copying passages from R. Tagore.

'My headache!' she now protested. 'My rest destroyed! Oh, my God! My conjunctivitis!'

On account of the conjunctivitis Aunt Thalia was wearing her bottle-green eye-shade, which made her appear especially tragic. Altogether Aunt Thalia was like a masked figure in a tragedy.

So that I was shocked, and Titina Stavridi even more so.

On the next occasion when I fetched her, her mother took me aside and instructed me in detail.

'Your poor Aunt Thalia!' She sighed. 'Night and morning,' she made me repeat. 'Bathe the eyes. Undiluted.'

'What is this bottle you have brought me?' asked Aunt Thalia when I presented it.

She was standing in the big *salon*, and the sleeves fell back from her rather thin, but elegant arms.

'It is for the conjunctivitis.'

'Yes! Yes! But what is it?'

Aunt Thalia could grow so impatient.

'It is a baby's water,' I replied. 'Night and morning. Undiluted.'

'Oh! Oh!' moaned our Aunt Thalia as she flung the bottle.

It bounced once on the polished floor.

'Disgusting, disgusting creature!'

'It's probably a very clean baby,' I said.

It sounded reasonable, but Aunt Thalia was not consoled.

Nor did I fetch Titina again. I must say that, even without the episode of Kyria Stavridi's prescription, we should not have been allowed to see Titina. For the Stavrides were always becoming involved in what our aunts considered undignified, not to say repulsive, incidents. For instance, Kyria Stavridi was butted in her broad behind by a piebald goat in the middle of the Rue Goussio. Then there was the thing that happened in our own street as Despo and Aphrodite, the maids from Lesbos, were returning home at dusk. The two girls were panting and giggling when they arrived. We could hear them already as they slammed the gate. What was it, Despo, Aphrodite? we called, running. It was to do with the Kyrios Stavridis, we gathered, who had shown them something in the almost dark. Long afterwards it was a matter for conjecture what the Kyrios Stavridis had shown our maids, though our sister Phrosso insisted from the beginning that she knew.

In any case, Titina Stavridi withdrew from our lives, to a distance of windows, or balconies.

Once, indeed, I met her outside the grocer's, when Titina said:

'It is sad, Dionysi. You were the one. You were the one I always loved.'

So that I experienced a sensation of extreme horror, not to say terror, and ran all the way home with the paperful of sugar for which Kyria Smaragda had sent me.

But I could not escape Titina's face. Its dreadful oblong loomed in memory and at open windows, at dusk especially, as the ripening dates fell from their palms, and a camel grunted past.

So much happened all at once I cannot remember when the Stavrides went away. For we, too, were going. Our Aunt Ourania had paused one evening in doing the accounts, and said it was time to give serious thought to education. So there we were. Packing. Fräulein Hoffman began to cry.

Once I did happen to remark:

'Do you suppose the Stavrides have left already? One sees only shutters.'

'That could be,' said Aunt Ourania.

And Aunt Thalia added: the Stavrides were famous for moving on.

Anyway, it was unimportant. So many events and faces crowded into the next few years. For we had become Athenians. In the dry, white, merciless light, it was very soon recognised that I was a conscientious, though backward boy. Time was passing, moustaches growing. Often we children were put to shame by the clothes our Aunt Ourania would make us wear, for economy, and to contain our pride.

Most of the other boys had begun to think of going to brothels. Some of them had already been. Their moustaches helped them to it. But I, I mooned about the streets. Once I wrote on a wall with an end of chalk:

I LOVE   I LOVE   I LOVE

And then went off home. And lay on my empty bed. Listening. The nights were never stained with answers.

It was soon the year of the Catastrophe. We moved to the apartment at Patissia then. So as to have the wherewithal to help some of those poor people, our Aunt Ourania explained. For soon the refugees were pouring in from Anatolia. There were cousins sleeping on the tiled floors, and our Aunt Helen and Uncle Constantine in the maids' bedroom; the girls from Lesbos had to be dismissed. Give, give, ordained Aunt Ourania, standing with her arms full of cast-off clothes. My youngest sister Myrto burst into tears. She broke open her money-box with a hammer, and began to spend the money on ices.

Oh, everything was happening at this time. Our eldest brother, who had given up all thought of becoming a film star, was in Cairo being a business man. Our sister Phrosso had stopped falling in love. She was again in Alexandria, trying for one of several possible husbands. There were the many letters, which filled me with an intolerable longing for damp gardens and ficus leaves. Once I even wrote a poem, but I showed it to no one, and tore it up. It was sometimes sad at home, though Agni might sit down at the piano, and bash out *Un baiser, un baiser, pas sur la bouche* ... while the aunts were paying calls.

Then it was decided—it was our Aunt Ourania who decided things—that as Dionysios was an unexceptional, but reliable boy, he should leave school, and go to our Uncle Stepho at the Bank. Then there would be so much more to give to those poor people, the refugees from the Turks in Anatolia. It was exciting enough, but only for a little. Soon I was addressing envelopes at the Bank. The dry ledgers made me sneeze. And my Uncle Stepho would send for me, and twist my ear, thinking it a huge joke to have me to torture at the Bank.

So it was.

Summer had come round again: the eternal, powdery, white Athenian summer. The dust shot out from under my shoes as I trudged along Stadium Street, for although I had intended to spend my holiday at Pelion, Aunt Ourania had at once suggested: will your conscience allow you, with all those refugees sleeping on mattresses in the hall? So I had stayed, and it was intolerable. My clothes were damp rags by eleven o'clock in Stadium Street.

When I heard my name.

'Dionysi! Dionysi?'

It was a young woman. Or girl. Or girl. Who sprang from one of those little marble tables, where she had been eating a water-ice, on the pavement, at Yannaki's.

'Oh,' she continued, 'I thought. I thought it was *some* one. Dionysios Papapandelidis. Somebody I used to know.'

I must have looked so stupid, I had caused this cool, glittering girl to doubt and mumble. She stood sucking in her lips as though to test to what extent her lipstick had been damaged by the ice.

When suddenly I saw, buried deep inside the shell, the remains, something of the pale, oblong face of the child Titina we had known at Schutz.

My surprise must have come pouring out, for at once she was all cries and laughter. She was breathing on me, embracing even, kissing the wretched beginnings of my thin moustache, there in the glare of Stadium Street. I had never felt so idiotic.

'Come,' Titina said at last. 'We must eat an ice. I have already had several. But Yannaki's ices are so good.'

I sat with Titina, but was nervous, for fear I might have to pay for all those previous ices.

But Titina almost immediately said:

'I shall invite you, dear Dionysi.'

She was so glad. She was so kind. The curious part of it was: as Titina fished in her bag for a cigarette, and fiddled with the stunning little English lighter, and a ball of incalculable notes fell out on the marble table-top, *I* had become the awkward thing of flesh Titina Stavridi used to be.

'Tell me!' she begged; and: 'Tell me!'

Dragging on the cigarette, with her rather full, practised lips.

But I, I had nothing to tell.

'And you?' I asked. 'Do you live in Athens?'

'Oh, no!' She shook her head. 'Never in Athens!'

This goddess was helmetted only in her own hair, black, so black, the lights in it were blue.

'No,' she said. 'I am here on a short visit. Jean-Louis,' she explained, 'is an exceptionally kind and generous man.'

'Jean-Louis?'

'That is my friend,' Titina answered, shaping her mouth in such a way I knew my aunts would have thought it common.

'This person, is he old or young?'

'Well,' she said, 'he is mature.'

'Does your mother know?'

'Oh, Mother! Mother is very satisfied things have arranged themselves so well. She has her own apartment, too. If this is the world, then live in it. That is what Mother has decided.'

'And your father?'

'Papa is always there,' Titina said, and sighed.

As for myself, I began to fill with desperate longing. Here was Titina, so kind, so close, so skilled, so unimaginable. My clothes tightened on me as I sat.

And Titina talked. All the time her little bracelets thrilled and tinkled. She would turn her eyes this way and that, admiring, or rejecting. She would narrow her eyes in a peculiar way, though perhaps it was simply due to the glare.

'Tell me, Dionysi,' she asked, and I experienced the little hairs barely visible on her forearm, 'have you ever thought of me? I expect not. I was so horrible! Awful! And you were always so very kind.'

The fact was: Titina Stavridi did sincerely believe in her own words, for she had turned upon me her exquisitely contrived face, and I could see at the bottom of her candid eyes, blue as only the Saronic Gulf, I could see, well, I could see the truth.

'There is always so little time,' complained Titina, both practical and sad. 'Dionysi, are you free? Are you free, say, this afternoon? To take me to the sea? To swim?'

'But this is Greece,' I said, 'where men and girls have not yet learnt to swim together.'

'Pah!' she cried. 'They will learn! You and I,' she said, 'will swim together. If you are free. This afternoon.'

And at once time was our private toy. We were laughing and joking expertly as Titina Stavridi pared away the notes, to pay for all those ices we had eaten at Yannaki's.

'First I have an appointment,' she announced.

'With whom?' I asked.

I could not bear it.

'Ah!' She laughed. 'With a friend of my mother's. An elderly lady, who has a wart.'

So I was comforted. There were *youvarlakia* for lunch. Nobody could equal Eurydice at *youvarlakia*, but today, it seemed, sawdust had got into them.

'You will offend Eurydice,' Aunt Thalia had begun to moan. 'You have left her *youvarlakia*.'

I decided not to tell my two, dear, stuffy aunts of my meeting with Titina Stavridi.

It became the most unbearable secret, and to pass the time—to say nothing of the fact that I should probably have to pay Titina's fare on the rather long journey by bus.

'Oh, no,' she was saying at last, there on the steps of the Grande Bretagne. 'Call a taxi,' Titina insisted, which the man in livery did.

'Money is for spending,' she explained.

On the way, as she rootled after the lovely little lighter, I was relieved to see her bag was still stuffed with notes.

For the afternoon she was wearing a bracelet of transparent shells, which jostled together light as walnuts.

'That,' Titina said, 'is nothing.'

'My friend,' she added, 'advised me to leave my jewels in a safe deposit at the Crédit Lyonnais. One never knows, Jean-Louis says, what may happen in Greece.'

I agreed that the Crédit Lyonnais offered greater certainty.

It was like that all the way. As her body cannoned off me, as lightly as her bracelet of shells, Titina revealed a life of sumptuous, yet practical behaviour. She accepted splendour as she did her skin. All along the beach, that rather gritty Attic sand, Titina radiated splendour, in god-like armour of nacreous scales, in her little helmet of rubber feathers.

'Do you like my costume?' she asked, after she had done her mouth. 'Jean-Louis does not. *Ça me donne un air de putain*. So he says.'

At once she ran down into the sea, shimmering in her gorgeous scales. I was glad to find myself inside the water.

Then we swam, in long sweeps of silvery-blue. Bubbles of joy seemed to cling to Titina's lips. Her eyes were the deeper, drowsier, for immersion.

I had asked the taxi to drop us at a certain bay along that still deserted coast. The shore was strewn with earth-coloured rocks. The

Attic pines straggled, and struggled, and leaned out over the sea. It was a poor landscape, splendid, too, in its own way, of perfectly fulfilled austerity. I had hoped we should remain unseen. And so we were. Until a party of lads descended half-naked on the rocks. Several of them I had sat beside in school. Now they seated themselves, lips drooping, eyes fixed. They shouted the things one expected. Some of them threw handfuls of water.

But Titina squinted at the sun.

Faced with these gangling louts, of deferred muscle and blubber-lips, anything oafish in myself seemed to have been spent. Was it Titina's presence? My head, set firmly on my neck, had surveyed oceans and continents. I had grown suave, compact, my glistening moustache had thickened, if not to the human eye.

Presently some of the boys I knew plunged in, and were swimming around, calling and laughing in their cracked voices. Their seal-like antics were intended to amuse.

But Titina did not see.

Then, as we were standing in the shallows, squat, yellow Sotiri Papadopoulos attempted to swim between Titina's legs.

'Go away, filthy little boy!'

How she pointed!

Titina's scorn succeeded. Sotiri went. Fortunately. He had often proved himself stronger than I.

Afterwards I sat with Titina, dripping water, under the pines. She told me distantly of the visits to Deauville, Le Touquet, and Cannes. Reservations at the best hotels. I was only lazily impressed. But how immaculate she was. I remembered Agni, her goosey arms, and strings of wet, swinging hair.

Titina produced *fruits glacés*.

'We brought them, Jean-Louis and I, from the Côte d'Azur. Take them,' she ordered.

First I offered her the box.

'Ach!' she said. 'Eat! I am sick of them. The *fruits glacés*!'

So I sat and stuffed.

For a long time we remained together beneath the pines, she so cool and flawless, myself only hot and clammy. She began to sing— what, I really cannot remember.

'Ah,' she exclaimed, lying back, looking up through the branches, 'they are stunted, our poor pines.'

'That is their way,' I told her.

'Yes.' She sighed. 'They are not stunted.'

I walked a short distance, and brought her *vissinada* from a roadside booth. We stained our mouths with the purple *vissinada*. All along the Saronic Gulf the evening had begun to purple. The sand was gritty to the flesh. I believe it was at this point the man with the accordion passed by, playing his five or six notes, as gentle and persuasive as wood-pigeons. Unlike the boys earlier, the man with the accordion did not stare. He strolled. I think probably the man was blind.

'*Ach, Titina! Titina!*'

I was breathing my desperation on her.

The darkness was plunging towards us as Titina Stavridi turned her face towards me on the sand. A twig had marked her perfect cheek. She lay looking into me, as though for something she would not find.

'Poor Dionysaki,' she said, 'at least it is unnecessary to be afraid.'

So that I had never felt stronger. As I wrestled with Titina Stavridi on the sand, my arms were turned to sea-serpents. The scales of her nacreous *maillot*, which Jean-Louis had never cared for, were sloughed in a moment by my skilful touch. I was holding in my hands her small, but persistent buttocks, which had been threatening to escape all that afternoon.

'*Ach!*' she cried, in almost bitter rage, as we heard her teeth strike on mine.

Afterwards Titina remained infinitely kind. The whole darkness was moving with her kindness.

'When will you leave?' I dreaded to ask.

'The day after tomorrow,' she replied. 'No,' she corrected, quick. 'Tomorrow.'

'Then why did you say: *after* tomorrow?'

'Because,' she said, simply, 'I forgot.'

So my sentence was sealed. All the sea sounds of Attica rose to attack me, as I thrust my lips all over again into Titina's wilted mouth.

'Good-bye, Titina,' I said, on the steps of her hotel.

'Good-bye, Dionysi. *Dionysaki!*'

She was so tender, so kind.

But I did not say anything else, as I had begun to understand already that such remarks are idiocy.

All the way to Patissia, the dust was thick and heavy on my shoes.

When I got in, my Aunt Calliope, the professor, had arrived from Paris.

'Our Dionysi!' cried Aunt Calliope. 'Almost a man!'

She embraced me quickly, in order to return to politics.

We had never cared for Aunt Calliope, who had made us write essays and things, though her brothers loved her, and would quarrel with her till the white hours over any boring political issue.

'The Catastrophe,' my Aunt Calliope had reached the shouting stage, 'was the result of public apathy in one of the most backward countries of the world.'

My Uncle Stepho was shouting back.

'Hand it over to you and your progressive intellectuals, and we might as well, *all*, decent people, anyway, cut our throats!' bellowed Uncle Stepho, Vice-President of our Whole Bank.

'But let us stick to the Catastrophe!'

'The Generals were to blame!' screamed my Uncle Constantine.

'All Royalists! Royalists!'

Aunt Calliope was beating with her fists.

'What can one expect of effete Republicans? Nothing further!'

'Do not blame the Republicans!' Aunt Ourania dared anyone.

'The Royalists have not yet proved themselves.'

Aunt Calliope started to cackle unmercifully.

'Better the Devil,' thought Constantine.

Aunt Ourania frowned.

'Still, Kosta,' she suggested, very gravely, in the voice she adopted for all soothing purposes, 'you must admit that when blood flows our poor Greece is regenerated.'

My Aunt Thalia, who had been crying, went to the piano. She began to play a piece I remembered. Sweet and sticky, the music flowed from under her always rather tentative hands.

The music gummed the voices up.

Then my Aunt Calliope remarked:

'Guess whom I saw?'

Nobody did.

'That little thing, that Titina Stavridi, to whom you were all so kind in the old days at Schutz.'

'Living in Athens?' asked Aunt Ourania, though the answer must remain unimportant.

'Not a bit of it,' Aunt Calliope said. 'I have run into her before. Oh, yes, several times. In Paris.' Here Aunt Calliope laughed. 'A proper little *thing*! A little whore!'

It was obvious from her expression that Aunt Ourania was taking it upon herself to expiate the sins of the world, while Aunt Thalia forced the music. How it flowed, past the uncles and out of the room, all along the passages of our shrunken apartment, which seldom nowadays lost its smell of *pasta*. The intolerable Schumann pursued me as far as my own room, and farther.

Outside, the lilac-bushes were turned solid in the moonlight. The white music of that dusty night was frozen in the parks and gardens. As I leaned out of the window, and held up my throat to receive the knife, nothing happened. Only my Aunt Thalia continued playing Schumann, and I realised that my extended throat was itself a stiff sword.

Towards a Modernised View of Mass Media (1962)

Robert B. Rhode

It was that very astute and remarkable journalist, C. P. Scott of the *Manchester Guardian*, who said 'a newspaper has a moral as well as a material existence, and its character and influence are in the main determinated by the balance of these two forces'. This could be said of all individuals, all institutions, all businesses, all industries, all professions in a free society, but it applies with particular emphasis to some individuals (journalists are an example) and to some institutions (the press, radio, and television). Scott found the balance struck between the moral and the material existence of newspapers particularly significant because the newspaper 'plays on the minds and consciences of men'. So, too, do the other mass media of communication.

Phrased in different terms, the problem of balance involves freedom on one side of the scale and responsibility on the other. Some publishers deny that this problem exists. They claim the freedom but reject the responsibility. Such is the attitude of the American publisher who said, 'A newspaper is a private enterprise owing nothing whatever to the public, which grants it no franchise. It is emphatically the property of the owner, who is selling a manufactured product at his own risk.' This perhaps, would have been a defensible view for a shoe manufacturer in the *laissez-faire* economy of the 19th century but seems to be out of step with the social trends of the 20th. But, at least, it has the merit of frankness.

Every school child in America learns of the first amendment to the U.S. constitution which 'guarantees' free speech and a free press. The revered first amendment, in the words of historian Charles Beard, granted the 'right to be just or unjust, partisan or nonpartisan, true or false'. Newspapers without government were preferable to government without newspapers, Thomas Jefferson said. But Jefferson and the framers of the U.S. constitution were children of the Age of Enlightenment and they followed the libertarian theory of the press based on John Milton's self-righting process, that process by which truth bests falsehood in free and open encounter. United States history in the late 18th century and early 19th, and Australian history in the second half of the 19th century, provide examples of this theory put into journalistic practice. These were periods of extreme partisan journalism when newspapers concentrated on opinions, not news, and nearly every shade of opinion had its organ. Some other journalistic philosophy might have served us better, but hindsight testifies that the babble of voices did not, on the whole, serve us badly. A political, economic, and social climate existed in which a multiplicity of voices could and did flourish.

In the second half of the 19th century came the development of what has been called 'objective reporting', the technique of the reporter as aloof spectator. Objective reporting had its origins in the demands for nonpartisanship created by cooperative news gathering for a number of publications otherwise unassociated and often diametrically opposed in political outlook. Objectivity was accelerated by the decline of the purely political journal and the rise of the medium devoted primarily to 'scorekeeping', a factual recounting of overt events judged to be news. And inevitably, then, news came to mean not what the editor judged as significant, but what he judged most consumers would most likely read. The skilful at guessing the current state of reader taste gained the seemingly incontrovertible evidence of success—the biggest circulation. Thus, the theory of journalism for the masses: 'Give them what they want.' Interestingly enough, this theory is defended, when anyone feels called upon to defend it (which is seldom), by appealing to the hallowed phrases of the libertarian philosophy: Man is a rational creature and is best left to judge for himself what is best for himself, and it is a free country so if he doesn't like this newspaper or this television programme then he can read that magazine or that book, or go and play the poker machines at the club.

But the libertarian formula—from the self-righting process comes truth—assumes a multiplicity of voices, each with an equal chance to be heard. This assumption has never been in complete accord with the facts and has become increasingly less so as society has developed greater complexity with an inevitable greater reliance upon mass rather than individual communication as a thread for weaving the social fabric.

Some persons have superior ability in communication; some have or have created for themselves direct access to a large, even vast, audience, which, through the unavoidable facts of modem economics, is denied to others. And with the mass media all pervasive the truth-seeker finds himself so overwhelmed with pap he has little stomach for the search. Communication today is dominated by publishing and broadcasting giants and, even assuming that these are benevolent despots, it is idle to argue that bigness and monopoly represent no danger, either current or potential, to the unhampered and undistorted dissemination of information. However, it is equally as idle to charge with Quixotic lance the combination which the forces of modem society have created in communications as well as in industry, and in labor. A new philosophy, a new theory, must be formulated to fit new conditions. The mass media must be assessed in terms of how well they serve and fit the society of the 20th century. Any theory of the mass media must be tested against the mentality of today's age, not yesterday's. Any institution which persists in operating in a new age, on the theories of the old, risks being modified or even scrapped by a dissatisfied society. The wreckage of discarded publications which strews the history of journalism would seem to be relevant evidence on this point.

The libertarian theory of the press developed out of the mentality of the Age of the Enlightenment. This was the age characterised by Newton's theory of a perpetual motion world which ran timelessly according to immutable laws of nature, by John Locke's philosophy of natural rights, by the theories of classical economics that a minimum of governmental interference would inevitably result in the equating of self-interest with public good, and by John Milton's principle of the free market place of ideas. These theories, and others, produced a revolution in thought, in industry, in social organisation, and a revolution in mass communication. But revolutions are not solely a characteristic of the pre-20th century. Thought has continued and from it have come changes which have all but demolished the theories of the libertarian mentality. Evolution and the dynamic concepts of modem physics have shattered the Newtonian world; modern social science and philosophy have outmoded Locke's natural rights theories; modern societies have repudiated classical *laissez-faire* economics; the freedom of the market place for ideas is suspect.

The intellectual climate of the mid-20th century seems to favor what has been described as the social responsibility theory of the press. This is a new theory only in a limited sense since it amounts to only a variation of the libertarian theory. Both theories emphasise the notion of freedom, thus rejecting governmental control and accepting the theory of a free idea market. But the new theory, recognising that modern-day economics limits access to the market place, emphasises that freedom must be balanced with a sense of responsibility.

A number of technological developments are behind the social responsibility theory. These include the increased size, speed, efficiency, and scope of the old media (primarily products of the printing press), the creation of new media (primarily products of electronics), the growing volume of advertising, the demand for communication threads to hold together an increasingly urbanised society, and the increasingly centralised control in the mass communication industry. These developments have paved the way for a view of the mass media, not as voices in the market place, but as profitable industries.

Also behind the social responsibility theory is development in thought which departs from the basic philosophy of the libertarian view in that it appears to place significantly less faith in man as a rational creature who can be depended upon to apply his reasoning faculties to the unending and difficult search for truth without prodding. But is this rather less optimistic view of the nature of man a radical or unprecedented departure from our cherished inheritance from the Age of Enlightenment? Or is it merely a logical extension of a notion which has already had its expression in such accepted but widely diverse developments as laws decreeing compulsory education, compulsory voting, driving tests, prohibiting pornographic literature, establishing an Australian Arts Council?

Constitutions declare the press free; could they also guarantee responsibility? There are examples. Article 22 of the constitution of Portugal: 'Public opinion is a fundamental element of the politics and administration of the country; it shall be the duty of the state to protect it against all those agencies which distort it contrary to truth, justice, good administration and the common welfare.' Or Article 187 of the Constitution of Ecuador: 'The primary aim of journalism is to defend the national interests, and it constitutes a social service worthy of the respect and support of the state.' But these are modern-day authoritarian views of the press which, in effect, deny freedom while defining responsibility. Any attempt by government to define responsibility of the press is too dangerous because it is only one short step more to 'big brother' and state regulation of ideas.

How then to achieve wide-spread responsibility in the mass media while preserving freedom? To the mass media themselves this question often poses itself as a conflict between public service and the need to survive without being obligated to government, public pressure groups, or subsidising agencies. Reports of the Commission on Freedom of the Press (in America), the Royal Commission on the Press (in Britain and Canada), and studies of such competent researchers as Wilbur Schramm suggest three general approaches to this problem.

Responsibility has been defined and adjured by organisations within the communication industry through codes of ethics. Examples include the code of the Australian Journalists' Association, the 'Canons of Journalism' adopted by the American Society of Newspaper Editors, and the code of the American Broadcasters' Association.

But there are difficulties involved in attempting to punish irresponsible behaviour through a code of ethics. It seems to be more troublesome to pinpoint precisely unethical behaviour in the realm of communication than in the realm of medicine or law, where the scope and form of practitioners' activities can be defined with relative precision. There is a seeming reluctance, too, on the part of newspapermen to discipline or even publicly criticise fellow club members—a rather strange and abnormal sensitivity to criticism, in fact, whether from internal or external sources, for an institution which generally seems to assume it has the right and even the duty to criticise most other elements of society.

The American Society of Newspaper Editors' 'canons' have never been applied as a disciplinary measure against a member in any really serious case. The one time when there seemed to be a probability that the code would be employed, the accused member was allowed to resign before any formal action was taken. In Australia, the Journalists' Association code has been applied in a few cases, making it evident that this group regards its code as something more than mere words such as are pronounced solemnly at a fraternal initiation. But the difficulty in the Australian case lies in the fact that the A.J.A. code has no jurisdiction over proprietors and top-ranking editors.

Also suggested, and in one case being tried, is the establishment of independent agencies to appraise and report publicly on the performance of the mass media. This method is now being tried in Britain and has been proposed in both Australia and the United States, but prevented in both countries largely through the opposition of some, but not all, newspaper proprietors. An argument advanced in favor of these 'watch-dog' agencies, independent of mass media control, is that these media have claimed for themselves time and again the mantle of leadership. Their nature, in fact, forces them into this role. It is basic in a democracy that the citizenry has the right to appraise and criticise the performance of its leaders.

The third proposal involves education of the consumer to a more wholesome and informed interest in the mass media of communication. A great many individuals among the consuming public have still to learn that it is not the primary function of the mass media to provide mass tranquillisers. Many of the shortcomings of the mass media are in truth only reflections of the existing political, economic, and social climate. Some responsibility for the escapism and delusion pumped into society in massive doses by the mass media must rest with the consumers, but only some. The primary responsibility rests with those who control the media, since they have assumed, willingly or not, roles of leadership, and also because the still increasing tendency toward centralised control in the communications industry has here again emphasised the responsibility side of the balance scale. The tremendous power concentrated in the hands of a relatively few persons is an aspect of the 20th century's communications revolution which most people do not appreciate—if, in fact, they are even aware that a communications revolution has taken place.

What is needed is informed consumer comment on the mass media, not consumer control. Communications magnates are fond of quoting the cliché about the public being the final judge and jury, implying that no newspaper, no magazine, no television programme will survive sustained public disfavour. But this is only the power of final veto, works erratically and slowly at best, and offers but a very meagre guide to what the public considers to be a responsible performance. On the other hand, danger lies in any organised consumer group since such tend to become pressure groups that advance the moral, economic, or political standards of only a limited section of the public. It is only too clear in the evidence of today's movies and television programmes what the intervention of pressure groups can do in helping such media achieve a new level of shoddy art characterised by almost incredible inanity and pointlessness.

There is no easy way to force responsibility upon anyone or any institution. It can be accomplished to some degree in, for example, drug manufacturing and banking through legislation, but we have already seen that this has been rejected as a precedent too dangerous for serious consideration in the realm of ideas where the mass media, to serve a free society, must operate. This leaves us with only the possibility of falling back on the techniques and traditions of democracy, developing a flexible system of checks and balances that will provide not an infallible but at least a reasonably reliable appraisal of and guide for improvement of mass media performance. This would seem to involve all of the methods proposed, other than legislation, each functioning independently but with interaction: internal surveillance by the communicators themselves plus external surveillance by an independent agency or agencies and by unorganised but informed consumers. Formation of internal and external groups which make public in detail their investigations of and reports upon the performance of the communication media should aid greatly in achieving the third goal, an informed and critical public. Both internal and external agencies should make it part of their business to see that publications and broadcasts are regularly available that ignore the common-denominator-of-taste criterion but appeal directly to specialised tastes which now tend to be ignored (in fact sometimes seemingly deliberately insulted) by the mass media.

Coupled with all this must be a programme to exploit the resources of universities for the best possible preparation of journalists, and for advanced study, research, and critical evaluation of the communications field. Some might feel that such a programme for improvement of the product of press and airwaves could only result in cramming both with intellectualised wailing over the state of world culture, but a much more likely and to be hoped for result would be a more effective challange to the mental worlds people carry about with them by exposing them more frequently to the harsh and the lovely in the world of reality.

The press and the other mass media of communication, whether they realise it or not, long ago passed the point where the rising tide of criticism can be stayed by arrogant indifference, born of absorption in their own importance, or by the flip comment: 'We give the people what they want.' That comment, taken at its face value, is irresponsible (if not immoral) in that it denies responsibility, attempts to shift responsibility to the shoulders of the customer. Just as the press holds the concert artist responsible for programme selection as well as performance, so should the press be held responsible for what it prints and how well it presents it.

Shadow of War (1967)

Thomas W. Shapcott

We had never seen black cockatoos, though in the park
at home sometimes we'd begged our mother along
to the safe wire to stare at the white cousins
for a taunt of trained vowel and diphthong;
but here, up in the country where our father had sent us
(evacuees from a real and newspaper terror),
one morning we were shown on the dead tree near the kitchen
black cockatoos gathering, over and over,

crowded in warfare of black wings, black feathers,
quarrelling for a few stiff branches in their thick dozens.
'Look at them!' we cried to the farmer, our taciturn host,
as they covered the charred tree with acrid blossoms,
jagged and torn by red shadows, red crests.
He stood in the dry yard where we shouted and pranced.
'I see them' he said, then, 'It's the corn they're after.
A gun would shift them.' But he only walked away, and cursed;

while we crowded and shrieked to see the birds keep the tree,
not like the sleek crows, sly and silently,
but angrily, arrogantly, with black and red noise,
forcing their own terms triumphantly.
We were too young to price the waste of a crop,
or the shrug of that grim man—whose son was newly dead
in a battle out of reach. On the dead verandah
we played at soldiers, khaki and black and red,
and our cries were birds on fire overhead.

The Inquisitors (1968)

Thomas Keneally

So that next morning Maitland was firmly *persona grata* again. He was glad. To live in that grey elephant of a house on any other terms would have been a test of sanity he did not wish to undergo. Yet his success had its blemishes, as when Costello bombarded him with applause. Nolan, having carried so funereal a face on the question, kept clear. It was not until two mornings later, himself and Maitland passing in the corridor behind the high altar, both vested for Mass and bearing chalices, that Nolan smiled with an aged wistfulness and whispered, 'So you talked His Grace round to your view of things.'

During that brief springtime when Maitland seemed to bear His Grace's cachet, Costello came to him a second time and said, 'It seems there's a nun in St Thomasine's College—that's across the city. She's apparently a little unorthodox but the mother-superior has tended to be tolerant of her. However, two parents have complained now, and mother is shaken. His Grace is so far on your side over this other matter that he wants you to be one of the three members of a sort of informal enquiry.'

Maitland, caught in his shirtsleeves and in a contemplative mood, said, 'I'm not a good inquisitor.'

'It doesn't matter. I'll be there. I've done this sort of thing before. You just sit back and look as magisterial as get-out and learn the ropes.'

Moored on a hill against a high wind and vibrant south-easting clouds, St Thomasine's was neither as huge nor as Lord Alfred Peacock as the house-of-studies, yet fit to make hysterical any girl returning from summer holidays. Down to the last digit on its crass garden statuary, it seemed exemplary, the last place to harbour a radical nun. Inside was the browning winter light of institutions, waiting for them in the parlour like something they had been unsuccessful at leaving at home. Also waiting were Monsignor Fleming, the third member of the committee, and the mother-superior. Both were young sixty-year-olds. Their serge clothing lapped them about in unchallengeable snugness as they spoke of the signs of decline, angina and gall and kidneys, in old nuns and priests known to both of them. Introductions over, the mother-superior began to present the dossier on Sister Martin, the danger. She asked them to sit at the head of the table so that the thing would look judicial. She said reluctantly that she thought it had come to that.

'Sister Martin is a brilliant young woman, university trained. If I say that I'm alarmed at her cynicism about questions of church administration and history, you'll receive the wrong impression. She's gentle and pleasant and, practically speaking, docile. What I'm trying to say is this—I don't think that a church history period should be an opportunity to describe how a medieval Pope got in such a hurry to go out hunting that he ordained some poor priest in a stable instead of a church. Nor to look into the lives of some of those cardinals of pre-reformation days.'

Costello chuckled. 'The sins of the fathers ...'

'Yes, doctor. But you see, one of the girls' parents complained. Two excellent Catholics. The mother is a member of the Catholic Women's Guild Committee, the father is an executive of the Knights of St Patrick ...'

Maitland blinked. He said, 'Excuse me, mother. Not that it matters, but is the name of these people Boyle?'

The nun frowned as if an effort of memory were involved. 'No ... no. Not Boyle, father.'

His sigh was too audible. He settled back to suffer the dull malaise that the brown light, the buffed pearliness of the oak table, the terrifying cleanliness-next-to-Godliness of the cedar floorboards awoke in him. (The cobbler allergic to leather, the claustrophobic miner were not more star-crossed than Maitland.) Beyond the window, girls yelped on the tennis-courts; the resonance of nylon racquets came to him; and in some music room a child with a violin assaulted the jolly scarps of *Humoresque*. None of it failed to add layers to his discomfort.

'They were very reluctant to complain,' said the mother-superior of the exemplary parents. 'They claim, however, that Sister Martin has criticised the traditional formulas of belief—not violently. Firmly. I must make that clear to you. There is no arrogance in Sister Martin. Absolutely none.'

'Have you questioned her about these matters?' Costello asked.

'Yes, doctor. That is how I know—not violent, but firm. She uses terms for almighty God which, it seems, were coined by Protestant theologians. She speaks of 'the ground of our being', although she has reservations about that term, as about all other terms.'

Costello's eyes narrowed.

The nun said with a hint of pride, 'I thought of letting old Father Royal speak to her, but the trouble is she'd run rings around him. Shall I fetch her now? Oh, her views on the sacraments are a little revolutionary.' Her eyes dropped. She had the grace not to like what her conscience demanded, not to like giving up her sister to theologians.

'Before you go, mother, did the parents complain on all these points?'

'No. Actually, their sense of outrage centred mainly in that she'd called perpetual novenas magic.'

'Did you ask her about that point, mother?' Monsignor Fleming asked.

'Yes, monsignor. She said that—well, that for her, magic wasn't necessarily a nasty work, that mankind deprived of magic wouldn't be the richer.'

'You seem to be careful not to misquote her,' Costello decided.

'Yes, I took notes of our interview and allowed her to reread and amend them. However, I am no expert, so I didn't think it quite just to burden you with them.'

'You *have* been merciful, mother.'

'She's a lovely girl ...'

'Sister Martin?'

'Yes, doctor.'

Costello closed his eyes and made a harsh male sound with his sinuses. 'There are questions, mother, on which we cannot yield an inch even to those we love.' Maitland noticed for the first time that the theologian had actually been taking notes of his own.

'I had better let her speak for herself,' the reverend-mother decided.

Waiting for Sister Martin, Costello and the monsignor sat up straight and ready, knowing that theology was a man's world and that here were men enough for the job. Maitland wished on the poor girl the guts of Joan of Arc, the wit of Heloise.

Costello told him, 'James, we may not be able to observe all the amenities with this young lady.'

'Why not?' Maitland was preparing to say. 'She sounds civilised enough.'

But that was when she came in; and in an attempt not to look judicial, he took to playing with the cuff of his coat. It was impossible though, massed at one end of a long table with an august theologian and a monsignor in purple stock, not to seem to be what he was. Which was, of all things, a judge.

She was young with pale, fine-grained skin that reminded him of Grete's. She said, 'Good afternoon monsignor, fathers,' and waited like a schoolgirl to be invited to sit. Maitland blushed but lacked the courage; and in the end Costello glanced up and ordered her to take a seat. It was rudeness justified by the need for orthodoxy. Maitland became so angry at it that all he could do was sit on the rim of his chair and swallow. He thought, 'One day, when you're a bishop, you'll be all worldly grace to the baggy wives of Q.C.'s.'

As it was, the expanse of table between the three priests and Sister Martin too clearly imposed the status of culprit on the woman. The monsignor unexpectedly found it alien to his nature that it should be so, that the girl should be kept at such an inquisitorial distance. He pointed to the gas-fire glinting inappositely under an antique mantel-piece.

The chair being massive, Maitland helped her shift it. 'Here?' he asked, grounding it. 'Thank you, father,' she said. 'Father' came out broken in two by a nervous lack of breath at the back of the throat. Maitland felt his profound lack of innocence. He was glad to return to Costello's side.

'What's all this then, sister?' Costello wanted to know. He smiled leniently, the sort of male leniency that provokes feminists. His fingers played sensitively with the edges of his notepaper. 'Been scandalising the parents?'

'It is possible for these things to be reported out of context by children,' said the nun. 'I believe I may have been reported a little out of context, father.'

'Of course,' the old monsignor said pacifically. 'It happens.'

Costello raised his voice. 'Just the same, aren't some of the things you've said rather rash whether in or out of context?'

The nun told them, 'When a class hasn't been fully prepared, it's unavoidable that something rash will be said.'

'And you don't prepare your classes fully?' Costello asked her in a voice that only just managed to maintain basic human trust in her.

'We're very understaffed. It's impossible to prepare every class fully at the moment, father.'

As a first principle to which he required her assent, Costello stated, 'The teaching of the one true faith comes first, sister.'

Seeing that she was not meant to win, 'Of course,' she said.

'Let us begin at *the* beginning,' Costello suggested. 'I have always thought that God was God, sister, that we confuse the faithful by calling him by any tautologous terms as "The ground of our being", and that other meaningless and downright blasphemous title, "the God beyond God".'

Tautologous terms such as 'Our father who art in heaven', Maitland thought. He began to wonder if he also were not the object of the enquiry—two anarchists for the price of one.

'Don't you agree, sister?' Costello persisted.

'When one spends all one's energies pursuing the vision of God, one is disturbed when people find it possible to say that God is dead.'

'That God-is-dead business is just a university fashion.'

'Partly, father, yes, but fashion is an extension of society. So that one is still alarmed.'

The nun, her skin smooth with those cosmetics which mother-church considered best for her—these being humility in argument, the seeing of God's will in the decrees of people such as Costello, modesty about the eyes—nevertheless managed her small ironies; mainly by speaking to the tribunal as a whole, trusting to its joint good reason, using 'father' in a collective sense. There was a marginal hint about her manner: that she did not trust entirely to Costello's good reason, that she did not consider him unqualifiedly as her father. This was so tenuous an implication that Costello would lose dignity by responding to it. Yet, while tenuous, it was also unmistakable. Maitland felt very pleased with this nun. She underlined one of the few things he knew about women: that they were essentially ungovernable.

He himself broke in. 'What do you think people mean when they say that God is dead, sister?'

'I hardly dare say,' she answered immediately, but gave signs of being about to show considerable daring. 'But human organisations limit God by identifying themselves with him. They express him in terms that accord with their nature and needs. Then the terms get old—like the organisations. The terms die.' She glanced at Costello. 'If I used the term "God beyond God", which I can't really remember doing—but we're very busy—if I used it, it was to make the girls realise that no matter how old terms and organisations grow, the real God is still untouched and unknowable and speaks in silences.'

Quickly, she sat back, alarmed to discover herself eloquent before priests. She had, in fact, given the word 'unknowable' a ring of triumph, of passion and blood. This helped bring all that was most arid to the forefront of Costello's mind.

'You say "unknowable", sister,' he observed. 'What do you mean by unknowable?'

She tried to say, grimacing. 'Words are a trap, father. Yet I suppose it is what you theologians would call unknowable in his essence.'

That particular theologian became taut with delight.

'The first Vatican council rejected your opinion as heretical.'

'Did they, father? It's so hard to express oneself, but then if one is a teacher one has to try. However, I'm sure we both ultimately agree, Vatican I and myself. So many of these theological squabbles are only matters of semantics.'

'Are they just?' said Costello.

'I was reading last week,' the girl began; and then, 'Did you want me to continue speaking, father?'

'Why not? You're the informed member of the panel.'

'Oh no,' she said softly. 'I'm sorry. I realise how annoying it must be for a professional theologian to have to listen to me.'

'At the moment you must speak. That is why we are here.'

The monsignor smiled and assured her. 'We're fair game.'

For a second, a small girl ran beneath the window taunting, 'Boarders are getting cabbage for tea.' The nun took her crucifix out of one place in her girdle and stabbed it back into another. Her flummoxed hands found this the first thing available for the doing.

'I was merely going to say that I read an article last week in an English review about Luther and Aquinas—that Luther meant by faith what Aquinas meant by hope, that Luther needn't have been excommunicated and all that religious and political agony could have been prevented. The predicament we are in with words, you see. Now, when one speaks of God, one has to apologise for the poverty of words, one has to mistrust them. Yet we have to speak about the unspeakable, don't we?'

'Of course,' old Fleming said, as if for the sake of keeping well in the game. 'But a teacher of the young has to be so careful, sister, so very careful ...'

In the meantime, Maitland, though not expert on legislation, decrees and anathemas, saw reason to suggest, 'If I might correct an impression sister may have taken from what you said a moment ago, Doctor Costello ... I don't think that either yourself or the Vatican council intend to imply that Sister Martin is a heretic because she believes God is, as she says, untouched and ultimately unknowable.'

Costello sighed. 'Let me assure you, Dr Maitland, that that *is* what the Vatican council condemned.'

'Of course, the relationship between man and God is personal and can't be legislated for,' said Maitland. 'All the council claims is that God can be known by reason. But surely not in his essence— whatever that word means.'

'That is casuistry!' Costello cried out. He stared ahead of him. There was an unwonted pallor in the eye-pouch and cheek that Maitland could see. 'How can something be known if it is not known in its essence?'

'Indeed,' said the monsignor, who had none the less lost track of the hounds.

Costello announced, very loudly but to no one in particular, 'What I have said is aimed at proving the dangers of playing inexactly with theological terms.'

Monsignor Fleming nodded. 'It's done for many a good man. Look at the great Père Lammenais in nineteenth-century France ...'

But the other three had too much on hand to take this invitation.

'I must say in fairness to Sister Martin,' Maitland enjoyed observing, 'that she seems to have a profound sense of these dangers.'

'No,' said the nun herself, and meant it absolutely. 'Not enough sense. Not enough.'

'*Ipse dixit*,' said Costello. 'Or should I say *ipsa*?'

There was a silence. The nun bowed her head, obviously accepting on it the blame for having spoken inexactly of the diety. Since this same guilt was shared by Moses, Augustine, John of the Cross, Teresa of Avila, Joan of Arc, and an army of other master spirits, Maitland hoped she was proud of the crime. She gave no sign, however.

'And now what about these sacraments?' Costello asked, restored to victorious joviality.

After listening to Sister Martin on sacraments for a short time, and having watched that fool Maitland nodding his lean head, forebearing, perhaps even approving, Costello cut the drift of the girl's pleadings with one downward stroke of his hand. Passionless, breathing hard, he spoke.

'I have something to tell you, Sister Martin. I tell it without malice, merely with some sadness.'

He once again made that sinusitic rumble already tested on the mother-superior. It sounded, and was almost certainly meant to be, male and harsh and mastering, gruff as a navvy's fart and, to Maitland's mind, even less creditable. '*You* are a modernist. And modernism is a heresy.'

The woman sighed. *She* sounded feminine and soft as any deep waters; and indicated ever so slightly the vulgarity of the doctor's nasal cavities. 'Do you wish to conclude I am a heretic, father?'

'Not yet.' He waved his right hand spaciously. 'We presume your good faith up to this moment. However, now that you have been warned … I beg you, my daughter, in this hour of your extreme need, to prostrate yourself before Christ your Spouse and His Blessed Mother.'

Maitland, speechless, battled for composure; as Monsignor Fleming quoted, '*Woe unto him who scandaliseth a little one …*' He was sure that she had not merited mill-stones. But all those who dealt with the young had to be careful, so very careful.

Suddenly, Costello became therapeutically kind. He said that he would draw up, prayerfully and with specific attention to her peril, a list of theology texts she was to con thoroughly. In the meantime she should not teach the one true faith to children. After some months he would return and interview her once again. 'Agreed?' he asked the monsignor, who certainly didn't want to seem severe, but thought that such a course was proper. Not that he didn't realise she did her level best. But until her small inaccuracies were cleared up …

'Remember that you are the bride of Christ,' Costello demanded of her, and shut his awe-struck lids.

Something began to pulse in Maitland's throat, and out of the pulse, full of the rhythms of his blood, grew unaccountably his voice. It swung across the room like a pendulum.

It said, 'The bride does not need a formula for the bridegroom, her knowledge of him surpasses formulas.'

'That's all very well for the bride,' Costello agreed after a silence.

'Exactly', said Maitland.

He told the nun, 'I know each of the books Dr Costello has recommended to you. Let me say that you will find them alien, legalistic, sterile. None the less, perhaps mother-superior will order you to read them, and in that case you must not let them influence your life as a nun or give you despair.'

The nun said, 'I'd prefer you didn't continue, father.'

'Ah, but preferences aren't your business. Dr Costello has made that clear enough. However, the only other thing I wanted to say was that I disassociate myself utterly from Dr Costello's concerted rudeness to you.'

'Thank you,' she told him with classroom firmness. 'But, of course, I understood from the beginning that none of you were acting from spite.'

As she was going, Maitland opened the door for her to pass into the hall. Here the lights shone. Two barbarous statues, lolly-pop coloured, postured across the void of carpet and stained boards, and from a place where showers and taps ran, boarding students could be heard giggling towards cabbage-time.

'Sister Martin,' Maitland called after her from the door. 'I haven't time to stand on ceremony. Have you—' He lost his temper at his powers of speech and ended in saying lamely, 'Have you *seen* God?'

Behind them, at the far end of the parlour, Costello could be heard rumbling in judgment of this flourishing woman.

She smiled. 'If I said yes, father, I could hardly blame you for calling me a liar.'

'In this frantic world, how can a person be sure he isn't pursuing a nullity, or worse still, himself?'

'But what would you expect to be told, father? That you see God as you see a town clerk, at a given time on a given day. And as if by appointment?' She frowned. 'Father, I don't think there's one being that pursues a nullity.'

Costello coughed a summons to him. The nun formed a sudden resolve. She told him, 'One knows by the results. Nothing is the same afterwards. Everything has a special—luminosity. You are able to see, well, *existence* shining in things.' She shrugged, 'Words again!' and seemed very sad.

'I have never experienced a more blatant attack on religious obedience,' Costello told his notepaper softly as Maitland once more took the seat beside him. 'If I were the type, I would count the number of times I have attempted to make you feel welcome in the happy brotherhood of this archdiocese. This is the second time I have been fanged as a result. I know that there'll be a seventh and eighth time. Therefore,' and he made an ample gesture of cancellation, 'I wash my hands. Of course, I may relent—Christians are meant to be professional relenters—but I have rather genuine hope that once and for all, I have left you to your own juice.'

The old monsignor chewed his lips and concentrated upon surviving the contretemps. Maitland did not make this task easier, contending, 'No doubt, when the Holy Spirit sees fit to raise you to the episcopate, you'll treat the society wives at charity openings with the same honest brutality you showed that girl.'

'If ever it becomes necessary I will. Oh, what's the use of explaining old methods to novices. Do you know how to begin to rehabilitate a woman? Do you know what the basic step is? To make them weep. Once you have, the work can begin.'

'That's barbarism.'

'Ask any long-service husband,' the doctor advised.

'Might I be excused? From the room, I mean. From the whole turnout.'

'You had better wait till mother shows.'

Costello kept working on the list of texts for Sister Martin, and when he was finished, showed it first to the monsignor, then to Maitland. In a short time the mother-superior returned.

'Would a retreat be possible?' he asked her. 'I believe *that* sister should make a retreat soon. There is a crisis of faith pending there, and it should be brought on quickly.'

'My God!' Maitland said loudly.

'There are crises of faith in all directions,' the doctor opined tangentially and gazed into the ordered depth of the gas-fire.

Maitland stood and turned to the mother-superior. 'Mother, thank you for having me. If I might be bold enough to say so, you gave signs earlier of thinking that perhaps you owned a jewel in Sister Martin. I concur utterly in your suspicions. Please don't burden her with those deathly books on Dr Costello's list.'

'I don't think you can go that far, young fellow,' the monsignor protested behind him.

'Believe me,' said Costello, 'he'll go all the way one of these days. All the way.'

Maitland certainly went further there and then. 'As for a retreat, silence can't hurt *her*. How far is it to the bus-stop, please?'

'But surely Dr Costello would drive you …?'

'Dr Costello is not safe at intersections,' said Maitland. 'Monsignor, it was a pleasure to meet you.'

Outside, it was night in an avenued suburb. The leaves spoke elementally in the wind, you would never have known that they were all tame and pampered vegetables pollarded yearly by the municipal council. Maitland felt refreshed and free.

The Monstrous Accent on Youth (1968)

Thea Astley

Two years ago at a middle-class girls' high school in Sydney, I set the top-level stream of students the task of writing about their attitudes to conscription for Vietnam. Seventy per cent favoured conscription for boys. They used anachronistic phrases like 'question of courage', 'man's duty to defend his family', 'making the world safe for democracy'. As the mother of a son I was perturbed and interested. After an interval of two months I suggested they write on conscription for girls, conscription to national service which would use them for nursing (perhaps in Vietnam), relief work for two years overseas, and so on. This time less than ten per cent favoured conscription. Girls, like female spiders, want to have their men and eat them, too. I was appalled by the selfishness of their reactions and wondered if this were merely a by-product of thinking in a Liberal Party voting area.

I cite this incident merely as an introduction to the attitudes of this generation which, despite engaging frankness on matters like sex and drug-taking, still has a hard conservative core. Perhaps they are only hard and conservative when it is a question of unselfishness. Perhaps they are tolerant merely in matters that concern self-indulgence.

In my evening tutorial classes at Macquarie University, I found more liberal discussion standards prevailed, a trait particularly noticeable in the nuns (I speak as one who recalls with some anguish the narrow dogmatism of the Irish teachers of my youth). General reading standards were low—again except for the nuns. This is an interesting point! Writers such as Compton Burnett, Cheever, Edmund Wilson, Nabokov, Gordimer (even funny men like de Vries) were literally unknown as names. (I clutch a handful at random.) Discussing D. H. Lawrence and the war between men and women, only one in sixty had read Thurber's *The Unicorn in the Garden*.

Maybe the average of this generation have not the time for reading or perhaps not the interest. They drink much more. (I went through university on four sweet sherries.) And they have more money to do it with. Where my generation enjoyed faculty picnics up the Brisbane River with bottles of lemonade and a lot of earnest conversation, final year students at leading Sydney private schools prefer pub crawls and regard a party where the drink runs out early as a wash-out. I don't know what this proves. I feel their livers are in more danger than their morals. But I do deplore the jaded attitude that can only get its kicks in a semi-inebriated state.

The generation before mine was probably sour-puss because the Depression made every personal achievement heroic. We still tend to think the young should fend for themselves when, as everyone is aware, nepotism and privilege, the unsubtle play of 'influence', are at work all the time. One is sorry life is so easy for the young and, because of this, so difficult.

The permissiveness of our generation to the younger has created the monstrous over-rated importance of youth. Oldies—pregnant, sick, reeling—can tremble vertical upon trains and buses while thick-thighed youngsters cling to their seats. There is no reverence for age as such and while this is understandable and not expected, one longs for a little sympathy such as might be meted out to the under-privileged.

Recently I said to a colleague and his wife after we had been discussing youth, 'Oh God, sometimes I loathe the young!' Instantly and together they cried, 'Yes, so do we!' But of course they don't. And I don't. They adore their children and students as I do mine. It's only that at times we grow a little fearful of the Frankenstein we have created.

Protest and Anaesthesia (1968)

Douglas Kirsner

Herbert Marcuse has described modern man and his society as 'one-dimensional'. Establishment mores are all-pervasive. It is difficult now to differentiate individual from social needs, what the individual actually wants from what society wants him to want. True, these 'needs' are not imposed on him by force. Ideology, having extended itself everywhere, becomes even more insidious because its presence so often goes unnoticed. Values are thought of as facts to be known, rather than as preferences to be decided.

Those who disagree with the basic functioning and structure of society are regarded as neurotic, irrational, in need of adjustment and understanding. Society no longer locks up its critics; it renders them ineffectual by more subtle means. There is an accepted arena of rational discussion and action, and anything outside this is deemed irrational—or at least unalterable. Thus the foundations of society cannot seriously be questioned since they are assumed to be rational.

By being translated into more ameliorable terms genuine problems about society are gutted of real content. Work problems are solved by higher wages, Vietnam by more or fewer troops, boredom by more television. Problems about the quality of life are redirected on to quantitative and thereby more manageable grounds.

Society is paternalistic. The people are passive recipients of goods and governments. Apathy is regarded as good, a sign of stability. Intensity of experience eludes modern man. When it occurs it is regarded as unusual or neurotic; it is institutionalised so that others will not be infected. Creativity and spontaneity are packaged together with artists and ardent lovers. The happiness of ordinary people is equated with a 'high standard of living'; freedom with a choice between fundamentally similar automobiles or political parties. 'He has no cause to be unhappy—a family, a good position, house, car, education. What more could a man ask for?'

We seldom realise just how far we are the objects of manipulation and management. By giving the illusion of free, individual choice, democratic capitalist society provides one of the most effective forms of domination yet devised. Freedom has hitherto performed a critical function, but now it is formalised, it is empty, itself enhancing man's alienation. But the 'otherness' of society is still felt. Whatever it is, it is not ours in any but a formal sense. Man's alienation is becoming increasingly objective. There are enormous areas of society over which we have no control. Democracy is always defined as 'political', which means that we are allowed to have a say in certain *political* decisions. But what about industrial democracy? What control has the worker over his product or the way it is produced? Or economic democracy? The major investment decisions are taken by the large companies and corporations. Huge profits go to a numerically insignificant section of the population. The consumer is not sovereign since his 'needs' are manufactured for him by the corporations and their advertising agents. Or social democracy?

Even within the strictly limited ambit of political democracy how much power has the electorate? Irrational factors such as chauvinism and the 'downward thrust' of communism can win elections. The elected government often does not put its platform, if it has one, into effect.

More lies are told to this generation than to any previous. The Vietnam war has made this clear. Many governments have been so exposed on this issue that there is now an accepted 'credibility gap' on a great number of other matters. Youth everywhere—from Tokyo to Paris—are rebelling, and even where the aims of the rebellions are not precisely enunciated, a feeling of abhorrence for what is happening in society can be sensed. Never has the Establishment been in a better position to mould the individual to its wants from birth. With the aid of the mass media the government can deceive the people most effectively on a large number of matters. The Gesture has become very important. Demonstrations, if not always of any immediate perceptible effect, are a means of searching for the truth denied the young demonstrators by a society whose watchword is 'deceit'.

Youth are faced with a reprehensible, deceitful society which does not seem capable of fundamental change through the accepted methods of transformation (such as political parties seeking parliamentary power). Many withdraw and go about the life-work of raising a family, others seek change through public and unconventional methods. Students certainly seem to receive a press coverage and influence vastly incommensurate with their numbers. The riots in France and civil disobedience in Australian capital cities imply strong beliefs among the protesters about the inherent dignity of man which is being stifled by society.

The overt and direct physical 'violence' of some of the students is a reaction against the more sophisticated 'violence' of the Establishment which injures or destroys its subjects in one way or another. Rationales for protest such as the 'Situationist ethic' do not lead to anarchism or chaos. They look at society in a fundamentally *social* way and view the present set-up as so immoral that it has to be changed so men can really live their own lives in their own ways. Many protesters cite the Nuremburg charter as evidence that it is the moral duty of man to protest against an immoral state of affairs.

Those who criticise students for breaking the traditional patterns of behaviour should ask themselves: if they were faced with situations which they regarded as morally iniquitous and not the subject of change by traditional means, which have turned out to be useless by themselves, and they felt very strongly about the evil being done, what would they do? If they did nothing, would they not be morally responsible for the persistence of the evil state of affairs? The revolt of youth is a moral one.

The inevitability of violence is accepted in our society. Television screens tell us what is happening or has happened. Although the bomb dropped over Vietnam explodes also in our room, we know we are safe. But we also know we are powerless to prevent it. Instantaneous communication may only increase man's sense of impotence.

Although accustomed to vicarious physical violence, the young generation has not known war. We may know somebody who was conscripted to Vietnam, and we glance through the latest casualty lists. In Australia at least, the war has changed our lives very little.

The nature and type of war have changed. Weapons have become far more sophisticated, with the result that soldiers rarely see the 'enemy'. Since World War II the oppressed have not been on 'our' side and we have not been able to identify with them. The wars have largely been anti-colonialist, or wars of national liberation. We cannot identify with the Vietnamese because they are either on 'our' side fighting against the North Vietnamese, or they are slant-eyed Viet Cong. What has not struck home is that the people 'we' are fighting are on 'our' side.

There are many more radicals among the young today than there were during the thirties. The enormous rise in the size of universities has brought many of them together. Despite its numerous faults, mass education has put people in a better position to think about issues. The modern radicals generally read more than their predecessors. The massive growth in communications and travel has made the radicals more aware of an international responsibility. The hydrogen bomb, which has brought about the imminent possibility of almost total destruction, has made the concepts of internationalism and humanism more real. Compared with the radicals of the thirties, those of today are very wary of organisations and dogmas and often do not present positive alternatives to the present society.

Nevertheless modern radicals feel transformation of society in a socialist and democratic direction to be essential. But they are faced with no acceptable model. Although certainly not on the same basis as the U.S.A., the U.S.S.R. is undemocratic and bureaucratic and in many ways as remote from democracy (meaning the individual's control of his own destiny) as is America. Some young radicals seek inspiration from the national liberation movements of the Third World. Che Guevara, Ho Chi Minh, and Chairman Mao are seen as

the charismatic symbols of the new world. Change from within exist-
ing western society is seen as almost impossible.

But that does not mean that radicals subscribe to the 'end of
ideology'—that belonged to the 'silent Fifties'. Unrest, rebellion, dis-
satisfaction with the Affluent Society have reached new peaks. The
New Left is gaining greater influence. The emergence of (say) Dr J.
F. Cairns, Senator Eugene McCarthy (U.S.A.) and Prime Minister
Trudeau (Canada) symbolises a turn to a more *moral* view of society.
People are becoming sick of the mundane, useless, often immoral
machinations of the old politicians and are beginning to seek some-
thing new.

The need to transcend the present is now accepted by many of the
young. They cannot do this by using the system's own methods—by its
own self-seeking definition of 'rational action'—but rather by entirely
new modes of action, more akin to poetry than to prose, existentialist
rather than linguistic, 'utopian' rather than 'realistic'. Some live a type of
transcendence by the 'turn on, tune in, drop out' formula; others by par-
ticipating in movements to change society. If they have not articulated a
complete programme to replace the existing system, they at least know
that the system must be changed. It is this 'moral' thing that fires rad-
icals. They are incensed with the Napalm State. They do not want to
be the subject of a total (albeit 'pluralistic') administration. They attack
liberals not because they disbelieve in liberal ideals, but because these
ideals have been and can only be vacuous within the present society.
They do not believe that alienation is an unalterable fact about man
and his relations with his society and his world. They believe that the
individual's potentialities are stifled in our society, and that the general
monochrome level of apathetic existence can be replaced with a soci-
ety of free persons in which the individual's capacities can be fulfilled.
They believe in an intense, multi-dimensional existence. They are
utopian only in the sense that their demands cannot be satisfied within
the present framework. The radicals want to have real control over the
decisions of the community upon which they are dependent.

That's what the New Left is all about.

1970s

King Tide (1970)

Peter Steele

An hour ago the light could glaze alive
a dozen crumbling peaks to the green sand,
and fuse your mind with water into dream.
Later tonight, omnivorous, lurching inland,
a salient nightmare breeding darkness in darkness,
the tide will pulse its own anabasis,
fretting at pasture, a savage timed by the moon.
But now, the rough grown smooth enough to place,
the flow is neither, washing the river's mouth,
not poise or throb, the brazen or bestial serpent,
but only most of the world shifting a little,
unobliging, unobliged, vulgar and fecund,
fuming gods and death. Hock-deep in sand
I plough the wind, my mouth pebbled with prayers,
waiting for king-tide, slurring over and over
the lone unlikely epithets of God.

Sturt and the Vultures (1970)

Francis Webb

Mincing, mincing we go. And it follows, follows,
This hot nor'-easter: sometimes even a little testy at us
So that these poor horses sprocketed to its whirring coils
Slew away, working at the bit. Browne may be dying.
Little hot tantrums of wind and tiny pebbles
Desiccate and annul the few words I toss to him.
My thoughts skip among the stones. And it follows, follows,
This hot nor'-easter.
                    Back at the Depot
Our old Grandsire, misunderstood, is moping with Poole.
I gave Him his text at five sharp.
Feel for Him there, old bearded Predestinator
Trying to look kind … it's the plan He's tied to:
The elect and the—the—*wind, stones, pebbles.*
Browne may be dying.
                    Remember, my father's fireplace,
That lithograph beside the clock (Him there, as if the good Calvin
Had set Him there with St. Michael and a sword):
Yes, once at tea when prankful vermilion spat
And wriggled up out of the grate
I was solidly in the army—*Browne may be dying*—
There were cannonballs and bolting horses
And heathen by the barrel converted (I was about fourteen),
A girl, and benighted beachheads named after me
(*Hullo, Mr Browne*) and always the Search for something,
An opal, a prisoner …

Yes, I saw that prankful vermilion
Frisk up almost to His face. At the Search it was.
—*Wind, stones*—for an instant the Old'un looked hopeful
And about my own age.
Every morning now, the same:
I give Him His text early and wander off from Him
Leaving Him sob over the dear sacred scheme of His dotage
Dispositioning the just and the damned. *Stones, stones, stones.*
… Picture His poor tired old hands working away at the bellows
To keep up this hot nor'-easter. How it follows, follows.
Mincing we come, we go. Sand, pebbles all frills and furbelows.
Browne may be dying. *Water back at the Depot.*
—If only to rest His poor old hands a little … How it follows
This hot nor'-easter … the Void, the sand, the pebbles,
Little tattered pockets of the Void …
Browne is calling,
I was dreaming.
—The birds, the birds! Crying like children,
Closer, wheeling, wheeling, descending, closer!
They come in ecstatic flight, rapturous as the Paraclete,
Tongues of fire—it's a well of voices. Crying like children.
My horse props, makes to rear, shivers, and cannot move.
They come at us, begging, menacing, at eye-level, above.
I lash at them with my hands, filled with terror and love.

Fire a shot, Mr Browne. And, poets, you wheel away.
You are lost, gone. Where do you come from? (Feel the caressing
    nor'-easter
Following, following, chanting.) Are you from the Void?
Poets of dry upper nothingness, you are hunger, we are hunger,
You are thirst, we are thirst.
We go mincing along followed by the hot nor'-easter
—But sometimes we stray towards Sacrament, creek-bed, Virgin—

You stray, poets. But you ride neither high Heaven
Nor the earth of statuesque stones. Something lures you down,
Quartz, slate, limestone, an eyeball, an opal, a prisoner,
Till hunger and thirst wheel into madness within you,
Your immaculate Words, cryings (O hear the sweet nor'-easter)
Piping to us, see the lovely Madonna-faces in the gilt
Frameways of pure sand and pebbles!

                                       But neutralities or wrath
Of man—or is it of God!—expel you again from earth
Driving you out of sight and mind like exhausted breath,
The wing-whimper, the talon. Only something far beneath
Cowers away when you come.

                              And its name is Death.

'The revolution will not be televised'
(1971)

Craig McGregor

You will not be able to stay home, brother.
You will not be able to plug in, turn on and cop out.
You will not be able to lose yourself on scag
and skip out for beer during commercials.
The revolution will not be televised ...

Gil Scott-Heron

New York

Nothing's simple, of course, and even though Gimme Shelter, the Maysles Brothers' *cinéma vérité* account of the Rolling Stones' disastrous tour of America, is indeed a ritualistic tragedy over which Professor Albert Goldman, at New York's Columbia University, can rub gleeful hands ('They blew it!') and Michael Goodwin, in the underground magazine *Rolling Stone*, can achieve the self-propelled orgiastic martyrdom which *Easy Rider* has made fashionable ('We blew it!' says Goodwin-*né*-Fonda), it was sort of nice to find the cinema so grass-filled the other night that you could get a contact high and to rediscover that, even second time round, when Jagger blasts off at Madison Square Garden with *Jumpin' Jack Flash*, the fantastic, exhilarating power of hard rock slams you back in your seat yet again and your body lifts blood lifts and reels and even though you know how it all ended, like those Greek audiences in their stone Madison Squares, yet you still vouchsafe the music its life-dynamic and are forced to confront, once again, the paradox at the heart of what is still optimistically called the Revolution: that even within this particular sub-culture, there still exists all the terror, egotism, peacefulness, extremism, beauty and delusion—in a word, *plurality*— which makes the human situation human, and that in America today these contradictions are magnified a millionfold by their incarceration within the most violent and bloody-minded Empire State since Rome. Which was the message, beaten in with billiard cues and diffused on 300,000 bad vibes ('It's scary, really weird, man, really weird': Jefferson Airplane even before the Jagger debacle) understood at last at Altamont.

Please people please stop hurting each other.

The voice is Grace Slick's and she is trying to cool it at Altamont. But people have been hurting each other for a long time, they have been hurting each other ever since Cain slew Abel with a Stanley Kubrick jawbone and it is perhaps only this generation of young Americans who have been able to foster the self-delusion that if you turn your back on violence, which Rap Brown thinks is as American as cherry pie, it will like the bogeyman simply disappear in a whiff of good vibes and grass smoke. 'If we're all one let's fucking well show we're all one,' Jagger complains petulantly into the mike, his Superhype cloak drooping from his shoulders.

All one? That's another of the myths which the mainstream counter-culture has been assiduously propagating these last few years, what with George Harrison going on a treat about Within You Without You and the Maharishi preaching a sort of transcendental Oneness with the Unity or whatever other bloody Oneness we are supposed to be at One with—while in front of Jagger a black guy, a college student, is just a few seconds away from being stabbed and stomped to death and Hells Angels are leaping out into the crowd like killer whales, battering and smashing people's heads open with pool cues, blood everywhere, kids flashing pathetic V signs or scrambling for their lives and bearded guys like Hashidic rabbis trying to get between the Angels and their victims and next to the stage two guys who look like students are looking up at Jagger with pain in their eyes shaking their heads NO NO NO NO ('Twerpy hippies … demanding punishment,' sneers Goldman) and next to them there's a girl with an utterly immobile face and tears streaming down on to her neck and later there is this hysterical girl standing next to the stretcher (Meredith's girlfriend?) screaming 'I don't want him to die, he isn't going to die' but Meredith Hunter already has a blanket over his face and blood has soaked right through his hip green jacket and the chopper is waiting and he is dead.

We are not One, we never have been One, there in conflict Within Us and Without Us, and the lesson the counter-culture(s), hopefully, will carry away from Altamont is that deluding ourselves we are One is a surrogate for working out how to deal with the fact we are not. 'I ain't no peace creep,' snarls Hells Angel Barger afterwards—'they got got'. 'That was insane,' says drummer Charlie Watts, looking at the re-run of Angels gunning their hogs through 300,000 peace creeps. 'The Angels … seem more like heroes than villains,' says Michael Goodwin of *Rolling Stone*.

> *Don't follow leaders*
> *Watch the parkin' meters*
> Bob Dylan

In its desperate search for heroes the rock culture some time ago seized on, of all people, Mick Jagger … Jagger! Ole Mr Mephistopheles himself, the showbiz Lucifer who dabbles (Whist! dare we mention it?) in black magic and phony Satanism (*Their Satanic Majesties*), him of the Mandrake costume and liver-lipped *fin de siècle* decadence of Performance Oc-cult, him of the painted face and Regency kisscurls who opens his set at Altamont *opens* it for Chrissake with kids being chopped unconscious in front of him and people screaming and running and falling and that terrifying roar you get at football crowds and fight crowds when the blood shows yes *opens* it with *Sympathy for the Devil* and who when the song finally stumbles to a halt with

Angels his own mock-Satanic hirelings stalking the stage and the rest of the Stones transfixed over their guitars at the mayhem at their feet can only blurt out 'Something very funny happens whenever we start that number' (giggle). And a few minutes later Meredith is dead for Chrissake Jagger DEAD you bloody fool—how does that fit with your phony devilry? Meredith who is one of the few black guys in that colosseum of 300,000 roaring onlookers who made the mistake of taking a gun to a love-in given by the love generation and made the further mistake of pulling it to ward off The Wild Ones and ended with a knife in his head and a mouthful of blood likewise of years and then—nothing. 'Love is coming, love is coming to us all,' sing Crosby, Stills, Nash & Young. It is an elegy. There has always been murder in the Garden. *'Because your Adversary the Devil walketh about as a Roaring Lion, seeking whom he may Devour.'* At least Meredith picked up the gun. And in a single terrible act confronted the dilemma which haunts the 'counter-culture': when face to face at last with the death-dealers, whether at Altamont or in the White House, what do you do?

> *The revolution will not be televised.*
> *There will be no pictures of pigs shooting down*
> *brothers on the instant replay ...*

What the hell were the Angels doing there? We all know the answer to that: they were hired, in a bizarre showbiz stunt, as bodyguards for the Stones. But it isn't just Jagger's fault, or the Stones'. Altamont wasn't an accident. The rock culture's long-standing flirtation with the Angels is just another facet of the we-are-one myth, the secular monism which preaches that everyone who is outside straight culture is the same. If *Gimme Shelter* demonstrates anything it is that at Altamont there were two different and explosively opposed cultures—a fact which is dramatised in those climactic sequences in which Jagger, the ass-wiggling unisexual hero of new-found liberation, prances around the stage with his little tailfeathers quivering in cockerel-invitation ('I think Mick's a joke, with all that fag dancing,

I always did': John Lennon) while a few inches away Hells Angels in insignia-splattered leather jackets and Herakle lionskins stare at him with disgust and contempt. The Angels are outsiders, sure, but their alienation is the only thing they have in common with the 'peace creeps' who trod on their precious bikes ('Something which is your *whole life*,' says Sonny Barger) or with the brave new wave of sexual freedmen whom Flash Mick represents. Jagger's right to do his thing: every gain in liberty, personal or social, is precious. But the Angels belong to a more brutal and repressive culture, one which has yet to be liberated, in which violence is the central motif: it is the only thing which gives their lives (working class 'proles', no future, a worse past, the discarded offal of the technocratic society) any meaning. Violence and hogs provide the power which a merciless System has stripped from them: and in their brutal reaction they enact, vicariously, the violent rebellion which the Woodstock Nation has so resolutely turned its back against. And so the Angels, like Jagger, become yet another surrogate ...

> *The theme song will not be written by Jim Webb or*
> *Francis Scott Key nor sung by Glen Campbell,*
> *Tom Jones, Johnny Cash or Engelbert Humperdinck.*
> *The revolution will not be televised ...*

There is no counter-culture: there are many. There is no Hero: everyone must be his own. There is no One: there are only ones, and it is only our differences which make the command 'come together' meaningful. We must beware of surrogates. We must beware of surrogate heroes like Jagger, whom we idolise because we have more sense than to idolize ourselves and not enough guts to make ourselves worthy of idolatry; we must beware of surrogate violence, because then those whom we vest it in will turn it, Angelically, against ourselves; we must beware of surrogate prophets and doomsayers, who lose heart and blow it secondhand to fulfil their own Jeremiads. Above all, we must beware of surrogate Revolutions, the portable apocalypse of the rock festival and the mass freak-out—because what America, and the world, needs right now is the real thing.

> *The revolution will not go better with Coke.*
> *The revolution will not fight germs that may cause bad breath.*
> *The revolution will put you in the driver's seat.*
> *The revolution will not be televised.*
> *The revolution will be no re-run.*
> *The revolution will be live.*

Peeling (1972)

Peter Carey

She moves around the house on slow feet, her footsteps padding softly above me as I lie on my unmade bed of unwashed sheets, listening. She knows, as she always knows, that I am listening to her and it is early morning. The fog has not risen. The traffic crawls outside. There is a red bus, I can see the top of it, outside the window. If I cared to look more closely I could see the faces of people in the bus and, with luck, my own reflection, or at least the reflection of my white hair, my one distinction. The mail has not yet arrived. There will be nothing for me, but still I wait. Life is nothing without expectation. I am always first to pick up the letters when they drop through the door. The milk bottles, two days old, are in the kitchen unwashed and she knows this, too, because she has not yet come.

Our relationship is beyond analysis. It was Bernard, although I prefer to name no names, who suggested that the relationship had a boy scout flavour about it. So much he knows. Bernard, who travels half way across Melbourne to find the one priest who will forgive his incessant masturbation, cannot be regarded as an authority on this matter.

And she walks above my head, probably arranging the little white dolls which she will not explain and which I never ask about knowing she will not explain, and not for the moment wishing an explanation. She buys the dolls on Friday mornings. She has not revealed where, but leaves early, at about 5 a.m. I know it is a market she goes to, but I don't know which one. The dolls arrive in all conditions, crammed into a large cardboard suitcase which she carries on her expeditions. Those which still have hair she plucks bald; those which have eyes lose them; and those with teeth have them removed, and she paints them, slowly, white. She uses a flat plastic paint. I have seen the tins.

She arranges the dolls in unexpected places. So that, walking up the stairs a little drunk, one might be confronted with a collection of bald white dolls huddled together in a swarm. Her room, which was once my room, she has painted white; the babies merge into its walls and melt into the bedspread which is also white. White, which has become a fashionable colour of late, has no special appeal to her: it is simply that it says nothing, being less melodramatic than black.

I must admit that I loathe white. I would prefer a nice blue, a pretty blue, like the sky. A powder-blue, I think it is called. Or an egg-shell blue. Something a little more feminine. Something with—what do you call it?—more character about it. When I finally take her to bed (and I am in no hurry, no hurry at all) I will get some better idea of her true colour, get under her skin as it were.

I have found her on numerous occasions playing Monopoly in the middle of her room, drinking Guinness, surrounded by white dolls.

Several times a week she comes to wash my dishes and to be persuaded to share a meal with me. The consumption of food is, for the moment, our most rewarding mutual occupation. We discuss, sometimes, the experience of the flavours. We talk about the fish fingers or the steak and kidney pies. She is still shy, and needs to be coaxed. She has revealed to me a love for oysters, which I find exciting. Each week I put a little of my pension aside. When I have enough I will buy oysters and we will discuss them in detail. I often think of the prospect.

At an earlier stage I did not understand myself so well, and achieved on one or two occasions a drunken kiss. But I have not pursued the matter, being content for the moment with the meals and the company on these quiet nights now that the television has been taken away and now that I, unemployed, have so little money to spend on the ladies of Fitzroy Street, or the cinema, or a pot or two in the Bricklayers Arms which, to tell the truth, I always found dull.

I am in no hurry. There is no urgency. Sooner or later we shall discuss the oysters. Then it will be time to move on to other more intimate things, moving layer after layer, until I discover her true colours, her flavours, her smells. The prospect of so slow an exploration excites me and I am in no hurry, no hurry at all. May it last forever.

Let me describe my darling. Shall I call her that? An adventure I had planned to keep secret, but now it is said. Let me describe her. My darling has a long pale face and long golden hair, slightly frizzy, the kind with odd waving pieces that catch the light and look pretty. Her nose is long, downwards, not outwards, making her appear more sorrowful than she might be. Her breasts, I would guess, are large and heavy, but she wears so many sweaters (for want of a better term) that it is hard to tell, or likewise of the subtleties of her figure. But she moves my darling, with the grace of a cat, pacing about her room surrounded by white dolls and her Monopoly money.

She seems to have no job and I have never asked her about her occupation. That is still to come, many episodes later. I shall record it if and when it is revealed. For the moment: she keeps no regular hours, none that I can equate with anything. But I, for that matter, keep no regular hours either, and never having owned a clock, have been timeless since the battery in the transistor radio gave out. Normally it seems to be late afternoon.

She is making up her mind. I can hear her at the top of the stairs. Twice in the past few minutes she has come out onto the landing and then retreated into her room. She has walked around her room. She has stood by the window. Now she moves towards the landing once more. There is silence. Perhaps she is arranging dolls on the landing.

No. She is, I am almost positive, descending the stairs, on tip-toe. She plans to surprise me.

A tap at the door. My stomach rumbles. I move quickly to the door and open it. She says hello, and smiles in a tired way.

She says, phew. (She is referring to the smell of sour milk in the unwashed bottles.) I apologise, smooth down my bed, pull up the cover, and offer her a place to sit. She accepts it, throwing my pyjama pants under the bed for the sake of tidiness.

She asks, how is your situation.

I relate the state of the employment market. But she is a little fidgety. She plays with a corner of the sheet. She is distracted, seems to be impatient. I continue with my report but know she is not fully listening.

She leaves the bed and begins to wash up, heating the water on the small gas heater. I ask her of her situation but she remains silent.

The water is not yet hot enough but she pours it into the sink and begins to wash-up, moving slowly and quickly at the same time. I dry. I ask about her situation.

She discusses George, who I am unsure of. He was possibly her husband. It seems there was a child. The child she visits every third Sunday. For the hundredth time I remark on how unreasonable this is. The conversation tells neither of us anything, but then that is not its purpose. The dishes she dispenses with quickly; an untidy washer, I could do better myself—she leaves portions of food behind on plates, bottles and cutlery. But I do not complain—I keep the dishes to attract her, like honey.

I relate a slightly risqué joke so old it is new to her. She laughs beautifully, her head thrown back, her long white throat like the throat of a white doll, but soft, like the inside of a thigh. Her throat is remarkable, her voice coming gently from it, timorously, pianissimo.

She is—how to call it?—artistic. She wears the clothes of an ordinary person, of a great number of quite different ordinary persons, but she arranges them in the manner of those who are called artistic. Small pieces of things are tacked together with a confidence that contradicts her manner and amazes me. Pieces of tiny artificial flowers, a part of a butcher's apron, old Portuguese boots, a silver pendant, medal ribbons, a hand-painted silk stole, and a hundred milk bottle tops made unrecognisable. She is like a magpie with a movable nest.

Her name, which I had earlier decided not to reveal, is Nile. It is too private a name to reveal. But it is so much a part of her that I am loathe to change it for fear I will leave out something important. Not to mention it would be like forgetting to mention the white dolls.

The washing-up is finished and it is too early yet to prepare a meal. It is a pleasant time, a time of expectation. It needs, like all things, the greatest control. But I am an expert in these matters, a man who can make a lump of barley sugar last all day.

We sit side by side on the bed and read the newspapers. I take the employment section and she, as usual, the deaths, births and marriages. As usual she reads them all, her pale nail-bitten finger moving slowly over the columns of type, her lips moving silently as she reads the names.

She says, half to herself, they never put them in.

I am at once eager and reluctant to pick up this thread. I am not sure if it is a loose thread or one that might, so to speak, unravel the whole sweater. I wait, no longer seeing the words I am looking at. My eardrums are so finely stretched that I fear they might burst.

She says, don't you think they should put them in?

My stomach rumbles loudly. I say, what? And find my voice, normally so light, husky and cracked.

She says, babies … abortion babies … they're unlisted.

As I feared it is not a loose thread, but the other kind. Before she says more I can sense that she is about to reveal more than she should at this stage. I am disappointed in her. I thought she knew the rules.

I would like, for the sake of politeness, to answer her, but I am anxious and unable to say more. I do not, definitely not, wish to know at this stage why she should have this interest in abortion babies. I find her behaviour promiscuous.

She says, do you think they have souls?

I turn to look at her, surprised by the unusual pleading tone in her voice, a voice which is normally so inexpressive. Looking at her eyes I feel I am being drowned in milk. She pins back a stray wisp of hair with a metal pin.

I say, I have never thought of the matter.

She says, don't be huffy.

I say, I am not huffy.

But that is not entirely correct. Let us say, I am put out. If I had any barley sugar left I would give her a piece, then I would instruct her in the art of sucking barley sugar, the patience that is needed to make it last, the discipline that is required to forget the teeth, to use only the tongue. But I have no barley sugar.

I say, I am old, but it will be a little while before I die.

She says (surprisingly), you are so morbid.

We sit quite silently, both looking at our pieces of newspaper. I am not reading mine, because I know that she is not reading hers. She is going to bring up the subject again.

Instead she says, I have never told you what I do.

Another thread, but this one seems a little less drastic. It suits me nicely. I would prefer to know these things, the outside layers, before we come to the centre of things.

I say, no, what do you do?

She says, I help do abortions.

She may as well have kicked me in the stomach, I would have preferred it. She has come back to the abortions again. I did not wish to discuss anything so … deep?

I say, we all have our jobs to do, should we be so lucky as to have a job, which as you know …

She says, the abortionist is not a doctor, there are a number of rooms around the city, sometimes at Carlton, Fitzroy, there is one at Richmond, a large house … it is for poor people … very cheap … in comparison.

I have not heard of this sort of thing before. I examine her hands. They are small and pale with closely bitten nails and one or two faintly pink patches around the knuckles. I ask her if she wears rubber gloves. She says, yes. I am quite happy to discuss the mechanics of the job, for the moment.

She says, I have always thought that they must have souls. When she … the woman I work for … when she does it there is a noise like cutting a pear … but a lot louder. I have helped kill more people than live in this street … I counted the houses in the street one night … I worked it out.

I say, it is not such a large street … a court, not very large.

She says, twice as many as in this street.

I say, but still it is not so many, and we have a problem with population. It is like contraception, if you'll excuse the term, applied a little late.

My voice, I hope, is very calm. It has a certain 'professional' touch to it. But my voice gives no indication of what is happening to me. Every single organ in my body is quivering. It is bad. I had wished to take things slowly. There is a slow pleasure to be had from superficial things, then there are more personal things like jobs, the people she likes, where she was born. Only later, much later, should be discussed her fears about the souls of aborted babies. But it is all coming too fast, all becoming too much. I long to touch her clothing. To remove now, so early, an item of clothing, perhaps the shawl, perhaps it would do me no harm to simply remove the shawl.

I stretch my hand, move it along the bed until it is behind her. Just by moving it … a fraction … just a fraction … I can grasp the shawl and pull it slowly away. It falls to the bed, covering my hand.

That was a mistake. A terrible mistake. My hand, already, is searching for the small catch at the back of her pendant. It is difficult. My other hand joins it. The two hands work on the pendant, independent of my will. I am doing what I had planned not to do: rush.

I say, I am old. Soon I will die. It would be nice to make things last.

She says, you are morbid.

She says this as if it were a compliment. My hands have removed the pendant. I place it on the bed. Now she raises her hands, her two hands, to my face. She says, smell …

I sniff. I smell nothing in particular, but then my sense of smell has never been good. While I sniff like some cagey old dog, my hands are busy with the campaign ribbons and plastic flowers which I remove one by one, dropping them to the floor.

She says, what do you smell?

I say, washing up.

She says, it is an antiseptic. I feel I have become soaked in anti-septic, to the marrow of my bones. It has come to upset me.

I say, it would be better if we ceased this discussion for a while and had some food. We could talk about the food, I have fish fingers again.

She says, I have never told you this but the fish fingers always taste of antiseptic. Everything …

I say, you could have told me later, as we progressed. It is not important.

She says, I'm not hungry, I would rather tell you the truth.

I say, I would rather you didn't.

She says, you know George.

I say, you have mentioned him.

My hands are all of an itch. They have moved to her outermost garment, like the coat of a man's suit. I help her out of it and fold it gently.

She says, George and my son … you remember.

I say, yes, I remember vaguely, only vaguely … if you could refresh my memory.

She says, you are teasing me.

I have begun with the next upper garment, a sweater of some description which has a large number 7 on the back. She holds her arms up to make it easier to remove.

She says (her voice muffled by the sweater which is now over her head), I made up George, and the son.

I pretend not to hear.

She says, did you hear what I said?

I say, I am not sure.

She says, I made up George and my son … they were daydreams.

She should have kept that for next year. She could have told me at Christmas, it would have been something to look forward to.

She says, how can you look forward to something you don't know is coming?

I say, I know. I knew that everything was coming, sooner or later, in its own time. I was in no hurry. I have perhaps five years left, it would have filled up the years.

She says, you are talking strangely today.

I say, it has been forced on me.

There is another garment, a blue cardigan, slightly grubby, but still a very pretty blue.

I say, what a beautiful blue.

She says, it is a powder-blue.

I say, it is very beautiful, it suits you.

She says, oh, it is not really for me, it belonged to my sister … my younger sister.

I say, you never mentioned your younger sister.

She says, you never asked me.

I say, it was intentional.

The conversation goes on above or below me, somewhere else. I have removed the powder-blue cardigan and the red, white and blue embroidered sweater beneath it. Likewise a blouse which I unfortunately ripped in my haste. I apologise but she only bows her head meekly.

She says, you have never told me anything about yourself … where you work…

I am busy with the second blouse, a white silk garment that looks almost new.

I say, distractedly, it is as I said, I am unemployed.

She says, but before …

I say, I worked for the government for a number of years, a clerk …

She says, and before that?

I say, I was at school. It has not been very interesting. There have been few interesting things. Very boring, in fact. What I have had I have eked out, I have made it last, if you understand me, made my few pleasures last. On one occasion I made love to a woman of my acquaintance for thirty-two hours, she was often asleep.

She smiles at me.

I say, the pity was it was only thirty-two hours, because after that I had to go home, and I had nothing left to do. There was nothing for years after that. It should be possible to do better than thirty-two hours.

She smiles again. I feel I may drown in a million gallons of milk.

She says, we can do better than that.

I say, I know, but I had wished it for later. I had wished to save it up for several Christmases from now.

She says, it seems silly … to wait.

As I guessed, her breasts are large and heavy. I remove the last blouse to reveal them, large and soft with small taut nipples. I transfer my attentions to her skirt, then to a second skirt and thence to a rather tattered petticoat. Her stockings, I see, are attached to a girdle. I begin to unroll the stocking, unrolling it slowly down the length of her leg. Then the second stocking. And the girdle. Now she sits, warm and naked, beside me, smiling.

There is only one thing left, an ear-ring on the left ear. I extend my hand to take it, but she grasps my hand.

She says, leave it.

I say, no.

She says, yes.

I am compelled to use force. I grasp the ear-ring and pull it away. It is not, it would appear, an ear-ring at all, but a zip or catch of some sort. As I pull, her face, then her breasts, peel away. Horrified, I continue to pull, unable to stop until I have stripped her of this unexpected layer.

Standing before me is a male of some twenty years. His face is the same as her face, his hair the same. But the breasts have gone, and the hips; they lie in a soft spongy heap on the floor beside the discarded pendant.

She (for I must, from habit, continue to refer to her as 'she') seems as surprised as I am. She takes the penis in her hand, curious, kneading it, watching it grow. I watch fascinated. Then I see, on the right ear, a second ear-ring.

She is too preoccupied with the penis to see me reach for the second ear-ring and give it a sharp pull. She sheds another skin, losing this time the new-found penis and revealing, once more, breasts, but smaller and tighter. She is, generally, slimmer, although she was never fat before.

I notice she is wearing a suspender-belt and stockings. I unroll the first stocking and find the leg is disappearing as I unroll. The right leg has now disappeared. I begin to unroll the left stocking. The leg, perhaps sensitive to the light, disappears with the rolling.

She sits, legless, on the bed, seemingly bemused with the two coats of skin on the floor.

I touch her hair, testing it. A wig. Underneath—a bald head.

I take her hand, wishing to reassure her. It removes itself from her body. I am talking to her. Touching her, wishing she would answer me. But with each touch she disassembles, slowly, limb by limb. Until, headless, armless, legless, I carelessly lose my grip and she falls to the floor. There is a sharp noise, rather like breaking glass.

Bending down I discover, among the fragments, a small doll, hairless, eyeless, and white from head to toe.

Brown Paper Bag (1977)

Carolyn van Langenberg

1

Children milled in the house, laughing at me, a strange and pregnant woman lying in a dishevelled bed in the upstairs of a quivering summer-house, afraid of the violent weather, the blackened sky, the wind, the sea, its spray visible on the windows—sea pounding into my reasoned belief that the village was at least four centuries old and had never been awash in a frothing tide.

But she opened the door. She let the wind hiss through the house and around the chairs and tables and under my bed, rocking it. The wind forcing open the doors and windows. She leant over her great belly to pat a child on the head, smiled at another. So ridiculous, that great belly. She grabbed her coat and hat, and I saw her elevate and ride with the wind behind some houses in the direction of the Huis Ter Duin.

I struggled out of bed. The children, these centuries old children, clustered round me, their wizened faces hard-pressed against my pregnant body. They were ugly. Small and gnarled. Foetal ugliness.

I forced them back. Forced them away from me. I wanted my coat and hat. I had to follow her.

The children clung to me. Their hot breathing wetted my dress. The wind swept through the house and strengthened in gusts that sent the children reeling against the walls and furniture. Their ugly faces wrinkled with pain. The wind freed me of them.

But, as I began to walk to the esplanade, the wind tugged at me. Pulled at my legs. Tangled my clothes. Sand and ice pitted my face. I began to panic. The wind was too strong. I would lose her if I could not follow her. Then the baby inside me kicked savagely and locked across my abdomen, stopping me with pain. I held the rail of the steps to the esplanade and waited for the pain to pass, for the baby to move again. The wind was too strong, and I would have to turn back.

2

The children had left the house, and the doors and windows were shut, the furniture in place. The bed upstairs was unmade and empty. Its familiarity calmed me.

3

I fixed myself some bread and cheese, ate an apple and a pear, and drank a glass of milk. I wrote a letter home about the storm. The house was warm and, outside, disregarding the strong wind and the sleet, children were walking and cycling home from school. A neighbour's cat pushed against a window pane, curled round twice and leapt to the ground, glowering over its shoulder at the unrelenting window as it slunk across the yard. A woman across the road took her two poodles out for a walk on long leashes. A man strolled past with his glossy Great Dane ... Framed by the curtainless glass doors of my house ... A moving picture of suburban forms, windswept ... I reread my letter's description of the storm, drew fresh paper towards me and wrote as follows:

4

The Huis Ter Duin stands above the sea which belts into the dunes under it, eats out its foundations, rages round the ballroom built over the beach for romantic European aristocrats of an era remarkable for its indifference and elegant repose. As I approach, I feel the lack of pink chiffon and a corsage of irises.

The wind drops. I walk quickly towards the house. The enormous pleasure house straddling the dunes, obvious on the height of the dunes, obvious by its blackness on the dunes. Horribly black. Stark. Its doors and windows small against the magnificence of its size.

Inside there is rubble and dampness. The sea echoes, pounds, belts, crashes under the house, frighteningly loud, shaking the structure and each step I take.

I find her there. She stands enraptured.

She knows I can see her. I see her pout and roll her eyes, coquettish and ludicrous above her belly, her fingers feathering the air. She reaches across her belly to touch the hand of a black man, a beautiful black dancing man. He throws back his head, mocking her with a silent laugh, and dances from the room.

A white man comes in. He circles the room and watches the sea from a window before he sits in a corner, at his ease, as if he were waiting for someone, or something. He does not appear to see either of us.

She has seen me. Though she has not acknowledged my presence she knows I am here. She likes to berate me with her insolence. Her free-spiritedness. And I wish I were able to blend my earthness with her gaiety. I want her to be me, an earth spirit, earth-bound, with no relief from my earth's clichéd expectations. I want her to know the small globe of madness that explodes into cruel splinters of disbelief, the pain exceeding even a body's suffering.

I hear her groan and see her face twist. She lies down on the rubble, rubbing her belly and pushing, sweat dripping from her face and through her hair. The white man sits beside her, smiles encouragement and rubs the contours of her belly. Tender. Gentle. He watches and smiles and rubs her belly, and she pushes and heaves and sweats. And when the baby crowns he begins to ease it out, carefully, without tearing her skin.

She nuzzles the baby to her breast and, after some minutes, he cuts the cord. She puts it in a brown paper bag. Then, hand in hand, they step outside the Huis Ter Duin. They send kisses to each other which run along the wind's currents, into the wind's force. Children gather round them, chattering loud incoherencies.

I watch them walk away over the dunes until they disappear. Behind a wall of sea, it seems. And I think I see a brown paper bag tumble on the wind. I stretch my hands across my belly and feel the baby rolling and kicking there. The weight of my body crushes my feet.

I am impatient to be her.

5

I pushed my writing aside and drank some tea. I felt a stickiness in my pants and a tightness gripping my belly. I began to feel the force of contracting muscles.

Fear of inevitable pain wracked my body terribly. Trembling with no control, unable to stop my body's fear, I called a neighbour who understood enough of my English and my terror. Her children and her dogs tripped her feet. She rang my husband and a doctor who came through the storm to the house. He sat beside me. I could see the broken vessels that coloured the white skin of his cheeks red. He sat beside me, waiting, easing the contractural pains with advice and gentleness, fatherly towards my husband when he came home from the Institute with an American companion, a tall black dancing man who slanted a smile at me before he walked through to the other room.

The baby crowned and the doctor delivered it and the neighbour washed it. They handed me a prune coloured thing rapidly changing to red, and wrapped in white. I fed it, giving myself over to a delicious primitivity, until I grasped that the voices above me were discussing the sea flooding the fields between our village by the dunes and the village below us.

Queensland: A State of Mind (1979)

Humphrey McQueen

For a majority of Australians, Queensland is more a state of mind than a state of their nation. As such, 'Queensland' excuses them from doing much about what is wrong in their own states: 'If things are so bad there, then we can't be too bad here'. A similar process works inside Queensland, where the awfulness of Joh is occasionally used as an excuse for not doing anything about him. A mood of waiting for Joh to go has been broken by Aboriginals, by strikes, and most recently by opposition to the street march legislation. Yet a commonly encountered response is either a despairing 'Anything's possible in Queensland', or an incredulous 'Were you born in Queensland?', as if nothing radical ever came out of Brisbane.

Against Joh's attempt to convince Queenslanders that they live in a sovereign state and are in some way superior to the rest of their fellow Australians, ALP apologists push the counter-view that Joh is the odd man out and that Queensland is, and has been, very much the same as the rest of Australia. For party political reasons neither side in this argument can face up to the facts of the situation. The past is too embarrassing for present-day Labor reformers, while the present is too revealing to be good propaganda for a premier seeking re-election.

On a number of important counts Queenslanders are different, although no one has yet suggested that, like Tasmanians, we all have pointed ears. As Byron implied, inbreeding is usually not the problem where the climate's sultry. The differences which exist are in population distribution, educational attainments and work-force participation, all of which are anchored in the primary industry bias of Queensland's political economy. Queensland's economic pattern is not unique; Tasmania's and Western Australia's are fairly much the same. What is unique is the spread of primary industries and population across so much of the state.[1]

Brisbane is the only mainland capital to contain less than half its state's population: 857,066 out of 2,037,197. The percentage of Queenslanders living in rural areas is the highest for all mainland states: 20 per cent against a national average of 14. Brisbane is closer to Melbourne than to Cairns, and closer to Canberra than to Townsville. Compared with either far northern city, Kingaroy is just another outer Brisbane suburb.

It is the economic matrix and not distance which makes regionalism more significant in Queensland than in any other state. Even before separation from New South Wales in 1859, there were proposals to slice Queensland horizontally into three. The sugar industry's demand for Pacific Island labour was at the root of separatist, anti-Federal, and finally secessionist movements in the far north. Regionalism was bolstered by a rail system which spread inland out from a string of ports from Brisbane up to Cairns, which were not linked to each other by rail until 1924. Brisbane was never the focus of Queensland's economic life. Indeed, there never has been such a focus. As well as competing against Brisbane for the state's trade, eight ports battled their nearest neighbours for regional supremacy. Bowen's annoyance at the Cloncurry-Mt Isa railway ending in Townsville helps to explain why Bowen returned Australia's only acknowledged communist parliamentarian, between 1944 and 1950.

Twenty years of non-Labor rule have not altered the primary bias of Queensland's economy. With 13 per cent of Australia's civilian

---

1 Well into the 1920s, Queensland's tropical and semi-tropical latitudes were considered by many scientists to be a major cause of mental and physical debilitation amongst its population. The 1920 British Medical Association Congress , held in Brisbane, was specifically charged with determining if whites would thrive in the tropics; the Congress found that they could, but only with more and better sanitation (most of Brisbane was not sewered until the mid-1960s). The University of Queensland has collected a large body of evidence showing that some people still find it hard to work and think in hot and humid conditions and often drink too much.

employees in 1976, Queensland had 19 per cent of the nation's rural workers but only 10 per cent of those engaged in manufacturing. Moreover, the structure of manufacturing is skewed towards rural products. Food, beverage and tobacco processing employ a third of Queensland's manufacturing workers, twice the national figure. The proportion of working wives is lower: 37.5 against 42 per cent. The population is very slightly weighted towards the under 20 year-olds and the over 55 year-olds, suggesting that people leave the state to work but go there to retire.

The reluctance to industrialise meant that fewer migrants went to Queensland. Between 1947 and 1961, Queensland's overseas-born rose by 56 per cent, against an Australian average of 139 per cent. The proportion of overseas-born remains substantially lower: 13 per cent for Queensland and 20 per cent for Australia; 16 per cent for Brisbane and 25 per cent for all major urban centres in the country. The percentage of Italians and Greeks in Brisbane is 1.4, compared with a mainland range between the next lowest of 4.4 in Perth up to 7.7 in Melbourne.

Partly because of the economic pattern outlined, but more because of a complex cultural inheritance discussed below, educational levels are markedly lower: 36 per cent of Queenslanders left school after only five or six years, compared with a national average of 24 per cent; only 12 per cent of Queenslanders have more than nine years schooling, as against 18 per cent for Australia as a whole. Inevitably, the number of people with qualifications and degrees is noticeably smaller. And this pattern of early school leaving is continuing, so that while only 43 per cent of sixteen year-old Queenslanders are still at school, the Australian average is 57 per cent.

So there is something to the view that Queensland residents are different; on average, they are much less educated, very much less urbanised, more likely to be Australian-born, and less likely to work in a factory.

In no sense do I wish to argue that centralisation and industrialisation make people good, or that schooling and migrants will, of themselves, make us better. Yet, irrespective of the value of these experiences, people who possess them will have values which differ from those who do not, especially where such differences have existed for three or more generations, as they have in Queensland.

Important as economic and geographic forces remain, they always have to work through politics, of which parliament is only one small part. Queensland is different because arrangements made out of rural circumstances largely held in place until the mid-1950s. Underneath the accommodations reached in the 1920s and 1930s with the major companies operating in Queensland—Colonial Sugar Refinery, Mt Isa Mines, Vestey's meat, and the London bond market—a governing stratum of Labor party politicians, Australian Workers Union officials, state public servants and Catholic clergy built a political culture that offered most Queenslanders some of what they then wanted most: for example, public instruction rather than education, and free hospitals rather than more of either. The repressiveness of this alliance grew as the old grouping was challenged by militant workers. When Bjelke-Petersen declared a State of Emergency during the 1971 Springbok football tour, he used a section of a strike-breaking Act that Labor had introduced in 1938, and had buttressed during the 1948 rail strike. The police bludgeoning of communist MLA, Fred Paterson, while he stood on the footpath watching a protest march against these 1948 amendments, is only the most notorious example of how Labor governed.

The linkages are clear. At root, there was a shared commitment to rural life as morally, politically and economically sound. The A.W.U. machine was a prize in itself but its voting strength extended its officers' ambitions to the Labor party, and through it to the government. Industrialisation threatened this power flow by strengthening craft unions open to 'communist' influence. The A.W.U. believed that it could be secure as Queensland's one big union, covering all kinds of unskilled and all grades of semi-skilled labour, only if Queensland's rural bias was maintained. The Labor party was Labor in name but represented more rural seats than city ones; its leadership was non-metropolitan and usually derived from within the A.W.U. The Catholic Church favoured farming as the best bulwark against the Syllabus of Errors, arguing that everything from 'race suicide' to communism was less likely away from urban industry.

The Church had a special interest: state aid, which it had got for its secondary schools in 1900 by having the Scholarship moneys won in competitive public examinations paid directly to its schools. Thereafter, proposals to raise the school leaving age above 14, or to open secondary education to everyone, were opposed by the Church: such reforms would undermine the Scholarship system upon which its colleges and convents depended. The Church also opposed modernising the curriculum because such changes were invariably subversive and often beyond the teaching capacities of their own poorly educated religious orders. There was no Jesuit college in Queensland. Support for the Scholarship became a question of faith and morals. As so often before, the Church had adapted a pagan instrument, in this case, of liberal progress, to its own conservative ends.

In addition, the Scholarship system offered some social advancement, especially into the state's teaching and public services, whose recruitment standards were kept at Junior (Intermediate) level in order to aid this emancipation. One result was that the public service and the state's teachers became defenders of the Scholarship and of low entry requirements, if only because their promotion prospects were threatened by matriculants and graduates. At the close of Labor's rule in the late 1950s, two-thirds of Queensland's 91 senior public servants had entered the service with Junior or lower qualifications. Senior did not become the entry standard for clerks until 1974. The public service tended to be not only catholic and Labor, but also rural-minded and inept. Even when Labor governments recruited outside experts, they brought similar attitudes: Colin Clark and Raphael Cilento.

Between 1938 and 1953, Colin Clark was Queensland's economic brains trust. His religious commitment to small scale rural production gave a veneer of respectability to the prejudices of and problems that were the Queensland economy. By 1921, employment throughout Australia in manufacturing almost equalled employment in pastoral pursuits and agriculture combined. Not so in Queensland, where pastoral and agricultural employment were each greater than that in manufacturing. In the first quarter of the century the state's railway mileage was more than doubled. This massive public underwriting of rural expansion meant that the government had no funds to join in Australia's limited industrialisation in the 1920s, even if it had really wanted to. The rural bias of the economy helped to conceal under-employment throughout the 1930s while the assured domestic sugar market, although at reduced prices, somewhat sheltered Queensland from the depression's worst effects. The lesson learnt was that agriculture was sounder than manufacturing. The 1940s reinforced this experience with its great demand for food to supply Australian and U.S. armies, and later, British civilians. Queensland was considered unsafe for war industries and so missed out on another stimulus to manufacturing. A committee which reported on the Development of Secondary Industry in 1946 was soberly optimistic because the war had left Queensland with one empty munitions factory to lease to manufacturers. The government equated mining with machinery and most of the loans from its Secondary Industry Division went to copper, tin and cement extracting firms.

Cilento's 1936 appointment as Director-General of Health saw the start of a public hospital program, especially concerned with maternity cases, in which the government's desire to populate the whole state coincided with a Catholic concern for large families. There can be no doubt of the program's popularity, indeed, of its almost mystical presence. One of my firmest childhood memories is of being reminded that the professor of gynaecology had delivered me free of charge in a public ward. Ned Hanlon, the then Health Minister, is remembered less for his premiership (1946–1952) than for the building of Brisbane's Women's Hospital, in whose forecourt stands his statue. After Commonwealth finance ended in 1950, Queensland was the only state to keep free hospitals, which it managed to do at the expense of secondary education. Such priorities suited the Catholic ascendency, and did not conflict with the ailing non-industrial economy.

The free hospitals versus high schools question captures the spirit of Labor's rule because its remoteness from immediate political and economic demands shows how pervasive the rural-Catholic outlook became, even under the premiership of a Scottish Protestant, William Forgan Smith, who added four faculties to the University: Agriculture, Medicine, Dentistry and Veterinary Science.

Although the constituents of the ALP-AWU-Catholic alliance came with the Labor government in 1915, it was during Forgan Smith's decade as premier from 1932 to 1942 that they were consolidated. His initial cabinet of ten comprised nine non-metropolitan members, seven catholics and six AWU men. In the first period of Labor's rule from 1915 to 1929, there was substantial internal opposition to the dominant clique, who were occasionally brought into line. Under Forgan Smith, these elements were eliminated from the ALP and the AWU but they reformed around the Trades and Labour Council and the Communist party.

Labor's ferocious anti-communism delighted that political architect and admirer of Mussolini, James Duhig, who had been priest and bishop in Queensland for twenty years before being Archbishop of Brisbane from 1917 to 1965. Duhig's ideological contribution to the Labor alliance is not surprising until his conservatism is recognised; unlike most Australian Catholic bishops, Duhig was a Tory. What is no less surprising was his involvement in the administrative side of the state's political and economic life. Like Theodore, whom he greatly admired, Duhig promoted the development of primary industries, and his presidency of the Royal Geographical Society was in keeping with his enthusiasm for oil exploration. Duhig took care to court the Anglican hierarchy and to avoid offending Protestant sensibilities, but his political successes made it inevitable that the Nonconformists would be implacably resentful. At the 1938 elections, a Protestant Labor party polled well enough to gain one seat.

Sectarianism was no less bitter in Queensland than in Victoria, even if Duhig could be more gracious in victory than Mannix was in defeat.

Thus Queensland was administered by a Catholic rural movement long before Santamaria met Archbishop Mannix. The Hanlon and Gair governments (1946–1957) did not need the Industrial Groups to show them the shortest way with communists. Santamaria's early ideal of 'The Earth—Our Mother' was being realised in Queensland, though almost everyone involved there would have been embarrassed by the intellectual pleading which Santamaria provided. A general mentality of feudal clericalism proved as good a way as any of sustaining the rule of monopoly capital on behalf of Mt Isa Mines and CSR. Colin Clark recently reported that when he returned to Queensland in the late 1930s he found that the Labor government 'purported to control the entire production and distribution of sugar, using the C.S.R. Company as agent. But it very much looked as if the reverse was taking place ...'[2]

The potential for northern development to puzzle outside observers is indeed great, and several writers confuse it with the corruption practised in other states. In 1883, the premier, Sir Thomas McIlwraith, showed his faith in Queensland by proposing that his government allow a land grant railway company 12 million acres. In 1896, McIlwraith was acutely embarrassed by the unexpected death of the general manager of the Queensland National Bank, which had lent him £255,000 on securities of £60,700. This lesson in public finance was not lost on a subsequent Treasurer who, in 1899, concealed the colony's bankruptcy by using £500,000 of Government Savings Bank deposits without any authority. It was from this stimulating intellectual climate that E. G. Theodore emerged as a pre-Keynesian mine-owner, although his failure to anticipate the multiplying effects of public expenditure on his private enterprises cost him the Federal treasurership.

---

2 *Quadrant*, December 1978, p. 9.

Not all Queensland politicians have been so large-minded. In 1946, Commonwealth police found 250 kilos of black market tobacco stored in the garage of the house occupied by the Minister for Health. Ten years later, a Royal Commission found the same minister guilty of collecting bribes for Labor party funds. Magistrates acquitted him on both occasions. Most rumours and allegations of corruption were either not investigated or were dismissed. In 1940, when bridge contractors presented the premier with a portable radio, the main point of public dispute was the value of the banknotes inside: £10,000 being a favoured sum. The frequency and grandeur of such allegations made it too easy for the opposition to suggest that only Labor politicians operated with one hand in the till and the other in the ballot box. Time has not weakened nor coalition government stifled the venality of public life. In 1966, the state parliamentary Labor leader resigned on the day before the *Courier Mail* announced that he had understated his taxable income by over $66,000 as a result of importing tin plates from Taiwan. The 1970 Comalco share handouts went to cabinet ministers, public servants, ALP officials and the Labor member for Gladstone.

Many of the checks on government available in the Westminster model have long been absent from Queensland. The Legislative Council was abolished in 1922 under Gilbertian circumstances and preceeded by one of the most remarkable devices ever: a proxy voting bill which allowed Theodore to exercise personally the vote of absent members. In the words of an opposition squib,

> *Whenever the government is found in a fix*
> *My voice shall carry for those of six.*

Significantly, Bjelke-Petersen has not demonstrated his loyalty to the British way by re-establishing a house of review. Two innovations which he has been forced to live with are a few parliamentary committees, and questions without notice, which are answered in kind.

Labor's grand old alliance was broken from outside in the aftermath of Evatt's splitting the Federal party, and from within when the AWU temporarily allied itself with the communist-led Trades and Labour Council following the 1956 shearers' strike. When Labor was defeated in May 1957, it was succeeded by Australia's only Country Party-dominated government, which had no more idea of how to break out of Queensland's malaise than had.its predecessors. These economic difficulties were highlighted by the Federal government's 1960 credit squeeze and the 1961 swing to Labor which brought Calwell within one seat of forming a government. The credit squeeze blinded some commentators to the state's chronic unemployment, which had been much higher than the Australian average throughout the 1950s, despite (or because of) a relatively slower rate of population increase. In 1962–63, an investigation of Queensland's manufacturing industry found too few new factories to draw statistically significant conclusions.

The 1961 swing to Labor has been added to a list of alleged proofs that, despite the past decade, Queensland is inherently radical. To support this cheeriness, a long tradition is established from the armed camp at Barcaldine in 1891, through the world's first Labor government in 1899, Australia's first general strike in 1912, the anti-conscription stance of premier Ryan, forty years of nearly continuous Labor rule, Australia's only communist parliamentarian, and the militancy of certain Queensland unions in the 1920s and 1940s. Just as it has been shown that the Labor party was in reality a country party, so it can be argued that most of the other examples cited are either misinterpreted or extrapolated out of context. For example, the militancy of the Twenties and Forties was directed against the Labor government's reactionary policies. Other dissenting highpoints were protests by depressed rural producers or disadvantaged regions, that is, by forces which today are marshalled behind Bjelke-Petersen's government. Change over time is history's divisive equation. Broken or blunted are the tough realities which once brought forth shearing-shed anarchism and bush populism, or determined railway workers in their militancy.

Likewise, the experience of Queensland's blacks is not only different from that of whites, it is also more of a piece than that of blacks elsewhere. Well before other colonies started, and long after other states stopped, Queensland's government took an activist approach towards Aboriginal management. Despite some recent window dressing, the philosophy of preservation and protection, first enacted in 1897, still prevails. The health of the whites was protected by locking away on penal settlements, like Palm Island, those blacks to whom whites had given tubercular, leprous and venereal infections. The wealth of pastoral companies was preserved by using other settlements as breeding grounds for cheap station labour. Blacks under this system acquired a healthy respect for a law which was custodian of such wealth as they were allowed to earn and able to keep from swindling police sergeants. Under this régime, Aboriginal numbers increased, the militant moved to Redfern, those under church control developed centres of resistance, and Uncle Toms abounded. Today, the militant are driven out of, rather than into, the camps which officially are hailed as the antidote to the apartheid of land rights. Within that old framework, change has moved slowly over time, establishing new forms of oppression before provoking fresh resistance.

Bjelke-Petersen is both inheritor and destroyer of these old ways. He uses ALP laws from the 1930s and 40s to bolster the transformation of Queensland from being a hillbilly Tennessee to become a Texas bonanza. The over-used metaphor of a 'Deep North' entirely misses the point. Queensland is no longer like the Deep South, but is the New South. Its faults are those of progress, growth and development —as foreign monopoly capital understands those words. Under post-depression ALP governments, Queensland was indeed like Tennessee, or, more accurately, like County Clare in Ireland. To label Queensland by its civil liberties is to ignore the substance of Bjelke-Petersen's régime, which cannot be as easily authoritarian as some of its Labor predecessors were precisely because it has unleashed on Queensland that 'Constant revolutionising of production, uninterrupted disturbance of all social conditions, everlasting uncertainty and agitation'[3] which Marx identified in the bourgeoisie.

History judges Bjelke-Petersen to be the farmer who killed rural idiocy, the lay preacher whose policies ensure that all things holy will be profaned. (Hasn't Joh himself started to take a little white wine with his meals?) From his first equipment-hiring ventures and aeroplanes to his current use of a professional image-maker, Bjelke-Petersen is stamped as capitalist moderniser, not as feudal throwback. He knows the relative significance of mineral and peanut oils, even if his opponents do not. The votes of a few small farmers help him to realise the interests of certain big corporations. His party's name change from Country to National and the votes won by National Party candidates in urban areas are the signs to read. It is the Liberals, not the ALP, who have lost most and have the most to fear, in parliamentary terms, from Joh's successes. Forget about Joh Bananas, and remember that his life-long hero has been Henry Ford.

Not that Bjelke-Petersen wants to industrialise. He ridicules southern manufacturing as a charge against Queensland's wealth. To the extent that he has any long-term economic plan, it is that growing mineral exports can lever overseas meat and sugar contracts; will need construction work; can support service industries; and be supplemented by tourism. As evidence he can point to state government expenditures which have quadrupled since he became premier in 1968, while mining royalties are twenty times greater. Beyond a pride in these superficial trends, he places his faith in foreign investors rebuffed by the Commonwealth, which has to watch the broader and longer-term interests of Australia and of capital.

As an advocate of states' rights, Bjelke-Petersen runs a poor third to Labor premiers Forgan Smith and Hanlon. His far greater success

---

3 K. Marx & F. Engels, *Collected Works*, Volume 6 (Lawrence and Wishart, London 1976) p. 487.

derives from those people whose rights he actually is defending, namely, anyone avoiding Commonwealth regulation, or with speculative capital: Utah and CRA; Wiley Fancher and the Moscow Narodny Bank; Mr Iwasaki's Yeppoon resort and—in time to come—Great Barrier Reef Oil Drilling (Aust) Pty Ltd. They are Joh's constituency. The book-burning biblebashers who want to castrate poofs and shoot reds merely get the pleasure of playing with his gerrymander. States' rights have always been a mask for class interests, or more usually, for the interests of some section of capital which is on the outer at Melbourne and Canberra. United secession by Western Australia, the Northern Territory and Queensland would serve Japanese capital better than the old Brisbane Line.

In encouraging miners and speculators, Joh has attached himself to one predicted Australian future. The small farmers and bush workers who kept Labor in office are going, and Joh is using their dying resentment to reward the very people who have killed them off and who are already undermining factory and office jobs. The regrowth of massive opposition in Queensland is coming from such newly threatened groups, as well as from Aboriginals and mine workers, who are once more in the front line of the profit-making. Radicalism cannot be born again from the glory that was Labor's Portuguese-style fascism.

If mining is allowed to conquer manufacturing until all of Australia becomes, in Sir Roderick Carnegie's words, 'the Uruguay of the South Pacific', then fascist will be a far more appropriate description of all of Australia than it ever has been of Queensland. The rule of capital could not survive such a total economic reverse without open dictatorship. In such a pass we might be tempted to apply to Bjelke-Petersen, and even to his Labor predecessors, the *Bulletin*'s 1922 obituary judgement of an earlier Queensland Premier: 'We had no idea how good a man he was till we found out how rotten subsequent men could be.'[4]

---

4 *Bulletin*, 22 June 1922, cited by G.C. Bolton, 'Robert Philp', in D.J. Murphy & R.B. Joyce, (eds.) *Queensland Political Portraits* (University of Queensland Press 1978) p. 220.

1980s

Yugoslav Story (1980)

Sue Hampton

Jože was born in the village of Loški Potok,
in a high cheek-boned family. I remarked
that he had no freckles, he liked to play cards,
and the women he knew were called Maria, Malčka, Mimi;
and because he was a 'handsome stranger'
I took him for a ride on my Yamaha
along the Great Western Highway
and we ate apples; I had never met someone
who ate apples by the case, whose father
had been shot at by Partisans in World War II,
who'd eaten frogs and turnips in the night,
and knew how to make pastry so thin
it covered the table like a soft cloth.
He knew how to kill and cut up a pig,
and how to foxtrot and polka. He lifted me up in the air.
He taught me to say *Jaz te ljubim, ugasni luč*
('I love you, turn off the light')
and how to cook *filana paprika, palačinka,*
and *pražena jetra*. One night in winter
Jože and two friends ate 53 of these *palačinke*
(pancakes) and went straight to the factory
from the last rummy game. Then he was my husband,
he called me '*moja žena*' and sang a dirty song
about Terezinka, a girl who sat on the chimney
waiting for her lover, and got a black bum.
He had four brothers and four sisters,
I had five sisters.

His father was a policeman under King Peter,
my father was a builder in bush towns.
Jože grew vegetables and he smoked Marlboros
and he loved me. This was in 1968.

Our Lady of the Beehives (1984)

Beverley Farmer

1

Tomorrow, thought Kyria Eirini, waking as the house sighed and crackled in the dark, tomorrow I'll go to the church. To the Panagia of the Beehives. For Varvara's sake.

The Panagia *sta Melissia*, as it was known, was hardly a church at all, compared to the proper one in the town square, Agios Nikolaos, the patron saint of sailors. The Panagia's was little more than a *parekklesi*, a chapel built to honour a promise by the grandfather of the man who kept the bees now. If the Panagia would save his sons in the storm that had wrecked the fishing boats—he stood watching from the hill among the torn acacia trees—he would build Her a chapel, he vowed. He built it in the shape of a bee box, but with a small square tower, and mixed blue in the whitewash to make it the same colour as the hives. The oil lamp before the ikon of the Panagia would never go out, the old mothers of the town made sure of that.

Inside there was a rustling, never pure silence, even when no one was there; and when the lamps were lit for a *litourgeia* an amber light filled it. The candles on sale at the entrance were made of the pale beeswax, and smelled of honey as they burned. An itinerant artist, having covered the walls and ceiling with images of haloed saints, had painted the shawled Panagia Herself with a gilded Child in skirts, in a garden full of lilies and large brown bees.

Kyria Eirini, turning over on her bed in the hot house, told herself to go and light a candle to the Panagia in the morning. Two candles: one for her dead Vassili, whose sins were forgiven; and one to ask Her to do something. And this morning I won't wake Andoni to go and buy fish, I'll let him off. I'll make *imam bayildi* for lunch instead, she thought; and fell asleep again.

Barbara, in the dark beside Andoni, felt swollen all over, raw and gritty from the day's sun and salt and sand. Like a hard-boiled egg her body held the heat in. She had dreamt again that some great whining insect, a bee or a wasp, had stung her. In this dream she was asleep on the beach in the noon sun. Waking as the sting pierced her, she was alarmed to see darkness. The harsh slow sound she heard was not waves, but Andoni's breathing.

Vassilaki cried out in his sleep. She got up and knelt with her cheek against his. 'Mama?' he murmured.

'*Nani,*' she said. 'Go to sleep.' But he was fast asleep.

She sighed. It was too hot to lie awake. Instead she crept into the shadows of the sitting room, switched on the hard light and tore two pages out of her diary to write a letter to her sister.

> Dear Jill (she would address it Poste Restante),
>
> I hope you arrived safely and love Athens. We're all fine here. It was great to see you and Marcus. We've just moved into a better house, the Captain's, no less, two floors furnished. The bedrooms are upstairs, with homespun sheets and lots of chairs, a table, but the rooms are large and full of heat— bare planks for floors. Downstairs we cook and eat and keep cool. We have a marbleslabbed bench with a sink and a *tap*—running water!—and a portable gas stove-top with two large burners and a little one for the coffee *briki*. (If we run out of gas a neighbour's child will run to the *kafeneion* for us and along will come the *kafedjis* with a new bottle on his motor scooter.) The Captain and family have moved next door. His wife has left us plates, cups, glasses, cutlery, pots, pans, baskets … There's a large round dining table, painted shiny green, and ten rush-bottomed chairs. There are spiky bundles of herbs—mostly *rigani*—hung like birch brooms on the wall, and plaits of onions and garlic, and shrivelled

hot red peppers on a string; we are to help ourselves. Her yellow tabby sits on guard day and night.

And as if all that were not enough, this house has a lid!

Well, it has an indoor staircase, as well as the usual cement outside one: an indoor ladder, really, fixed into the floor and leading to a trapdoor set in the planks above. The *kapaki*, they call it: the lid. The older houses all have one. It props open on its hinges, or there's a ring in the wall to hook it into, or you can keep it shut—the sensible thing, Andoni's mother says, when there's a child to worry about. The lid looks too heavy for Vassilaki, but it's not, only awkward to lift. Besides, any one of us, being unused to houses with lids, might step into space where floor should be. (She looks on the dark side.) So we don't let Vassilaki go near it. (The Captain's wife agrees.)

It's like *Treasure Island*!

For the rest: no bath, but as the Captain said, with the sea so near who needs one in summer? And in an annexe behind the kitchen there's a cubicle with a sit-down toilet, a sewered one, a bucket of water to flush it, and a plastic waste-paper basket for the used paper which we mustn't ever flush, only burn.

As for the washing, we heat water in a sooty pan of the Kapetanissa's, kindling a fire under it in the yard with twigs and brambles, wads of newspaper and (yes) used toilet paper. We wash the clothes in plastic basins and rinse them in the wheelbarrow with the hose … In short, it's bliss!

I wish you could come and see, but of course you have to get back to London. Tell Marcus the whole town asks after him ('that brother of yours, is it, that Marko') and please write soon.

Much love,
Barbara.

It was not what she had meant to write, but it would have to do. In the yellow glare she flicked over the pages she had written when Vassilaki was a baby. A couple of pages, that was all, in two years. She was always tired.

He lies in my arms (she read).

To sleep he has to suck one fist and clamp the other in my hair, or in his own.

When he cries and I pick him up he sobs, pushing his face into my armpit, like our old cat.

I unwrap his heavy napkin. He has a small pink bag, seamed and ruched, and above it a pink stalk that extends itself and squirts, like some sea creature.

With a grunt he squeezes out mustard, soft lobster mustard. He presses on the white bags that give him milk, and opens and shuts his vague eyes.

It might be a girl this time, she thought We can call her Eirini and that will gratify Andoni's mother. Andoni would have to be told soon, when the time was right. It was a wonder he hadn't guessed. He had something on his mind.

When she sank back on the bed in the dark, Andoni took her in his arms and drove fiercely inside her. Neither of them spoke. He was slippery all over. He hissed like a dolphin surfacing, and then subsided. They drifted back into sleep.

The Captain's daughter, Voula, lying awake in her room next door, saw the gold lozenge of their sitting room light fall on the balcony, and later disappear. It was Andoni, she thought. 'I love you, Voula, my darling,' she whispered in English, though she had only ever heard Andoni speak Greek. She saw herself on the balcony again, brushing out her hair in swathes, hair smelling of rain water; and Andoni looking on. How could such a man have married a thin ginger-yellow oblivious foreign broomstick of a woman like Barbara?

It was almost as if he were not married at all.

She stood up. Her mother was snoring in the next room. She crept out of the cracking house, past other moon-white houses and along a dusty path fenced with sharp thistles to a beach out of sight of the town. The lights of the gri-gri boats were as small as the stars. She dropped her clothes on the dry sand and padded across the black suede of the wet sand with its cold pools of stars, knotting her hair in a crown as she went, to keep it dry. Then she ran straight into the thick water. The shock of it made her shudder. It was so cold it was as if she had been cut in half: she could neither feel nor see herself below the waist. She bobbed down and quickly up. Her breasts glowed, dropping glints of water. Her feet stung now where thistles had scratched them. Blood pounded in her head.

If she floated, her face lying on the water would be a mirror of the moon. But then she would wet her hair. She would be found out. A moon afloat in black ice.

The heroine of a book she had read swam alone at night. She was a sea-girl too, a fisherman's daughter, the foundling child of a mermaid; and a man watched her, watched Smaragdi in the water. But that was not why, Voula insisted to herself: I love swimming at night and I always have and I always will.

But she knew that this time she was hoping that Andoni, unable to sleep, would sense where she was and follow her.

'Who's there?' she would say, splashing to make a surface of froth to cover her.

'Andoni,' he would say. 'Did I frighten you?'

What would she say? 'No. It's all right.'

'What?' He would falter. He would not be sure.

'A little. But don't go. It's all right.' She moved her cold hands over her breasts. His hands would be dry, warm.

A whimper came from the shore. She stiffened, horrified. On the grey sand a shadow was moving towards her clothes. With a gasp she sank to her nose to hide. She could see a white body, long-legged, white-scarved: no, it was a goat. 'Meh,' it said.

With a snort of alarmed laughter Voula splashed out. '*Fige*,' she hissed, and it stared at her. '*Fige!*' She slapped its burry rump and it trotted off, its frayed rope hopping behind it. Glancing anxiously at shadows, she dragged her clothes on to her wet skin and hurried along the path. Thistles slashed her. The goat, looking back, leaped and was gone. Moonlight lay heavy and white on shuttered walls. Nothing moved. Her shadow was sharp, and at every streetlamp a dim one joined it, grew and dwindled away. It reminded her of the game she played with Vassilaki's shadow when they went to the beach; Andoni's little boy. Her step was light as the shadows falling. No one seeing her out at this time of night would doubt why.

The door creaked, but her mother snored on. She laid herself cool and dry on her bed, and yawned. Bubbles of blood stung on her ankles. The moon was blue stripes on a wall.

A loud door creaked, waking Barbara, but no other sound followed. The house creaked a lot as the night cooled. She lay and thought that the air in the room was like coal in a fire, black and steadily smouldering. It would be good to walk through the grey dust of the streets now. The boats would be converging out at sea, gathering in the net. *Savridia*, she thought; *kefalopoula, marides, barbounia, fagri, sardelles*. She knew more fish in Greek than in English. It would be good to wade into cold black water flickering with fish. But there would be a scandal if anyone saw her. Besides, she was tired.

With a sigh she turned her soaked body over. A donkey sobbed, a goat gave a sudden meh-eh-eh. Soon the roosters would wake. Soon Andoni's mother would knock on the door and call Andoni to go and buy fish, unless she slept in. Soon Vassilaki would wake, waking them all.

She closed her eyes and slept.

2

Voula met Andoni coming out of the water with his speargun and flippers, pushing his mask up on to his rough hair. 'Hullo, did you catch any?' she said.

'No. None there.'

'Bad luck.'

'You're looking very beautiful today.'

'I look very beautiful every day.'

'Is that so?'

She only smiled and swung away, ruffling the surface. That he was watching her made her aware of all her colours and shapes intensified in the morning sea. In a few minutes he waded back in and floated and swam lazily some metres away. But neither of them spoke again.

This morning as usual Barbara had clothes and napkins to wash, soaking in a basin on the back *taratsa*. She wrung them out and with a grunt hurled the dirty water into the vegetable garden. Hens skittered. She poured powder and hot clean water on the clothes and pumped and kneaded them. There were ripe grapes already in the vine above her head, and flies crowded in them. The morning sun shone through grapes and leaves; she looked on the ground for green reflections, as if they were made of glass; but the shadows were black. They were sharp in the still light. Strange, thought Barbara, brushing sweat off her eyebrows, how shadows look sharper on a still day, as if a wind would blur air as it blurs water. Bubbles catching the sun in her basins of clothes were like white opals.

Kyria Eirini swept the leaves and hens' droppings off the dry earth of the yard with a straw broom with no handle, then rinsed and wrung out the clothes with Barbara and helped her hang them out. Then she went in to tidy up. When she opened the shutters and panes to air the rooms, the sun fell in thickly and whatever was inside glowed, furred with gold. No matter how often she dusted, more dust drifted in and settled. At least it's fresh dust, thought Kyria Eirini. Insects buzzed in and out.

She was glad when Barbara and Vassilaki went to the beach at last, to the same spot as always, so she knew where to find them. She would rather stay and be alone in the Kapetanissa's kitchen. She boiled rice in milk and honey to make *rizogalo*, stirred it and poured it on to plates to cool before she tapped cinnamon over its tightening lumpy skin. Andoni and Vassilaki loved her *rizogalo*. She sliced doughy eggplants and salted them, sliced onions and garlic and tomatoes. She breathed in the smell as the olive oil smoked in her hot pans. 'God be praised,' she muttered. 'Everything we need. He gives us.' She slid slices of egg-plant in and the oil frothed over them.

Barbara came to life only in the sea. Her speckled body glowed, mag-nified, and made its green gestures metres above her shadow on the sea floor. Pebbles were suddenly large then small as the water moved. She dived to grasp one. A bird must feel like this, she thought as she dived and twisted, gasped, the bubbles pounding in her ears: a bird flying in rain. When she came up a white net of light enfolded her lazily.

When she came out of the water she lay on a towel with another towel over her to keep off the sun, and lay in a daze facing the sea. Whenever she blinked she saw a flare of red; then the green sea, then the red flare again, as regular as a lighthouse lamp.

Kyria Eirini bent over her eggplants arranged like small black boats in the pan, ladling the filling of onions and tomatoes more carefully than usual into each one: the pan would be on show in the baker's oven. Barbara would be annoyed with her for struggling down the hot road to the bakery with it, when they could have had something easy for lunch. The thought of Barbara's annoyance was almost as pleasant as the thought of how Andoni would carry it home, sucking his fingers cop-pery with oil when he arrived because he had picked at it on the way.

So she struggled, hot in her black clothes, down the road to the baker's, exchanging greetings as she went. She pointed out to the baker exactly where she wanted her pan, and he told her that he knew his oven as he knew his own hand. She bought a hot white loaf and went on to the Melissia to light a candle to the Panagia, which was after all the real reason she was there.

The church was stuffy and dim, with a rosemary smell of old burnt incense. The glazed faces of the saints stared. Kyria Eirini crossed herself and slipped her drachmas into the box for two candles. One she stuck in the tray of sand, for the dead; one in the iron bracket, for the living. The Panagia held her dwarfish Christ to one blue shoulder, her hollow eyes stern.

'It's not for myself,' she thought to the ikon. 'It's for my daughter-in-law. The Australian one. Fool though she is. *Aman*. Has she no pride? Enlighten her, help her, I pray. And the girl too, save her from temptation. Andoni is turning out just like his father was, whose sins are forgiven.'

As she was leaving, a bee settled on her sleeve. She shook it off. It hovered. 'Xout!' she said. They blundered together out into the sunlight.

At home she wrapped the bread in a cloth. Her dress was stuck to her. She swilled cold water from a bucket over the speckled kitchen floor to wash it. Its stones came to life, all their colours, like shingle on a sea floor. The cat that came with the house, and spent the mornings dozing under the table, sprang up on a chair and spat at her. 'Xout!' spat Kyria Eirini. The cat fled to the window sill and hunched there with a brazen scowl.

When Andoni walked in, Kyria Eirini was scrubbing spots out of the washing before Barbara got home. She started and looked guilty. 'You're home early,' she said.

'I said I'd buy the bread.'

'I bought it.'

'Why? When I told you I'd go!'

'I wanted to light a candle. It was on my way. I took a pan of *imam bayildi* as well. You can get that if you like.'

'*Aman*, Mama! You could just as easily cook it here.'

'Yes, but you like it better baked.'

'Not when it's so much more work.'

'But since it's better?'

'Tiring yourself out for nothing. It's madness.'

Andoni's reaction was all she could have hoped.

'Kyria Eirini?' came Voula's voice at the gate. Still in her bathing suit, she was hugging a pile of striped *kilimia*. 'We thought—my mother and I thought—do you need more blankets at night?'

'Ach.' Flustered, Kyria Eirini waved her soapy hands. 'Thank you. That's very kind.'

'I'll leave them upstairs, will I?'

'Yes, there's a good girl. Thank you.'

Voula, padding into the dark kitchen, ran into Andoni before she saw him, he was so dark himself.

'Careful.' He climbed up ahead to hold the *kapaki* open.

Voula laughed. 'I grew up in this house.'

'All the same.'

'My father fell through once. He was drunk at the time.'

'Didn't you ever fall through?'

'I wasn't allowed to go near it.'

'So you never did?' He followed her and shut the trapdoor.

'No, I was a good girl.'

'Was. And now you're not.'

'Is that what you think, is it?'

'I'm hoping to find out. How old are you?'

She blushed. 'Old enough.' No, this was going too far: she looked round for something safe to remark on, and saw waxy lilies in a vase of her mother's. 'Pretty,' she said.

'Take one.' He lifted one out, its curled stalk dripping.

'Oh, no.' She stepped back. 'Are they from Kyria Magda?'

'Why not? Some old woman with whiskers gave them to your mother. Her goat got out and ate half your mother's beans last night, haven't you heard? You will. You're getting a bucket of milk too. Your mother hates them, she says, so here they are.' He nodded the lily at her. 'Take it, come on.'

'They make her sneeze,' she explained.

'Too big to wear.' He held it up to her hair. 'Pity.'

'How can I take it? It would look—I can't.'

With a stare he dropped the lily out the window. Shocked, Voula ran into the sitting room with the *kilimia*. He climbed back down to wait, letting the *kapaki* slam shut. But Voula left the house, trembling, by the outside stairs.

Andoni trudged off to the bakery.

3

It was a relief when lunch was over. Barbara and Andoni assured Kyria Eirini that the *imam bayildi* was delicious. But the baker had burnt one edge of it, and besides she thought there was just a little too much salt. They didn't think so. Vassilaki refused to eat any and filled up on all the *rizogalo*.

The washing was dry by then, hooked on the barbed wire fence among the speckled pods, green and red, of the Kapetanissa's climbing beans. Drops of water, falling from their bathers, rolled and were coated with dust. A shirt and a napkin had fallen on to the red earth. They would have to be washed all over again. Barbara sighed. Nothing seemed to dry without its earth or rust or bird stain.

The Kapetanissa had green onions and garlic growing as well as beans, and eggplants with leaves like torn felt, and cucumbers, potatoes, tomatoes, wilting melon vines. Her hens and the rooster had squeezed through the wire and were scratching and jabbing among the watered roots. Brown papery birds, murmuring to themselves, their eyes half-closed. Weary of summer.

Vassilaki had seen them too. He ran in by the gate to chase them out, but they pranced loudly into hiding. 'Xout!' he shouted.

'Vassilaki?' She had folded the clothes and was up to the napkins now. 'Where are you?' He came padding out. She pulled the wire over the gatepost. He was holding a long funnel-shaped pale flower.

'*Kitta*, mama,' he said. 'Look.' His mother had different words for everything.

151

'Mm. It's a lily. Where was it?' she said. Then: 'Put it down quick. Quick! There's a bee in it.'

So there was, when he looked. A bee with brown fur was crouched, its legs twitching, in the buttery glow at the bottom of his lily.

'Why?'

'It wants that yellow dust, see? On those little horns? It wants to make honey. *Meli*. Put it down now.'

'Why?'

'It might bite.'

'Why?' He held it out at arm's length.

'It might think you want to hurt it.'

'*Nao*,' he told it.

'Just put it down.'

'*Echo melissa*,' he called over the fence to the Kapetanissa and Voula, who had come out to see why the hens were squawking, and were packing the earth back round the roots with their sandalled feet.

'Careful, she bite you!' Voula called back, but softly in case she woke the neighbours.

'*Ela*, Voula!'

'Put it *down*, Vassilaki!'

He dropped his lily. The bee flew out, made a faltering circle and then was lost among the oleanders.

'*Paei*,' he sighed.

'Yes. It's gone.'

'*Paei spiti?*'

'Yes, it's gone home.'

'*Pounto spiti?*'

'In a bee box. On the hill near the church.' He looked puzzled. '*Konta stin ekklesia.*'

'Why?'

'*Paei na kanei meli*,' smiled Voula, shading her eyes. She followed her mother inside.

'Mama?'

'Yes. It's gone to make honey.'

'*Einai kakia.*'

'Who's bad? Voula?'

'Bee.'

'No, it's not, it's good—*kali*. But you have to leave it alone. You can pick up the lily now it's gone.'

'Nao.' They left it lying there.

He went ahead of her up the outside stairs—the wall was too hot to touch—and through the empty sitting room behind the balcony. He had gone when she came up with the washing. '*Pou eisal?* she whispered. 'Keep away from the *kapaki.*' When there was no answer she looked in the bedroom: only Andoni, asleep. She found Vassilaki in the next room, on his back on the bed beside the black heap that was his grandmother. His eyelids fluttered as she kissed his cheek; he brushed the kiss away with a loose hand. His hair was damp. '*Nani,*' she whispered. He was already asleep. The room burned with a buttery glow like that inside the lily.

The floor creaked as she crept in, her soles rasped the planks, but Andoni stayed asleep, as if stunned, his mouth open. He had thrown the sheet off. He glistened, brown all over and shadowed with black hairs, barred as well with shadows that fell from the window over him. She lay down beside him in her dress: they would all be getting up soon. The rough cotton was stuck to her. Her breasts ached. Andoni muttered something indistinct. She sighed, hearing a mosquito whine. Our four bodies in the house, she thought, four bubbles of blood, and a fifth still forming, afloat on our white beds. A hollow light seeped through the shutters. Time and the sun stood still.

4

When they woke, the women always brought coffee and glasses of water up to the balcony. Andoni read the newspapers there. The shadows grew longer almost as they watched, until the street was filled with them. Sometimes a sea breeze rose: the *batis*. Ach, o *batis*, people would say to each other with relief. Sometimes—especially when there was no sea breeze—the family went back to the beach for a late swim, in water warmer and brighter, tawny-shadowed and full of reflections different from its morning ones. Then the sun shrank, spilling its last light along the hoods of the waves.

This afternoon there was no sea breeze.

'Will you drink a little coffee?' And Barbara woke with a start. Kyria Eirini's grey head was at the door. 'Sorry, Varvara. Were you asleep? Vassilaki's awake.'

'Oh, not just yet, Mama, thank you.'

'Well, whenever you like.' She closed the door. Barbara lay blinking in the hot stillness. There was a crushed hollow beside her; she had not heard Andoni go. Her wrists and ankles itched and had red lumps all over them. She found a mosquito on the dim wall, slapped it, and was trying to wipe off the red smear with spit when the door opened again.

'Varvara, sorry. Vassilaki wants to go to the beach. Ach, not a mosquito? I sprayed too.'

'One. Look at me.'

'It's your sweet blood, you see. Vassilaki is insisting. Can you see any more?' They both peered up. 'No, it was just that one, Varvara *mou*.'

Vassilaki was insisting. '*Thalassa, thalassa, thalassa*,' he chanted.

'We were there all morning,' Barbara moaned.

'*Thalassa pame*. Mama!'

'Mama *nani*,' reproached his grandmother, stopping him in the doorway.

'Let his father take him,' Barbara said.

'He go to buy newspaper,' came Voula's voice in English. 'I take him, if you like.'

'Voula, would you? Come in.'

Voula came to the doorway, a coffee cup in her hand, with the other hand gathering her hair at her nape then letting it flow free. Vassilaki pushed past her: 'Mama!' Kyria Eirini made an apologetic face at Barbara and plucked at his shirt. '*Mi, Yiayia!*' And he shook her hand off.

'Come with me today?' Voula squatted beside him.

'*Pou?*'

'*Sti thalassa?*

'Mama?'

'Mama *nani.*'

He faltered, scowling, but finally took her hand. They went down-stairs to the shadowed garden to get a towel from the wire fence and find his bucket and spade. Then they came hand in hand out into the yellow evening. When he started to drag his feet, Voula dodged to make her shadow cover his, and he laughed, remembering how she always played the shadow game; and she remembered the moonlit streetlamps. 'What! You have no shadow!' she said.

'I have so!' He made his shadow escape and caper ahead.

'You have not!' Hers pounced on it again. 'You see? Where is it?'

'There!'

Families sitting on balconies looked on smiling.

Going past Kyria Magda's Voula saw from the corner of her eye that the ivory-necked lilies had gone from the pots on the *taratsa*. The white goat, tied to a post, fixed its slit brass eyes on Voula and said, 'Meh-eh.'

'Meh-eh. Meh-eh,' said Vassilaki. '*Alogaki?* If it was a horse, then he could ride it.

'*Katsika einai,*' explained Voula, not knowing the English word. '*Echei gala.*'

'*Pou?*'

She pointed to the pink bag bouncing between the stiff hind legs; Vassilaki stooped to look, and giggled. Kyria Magda, screeching hullo, staggered across the yard with a bucket of water. 'All right then, drink, you little whore': and the goat, in its thirst, plunged its chin and ears deep, and sneezed, rearing. 'Run away, will you?' said Kyria Magda, her hands on her hips. 'I'll teach you. Yes, I'll teach her,' she told the watchers; a sour smile crossed her face.

'*Kakia yiayia,*' said Vassilaki when they were well past.

All the way to the beach Voula let him keep ahead of her with his shadow, making little rushes forward whenever he flagged, so that they arrived sweaty and out of breath. She dipped herself in the water, no more, not wanting to take her eyes off him for a moment; though he always paddled in the shallows and if he did stray further out there was a sandbank. Waistdeep, he was filling his bucket with water and spilling it on his head. It splashed all round him and sent ripples flickering up. From his hair, darker and flatter now, bright drops went on falling.

'Ooh! *Kitta*, Voula!'

She sprang to her feet. *Ti?*'

'*Kitta*! *Psarakia*!'

'*Pou?*'

'*Na!*' He pointed. There were the little fish, when she looked, first like silver needles, then like black ones. He sank his bucket in bubbles to the bottom to catch them. She lay down again, resting on her elbows. In the distance the boats were tied to the pier. A small one was pulled up on the sand nearby with an octopus spread to dry over its lamps, swarming with wasps. No one else had come down to the beach. I am beautiful, Voula decided; but he's not here to see. Over the sandbank the water was a honeycomb, a golden net. Vassilaki was intent. Now with his bucket, now with his spread hands, he bent to catch fish. '*Psarakia?*' he pleaded. '*Psarakia?*'

They stayed until the sun turned the long shoals red.

Andoni, hunched over a newspaper, saw them coming home along the street, its dark patches not only shadow now but wet dust where the shopkeepers had hosed it. At the other end of the balcony his mother and the Kapetanissa sat making lace with crochet hooks, each of them ignoring her own quick fingers to covertly watch the other's.

'When it's wet it smells like coffee,' remarked Kyria Eirini. 'The earth, I mean.'

'Here comes Vassilaki,' said Andoni.

'Ach, good!' She swung round. 'Yes, here they are!' Sounding too relieved, she knew: the Kapetanissa bridled. Did they think the child might not have been safe with her Voula, did they? She raised her heavy brows.

'Are they late, perhaps?'

'No! Not at all!' They were laughing, licking icecreams. 'Look, she bought icecreams.' Kyria Eirini made her voice soothing. 'She gets on so well with him, doesn't she?'

The Kapetanissa was not satisfied. Andoni picked a sprig of basil from the nearest pot, rubbed it and sniffed at the green mash his fingers made. His mother waved to Voula and Vassilaki, who waved back.

'I noticed yesterday what a beautiful swimmer she is,' Kyria Eirini went on, making it clear that of course he had been in good hands. 'May we not cast the Evil Eye on her,' she added, as custom demanded after praise, and pretended to spit. The Kapetanissa smiled at her, appeased.

'Yes, she's a genuine mermaid. Everyone says so.'

'Who's a mermaid?' Barbara called lazily from inside, having caught the one word *gorgona*.

'Voula. They're home,' answered Andoni's mother.

'Oh, good.' Barbara went on reading. She knew she was a better swimmer than Voula any day.

Vassilaki's chest had pink trickles on it where icecream had dripped through the soggy tip of the cone faster than he could suck it. Voula flapped the towel—it had lumps of wet sand on it—and hung it on the fence. 'Have a wash?' she said, and pulled the slack hose through from the garden. Vassilaki loved the first wash, the sun-warmed water in the hose. He pulled his shorts open and squeezed his eyes shut waiting for the silver water to come coiling over him. When it did he gave a yell. Voula stooped down to swill the sand and the icecream off him. But the water was running cold now and he squirmed away, giggling as if it tickled.

'Come here.' She was giggling too.

'Nao!'

'There is sand on you!'

'Nao!'

Neither of them had heard any buzzing or seen a wasp or a bee hanging, its wings rippling the air. But now Voula felt a searing stab in her thigh. She screamed with pain and shock.

'*Ti?*' shrieked Vassilaki.

Voula was slapping at her thigh, staring round wildly. Whatever it was fell twitching in a puddle. She bent over it: impossible to tell now if it was a wasp or a bee. She crushed it with her hard heel.

'*Melissa!*' Vassilaki shrieked again. He peered at the crushed shell. Was it his bee? Would it dart up and sting him next? A hen jabbed and took it, spraying mud on him as she skipped away. '*Paei!*' yelled Vassilaki. '*Voula mou!*'

But this was not his Voula, cupping her stung thigh, her face red and twisted. Vassilaki stared. This was not his Voula. He stumbled into the kitchen. No one. 'Mama *mou*! Mama!' He bolted up the wooden steps and raised the trapdoor.

'Vassilaki!' screamed his mother's voice. He swung round in bewilderment—where was she?—and the trapdoor fell shut with a thud above him, jamming his fingers. He screamed loudly, lost his balance and tumbled down the steps on to the floor.

5

At first everyone had thought that the screams they heard were part of the game with the garden hose. Now they all came running. Barbara scrambled through the trapdoor and down the steps to pick Vassilaki up. She sat on the cold floor of the kitchen holding him against her. For long moments he held his mouth open in a silent roar, turning dark red. Then at last sobs and tears burst out. 'Oh, oh, oh,' moaned Barbara in the Greek way that always soothed him best, rocking with each 'oh'.

'*Ponaei!*' he wailed.

'Oh, oh, *poulaki mou*,' she murmured helplessly.

Andoni crouched over him and ran his hands over the wet quivering little body, the yellow mat of hair. There was a lump there and blood seeping; grey splinters showed in the plump flesh of his arms and legs; but no bones were broken. Red tangles were printed on Barbara's dress where he had laid his head.

'What happen?' said Andoni.

'The *kapaki*. He fell downstairs.'

'I know that.'

'*Ponaei!*' Vassilaki touched his head and shrieked when he saw blood on his hands.

'Oh, don't cry, no, no. It'll be better soon.' She kissed his hair.

'*Melissa*, Mama,' he snuffled.

They looked, but there was no sign of a bee sting.

'*Ma pou, poulaki mou?*'

'*Ti* Voula.' He pointed.

Voula, her face swollen with crying and as red as his, was standing in her bathing suit at the kitchen doorway. 'A *melissa* bite me and he frighten,' she said. 'And he hurt his self. The *kapaki* fall on him.' Her thigh bulged with a lump as big as a tennis ball: she had found the barb in it.

'Luckily he's not badly hurt,' said Kyria Eirini.

'He got a fright. I'm sorry,' Voula explained gratefully, because Kyria Eirini spoke no English. With a gasp of pain she squatted on her heels to face Barbara. 'It happen so quick!' she said tearfully; and met with shock a bitter relentless glare from Andoni.

'*Kakia* Voula!' Vassilaki hid his face.

'No, no, no,' said Barbara.

'But it was an accident,' said Kyria Eirini to everyone. 'These things happen. They can happen to anyone.'

The Kapetanissa gave her a grateful look. She had warned them about the *kapaki*, but this was not the time to say so; and besides, she blamed all such accidents on the Evil Eye, but she could hardly say that either. Instead she hustled Voula home to take out the barb and dab vinegar on the sting, at the same time questioning her at length. Voula burst into more sobs: Andoni had blamed her without a word. She blamed herself, she told her mother, who stoutly told her she was being stupid. It was the Evil Eye, it was written, it was the will of God; she crossed herself.

'Yes, but they all hate me now,' said Voula.

Vassilaki, his sobs dwindling to sniffles and hiccups, was still clamped fast to Barbara on the floor. '*Ponaei*,' he whimpered now and then, when she tried to move; but it was clear that he wasn't badly hurt. When his gradmother knelt beside them with a bowl of milky antiseptic and a tuft of cotton wool, he knew what was coming: '*Ochi! Ochi! Ochi!*' he wailed, wriggling.

'Ach, *poulaki mou.*' His grandmother's eyes watered.

'I'll do it,' said Andoni.

'*Ochi!* Nao!'

'Vassilaki! Vassilaki *mou!*' His grandmother snapped on the light and ran up the steps, calling. He peered, blinking in the yellow glare, from behind his wet fists. '*Da da!*' she shouted, and punched the trap-door. '*Da da to kapaki! Da! Da! Da!*'

Vassilaki gave a wheezy laugh. '*Da da pali*, Yiayia!' he commanded; so she beat it again, and again, until her arms ached and he decided that the *kapaki* was punished enough. And by then Andoni had swabbed the blood away.

As soon as Vassilaki was asleep Andoni inspected his head with a bright torch he had found, parting the damp tufts.

'He's all right. Really,' Barbara said.

'He could get delayed concussion,' muttered Andoni.

'I don't think so.'

'It's your job to look after him. Why did you leave it to Voula?'

'She offered. Vassilaki wanted her to take him.'

'He could have been killed.'

'It was an accident. It could have happened to anyone.'

'Did you call him to go up that way?'

'No, of course not!' Barbara jumped up.

'But you called him.'

'That was after he lifted it up.'

'I hope that's true.'

'I don't tell lies, Andoni.'

'You don't do anything much any more, do you?'

'No? Do you know why? I'm tired.'

'Tired!' He turned away.

'Tired, yes. Because I'm pregnant.'

It was some time before he turned to her; the torch in his hand threw winged shadows. He stood staring.

'You're not pleased.'

'Yes, I am. Yes. Are you sure? When will it be?'

'Mid-January, I think.'

'Does Mama know yet?'

'Most likely.'

He smiled at that.

'He's sleeping normally,' she said. 'He really will be all right.'

'I might just go for a walk, then. Just down to the *kafeneion* for a while. I'll burst if I stay here.' He bent over Vassilaki, then handed her the torch and went down into the street. From the balcony she watched him appear under each streetlamp, and disappear again.

After searching all over the sitting room, she found her diary under a pile of *kilimia*, striped red and green and black, which she didn't remember having seen before; and took out the two pages of her letter to her sister. She had more to tell her. A moth flapped at the torch, its shadow rocking the gold walls.

> P.S.—Jilly, I'm pregnant. I was going to tell you when you were here, but somehow it never seemed to be the right time. They will wish me *kali eleftheria* when I tell them: it means *good freedom*—by which they mean good (easy) birth.
>
> Be happy,
> B.

As they did every night, Voula and the Kapetanissa watched the boats get ready to go out in a jumble of nets and crates and lamps. Half the town was wandering along the waterfront and up and down the pier by then, dressed in their best for the *volta*. The streets were very dark now, except under the lights: people tripped over stones and tree roots. The sea held its oyster colours of yellow and grey longer, even when the caique and its little boats were chugging across to the fishing grounds, lamps strung in a row over the ringed wakes.

Later they sat with the families of the crew sharing bottles of beer and ouzo and plates of *mezedes* at the *kafeneion*. Moths fell against them. Often there was no other sound but the thump of the hurtling powdery moths. At every table children insisted, to the men's satisfaction, on sipping the froth from every glass of beer; soon they fell asleep in their mothers' laps. Cats yowled under the chairs. Their fur twitching, they would put a calm paw on top of a cricket, then let it limp free, then cover it again. Their eyes flashed green. Beyond the yellow edges of the lamplight more crickets started creaking under the pines. Out at sea the boats gathered under a milky dome of colder light. A gull cried out; then another.

Voula, standing to pass her aunt a plate of *kalamari*, suddenly saw Andoni on the beach. But he looked away and walked on into the dark.

'Wasn't that your tenant? What's his name?' her aunt asked, munching loudly.

'No. I don't think so,' Voula said. She longed to be alone. Her stung thigh throbbed.

There were no lights on next door, when Voula and the Kapetanissa came home. They went straight to bed. The house was too hot for sleep, and held its heat and silence the whole night.

In the next room Vassilaki said in English a word like a bell, but woke only his grandmother. She could see the slatted moon from where she lay. There will be dew, she thought, by morning, and the houses will look like blocks of feta straight out of the brine, until the moon sets. At dawn they will be blue. I must wake Andoni to buy fish, she decided, because once the moon is full the boats know better than to go out with their little lamps. For a week we'll be without fish.

It was too hot to sleep, and besides she was no longer sleepy, having gone to bed earlier than usual when Barbara did. They had sat in the light of an amber lamp in the kitchen and eaten cold what was left of the *imam bayildi*, just the two of them mopping their plates with bread and talking quietly, almost secretively. They felt fonder of each other than they had for a long time, and they both knew this, and so were shy with each other. She thought of asking Barbara if she might be pregnant, but it was not the right time yet. When Vassilaki woke tousled and grizzling, they soothed and dandled him. They spoonfed him an egg that she soft-boiled for him in the coffee *briki* and on which Barbara drew a naughty face, a little Vassilaki. His pallor was gone. He sipped the egg greedily and then ate some bread with grainy honey and a peach like a yellow rose that she had saved for him. She wanted to read Barbara a prayer from the *Theia Litourgeia*, but the lamplight, heavy with moths and beetles, was making her eyes sore. They are like fish in a yellow sea, Barbara said, waving insects away. They carried Vassilaki, fast asleep, up the outside stairs to bed. She heard Andoni come up soon after.

For all she knew, good may have come of the child's fall, since Andoni blamed the girl for it; though who knew how long the good would last or what harm might come of it? In any case, it was not how she would have gone about it. The child hurt, the girl stung, the bee dead. A bee had come blundering into the sun out of the Panagia *sta Melissia*. Was it that bee? Was a bee's life of so little account to the Panagia, that she sent it to die? Thy will be done: she crossed herself. It's not for me to say. Maybe our lives are of no more account than a bee's, if the truth be known.

She must nail up the *kapaki* in the morning.

Out in the night a click of hoofs and a faint 'meh' made her sigh. There was a goat loose again. It must have come for the rest of the Kapetanissa's climbing beans; it would finish the lot off tonight, no doubt, and the Kapetanissa would talk of nothing else tomorrow.

How did the Garden of Eden ever survive with goats in it? Goats eat every green shoot that pokes up. They're a ruin, goats are, though the milk makes up for it.

Is that bee alive now in the next world, she wondered; and is there honey there? Water, and milk and eggs, bread and wine? Shall we all have other forms, or none and be made of air? We boil wheat with sugar to make the *kollyva* for the dead; but it's only we, the living, who eat it. Or so it seems. For us of this world, at least, it tastes good, salty and sweet together. Like sardines fried in sweet green oil; or watermelon with a slab of briny feta, or any dry cheese; honey on rough bread; grapes, rich heavy muscat grapes, dipped in the sea to wash them.

Pain is like salt, in a way, she thought: it can make the sweetness stronger, unless there's too much of it. Pain and sorrow and loss.

There was too much salt in the *imam bayildi* today. Never mind. Well.

My poor Vassili, whose sins are forgiven: that was a salty old joke he loved to tell, the one about honey. Only a man could have made that joke up. A man might even believe it, who knows?

A gypsy (he put on a wheedling voice) came to an old widow, I forget why, and said, 'What is your wish, my lady? I can give you one of two things. A fine young man to marry, or a pot of honey. Just tell me which you want.'

'Now what sort of a choice do you call that?' (And he cackled like an old widow.) 'I couldn't eat the honey, could I? There's not a tooth in my head, is there?' (At which he laughed angrily as if he knew all about old widows, and disliked what he knew.)

She breathed deeply of the shuttered air, cooler now with the dew towards daybreak, and pulled the rough sheet up over her folded throat. In the next world may we all be young again, she fell asleep wishing. All of us young and at peace by the sea for ever.

Stone Quarry (1986)

Gerald Murnane

I have just finished reading a piece of fiction about a man who insists on finding out how deep the bedrock is wherever he happens to be standing.

I would like to know the name of the woman who wrote the fiction. She has light-brown hair and interesting eyes, but her skin is rather weatherbeaten and her forehead is oddly wrinkled. I can never judge a person's age. This woman might be thirty-five or forty-five.

The woman's fiction is all in the first person, and the narrator identifies himself as a man. The author—the woman with the creased forehead—claims that the man in the story is based on her own brother, who suffers from what she calls an illness of the mind.

I will explain where I am and why I have to write this.

I am sitting at a battered garden-table on the back veranda of a ten-room stone house on a hilltop thirty-four kilometres north-east of the centre of Melbourne. A forest of rather skinny eucalypts grows all around the house and all down the steep gullies for as far as I can see. About once an hour I hear a motor-car on the gravel road deep down among the trees. Mostly I hear the cheeps and tweets and ting-tangs of birds and the swishings of leaves and twigs in the wind. If I walk along the veranda I can just hear, through the thick stones of the wall, the tapping of a typewriter. At two other places along the stone wall I can hear the same faint sound. Far inside the house, and quite inaudible to me, two people are using electronic keyboards and screens. A writers' workshop is in progress.

The stone house belongs to a painter (a painter of quite ordinary views of desert and savannah, to judge from what can be seen on the insides of these walls). At this moment the painter is somewhere on the road to Hattah Lakes. But these details are not important ... the artist's house is ours for the present.

We are six writers—three men and three women—who have undertaken to write and to show our writing to one another for seven days and six nights up here among the sounds of birds and the wind in the treetops. Five of us, so I believe, have had fiction published in magazines or anthologies. Myself, I am a poet (sparingly published) who is trying to break into prose. Our workshop is not meant to produce immediately a body of publishable writing. Our meeting here on this hill is meant to put us in touch with the deep sources of fiction.

Last night—Friday night—each of us had to write our first piece and then hand it to the person in charge of the session. This morning at breakfast each of us was given a copy of each of the five pieces written by our fellow writers.

In most writers' workshops the members sit around discussing their work; they talk about themes and symbols and meaning and such matters. The six of us do none of this. Ours is a Waldo workshop. The rules were devised by Frances Da Pavia and Patrick McLear, a husband-and-wife team of writers in the USA. In 1949 these two began a series of workshops at their summer house in Waldo County, Maine. Francis Da Pavia and Patrick McLear have both since died but they bequeathed their estates, including the house in Maine, to the Waldo Fiction Foundation, which continues to arrange annual workshops and to keep alive the Waldo theory of fiction in the USA and in other countries.

The rules for the Waldo workshops have hardly been changed since the first summer when the co-founders and four disciples shut themselves away for a week on a rocky peninsula looking across the water to Islesboro Island. As far as possible the writers have to be strangers to one another. (The co-founders were far from being husband and wife in the days of their first workshops, and after their marriage they were never again together as writers in the stone house.) Everyone is compelled to take a pen-name at the first session and to change that pen-name each day. But the most important rule is the absolute ban on speech.

In this matter a Waldo workshop is more strict than a Trappist monastery. Trappist monks are at least allowed to use sign language, but writers at a Waldo workshop are not allowed to communicate by any means other than the writing of prose fiction. Waldo writers may exchange any number of messages during their week together, but every message must be encoded in prose fiction. No other sort of message is permitted. Writers may not even allow such a message to reach them inadvertently: if one writer happens to intercept another's glance, the two must go at once to their separate writing-tables and write for each other a piece of fiction many times more elaborate and subtle than whatever lay behind either glance or was read from it.

Waldo writers are not even permitted to make the sorts of comment that writers in conventional workshops make about each other's work. Each morning in this house each one of us will pore over the latest batch of fiction, looking for scattered traces of our own stories in the manifold pattern of Waldo.

To preserve the ideal of unbroken silence, the Waldo manual recommends a certain gait for strolling around house and grounds and a certain posture for sitting at the dining-table or on the veranda. The eyes are kept lowered; each stride is somewhat hesitant; arms and hands are guarded in their movements for fear a hand might brush a foreign sleeve or, worse still, a naked wrist or finger. House and grounds, naturally, are required to be remote and secluded. The co-founders' house, in the one photograph that I happen to have seen, seems to belong in an Andrew Wyeth painting.

The theory behind the vow of silence is that talk—even serious, thoughtful talk or talk about writing itself—drains away the writer's most precious resource, which is the belief that he or she is the solitary witness to an inexhaustible profusion of images from which might be read all the wisdom of the world. At the beginning of each workshop, every writer has to copy in handwriting and to display

above his or her writing-table the famous passage from the diaries of
Franz Kafka:

> I hate everything that does not relate to literature, conversa-
> tions bore me (even when they relate to literature), to visit
> people bores me, the joys and sorrows of my relatives bore
> me to my soul. Conversation takes the importance, the
> seriousness, the truth, out of everything I think.

Every breach of the vow of silence must be reported to the writer-in-
charge. Even so seemingly slight a thing as sighing within earshot of
another person is a reportable offence, and the writer who catches a
hint of meaning in the sound of someone's breath escaping is there-
fore expected not only to write before long about a fictional sigher
and sigh but to draft a brief informer's report. Likewise, the sight of a
mouth being drawn deliberately down at the corners or even a distant
view of a head shaking slowly from side to side or of a pair of hands
being pressed against a face—any of these can oblige a writer to
amend the work-in-progress so that it includes a version of the latest
offence against Waldo and of the report of the offence and any other
documents to do with it.

A first offender against the Great Silence is punished by being sent
to his or her room to transcribe passages from writers whose way of life
was more or less solitary: Kafka, Emily Dickinson, Giacomo Leopardi,
Edwin Arlington Robinson, Michel de Ghelderode, A.E. Housman,
Thomas Merton, Gerald Basil Edwards, C.W. Killeaton … The Waldo
Fiction Foundation keeps a register of all those who for at least five
years of their lives wrote or took notes but talked to no friend or lover.

A second offence brings immediate expulsion from the workshop.
The expulsion is never announced to the group, but suddenly among
the buzzings and clickings of insects and the chirrups of birds on a
drowsy afternoon a motor-car engine starts up, and perhaps you notice
an hour later that a certain pair of creaking shoes are no longer heard
in the corridors; or perhaps, standing at a certain point on the veranda,

you see the same trail of ants flowing up and down the yellowish stone and the same tiny spider unmoving in its cave of crumbled mortar but you no longer hear the faint rattling of a typewriter through the wall; or later at the dinner table a bread roll lies unbroken by a pair of hands that you formerly watched from under your eyebrows.

Does anyone reading this want to ask why the workshop should expel a person whose presence had made the fiction of at least one writer daily more bulky and more complex? Anyone who could ask this question has not even begun to understand what I have written so far. But Waldo can answer for me. What might have seemed to the objector a grave objection earns a sentence in the manual. *Just the one room becoming empty will make the echo of the fiction of the house more lingering still.*

No one questions the rules concerning silence, but newcomers to Waldo sometimes wonder why no rule forbids a writer in a workshop from sending urgent letters or manifestoes or apologias after someone who has just been expelled. How can the purpose of the workshop be served, the questioner asks, if the bereft writer, instead of working at fiction, drafts long addresses to someone who has seemed to undermine the basic principles of Waldo?

A little thought usually reassures the doubter. The writer in a workshop has to deliver each day to the writer-in-charge not only the finished drafts of fiction but any earlier drafts or page of notes or scribble and certainly any letter or draft of a letter written that day. No one may send out from a Waldo workshop any letter or note or any other communication without first submitting it to the writer-in-charge. In short, the writer sending messages after an expelled fellow-writer may be writing to no one. Even if Waldo, in the person of the writer-in-charge, actually forwards the letters, there is no obligation to reveal to the person who wrote them the true name, let alone the address, of the person they were sent to. And the ritual bonfire at the end of every workshop is not just for all the writing done during the week but for all of Waldo's records—every scrap of evidence that might otherwise be adduced some day to prove that this or that writer once, under half a dozen pseudonyms, learned the secret of true fiction from an eccentric American sect.

So, the writer who spends the last days of a workshop trying to reach someone who once or twice glanced or stared in a certain way before being expelled—that writer will usually understand in time that no letters may have been forwarded or that the letters were forwarded but with the sender identified only by a false name and the address 'Waldo'. The writer who reaches this understanding will then be grateful to the body of theory and traditions personified as Waldo. For if the writer had had his or her way at first, much precious writing time would have been lost and perhaps the workshop itself abandoned while the two strangers made themselves known to each other in conventional ways. But, thanks to Waldo, the writer stayed on at the workshop and began the first notes or drafts of what would later become a substantial body of fiction.

Those novels or novellas or short stories or prose poems would be widely read, but only their author would know what they really were and who they were addressed to. As for that person, the one whose motor-car had started up suddenly among the dry sounds of grasshoppers on a hot afternoon, that person would almost certainly never read any of the published fiction. That person would have been won over years earlier by the doctrines of Waldo, and in all the years since the founding of our group not a single apostasy has been recorded. The expelled writer is still one of us, and like every other follower of Waldo he or she would read no fiction by any living author. He or she might buy the latest books and display them all around the house, but no author would be read until that author was dead.

No living author would be read because the reader of a living author might be tempted one day to search out the author and to ask some question about the text or about the weather on the day when this or that page was first composed or about a certain year of the author's life before the first sentence of the text came into being. And to ask such questions would be not just to violate the most sacred tradition of Waldo; it would be as if to say that the old stone house by Penobscot Bay has never existed, that Frances Da Pavia and Patrick McLear are no more substantial than characters in a work of fiction, and that the Waldo theory of fiction—far from having produced some of the finest writers of our day—is itself the invention of a writer: a bit of whimsy dreamed up by a man at a writers' workshop and handed to the writer-in-charge so that a woman with light-brown hair and a frowning face would learn why the man had not yet told her how impressed he had been by her story of a man who worried about bedrock.

In an earlier draft of this paragraph—a draft that you will never read—I began with the words: 'You may be wondering about that ritual bonfire mentioned a little distance back ...' But if you had read those words you would have wondered not just how the words could have reached you if all the pages written during the workshop are ritually burned on the last evening; you would have wondered also who the word 'you' referred to. If these pages are being written on the veranda of a stone house during a writers' workshop, you might say to yourself, why are they seemingly addressed to me: to someone who reads them in very different surroundings? For the pages are much too explanatory to have been written for the other workshop members—why would five followers of Waldo have to be told in the opening paragraphs of a piece of workshop fiction all the rules and traditions so well known to them?

But you have almost answered your own objection. You have spoken of this writing as fiction. This is the truth. These words are part of a work of fiction. Even these last few sentences, which can be read as an exchange between the writer and a reader, are fiction. Any thoughtful reader would recognise them for what they are. And the writers at a Waldo workshop are the most thoughtful of readers. When these pages are put in front of them, my fellow writers will not demand to know why they have to read an account of things already familiar to them. They will read with even more than their usual alertness. They will try to learn why I have written in the form of a piece of fiction addressed to strangers far away from this hilltop a piece of fiction that only they can read.

And yet, you still want certain puzzles explained. (Or, to put this more clearly, if you existed you would still want those puzzles explained.) If the ritual bonfire consumes all evidence of the workshop, why should I write as though these pages are going to be preserved?

My first impulse is to answer, 'Why not?' One of the most cherished anecdotes among the followers of Waldo is of the writer who begged for a last few minutes while the other members of the workshop were already around the fire and making scrolls of their pages, tying bundle after bundle with the obligatory silk ribbons in the Waldo colours of pale-grey and sea-green, and tossing their bundles into the flames. During those last few minutes the writer crouched in the glow from the flames and scribbled over and over the same sentence for which the right order of words and the right balance among the subordinate clauses had still not been found.

With Waldo it is the spirit that matters rather than the form. No writer is stripped and searched before leaving a workshop. No luggage is forcibly opened on the front veranda on the morning of departure. If you still believe that I am writing these words to be read by someone outside the workshop, then you only have to imagine my slipping this typescript under the heap of my soiled underclothes on the last night …

Now the danger may be that I am making Waldo seem a mere set of conventions to be varied if occasion demands. I assure you that Waldo weighs heavily indeed on me. Every page that I write here on this veranda will be tied, five nights from tonight, in the colours of ocean and fog and burned in the view of five writers whose good opinions I value, even if I may never learn their true names.

And I follow the way of Waldo even more strictly for having read sometimes, on the last day of a workshop, the implication that we are not meant to take Waldo seriously after all: that these monastic retreats with their fussy rituals, the manual with all its rules, the house in Maine, although they are, of course, part of a solid world, are only meant to work on the imagination of writers and to suggest how seriously one *might* take the writing of fiction in an ideal world.

At this point someone who had never heard of Waldo before reading these pages might need to be reminded that the isolation of Waldo writers is not relieved during hours of darkness.

The co-founders in their wisdom decreed that the writers in each workshop had to be strangers and that the numbers of men and women must be equal. Some people have concluded from this that we provide a literary introduction service. Perhaps one of my readers, even after the careful account I have so far given, supposes even now that only half the bedrooms will be occupied each night during this workshop.

Even if my suspicious reader, like all my readers, is only someone I called into being this morning on this veranda, still I consider myself bound to answer truthfully. In any case, what do I have to gain by writing anything but the truth in these circumstances?

I spent last night alone in my room. I cannot imagine why I would not spend tonight and every other night of the workshop alone in my room—unless the whole of the history of the Waldo movement has been an elaborate practical joke of which I am the sole victim, and unless I am the only writer in this house who believes that if I were to try a certain door-knob tonight it should only be for the purpose of thrusting a little way into the darkness the thick bundle of all the pages I have written, with not even my true name on them, before I creep back to my room.

I cannot answer for any other writer, of course, but I hereby declare my faith in the doctrine that persuaded me to give up poetry and to come to this stony hill to learn how to write truly. I believe as a Waldo writer that my existence is only justified by the writing of prose fiction. And for inspiration I look to Campobello Man.

You Waldo writers reading this know very well who I mean. But my imaginary reader far from this hill could not have heard even the title of the book that explains everything.

Isles Fogbound: the Writer on the Wrong Side of America—have any of us read this book as it deserves to be read, and changed our lives accordingly? I am no better than any of you. I can expound the thesis of many a chapter, yet I have still not felt in my heart the joy that is promised in the last pages; I have still not seen the changed world that I ought to see all around me if only I could give myself wholly over to Waldo.

How can I think of everything I see as no more and no less than a detail in a work of fiction? I walked a little way down this hill before breakfast. From every outcrop of stones and gravel a small vine of *hardenbergia* grew: the same mauve that I look for in every garden I walk past in the suburbs of Melbourne. Yet I stared at the mauve against the golden-brown and could think of no place for it in any piece of prose fiction I might write. Perhaps the mauve and the brown belong in the fiction of another writer, and perhaps this is the sense of those ambiguous passages in the last pages of the inspired volume of Waldo.

When I knelt and touched the soil a surprising image came to me. The flaky stones had the look and the feel of a thick layer of face-powder plastered oddly on her face by a woman not quite right in the head. A different sort of writer might follow this image wherever it leads.

Of all I have read in Frances Da Pavia and Patrick McLear I remember mostly the smaller details and the quirky propositions. From the accounts of the first workshops I remember the custom of making the newly arrived writers walk all around the rooms and corridors counting windows. They could consider themselves for the time being dwellers in the House of Fiction, but they ought to acknowledge that the house had considerably fewer windows than Henry James had asserted. As for the windows, even though I have never set foot on the North American continent I can see the dark-blue sky, the green of Penobscot Bay, and above all, the pearly-grey of the fogs—even the painted fogs on the double panes of the rooms for those who wanted to live Waldo doctrine to the fullest.

I am familiar too with all the contrivances that were fitted to the house for those who wanted to spy on their fellow writers by day or night. (In these temporary quarters we have no opportunity for the intensive spying that Waldo has always permitted without directly encouraging. A Waldo writer is urged not so much to spy as to feel always under close surveillance, and the spy-holes and carelessly hidden cameras all around the house in Maine are to promote this feeling. How many writers make use of these things Waldo officially does not trouble itself to learn. No one on this hilltop would have drilled through the artist's walls, but anyone would have been free to bring their own equipment with them, and one of you five readers of the first draft of this may be reading it not for the first time.)

I have only sometimes glimpsed the world through Waldo's eyes, but I have meditated often on the map of North America as Da Pavia and McLear taught me to see it. The people of the continent are mostly going in the wrong direction.

The people are all being carried blindly westward. They are all hoping to reach a place of bright sunlight where they will see enacted deeds befitting the end of a long journey. But the people are all going the wrong way.

The coast of Maine is almost the farthest place where a group of American writers can stand and declare that they have gone, literally as well as spiritually, against the prevailing currents of their nation. But even in the stone house in Waldo County, the writers wanted to say more than this; and so began the game of the islands.

The people of America are being carried blindly along in the path of the sun, but not the writers of Waldo. They huddle on their clifftop and set their faces towards Penobscot Bay. America, these writers say, is a book. They themselves may be situated within the pages of America, but they stand where they stand to signify that the subject of their own fiction lies behind the readers and even the writers of America.

The man who wrote under the name of Stendhal is supposed to have said in 1830 that he wrote his fiction for the readers of 1880.

Frances Da Pavia and Patrick McLear announced in 1950 that their fiction of that year was being written for the reader of 1900. (To make their arithmetic quite clear: they were writing in 1960 for the readers of 1890; and if the co-founders were alive today in 1985 they would have in mind the readers of 1865.) Towards the end of their lives Da Pavia and McLear thought of themselves as privileged to be drawing still nearer to the putative age when no word of fiction had yet been written. And just before their sudden deaths, our founders were pre-occupied with the question what mode of fictional address the lucky writer would choose for that generation for whom a sentence such as *Call me Waldo* ... and all that it could possibly mean were solid items of a factual world.

This is what first drew me to Waldo of all the schools of fiction I might have joined: this earnest undertaking by Waldo writers to shape their sentences not according to habits of thinking in their own day but as though each writer is writing from a separate island just short of the notional beginning of the mainland.

In the early years of the game the writers chose from actual islands. Before beginning a workshop each writer would consult large-scale maps of the coast. Then, on the first morning in the stone house and while the fog outside was still unmoving, table and chair would be carefully aligned so that the seated writer faced the blank double-page of America and a word would be whispered in the monk-ish room. For the remaining six days of the workshop, *Monhegan*, *Matinicus*, or *Great Wass* would mark the place where the true story of America was being written; where a writer that the writer in the room could only dream of found the words to write; where the invisible was on the point of becoming visible.

Although every page of fiction purporting to have been written at these places was burned in due course, still rumours and gossip hung around the stone house, and each new group of writers seemed to know which islands had been claimed in earlier years and which dwindling few had never been written from. In the last year before the game changed its direction, members of the workshop had to choose from mere rocks and nameless shoals. Then someone who claimed afterwards not to have noticed the dots and dashes of the international border swerving strangely south-west across the inked ocean wrote that he dreamed of someone writing dreamlike prose on Campobello.

What happened during the following week enriched the theory and traditions of Waldo, it was said, immeasurably beyond the hopes of the co-founders. (I prefer to believe that Da Pavia and McLear foresaw confidently the scope, if not the details, of the Campobello Migration and wrote about it in some of the best of their lost typescripts.) In a word, the writers for that week were divided quite by accident into two groups. The first had consulted in the Waldo Library (can any of us in this house almost bare of books imagine what a treasury of recondite lore is the library in the original stone house?) an atlas in which coloured inks were used only for the nation or the state which happened to be the designated subject-matter for that page, surrounding areas being colourless, ghostly, almost bare of printed names. The second group consulted an atlas in which the colours reached to the very margins of every page, no matter what political or geographical borders crossed the page itself. So for one group Campobello—the island, the man supposed to be writing there, and the host of invisible possibilities behind the word itself—gave pleasure because it was perversely located in a place that a writer might actually visit if he or she was literal-minded enough to want to travel through the fog and even further along the schematic edge of America. (This group was further divided into those who recognised that Campobello Island is part of the Province of New Brunswick and those who believed it to be the utmost outpost of the State of Maine.) The second group, having seen a pale blob on their map and having deliberately refused to turn to the pages presenting a coloured Canada—not even to learn the name of the blob, supposed Campobello and everything arising from it to be the result of an ingenious invented cataclysm.

They supposed that at some time during the filling-in of the blank double-page of the continent and while the ink of America, so to speak, was still not dry, someone of far-reaching imaginative power had taken each page by its outermost edge, lifted the two pages upwards and inwards, and pressed them firmly together, even rubbing certain patches at random fiercely up against one another for simple delight.

How can the result of this be best described? America as a mirror of itself? America turned inside out and around about? America as a page in a dream-atlas? With this map in mind a writer could see in the forests of New England the colours of New Mexican deserts; could see, as I myself once saw (admittedly in an atlas published in England), the word *Maine* clearly printed near Flagstaff, Arizona, and the word *Maineville* near Loveland, Ohio. But of all the thousands of embellishments and verbal puzzles and aimless or fragmented roads and trails now added to America, what most appealed to the writers in the stone house was the simple notion of a Beautiful Plain as the primordial setting for fiction and the Handsome Plainsman as the original of all fictional characters, if not of all writers of fiction.

I could write an entire short novel on this subject, but I am only a minor poet taking his first stumbling steps as a writer of fiction; and in any case my first task is to finish this account of the most wonderful week in the history of Waldo.

After the bonfire of that week the writers meditated on the two versions of Campobello: the writer as finder of blank spaces on actual maps, and the writer as finder of quite new double-pages of maps. And what those writers never forgot was that the fiction from each of their two groups had been indistinguishable. The so-called Campobello Migration that followed meant simply that all Waldo writers were free from then onwards to locate the ideal source of their fiction in places even further east than New Brunswick or in places whose names or parts of whose names might have appeared on a map of Maine if certain pages of atlases were rubbed together, figuratively speaking, before their colours had finally dried.

The shadows of the nearest trees have now reached the yellow flagstones under my writing-table. The time is late in the afternoon. And just a moment ago I heard the sudden starting-up of a motor-car.

The artist who owns this house left a badly written note explaining how to operate the pumps that bring water up the hill from the underground storage tanks, and for some reason he scrawled at the bottom: *Late in day find spot on back veranda with terrific view of Melb skyline so long no smog.*

As I write these words, a motor-car is following the winding road downwards between these hard hills where off-blue *hardenbergia* sprouts wild between outcrops of dull-gold talc. In the motor-car is a writer who believes wholeheartedly, as I believe, in the claims of Waldo fiction. That writer has submitted to being expelled from this house as the penalty for sending a message to a fellow writer by means other than the inserting of an allusion into a passage of fiction. If I am the person who was meant to receive the message, I can write truthfully that I have never received it.

I do not know the name of the person in the motor-car. I will probably never know that name. If I could give all my time to reading all the fiction published in this country, I might read some day a passage recalling a piece of fiction I once read about a man who thought continually about the bedrock far under his feet, who studied the surfaces of all the stones he saw, who wanted to live only in stone houses, who would not have complained if he had been made to read fiction day after day, or even poetry ...

The rules of Waldo allow me only until sunset to finish what I am writing. If this were only a piece of fiction devised to amuse a few writers with tastes and interests like my own—if not only Waldo and the man who wondered about bedrock but even the woman with the light-brown hair was invented for the benefit of a group of writers who have not yet been mentioned in these pages, surely now would be the time for me to explain myself.

Until I was nearly twenty years old I thought I was meant to be a poet. Then, in December 1958, I saw in the window of Alice Bird's secondhand bookshop in Bourke Street, Melbourne, a copy of *Ulysses*, by James Joyce. After reading that book I wanted to be a writer of prose fiction.

In those days I knew only two people who might have been interested in my change of heart. I told the two people what I had decided while the three of us happened to be standing under an enormous oak tree in the grounds of the mansion known as Stonnington, in the Melbourne suburb of Malvern. Stonnington at that time was used by the Education Department of Victoria as part of a teachers' college. I was a student of the teachers' college, working to qualify at the end of 1959 for the Trained Primary Teacher's Certificate, after which I would teach in schools of the Education Department by day and write prose fiction during evenings and at weekends.

After I had announced my decision to write prose fiction I wanted to do more. I searched in libraries for information about Joyce. Somewhere I found a sentence that I still remember today: *He dressed quietly, even conservatively, beringed fingers being his only exoticism.*

I went to one of the pawnbrokers in Russell Street, Melbourne, and bought two cheap rings. Each was low-carat gold with a slab of black onyx. I wore the rings on my fingers but I did not otherwise change my threadbare style of dressing.

The first picture I found of Joyce was a reproduction of a photograph that I have rarely seen since. I believed the man I considered the greatest of prose writers had had a forehead sharply scored by lines of the same pattern—three parallel horizontals intersected by a single diagonal—as the lines I had drawn in my fourth year of secondary school in my general science notebook to represent a layer of bedrock.

I hid my rings from my father. In my father's eyes, rings and tiepins and cufflinks were of the style he called Cockney Jew. I hid *Ulysses* also. My father could not bear to hear such words as 'shit' or 'fuck' uttered in any context, and I assumed he would not want to read them either.

My father has been dead now for twenty-five years. He left behind him no prose fiction and no poetry, and not even a written message for any of his family. But on the wall of a sandstone quarry on the hill called Quarry Hill near the mouth of Buckley's Creek in the district of Mepunga East on the south-west coast of Victoria, my father's surname and his two initials are still deeply inscribed above the date 1924. When my father carved his name he was as old as I was when I made my announcement under the oak tree in the grounds of the building called Stonnington.

In 1924 James Joyce was forty-two and *Ulysses* had been published for two years. The young man carving his name in the stone-quarry had thirty-six years still to live; the man writing *Finnegans Wake* in Paris had a little less than half that time ahead of him. The man in the quarry knew nothing then of Joyce or his writing and still nothing of them when he died.

I have enclosed with my last will and testament five sheets of paper inscribed with what I consider useful information for my sons. One sheet tells them how to find the inscription made by their grandfather who died ten years before the eldest of them was born. One or more of my sons may care to inspect my father's writing twenty-five years after my own death, and then to note how much or how little of my own writing can still be read.

Out of the quarry on Quarry Hill came the blocks of sandstone that went into the building of a house known as The Cove about one kilometre from the quarry and within earshot of the Southern Ocean. My father's father built the house and lived in it until he died in 1949. The house stands solidly today, but it is owned and lived in by people whose name I do not know. I have not seen the house for nearly ten years. I hardly ever think of it. I did not even think of it while I was writing about the stone house of Waldo by Penobscot Bay. This is not a story about a house but about the space where a house could have been. I only mention my grandfather's house in this story because the digging of the stone for that house gave my father a page for his writing that has lasted for sixty years.

All my life I have looked around me for outcrops of rocks or pebbles or for any jagged place where the true colour of the earth is exposed. Even the crumbs around an ants' nest will make me stop and look. I watch the cuttings beside railway-lines, the bare patches at the bases of roadside trees, and the dirt thrown up from trenches; I like to be able to think clearly about the colours underneath me as I walk.

The man I read about today is not interested in the colours of soil. He wants to be sure the bedrock is deep and true for as far downwards as he can imagine it. He believes in a world of countless layers, most of them invisible, and he believes that a fault in any one of the layers has an influence on every other layer. He believes that what some people call his mental illness is a fault in one of the subtle, invisible layers of the world at about the level of his own head. He believes that the ultimate cause of this fault is a terrible creasing of the bedrock far below.

The man I am writing about is a character in a piece of fiction, but the woman who wrote the piece of fiction is a living woman whose forehead creases when she writes or reads. Until a short while ago that woman was with me in this house, but now she has gone and I do not expect to see her again.

The woman with the furrows in her forehead has left the house because she has already read what I am writing. The woman came up to my table this morning while I was crouched on the hillside staring at the mauve *hardenbergia* and fingering the brownish, powdery rocks. The woman read my pages and understood more clearly than I understand why I am writing them. Then she left a message for me—a clear, unambiguous message not encoded in prose fiction and therefore in serious breach of the rules of Waldo. And then the woman handed all her papers and drafts to the writer-in-charge and left this house.

To finish this piece of fiction I would only have to write that after the woman had gone I went in search of her message and found it in the most obvious place—in the nearest thing to a library in this house. I would only have to write that one volume on the artist's miserable shelf of books was oddly stacked, as though drawing attention to itself ...

The book is: *Berenice Abbott: Sixty Years of Photography*, by Hank O'Neal with an introduction by John Canaday, published by Thames and Hudson in 1982. On the front of the dust-jacket is a brilliantly clear picture of James Joyce at the age of forty-six. Two rings are clearly visible on his fingers. Inside the cover of the book the name Nora Lee has been written in ballpoint. My mother's mother had exactly that name but she owned no books. Towards the end of the book I found a photograph of a place called Stonington, which is on an island off the coast of Maine.

Or I might finish this piece of fiction by mentioning that I have always been drawn to writers who have felt their minds threatened. When I read Richard Ellmann's biography of Joyce in 1960 I studied carefully the account of his daughter's madness. I wondered whether Joyce could follow, as he claimed he could, the swift leaps in her thought.

One night in October 1960 I was drinking in the house of a man who boasted that he was welcome in the houses of famous artists in the hills north-east of Melbourne. Late in the evening, when the man and I were both very drunk, he drove me in his station wagon (it was the company car that he drove as a sales representative) first to Eltham and then along hilly back roads to the strangest building I had ever seen. I learned afterwards that the place was Montsalvat, but on that dark night in 1960 the man who took me there would only tell me it was an artists' colony. I learned afterwards too that the man I met in the stone castle was Justus Jorgensen, but I was introduced to him only as the Artist.

The Artist would have been justified in sending us away from his front door, but he let us in and dealt with us most politely. We must have talked for an hour, but all I remember is my learning that the Artist had been in Paris in the 1920s; my asking had he ever seen

James Joyce; his telling me that he had; my asking had he ever seen Joyce's daughter Lucia and had she seemed in any way strange; his telling me that Lucia Joyce had been a beautiful young woman with no imperfection that he had noticed.

I might have ended this piece of fiction in either of the two ways outlined above, but of course I did not. I have thrown in my lot with Waldo. If I am any sort of writer I am a Waldo writer. If what I write rests on any coherent theory it rests on those doctrines devised by starers into fogs and mutterers of names of islands on the wrong side of their country.

And so, trusting utterly in the wisdom of Waldo, and noting that the sun is at the point of sinking below the faint purple-brown blur which is the northern suburbs of Melbourne as seen from an artist's stone house far to the east of my own home, I end, or I prepare to end, this piece of fiction.

All the fiction I have written in the stone house has been an encoded message for a certain woman. In order to send this message I have had to imagine a world in which the woman does not exist and neither do I. I have had to imagine a world in which the pronoun 'I' stands for the sort of man who could imagine a world in which he does not exist and only a man steeped in the theories of Waldo could imagine him.

The Chook in the Australian Unconscious (1986)

Judith Brett

> *The dark haired girl said in the next*
> *Life she would choose to be a chook:*
>> David Campbell, 'Words with a Black Orpington'

Much has been made of the desert as a symbol for the precariousness of European civilisation's hold over both the Australian continent and the minds of those who dwell here, but for most Australians it is not the desert but the chook which symbolises the precariousness of our social order. Scratching out an existence from unyielding ground, collapsing into a flap when danger threatens, the chook not the desert haunts our dreams. And no one has gone into the national Parliament dressed as a desert, or even its ship. For the chook symbolises the forces, both inner and outer, which we fear we have not conquered, and it does so by being a uniquely Australian comic figure.

The word 'chook' is a symbol of our cultural difference; where the British have hens and the Americans chickens we have chooks, though as one moves up the social scale and ambivalence about Australia's difference from England increases the word is heard less frequently. Private school educated people nervously refer to hens; and when chooks were being discussed at an academic dinner party, a professor of lower middleclass origins remarked with surprised wistfulness, 'Chook, that's not a word you often hear around the university these days'. Social status is often expressed by one's distance from nature; the more nature is controlled, and the more of it one controls, the higher one is in the human pecking order. So, from chooks in the house, to chooks running free round the backyard, to chooks neatly penned, to the pinnacle of respectability where one is free from the foul altogether. Chooks are dirtier than hens, so the word, along with other images of dirt now banished, carries something of the allure of instinctual pleasures renounced for the dubious benefits of an upward mobility measured by one's distance from the dirt. Partridge describes the word as an Australian and New Zealand colloquialism derived from Irish and English dialect and current from about the mid nineteenth century, though the use of 'chook' as a pejorative referring to women is given as Australian only.

In his books *Totemism* and its successor, *The Savage Mind*, Claude Lévi-Strauss shows how human beliefs about and practices towards animals, which anthropologists had called the institution of totemism, are really systems of classification with which human societies think about their own social relations. Speculating on the relationships between human society and different species of animals he suggests that the bird world is the most perfect metaphor for human society that the natural kingdom offers.

> Birds … can be permitted to resemble men for the very reason that they are so different. They are feathered, winged, oviparous and they are also physically separated from human society by the element in which it is their privilege to move. As a result of this fact, they form a community which is independent of our own but, precisely because of this independence, appears to us like another society, homologous to that in which we live: birds love freedom; they build themselves homes in which they live a family life and nurture their young; they often engage in social relations with other members of their species; and they communicate with them by acoustic means recalling articulated language. Consequently everything objective conspires to make us think of the bird world as a metaphorical human society.

Lèvi-Strauss sees the society of birds as representing humanity's achievements—its love of freedom, its language, its caring family life, its sociability. But chooks are ground dwelling birds penned in our own backyards, made ridiculous by their lumbering efforts to grace the air with a flight that's more aspiration than achievement. They are birds slipped from their rightful element, an image not of human society's achieved harmony and completeness, but of the vulnerability of humans and their social forms to some of the less admirable characteristics of their nature. The pecking order, closely observed, is not a lovely institution; nor is the chook pen under threat an image of an ordered social world.

It is the chook's vulnerability that is perhaps the key to its role in the unconscious. In *The How to Teach Your Chicken to Fly Manual* (Kangaroo Press, Kenthurst, NSW, 1983) Trevor Weekes describes them as 'the birds evolution forgot' and gives detailed instructions for the building of a machine to exercise the domestic fowl's flying muscles. This little book, with its meticulous pencil drawings of chooks in mechanical contraptions and photos to show the machine in operation with a white leghorn called Gregory Peck, is evidence of both the sadism inspired by the chook's comparatively flightless fate and the laughter we use to defend ourselves against the knowledge of that sadism.

To visit the chook pen in the backyard is always to risk finding the devastation wrought by a marauding dog or fox—blood, feathers, dismembered chooks that couldn't fly away. The cruelty of nature's ethic of survival made manifest in suburbia; culture's fragile control over nature destroyed. Throw a rock on the chookhouse roof, run a stick along its corrugated iron sides, and you can recreate the blind panic of flightless birds trying to escape. Ned, in Olga Masters' *Loving Daughters*, returned from World War I not quite right in the head, beats the chookhouse wall with a lump of wood whenever he passes it, stirring the din and frantic flapping of the chooks within to an image of his own growing madness. And in the headless chook running round the backyard there is an image of panic not even death can stop.

This image is a vivid childhood memory for many Australians, particularly those over thirty-five who witnessed chooks being chased and killed for the family table. Perhaps for many their earliest experience of violent death, its impact was the greater because of the capacity for violence towards small living creatures it revealed in the parents.

The plucked carcass of the chook bears a remarkable resemblance to a human baby, or rather to its corpse—the beginning and end of the human life cycle brought together in a single image. After a difficult day with the new baby and cooking a roast chook for tea, a friend of mine had a dream: he trussed the baby, pink and vulnerable, for the oven. So in the Barrel routine on 'Hey, Hey, It's Saturday', in which numbered balls are replaced by numbered frozen chooks, there is a transformation of the symbolic equivalence of babies and chook carcasses to the world of the frozen embryo. In this transformation we see further evidence of the symbolic power of chooks and the need to give it cultural expression even within the urban world's attenuated relationship with nature. The particularly strong disgust evoked by battery hen farming is further witness to the chook's continuing power as an image of vulnerability.

In most cultures it is the male not the female domestic fowl which has been loaded with symbolic importance. The cock of European and Asian culture with its pride, courage, aggression and splendid plumage has been a rich source of images of masculinity. And cockfighting has been and still is, despite being banned in most countries, a popular male pastime. So although there are tales of the foolishness of the cock's pride, and talk of cocks gives great scope for sexual innuendo, the cock is only incidentally a comic figure. In Australia the cock scarcely figures; a hanger-on among the chooks, if it is singled out at all it is by the bowdlerised American word 'rooster'. Australia has replaced one of the central masculine symbols of the old world with a comic female figure, suggesting that it is female rather than male sexuality that is problematic in the Antipodes.

One must beware here of too glib an interpretation, resist the temptation to speculate about drooping cocks and other signs of national impotence. As Clifford Geertz has shown in his celebrated essay 'Notes on a Balinese Cockfight', cultural symbols are never simple reflections of social life. Rather they are parts of stories cultures tell themselves about themselves, and like all stories they could have been different. Australians' interest in chooks rather than cocks may have little to do with sex and more to do with their unease with nature; and of course human sexuality can both demonstrate and symbolise humanity's implication in nature, particularly female sexuality with all it implies about the physicalness of our birth and the consequent inevitability of our death. For as Lèvi-Strauss has argued, women have generally been seen by human society as closer to nature than men, their integration into culture more ambivalent.

Partridge notes that the use of 'chook' as a pejorative term for women is peculiarly Australian. When Reg Ansett called the air hostesses 'old boilers' they struck till he apologised. Pejorative terms express annoyance, generally caused by the speaker's inability to get someone so described to do what is wanted. They are a response to another's intractability, a railing against the limits of one's power. Intractable women, intractable nature. Female sexuality is particularly problematic here because nature is so problematic, both for those who try to farm it and for the urban majority who try to ignore it.

If nature were not so problematic here we would still have hens. Later in the poem of David Campbell's cited at the beginning a rural idyll is evoked, and like all rural idylls it refers to an English not an Australian landscape.

> And she said she would be a homestead hen
> With a nest under a damson plum
> In the windfall orchard back home.

Hens are at home in a cosy domesticated nature; always plump, never scrawny, they peck away in the orchards and solid stone barns of prosperous farms, red and black and speckled against the green fields of England; never dirty white mongrel chooks scrabbling between ramshackle corrugated iron and wood buildings in dusty paddocks.

The chook is an image of the tenuous hold Australians have over the land, its stubborn intractability and our ridiculous vulnerability. Whenever the word 'chook' occurs in conversations, at first people smile in the sophisticated way people smile at childish things they have put behind them; but if the topic is pursued most soon respond—with stories, memories, jokes and with the conspiratorial pride of sharing a cultural touchstone, of playing for a while with the secret identification in most Australians' hearts between themselves and the chook.

Essay on Patriotism (1987)

Peter Porter

Compared with my true patriotism,
the imperialism of my legs and bowels,
the suzerainty of my eyes,
grave hemispheric rulings
of the wide Porterian Peace,
my love of country is a pallid passion.

So when they say
we've dwindled to a Third Class Power,
a Banana Republic without
a decent satellite to spy from,
I recall those old inheritors
of fear, dirt, sickness, snot and rickets
who crawled out of their burrows
to hail Ladysmith's Relief
and bray the victories of their rulers
on air they couldn't warm.

Let us therefore handle the word 'great'
with circumspection. It fits Blake
and Milton, is much too big for Cromwell
and generally should watch itself in mirrors,
bearing down like Yeats's Nobel head.

When commentators write about
'the patriotic proletariat',
imagine week-end articles—
'from flat-cap to cat-flap

in one generation', 'Dinkies
are not toys today', 'Designer
Murder comes to Sicily'—
and hang wild garlic round your ears.

Let what people really love
invent an island tongue:
'a gemstone cantilever …
hearing it in Noel's SOTA/
Dynevector/Spectral/Threshold/
Acoustat/Entec …' no wonder
Rambo gobbled up the gooks
if he had such voices in his head.

Patriotism is not enough
of a scoundrel's last refuge
even if you love
your neighbour as yourself.
When I fell from the long tree of light
I didn't know it was going to be me
or I'd have checked all these quotations.
Where I landed I named ours
though it was never mine.

True patriots all,
the still-swimming lobsters in the tank,
the lambs that face the ocean through steel bars,
the opals in the open-cut—
I left my mother's and my father's house
and stepped on to a road beneath the stars.

Oyster Cove 1988 (1988)

Cassandra Pybus

In April 1855, J. E. Calder, Surveyor-General of Tasmania, set out to walk to the old convict station at Oyster Cove. So lovely was the day and so beautiful the terrain that Calder made detailed notes of his impressions for a Hobart newspaper. After passing through the hamlet of Snug on the southern edge of North West Bay, Calder followed the road upward into heavily wooded hills from which he caught the occasional glimpse of a spectacular landscape.

> Now and then only, when an opening occurred ... we greatly admired the varied and magnificent picture which lay before us. The dusky eminences of South Bruny stretched along the horizon, terminating in the bold and beautiful cliffs of the fluted cape. Adventure Bay on the east of Bruny—the place of anchorage of the famous old navigators Cook, Furneaux and Bligh, last century—lies fully in view, separated from the nearer waters of the D'Entrecasteaux Channel by the long, low thread-like isthmus that unites the two peninsulas of Bruny Island ... and a vast extent of undulating country in the east and north east, fronting on the most varied coastline in the world, forming altogether a picture which well repays the toil of a long journey to see it.

The huge eucalyptus and myrtle forests have now gone, but in essence the majesty and extraordinary beauty of the scene remain as Calder encountered it in the autumn sunshine a hundred and thirty-three years ago. This is the channel country, the home of my family for six generations. From where Calder stood he could possibly have made out the homestead Sacriston, built by my great-great-grandfather, Richard Pybus, who took up a large land grant on North Bruny Island in 1829. Below him, nestling at the very lip of Little Oyster Cove, but hidden from view, was the house and orchard of Calder's brother-in-law, Henry Harrison Pybus. This house, inherited by my great-grandfather, is still there behind its screen of trees, but only a huge scarred mulberry tree remains on Bruny to testify to the good fortune of that first immigrant from Northumbria. Not that physical presence matters. On my morning walks over the old station road I can feel my ancestral bonds to this place. It is my place: the landscape of my dreaming.

As I follow the path of my distant kinsman over the steep hills that divide North West Bay and the D'Entrecasteaux Channel, I have the same destination. It is a good long walk for my dog, while for myself it is a profound and constant source of psychic renewal. Like the tall timber, the old station is long since gone, and until recently the site was overrun with a tangle of bracken and blackberries. It was always sour and swampy ground, too low and damp for prolonged dwelling or productive use. Now it is cleared and signposted. The marker, pock-marked with dozens of bullet holes and defaced with spray paint, carries the Aboriginal flag. It is still possible to make out the words, a quotation from Xavier Herbert:

> Until we give back to the black man just a bit of the land that was his, and give it back without provisos, without strings to snatch it back, without anything but complete generosity of spirit in concession for the evil we have done to him—until we do that, we shall remain what we have always been so far; a people without integrity; not a nation, but a community of thieves.

The clearing and sign are the work of the Tasmanian Aboriginal community who have a repeatedly unsuccessful land claim on the old convict station site. Their reasons for such a claim are simple and unassailable: this damp glen and swampy inlet are where the remnant of the tribal people of Tasmania were brought to die. On that April morning in 1855, Surveyor Calder was on his way to visit the few Aboriginals who still remained at Oyster Cove.

Nearing his melancholy object, Calder found the glory of the landscape quite diminished by the forlorn spectre of the station. 'But if the view were a hundred times more prepossessing than it is', he wrote, 'its attractions would be scarcely observed ... when we know that within the walls of that desolate-looking shealing are all who now remain of a once formidable people, whom a thirty years war with our countrymen has swept into captivity and their relatives to the grave.' Within this dreary edifice, Calder found sixteen Aboriginal people living in a state of abject neglect and degradation, denied all but 'a naked sustenance ... to prevent them dying from want'. Mindful of 'the duties of man to his follows', Calder was indignant that 'even at this late hour' something should be done to improve the conditions of this pitiful remnant, 'for we cannot by mere maintenance in life repay the debt we owe a race whom we have forcibly dispossessed of everything but mere existence'.

Did this desire to soothe the dying brow, I wonder, bring with it any sense of culpability? Was Calder moved to reflect on the role he might have played while on his surveying explorations into various parts of Tasmania? Did he have cause to consider that, as a recipient of an original land grant on Bruny Island, he had actually dispossessed one of that remnant whose plight now so moved him? As he admired the impressive terrain of the D'Entrecasteaux Channel, did he observe that this temperate paradise contained both the beginning and the end of the fatal encounter of European and Aboriginal peoples? Did it matter to him that the virtual genocide of the Tasmanian people occurred within his own lifetime and that he was both witness to and participant in the process? Sadly, these are not the kinds of thoughts to which Calder's readers are privy.

It is a perverse desire to make the past bear witness, to own up to its grievous acts. After all, what difference could it possibly make now? What was done is done, the newspaper letter writers remind me. Those early settlers, my ancestors, were simply creatures of their time, which is to say they were men like other men; no better, no worse. The past is another country, things are different there. Ah, but that is not how it seems to me on this morning, when a delicate shift of wind across the channel brings me the smell of broom on dancing white horses. In that instant of pure joy I am awash with memory reaching back to smallest childhood and beyond to the accumulated memories of my father and grandfather. We have been very happy here in the territory of the Nuenone people. Has any one of us stopped to do a reckoning?

On 26 January 1777, Captain James Cook brought his vessels *Resolution* and *Discovery* into calm anchorage beneath the great fluted cape at Adventure Bay on Bruny Island. Here, as elsewhere in the Pacific, the great navigator was keen to cultivate friendship with the native people. He seized his opportunity when a party of ten Aboriginal men was sighted on the beach. Cook was agreeably surprised to find the men approach his party unarmed and confident. They showed little interest in the trinkets he proffered or the varieties of food with which they were tempted. Cook noted that the Aboriginal men were naked, with ornamental punctures and ridges on their skin. He found them to be sturdy, healthy and 'far from disagreeable'. There was nothing in this encounter to make him revise the opinion he had formed in New South Wales, that the Aboriginal people laid no claim to the land and would not oppose British settlement.

When d'Entrecasteaux sailed into the channel that bears his name almost exactly sixteen years later, he and his fellow scientists were also on the lookout for the local inhabitants. In a charmed encounter with a large mixed group, the naturalist Labillardière found them to be a spartan and friendly lot, with an openness he found most disarming. But his enthusiasm for these noble savages was not echoed by Péron and other scientists aboard Baudin's expedition, which called at Bruny Island eight years later. After an encounter with some twenty of the inhabitants, Péron described them as a miserable horde in a state of extreme primitiveness. This assessment concurred with the observations Péron had made elsewhere in Van Diemen's Land. In concluding that the Tasmanian Aborigines were further from civilisation than any other human race, Péron unwittingly provided scientific justification for their dispossession.

The presence of Baudin's expedition in Van Diemen's Land also provided justification for the occupation of the territory by the British, who feared the intentions of the French. Woorredy, a youth of the Nuenone band from Bruny, saw these first white settlers arrive:

> We watched the ships coming and were frightened. My people had seen ships like these before and knew about the white men and their pieces of wood that spat fire and killed. I was very young and I thought the ships were the Wragewrapper—the evil spirit my parents had said would come and get me if I did not behave well. Although we were frightened my people did not leave Nibberluna [Derwent]. We stayed hidden for a long time watching the strangers as they cut down trees, built their huts and planted their crops. (Reported to G. A. Robinson on 11 July 1833)

Woorredy's sense that these ships brought the evil spirit was not misplaced. Within twenty-five years of the first settlement at Risdon in 1803, the newcomers had taken all but the most inhospitable parts of the island for themselves, reducing the Aboriginal people to trespassers on their own hunting grounds. Though initially courteous and hospitable, Aboriginal reaction turned to violent resistance in the face of mindless killings, kidnappings and wholesale expropriation. Outraged at Aboriginal retaliation, the settlers declared an open season on killing the 'crows', as they commonly called the Aboriginal people.

In the midst of the lethal hostilities of the 'Black War', the channel district could still present an image of racial harmony. On 11 April 1828, a Captain Walsh reported that a party of about fifty Aboriginals from Bruny and the channel always gathered when vessels called at Recherche Bay, and would enthusiastically join the crews, hunting, fishing and making themselves useful. That the Nuenone people could be so benign is quite remarkable, as they too had suffered untold depredations and cruelty. On several occasions Nuenone men were captured and taken to Hobart as sociological exhibits. One man had escaped the Governor's pleasure to return to his people with a ball and chain still attached to his leg. Mangana, an important elder, had experienced the murder of his wife by whalers and the abduction of his two eldest daughters by sealers. His youngest daughter, Truganini, had been raped repeatedly by convict sawyers, and borne horrified witness to the gruesome murder of her betrothed and his friend by these same men.

Neither were the Nuenone free to regard Bruny Island and the channel as their hunting and fishing grounds. Whaling and logging had been established in the 1820s, and the government magnanimously parcelled up large sections of the island to be granted freehold to settlers. One such beneficiary was Richard Pybus, who arrived in the colony in 1829 with some two thousand pounds in gold and stores to be promptly granted title to 2560 acres of the fertile northern part of Bruny. There is neither surviving record nor family lore as to how this first Pybus regarded the dispossessed people who still clung to their traditional territory. Perhaps he gave them handouts of tea and flour, as did the overseer at Captain Kelly's farm on the point. Perhaps, like so many of his kind, he found them just a damned nuisance. I don't know. But I do know about his loquacious neighbour, George Augustus Robinson, whose voluminous and self-regarding journals represent almost the entire written record of the tribal people of Tasmania.

Lacking the social standing and material assets to guarantee him a land grant as an automatic right, Robinson was given 500 acres and a cottage in addition to his salary as the government-appointed storekeeper of an Aboriginal establishment on Bruny. Robinson had left his trade as a bricklayer to take this post, 'actuated solely by a desire to serve the aborigines, to do them good, to ameliorate their wretched conditions and to raise them in the scale of civilisation'. To this end he proposed the establishment of a native village where the principles of European civilisation could be learnt and Christian instruction given. As he explained in his journal of 30 September 1829:

> Though in point of intellectual advancement the aborigines of this colony rank very low in the savage creation, yet this defect is amply counterbalanced by the many amiable points which glitter like sunbeams through the shroud of darkness by which they are enveloped, and operate most powerfully in calling forth from the discriminating and philanthropic observer an irresistible feeling of sympathy on their behalf.

The concept of an Aboriginal settlement which would afford some protection to the indigenous people, and possibly some token recognition of their right to land, was part of Governor Arthur's strategy to find a solution to the native problem short of the genocide proposed by many vocal sections of the white community.

Arthur's strategy also included the deployment of roving bands whose mission was to capture blacks for a bounty of five pounds per adult and two pounds per child. Presumably Arthur intended these captives to be repatriated to Robinson's care on Bruny. Indeed, two Nuenone people, Jack and his wife Nelson, were used as trackers for one roving party in the central plateau. Their experience yields some dues about such parties' *modus operandi*. While Jack was repeatedly beaten by the soldiers, Nelson was forced to have sex with them. Jack was callously shot on attempting to escape, but Nelson managed to return to Bruny in a shocked and dazed state. There is no way of knowing just how many Aboriginals were killed by these bands. Certainly no-one grew rich on the bounty. According to Backhouse, such a successful operator as John Batman had killed thirty in the process of capturing five.

Some indication of the Governor's intention can be gleaned from the newspaper editor Henry Melville's report of a bizarre conversation between Arthur and Black Tom (Kickerterpoller), a guide for Gilbert Robertson's roving party. After an exchange concerning the policy of confining Aboriginals to specified areas such as the islands of Bass Strait, the conversation continued:

> Tom—You send him to dat hyland, and take't all him own country—what you give him for him own country?
> Governor—I will give them food and blankets, and teach them to work.

By mid-1829, Arthur seems to have decided on Bruny Island as the site. He ordered that all Aboriginals living with Europeans were to be sent to Bruny and soon after dispatched the few captured Aboriginals to join them. He was prepared to be generous in assisting the experiment. To Robert, an industrious fellow raised by settlers since a baby, he made a grant of twenty acres, as well as a boat, cart, bullock and farm implements. Likewise, Kickerterpoller was promised land and a boat. Perhaps these two, having learnt the rewards of European labour from childhood, were to be models for their fellow countrymen.

Whatever the intention, neither Robert nor Kickerterpoller became farmers. By the time they reached Missionary Bay, Robinson had despaired of Bruny for his Aboriginal establishment. Death had rapidly overtaken the Nuenone since Robinson's appearance among them. Mangana, on whom he had relied, had taken his second wife and son on an annual trip to Recherche Bay in August 1829. There his son was killed and his wife seized by mutinying convicts on the brig *Cyprus*. He returned to find that in his absence eleven of his people had died, as well as eleven visitors from Port Davey. To Mangana's further dismay, Robinson had shown himself to be unable to restrain the women, Truganini, Pagerly and Dray, from cohabiting with the European men who supplied them with tea and sugar, and all three were debilitated with venereal disease. Mangana himself died in December.

Not to be daunted, Robinson hit upon the audacious idea of taking the five surviving Nuenone—Woorredy, Myunge, Droyerloine, Truganini and Pagerly—as well as Dray from Port Davey, to conciliate the tribes of the west coast and bring them under the umbrella of his protection. To this group he added the newcomers Kickerterpoller, Eumarrah, Trepanner, Maulboyhenner, Pawaretar and Robert. They left Bruny Island on 28 January 1830. The Aboriginals never returned. What became of Robert's twenty acres, I have no way of knowing. Probably it was absorbed into the estate of some enterprising settler, to be passed on to his descendants and defended with the fierce determination and full force of the law that is so endearingly British.

Robinson did return to check on his own land on 5 April 1833. He dined with Richard Pybus, and they discussed property values and the cost of improvements. That evening in his journal Robinson had reason to query the veracity of Pybus's assertions on this score. They remained neighbours for another five years, although Robinson was perpetually absent. In 1838, when Pybus sold 1880 acres, Robinson's interest was aroused at the prospect of capitalising his property also. But it was not until 1848, just before he departed for England, that Robinson sold his Bruny Island holding, by then one of many land grants he had received.

Not Bruny but Flinders Island became the site of Robinson's philanthropic enterprise for the approximately three hundred Aboriginal people he was able to track down and conciliate between 1830 and 1835. There, at the dreary settlement at Wybalenna, he set about making them over into a Christian peasantry who laboured for a master and had no rights to the land they occupied, or to its products. 'Had the poor creatures survived', he wrote in his retirement at Bath, 'I am convinced they would have formed a contented and useful community.' Perceiving that Flinders had become one great graveyard, he threw in the towel in 1838 and took himself off to more lucrative prospects as the Protector of Aborigines in Port Phillip.

In October 1847, the forty-six survivors of Wybalenna made the longed-for return journey to the Tasmanian mainland. Among them were Truganini and Myunge, returning after seventeen years to the familiar territory of the Nuenone. The convict station at Oyster Cove was damp and dilapidated but it was in sight of their birthplace, their spiritual homeland. It was the proximity to home, much more than the beef and damper, that sustained Truganini for the next four decades of her increasingly lonely life.

Sir William Denison, the governor who had delivered the Aboriginals from their misery on Flinders, had his anxieties about the return to the mainland. Public protests had been held in Launceston; there was widespread concern that the blacks would endanger property. Having surveyed the thoroughly inoffensive group, Denison wrote to the Colonial Secretary: 'the mountain is delivered of a mouse indeed'. He gave instructions that the survivors be paraded before the citizens of Hobart and that 'respectable persons' be invited to visit Oyster Cove to observe them. In December 1847, Denison organised a Christmas party at New Norfolk where he entertained fourteen Aboriginal guests, and the following year six men were taken to visit Government House.

At Oyster Cove, however, the Aboriginals were largely left to their own devices, while the children were removed to the orphan school at Hobart. Occasionally there were hunting sorties as far afield as the Huon, which provided great pleasure in contrast to the chill and idleness of the station. Walter Arthur, undisputed leader of the community, attempted to farm the sour ground, and received a grant of fifteen acres near the settlement. He employed a European labourer to help him clear the land, but his later request for an assigned convict was refused. Subsequently, a request for more fertile land near the Huon was also refused.

Except for the social outings when the residents at Oyster Cove were dressed up in European finery, parsimony was the watchword for all government dealings with the Aboriginal settlement. By April 1855, only fourteen people remained at the station. Thirty-one had died. Fanny, daughter of Nicermenic and Tanganutura, had married a

European, William Smith, and had gone to live with him at Nicholls Rivulet. Despite complaints from both Calder and the visiting magistrate, the settlement's funding was pared to a minimum and nothing was done to repair the filthy, derelict buildings. Meat rations were 'often inedible, and blankets and clothing were traded for supplies, including 'strong drink' from local Europeans. Mathinna, once the pride and joy of Lady Franklin, who had taken her from Flinders to the pampered inner sanctum of Government House, drowned in a shallow creek beside the station in May 1855, having fallen facedown in a drunken stupor. She was twenty-one, but no longer anyone's pride and joy.

In 1859, *Hull's Royal Kalendar* listed the occupants of Oyster Cove as 'five old men and nine old women ... Uncleanly, unsober, unvirtuous, unenergetic and irreligious, with a past character for treachery and no record of noble action, the race is fast fading away and its utter extinction will hardly be regretted.' Such sentiments were not uncommon and helped to fan official concern for the cost of maintaining this despised remnant. Walter Arthur, already defeated by disappointment, drowned when he fell from a boat in 1861, leaving the eight remaining Aboriginals with no-one to represent their interests. Alternatives for their care were canvassed, including an intriguing offer from Henry Harrison Pybus to look after them for five hundred pounds a year on his adjacent property at Little Oyster Cove.

Henry Harrison and his sister Margaret, probably children from an earlier marriage, emigrated with Richard Pybus in 1829. Margaret married the surveyor J. E. Calder, and Henry Harrison prospered in various entrepreneurial enterprises, including the logging operations and saw mill he owned jointly with William L. Crowther at Oyster Cove. He was certainly not in straitened circumstances, so I might assume his offer sprang from benevolent impulse rather than mercenary considerations. It is possible that he remembered Truganini from his youth, or that his proximity had stimulated an affectionate concern for his Aboriginal neighbours, though he does not seem to have ever made a visit to the station. Maybe he was concerned about the moral tone of the neighbourhood, since he undertook to keep his charges from public houses and 'intimacies of an objectionable kind'. Yet another possibility is that it was his partner, Crowther, who instigated the offer.

Dr Crowther, among his varied pursuits, was a man of science with a particular interest in the original Tasmanians. He already had a collection of skeletal material and was keen to secure the skeletons of those he believed to be the last of their race. As joint owner of the property to which they were invited to move, Crowther would certainly have had prime access to the Aboriginal skulls and bones he coveted. With an arrangement of this kind, Crowther may not have needed to resort to breaking into the morgue to steal the skull from William Lanne's corpse, as he did on 4 March 1869. The *Examiner* reported a rumour that Crowther had taken a prospecting lease on the old convict station in 1867. His son, Edward, who had assisted with the operation on William Lanne, acquired the site in 1900, and with his own son proceeded to dig up the graves of its Aboriginal inhabitants in 1907.

Speculation about motives aside, Pybus's price was still too high for the Tasmanian government to pay. Instead, the settlement was allowed to continue in its deplorable condition under the despairing supervision of John Strange Dandridge, who did what he could with his meagre provisions. Despite the appalling conditions of their domicile, the remaining Aboriginals were increasingly being recognised as rare and valuable. William Lanne, who had joined a whaling crew, had been given the quite erroneous title of King Billy as a recognition of his importance. In 1864 the four women still living at Oyster Cove—Truganini, Wapperty, Goneannah and Mary Anne—were dressed up and taken to a ball at Government House. A newspaper social columnist reported the women to be 'charmed beyond measure by the position they occupied'. Along with Lanne, they then had their photograph taken so the Museum could record them for posterity. In 1868, William Lanne and Truganini, now called Queen Truganini, were presented to the Duke of Edinburgh as fellow royalty.

William Lanne died in 1869, having progressed from being a despised outcast to itinerant seaman to immensely valuable property. After Crowther and son stole his skull, the Fellows of the Royal Society cut off his hands and feet, then returned to the grave to cart off the rest of his remains after they had been buried. Such grisly scientific endeavour had a profoundly unsettling effect on Truganini, who was quick to perceive the interest her own body might excite. It was her fervent wish, reiterated to several people, that she be buried in the deepest part of the D'Entrecasteaux Channel in order to escape such a fate.

In 1874, after three years as sole Aboriginal resident at Oyster Cove, Truganini was transferred into the care of Mrs Dandridge at Battery Point and the settlement was closed. Truganini, last of the Nuenone, died on 8 May 1876, ninety-nine years after her people had their first fateful encounter with the inquisitive Captain Cook. She was buried at the Cascades in Hobart, and the following year her body was illegally exhumed to serve the interests of science. It was a further ninety-nine years before Truganini was to get her wish to be buried in the territory of the Nuenone. Her skeleton was on display in the Tasmanian Museum until 1947, then stored in the museum vaults. After considerable public pressure, Tuganini's remains were finally cremated on 1 May 1976 and the ashes cast upon the waters of the D'Entrecasteaux.

On the other side of Mount Wellington, well away from the public debate about the proper disposal of the body, Truganini was mourned in the traditional way by her friend Fanny Cochrane Smith, who had been born at Wybalenna and lived with her family at Oyster Cove. For many years Fanny had lived inland from Oyster Cove at Nicholls Rivulet, on a hundred-acre allotment granted to her in 1856, along with a lifetime annuity of twenty-four pounds. There she escaped public interest because of her marriage to William Smith, and because there was a suspicion that, like her sister Mary Anne, Fanny was a half-caste and of no scientific value.

Along with her husband and eleven children, Fanny ran a successful farm and timber business as well as continuing the traditional pursuits, hunting and gathering wild foods. Until 1874 she was often accompanied on her hunting trips by residents from Oyster Cove, especially Truganini. Until her own death in 1905, Fanny Cochrane Smith nurtured and promoted Aboriginal culture and traditions, giving performances of the songs and stories of her people. These she also passed on to her many children and grandchildren. Thanks to the wonders of technology, I can still listen to Fanny singing into a recording machine in 1903. She sings in honour of a great leader:

Papele royna ngongna	Lo with might runs the man.
toka mengha leah	My heel is swift like the fire.
Nena taypa rayna poonya	My heel is indeed swift like the fire.
Nena nawra peyllah	Come thou and run like a man.
Pallah a nawra pewylla	A very great man, a great man.
Pellanah, Pellanah	A man who is a hero! Hurrah.

The recording quality is very poor, but Fanny's strong voice never fails to make the hair rise on the back of my neck. Her photographs show a handsome black woman, assured and elegant in Edwardian clothing which she has adorned with shell necklaces and possum skins. By all accounts, Fanny Cochrane Smith was an impressive woman. She so impressed the Tasmanian Parliament that in 1884 they agreed to increase her pension to fifty pounds a year and give her full title to 300 acres. The land was actually granted in 1889. There is no doubt that both Fanny and the parliament regarded this grant as compensation for the expropriation of Aboriginal land.

While 300 acres was small cheese compared to Richard Pybus's 2560, there were those who felt that Fanny's claim to land was fraudulent. In the late 1880s, opposing voices raised the issue of her parentage, insisting that as a half-caste, by which they meant non-Aboriginal, she could have no claim on the land. Fanny's mother Tanganutura, known as Sarah, had lived with sealers for some years and had one child, Mary Anne, by a white man. Though Fanny was bom at Wybalenna after her mother had married Nicermenic, there was always a suggestion that she too was 'half-caste'. The Aboriginal people all regarded Nicermenic as Fanny's father, just as he was the father of her brother Adam. Fanny and her husband always maintained both parents were Aboriginal and presented convincing evidence to the parliament in 1889.

This would have been the end of the matter but for the Royal Society, which was never far away when Aboriginal issues were at stake. A paper read at the Society by Mr Barnard 'threw out the challenge to ethnologists' with the assertion that Fanny was of pure Tasmanian blood. Science rose to the occasion to prove she was not. Ling Roth, working from photographs and a lock of hair, definitively proclaimed Fanny a half-caste in 1898. His 'proof' was accepted over Fanny's own evidence and has been ever since.

Fanny did not lose her grant and pension, but the denial of her identity must have dealt a cruel blow to her, as perhaps it was meant to. Entering the twentieth century, Tasmanians were disinclined to dwell on the moral responsibilities of their past. Modern Tasmania had no place for Aboriginality outside of the classroom and the cherished story of 'Queen Truganini—Last of the Tasmanians'. By proving that 'half-castes' were non-Aboriginal, Ling Roth's curious science provided the underpinning for a continuing policy of denying Aboriginal rights in Tasmania. In granting land to Fanny Cochrane Smith, the government acted in error—so the logic runs. Since then, however, science has been on hand to ensure such errors are not repeated.

Leaving the grand sweep of vista, my walk descends into a perpetually damp gully of man ferns and musk trees, and I am conscious of the melancholy that always seems to emanate from Oyster Cove. But on crossing Mathinna Creek, named for Lady Franklin's darling, I catch sounds of revelry from the old station site. Smoke rises above the trees, and excited, high-pitched voices carry to where I stand, taken by surprise, with my dog. Closer scrutiny reveals a kids' barbecue, organised by the Tasmanian Aboriginal Centre. A game of rounders is in progress on the mudflats while huge quantities of chops and sausages are charring on the grill plate. My dog, keen to play, darts off to chase the ball, leaving me, the intruder, unsure whether to advance or retreat. I know these people, some of them at least. Several whom I recognise are the great-great-grandchildren of Fanny Cochrane Smith, who lived here with her parents, her brother and sister, all those years ago. We were close neighbours then, my family and theirs, but I fear I am not wanted here at this family picnic. I wave, call my dog and leave, somewhat belittled by the feeling that I have nothing to contribute.

On the homeward path, I crush leaves from the musk tree to immerse my senses in their pungent aroma. I do not know how to pay the dues I owe for my charmed existence in this place. I do know we cannot remake the past, but the promise remains that we can remake the future. With a head full of musk scent I remember the words of the American poet Robert Penn Warren, reflecting on his own country's brutal history:

> But if responsibility is not
> The thing given but the thing to be achieved,
> There is still no way out of the responsibility of
> Trying to achieve responsibility.

NOTE
In the preparation of this piece I have been especially indebted to Heather Felton, who has painstakingly compiled the life stories of many of the Tasmanian Aboriginal people.

Dreaming up Mother (1988)

Robert Adamson

Understanding is all, my mother would tell me,
and then walk away from the water;

Understanding is nothing, I think, as I mumble
embellished phrases of what's left of her story.

I carry her about like an old lung.
There is nowhere to go now but inside

though I keep battering myself against sky,
throwing my body into the open day.

Landscapes are to look at, they taught me,
but now the last of the relatives are dead.

Where do these walks by the shore take us,
she would say, wanting to clean up,

after the picnic, after the nonsense.
I have been a bother all the years from my birth.

Look out—the river pulls through day
and Understanding, like a flaming cloud, goes by.

Domain Road (1989)

Chris Wallace-Crabbe

Delph, our tangled spaniel, bounces
briefly up a steep backyard
and I am four years old, under leaves …
Where did that slice come from?

Somewhere inside my being
the enzyme calpain has played a part,
for every performative occasion
making a collage of neurones.

The dendrites frond like little trees.
My brain is a kind of Metro:
it would be really nice to have a ticket
to see me round and home.

A neurone accumulates its crop of signals
then fires a small gun.
Axon to synapse the signal goes,
molecules pushing out from their dark shore.

Receptors flush, the neurones are busy as bees.
Oh dear, none of that chubby frame
is left in me, all new process
fifty years on

but in what vein has that scene been buried,
nectarine tree and terraced carrots
with Delph panting on the back steps?
Channels are opening in the dendritic spine.

1990s

Professing the Popular (1990)

Simon During

A couple of months ago, on a research trip to Europe, I went to stay with an old friend of mine who teaches English at Cambridge. As it turned out, my visit came at an inconvenient time for him. I arrived during the Faculty's annual examiners' meeting, when undergraduate marks are decided. Traditionally it is a highly charged occasion; these marks don't only determine students' careers, but also whether or not they have (as they still say in Cambridge) 'first-rate minds'. That evening, after the meeting, a stream of apprehensive undergraduates flowed into my friend's rooms to learn their fate. Soon a little party was happening—at least for those whose first-rateness was now assured. Haydn came off the CD player, and David Byrne's Brazilian album went on. The men in particular lingered late and, as the night went on, conversation turned to matters unfamiliar to me. Why were Thomas Harris's thrillers so good, and which was the best of them? As I shuffled off to bed, everyone was crowded around some comic strips from the fifties, discussing their styles with not especially sober erudition and passion.

Visits to Cambridge have always been difficult for me. Even though I was a graduate student there, it is still the place where I feel most positioned as a colonial. This is more than just a personal, slightly paranoid response; the English departments in which I was first trained imitated Cambridge methods. And Cambridge people do have easier access to a larger world than Australians and New Zealanders—they can travel more, British magazines and television are better by almost any standard, they're close to the big museums and art shows, they tend to have a greater command of foreign languages and so on. But, strangely, on this stay my sense of my own provinciality came through my ignorance of what is—too easily—called 'popular culture'. I'd never read a Thomas Harris thriller; I don't know anything about postwar comics. This was especially disquieting because my Cambridge friends are less involved professionally in popular culture than we are at Melbourne, and take quite a different attitude towards it.

This became clear the day after the party. In the absence of students, the conversation turned to the differences between teaching at Melbourne and at Cambridge. Cambridge students study one subject for three years; they have two exams over that period, and written work outside the exam counts for comparatively little. Teaching is much more individualised than in Australia, and an English degree still requires both detailed knowledge of the canon and mastery of the methods of close reading. In Melbourne that just isn't so. Exams have almost completely disappeared. And in certain of my courses students can write on almost anything they want (David Croenenberg's movies or the difference between television and classic Hollywood film styles …). When I defended this, the argument became heated. My host insisted that university English teachers have a responsibility to the literary tradition, and ended the conversation by vehemently declaring that the thought of our pedagogical practices made him sick. Upset myself, I could only feebly and reductively reply that many of our students found it difficult to relate to old books, most of which are, to begin with, anti-democratic, patently sexist and set in places that Australians know, at best, only as tourists.

This somewhat unedifying anecdote is only worth recording because it highlights certain features of important shifts in the academic study of the humanities, and English most of all. These shifts follow the diminution of any firm sense that 'high' culture is of more value than 'mass' or 'popular' culture. This means that academic work is increasingly devoted to topics like, say, film noir rather than eighteenth-century poetry, or the history of nineteenth-century prostitution rather than the organisation of patronage in the Georgian House of Commons or, indeed, the influence of popular cultural forms on art previously considered independent of them—magazine illustration on modernist painting, for instance. As a result, whole areas of interest are disappearing from view. Icelandic or Old Norse, for instance, which were taught in most English departments up until about twenty years ago, are now difficult to study at all in Australia. But the new orientation is also methodological: the humanities are moving from *affirming* a more or less rigid cultural canon to *analysing* more localised cultural zones. It has been a long time since culture stood against anarchy (though it can still stand against violence and pornography). 'Culture' is itself broken down into sets of representations, narratives and ways of thinking and acting whose relation to wider social, economic and political formations can be studied. Cultural representations are also analysed in terms of their impact on everyday life: on the way, for instance, that they form people's sense and management of their bodies—their voices, their gestures, their clothes ... And the channels by which books, pictures, films move from the past into the present, so as to be preserved in the cultural memory as history, have also become objects of analysis and critique.

Here I want to concentrate on the effects of making popular culture central to academic study of the humanities. But some background is necessary. The disciplinary subdivisions of the humanities, which were mainly fixed in their current form during the 1920s, are losing their intellectual legitimacy, despite the fact that they continue to provide the framework for professional associations, certification and university funding and administration. 'Cultural studies'—to give a name to the discipline that is emerging as the embodiment of the shift in the humanities—breaks with the kind of thinking that defined differences between disciplines in terms of media (language, pictures, films ...) or between the always deeply uncertain distinctions between the political, the social and the cultural. This relaxation of disciplinary divisions leaves cultural studies with problems. How to negotiate its relations with established disciplines? How to be something else than an all-enveloping loose and baggy monster? The last is especially imposing because cultural studies merges the two main senses of the word 'culture'—the humanist meaning (what 'culture' signifies in phrases like 'high culture' or 'the cultural heritage') and the ethnographic meaning (as in 'Polynesian culture').

215

These different senses of 'culture' have come increasingly to overlap, especially as anthropologists have found it more and more difficult to find colonised societies untouched by the West: societies, that is, unable to tell their own story to the metropolitan centres or to register their own protests against the dominant world order (of which visiting anthropologists are an instrument). This situation in which our culture and other cultures come together is generally called 'postcolonial'. And the other side of the postcolonial moment is the increasing regionalisation of the old metropolitan centres: now their cultures don't belong unproblematically to world history either. As my Cambridge experiences show, one way in which the metropolitan centres have defined themselves as such is by their power to grade and preserve cultures for others. What made the Cambridge mastery of thrillers and comics so disquieting was that these popular genres still belong to a huge international system of publication and distribution. So that to claim the right to evaluate *these*, to be their greatest fans, is once again to stake a claim to centrality.

The role of popular culture was by no means simple that night at Cambridge. Although popular genres were sharply distinguished from the texts that my friend taught and examined, they could be shared between teacher and students in a social situation. They provided a field on which a hierarchy of tastes could be established and connoisseurship develop, so that an elite group of students could distinguish themselves from other students outside the official procedures of the university. Popular texts were available for this, of course, because they themselves belong to a highly differentiated field: a literate thriller writer like Thomas Harris is not 'popular' in the way that Jackie Collins is. Any particular popular text may be read in various registers too: the more ironical, the more cultural value. Only in theory is everyone equally armed to appreciate the popular. In fact my friend's authority, charm and intelligence was coming to mould his students' everyday, as well as their formally learned, tastes. I say his charm and intelligence but of course these traits also belong to, and are signs of, the university that produced them. The university's power was seeping outwards.

This particular function of the popular needs to be given a little historical depth. When English was established as an academic subject late last century, the relations between cultural zones were quite different from those that prevailed after the emergence of a highly centralised and commodified entertainment sector—the so-called culture industry. In the second half of the nineteenth century, classic texts were discussed in English Associations, in Browning Societies and in numerous courses in non-certifying institutions attended by those who could not go to universities. Great writers, alive and dead, were often discussed in the bourgeois press—especially in the so-called Reviews—as well as in families 'around the fire': literary tastes formed one basis of class and family identities. So university English departments provided their own ways of reading texts that were actively interpreted and distributed outside of them. What was the difference? In a university—but not outside—literature was taught historically, philologically. As the culture industry became stronger, literary criticism replaced literary history as the dominant form of academic English. Its task was to form tastes that could resist the new mass media, a function that became all the more urgent after the Second World War, when university education was extended to those for whom high literature was not part of a non-pedagogic heritage.

The new orientation in the humanities follows the relative decline of the educational institution's ability to form its pupils' tastes or 'sensibilities' against the media. The media have won—or, at any rate, are winning. Why is this decline stronger in Melbourne than in Cambridge? It's a worthwhile question because it helps us see that the entry of the popular into higher education is not just the expression of some general and progressive will, but the result of particular histories and social conditions. To begin with, in Britain literary high culture still retains stronger bases outside of the education institutions than in Australia. That's obvious—Britain is a society more tolerant of class and other social differences than its colonial offshoots. What is less obvious is that in Britain students tend to leave home to go to university (though recent changes in student financing will help change this). Students live in colleges away from their families and friends, forming strong (and often lifelong) social links with each other and with their teachers. It is in this context that a university education begins to mould not just tastes but also voices, gestures, clothes ... And in Britain (and the US) the university system is itself more hierarchical than in Australia—which means that to acquire an university (or college) educated manner is itself to gain a widely recognisable form of social capital. These factors enable and dispose such universities to teach material as far as possible from the popular, that is, as far as possible from the market. Though, after 1946, Oxbridge has become more accessible to students from families without high incomes, the university system's hierarchy has not disappeared. Thus, to use one of Pierre Bourdieu's terms, it shelters 'oblates'. In the Middle Ages oblates were children donated to (or abandoned at) the monasteries: modern oblates owe their way of life, their tastes and minds to the institutions that form them. Modern oblates want all their cultural preferences to be formed by the institution that guarantees their first-rateness: that is one reason why it is among them, most of all, that one encounters quasi-institutional discourse about popular culture.

In Australia things are different. Not only is the university system relatively unhierarchical, but most students live at home. This means that their tastes are formed not so much academically as by their families, their secondary schooling, their local social interactions and, most importantly, by the media. And quite small administrative changes can lead to dramatic intellectual shifts—including the transformation of the old humanities into cultural studies. Here university departments tend to be funded by student numbers, which means they must compete for students. Universities themselves actively seek to attract students by making trips into the schools. Unlike their US counterparts, most Australian humanities faculties feel no responsibility to the profession's reproduction: not only are they without graduate schools (through which scholars are directed towards fixed—historical—'fields') but the conditions of academic employment in general are being increasingly de-professionalised. So it is in a particular department's interest to offer courses that undergraduates will be most likely to choose—these preferences being determined by dispositions established through the media, students' families and social circle and so on. When the Melbourne English Department, in response to such pressures, cancelled core courses that had been based on the canon (Medieval Literature, Renaissance Literature, Romanticism ...) and replaced them by a 'smorgasbord' of smaller courses, which included topics like 'Popular Fiction,' 'The Novel and Film' and 'Postmodernism', enrolments increased sharply—and funding with them. Now students could take what courses they liked: indeed, it became quite possible to acquire a degree in English without having read a single book written before the First World War.

In this case the popular enters the academy as the result of a series of administrative reorganisations connected to Mr Dawkins' policies. But this is not the only way that an institution can be reorganised so that the canon begins to be dethroned. In the United States—despite its professionalism, and its hierarchical tertiary sector—questions of social justice have led to the widespread adoption of affirmative action procedures for student entry. To enter colleges at Stanford, Yale or Harvard, African Americans from the South, for instance, need much lower entry grades than those with East Coast Jewish backgrounds. Under federal and state funding pressure, such colleges welcome students from ethnic minorities. So they change their curriculum (never as radically as in Melbourne) not in response to the market-formed wants of their clientele, but to a sense that the university has a responsibility to other cultural heritages and to social justice (a sense apparently lacking in our university bureaucrats, if not in the Labor government itself).

What happens when popular culture becomes academised? First of all it is processed within the cultural studies tradition already in place—a deeply polarised and unsettled tradition that has not been able to unburden itself from the past or to detach itself from its early policing role. On one side, cultural studies stretches back to the work of Arnold and Leavis; on another to Richard Hoggart, E. P. Thompson and Raymond Williams; and on a third, to the so-called Frankfurt school. For the Frankfurt school (and, much more loosely, for Leavis), popular culture is an instrument of domination rather than an expression of genuine experiences and desires, because it is circulated and produced within a centralised and organised market. To use the terms of Adorno and Horkheimer's famous essay 'The Culture Industry', the widespread 'consent' given to commodified popular entertainment is itself part of the culture industry just because the market offers no alternative to itself. (Adorno and Horkheimer were writing, specifically, of America in the early forties—a society without television or public radio, in which Hollywood's production, distribution and exhibition arms were still vertically integrated, and where art movie houses did not yet exist.) In its 'technological perfection', the culture industry can manufacture narratives and representations powerful enough to substitute for reality so that 'to offer and to deprive [the consumer] of something is one and the same'. What keeps the culture machine going is the constant production of unsatisfiable wants that are simultaneously erotic and consumerist: the desires to look as good as (taking some modern examples) Madonna or Sean Penn, to be as funny as Robin Williams, to fall in love like Debra Winger, to have a house like one in *Dynasty*, or a mouth like Bardot's. Horkheimer and Adorno argue that the culture industry produces increasingly standardised products that form increasingly standardised tastes, values and desires; individuality becomes a floating signifier—as if I am me because I like Cary Grant and you are you because you prefer Spencer Tracy. Here, to prefer Cary Grant to Spencer Tracy is quite different from preferring, say, Frank Sinatra to Mozart—though even Adorno and Horkheimer have a popular canon, Greta Garbo and Betty Boop retaining traces of uncommodified and 'tragic' life in a way that Mickey Rooney and Donald Duck don't.

The British cultural studies tradition never fully detaches itself from the Leavisite and Frankfurt school view of the culture industry: it *cannot*, because the popular is not an expression of unmediated desires and choices. But it has presented a much more nuanced and less dismissive account. For it, popular culture is not a monstrous monolith, but contains many localised 'subcultures', some of which have long histories, often embedded in working-class life, and provide alternatives to hegemonic modes of representation. In writers like Dick Hebdige, the Birmingham School works within a frame where the difference between, say, John Lennon and Paul McCartney matters.

Yet the generation that follows Raymond Williams finds itself in a double bind. For them, high culture becomes increasingly just a marker and instrument of one class or region's domination over another, so that, unlike Leavis or Adorno, they have no set of fixed cultural values, texts and preferences to help them stand outside the cultural market. At the same time their methods and interests do not—cannot—belong to popular culture, which is defined against the academy. In this situation, cultural studies have tended either to read popular texts 'scientifically'—as examples to be analysed within established 'theories' (Lacanian, structuralist, Althusserian)—or symptomatically, as expressions of larger social formations (*The Towering Inferno* might be regarded as an allegory of American insecurity after Vietnam, for instance). Whereas for the old humanities high culture spoke for itself, as it were, through the critic, for cultural studies popular culture has to be interpreted as a sign or an instance of something else. To escape this bind, British cultural studies have taken their task to be a provisional and political one, working to increase the heterogeneity of cultural production, to enhance its connection to the lives that people actually lead. Such politics, however, are almost always gestural, both because they are not connected to any institutions that might actually change the structures of cultural production, and because the power of the market is so strong. More recently cultural studies academics like Hebdige or Constance Penley have attempted to identify with the popular by claiming to combine the role of the critic and the fan. This sounds like a neat solution; indeed it's one that returns us to the early days of English departments. But there are difficulties, not only because the critic (who works in or around academe) and the fan (who does not) must define themselves against each other in order to achieve their own identity, but also because if the critic did not maintain an identity different from the fan, then education—and the educational professions—would have no point.

There are, however, ways in which the popular and the academic do work together non-oppositionally. Teachers of popular culture find that their work bears upon everyday life in a way that it doesn't for those who work on texts that only the academy keeps alive. Their everyday tastes in films and television will be influenced by their critical practices. And as popular culture is increasingly absorbed into the higher education system, as journalists, arts administrators and so on are trained in cultural studies, then reviewing, especially in the up-market press, will move closer to those critical techniques—and vice versa. Equally, relations between teachers and students change in popular culture courses. An undergraduate may know more than an instructor—a lot more, particularly in a field that has not yet become the object of sustained academic research. Sometimes students may have read magazines or books distributed outside the academy, either through the market or through more specialised channels, like fanzine networks. Sometimes students can teach their teachers because they are close to what I'll call 'para-institutions'—computer groups, societies like the Trekkies, film societies even, or para-sciences like Vampirology. (Apparently there is a man on the local lecture circuit claiming a PhD in Vampirology.)

The interruption of the academy by other institutions of learning and connoisseurship is almost wholly productive, but it does induce certain anxieties. What is the difference between teaching or learning in the university and teaching or learning in a para-institution (leaving aside the all-important fact that the first has the power to give official degrees and the second does not).

This question is complicated because the popular, in its turn, defines (and sells) itself *as* popular against the academic. Negative images of academics and their institutions abound in highly marketed culture, especially where both it and pedagogy are most uniform and far-reaching—where they are directed at children. (The biggest-selling books in Britain during the 1980s were the Adrian Mole series, published by Routledge. They helped Routledge finance the academic journals most engaged in the new orientation in the humanities: *Cultural Studies*, *New Formations* and *Textual Practice*.) Education is demonised and ridiculed, not just in representations of the soullessness and pleasurelessness of schools and universities (see *Ghostbusters*) but in a plethora of images of mad or absent-minded professors and authoritarian or repressed schoolteachers (as in Pink Floyd's *The Wall*). Against this, pedagogical para-institutions are presented positively: the Ninja masters of the *Teenage Mutant Ninja Turtles* or Ben in the *Star Wars* trilogy, to cite two of many. (And when a movie wants to mark itself as serious and mature—as middlebrow—what better than nostalgia for the days when there were fans for old books and dead poets' societies still existed?) The strategy by which the popular defines itself as popular against the pedagogic can be repeated in 'popular critique', commentary on mass culture within the popular press. A recent article on the *Ninja Turtles* for the Murdoch press by Simon Townsend, for instance, sets 'fun', parental 'instinct' and children's desires against 'anal retentive teachers' who hate pleasure and who instead (how could anybody be so perverted?) 'love theoretical research'.

Popular culture produces mad theorists in two senses. As we have seen, it generates an imagery in which academics are vague, retentive, loopy, arrogant, live in ivory towers and so on. Though this imagery is rarely internalised, it does encourage academic self-doubt, even self-hatred. Certainly it makes the struggle to improve and legitimate education harder. But these popular images are not simply wrong. They are part of the organisation of the whole cultural system in (post)modern society: an organisation which requires that the popular can never speak for itself in the academy but must be interpreted, theorised, policed. And it is because the grounds for this theory, interpretation and policing are so insecure (partly because the market that carries the popular has more power than the pedagogical institutions) that professors who talk about the popular can begin to enact the popular image of the academic. For instance, in her recent book, *The Future of an Illusion*,

Constance Penley, one of the sharpest culture theorists, finds herself writing about *Pee Wee's Playhouse* like this: 'As a giant eyeball, Roger is the metaphorical and metonymical equivalent of what is threatened in the fantasy of castration (an unconscious fear of difference), yet he is also "our new friend Roger" from another planet (a social and conscious wish for the acceptance of difference).' (162) Surely there's a mad professor somewhere here: this is to culture studies what Doc's wild science in *Back to the Future* is to nuclear physics.

To recapitulate a little: in general terms there are three ways that the academy can host the popular. It can do so, as in those Cambridge rooms, in terms of the old tasks of evaluation and taste formation, which help consolidate a centre; or in terms of theories grounded on para-scientific truths (like psychoanalysis); or as part of a struggle against the market in the name of a different kind of popular culture. In my own teaching practices I try to modulate the first through the second towards the third. For me, what a teacher can do is to develop tastes that require political sensitivity, refuse conceptual simplification and retain a historical sense. And the reason why one has a right to attempt to form tastes is that popular critique is politically, historically and conceptually reductive. It does not make enough connections: its notion of pleasure is too detached from the pleasure—and the work—of thought. Saying this though does not help answer the question that has haunted this essay: what responsibility does one have to keep old books alive? It's not an abstract question: it affects decisions on what kind of staff departments hire, for instance. To some degree, the problem answers itself when one begins to historicise the popular. (To give an example: if one is interested in the relation between current 'sensational' reportage of domestic crime and literary fictions, one is soon led back to pre-Shakespearean drama and the 'domestic tragedy' genre.) Today's mass culture can also form tomorrow's cultural heritage, sometimes becoming the object of classical affirmative critical techniques—as in Stanley Calee's account of the Hollywood 'remarriage' genre in *Pursuits of Happiness*. Nevertheless, for about two hundred years canonical works have been written so as to avoid the obsolescence of the popular: they have consciously worked out strategies that will keep them alive in the future. And yet the struggle between the canon (and its claims on futurity) and the popular (and its claims on the present) is biased towards the latter in the current local organisation of culture and pedagogy. After Icelandic, Old English will disappear; after Old English, Middle English; after Middle English …

I began with a personal anecdote about appropriating the popular and I want to finish with one about losing the past. After returning from Europe, I took my seven-year-old son, Nicholas, to see *Ninja Turtles*. As much as the movie delighted and amazed me, I soon—inevitably— began to watch it as a theorist. It looked to me like an index of America's current situation: America's fear of a provincialisation that it can't avoid, its refusal to recognise the racism that organises its society and economy; its being torn by tensions between the popular, the pedagogical and the family as they compete to form the minds and manners of children. There may be good Japanese in the movie's narrative line, and the wisdom and technology are imported from Japan, but the only Japanese that we see are baddies. On the other hand, we see almost no blacks or Hispanics at all, though the movie is set on the streets. The gangs and vigilantes are replaced, on one side, by a bunch of middle-class white kids gone wrong, and, on the other, by four happy, anthropomorphised, pizza-guzzling turtles who, though they've never been to school and live in the sewers (literally an underclass), are very smart and have high-cultural icons for names (Raphael, Donatello, Michaelangelo and Leonardo). Despite these names, the turtles come straight out of patriotic popular knowledge: 'everyone' in America knows that the pizza was invented in New Haven, and that the sewers, rivers of the urban jungle, crawl with reptiles (though this 'information' was first disseminated by the avant-garde novelist Thomas Pynchon). The turtles' violence is beautifully choreographed; it's a party, a dance—they know no guns. The film is magical, and what its magic makes disappear is the difference between what America is and what the American dream would have America be.

Nicholas didn't see it like that. As we came out of the theatre he was already telling me the plot in some detail: for him the popular did not have to speak of something else. We headed into McDonald's, me for a Big Mac, him for a six-pack of Chicken McNuggets. Everyone was talking about the turtles. 'Who was your favourite?' a kid asked me. 'Donatello,' I said without thinking. 'Michaelangelo,' said Nicholas. When we sat down I realised why I'd chosen Donatello as *my* turtle. It had nothing to do with the character, who was hardly any different from the others. For me 'Donatello' is a resonant name: when I was a kid I heard it a lot. My father is a Jewish (in fact, half-Jewish) refugee from the Nazis and, like many such immigrants who came from bourgeois families, he had memories of an economically and culturally richer past. These memories turned into fantasies as the years went by. He often used to tell us that a relation of his had donated his art collection to the Vienna Kunsthistorische Museum and that one of the glories of the collection (which my father believed he should have inherited) was a Donatello. Years later, when I visited the Museum, I found out that the Donatello was in fact a Della Robbia—a very different kettle of fish. Nevertheless for me 'Donatello' signified what we as a family didn't have, *our* culture, lots of money, being like other families. For Nicholas, however, Donatello is a Teenage Mutant Ninja Turtle: it is as if the Renaissance sculptor, a source both of Western humanism and of our family's private fantasies, is called Noddy.

As far as I am concerned, that's a welcome change. Especially if his pleasure in the turtles one day comes to be connected to a sense of how that pleasure functions socially and politically. Which requires schooling. And to say that is to speak as a pedagogue rather than a fan or a dad.

Thanks, each in their own way, to Eric, Lisa and Nicholas.

Nothing has Changed: The Making and Unmaking of Koori Culture (1992)

Tony Birch

1

You get somebody coming in, a foreigner at that, trying to tell us to rename our mountains.

Bob Stone, Stawell town councillor.[1]

In March 1989 the Victorian Minister for Tourism, Steve Crabb, announced that the Grampians mountain range in western Victoria would 'revert to their Aboriginal name, Guriward' (which after further research was altered to Gariwerd). Although this initiative came from the Victorian Tourism Commission, and the local Koori community had not yet been consulted, the Minister felt that he could already announce the names that would be 'restored':

> I expect that the Grampians will be known as Guriward, the Black Range as Burrunj, the Glenelg River as Bugara, Halls Gap as Budja Budja, Victoria Gap as Jananginjawi and so on.

The local white community did not share these great expectations. An 'ex-Labor voter' wrote to Crabb accusing him of engaging in 'gutter level' politics, and warned of an electoral backlash: 'remember Mr. Crabb the tax payer pays your salaries not the lazy, dirty, counter-productive black sector of Australia'.[2] The Mayor of Stawell, Peter

---

1 Melbourne *Sun*, 27 March 1989.
2 Koori Tourism Unit file 9/7/76/3.

Odd, claimed chat behind the idea was a 'radical group' who had forced the proposal on the government:

> It seems to me more like a little group that can get what it wants like all the minority groups. The government just bows down to them and the government is ruled by the loudest noise all the time.[3]

Yet no 'noise' on the issue had come from the local Koori community. The five Koori communities in the Western District are represented by Brambuk Incorporated, which at the time was constructing the Brambuk Living Cultural Centre in the Grampians National Park. A spokesperson, Geoff Clark, criticised the government's continuing refusal to consult local Kooris on policies affecting their history and culture. Although he supported the 'refreshing and positive gesture' of the name restoration, Clark compared Crabb's approach with that of a fellow Scot: 'he and Major Mitchell are guilty of ignoring the Aborigines' past and present association and ownership of the Grampians area ... over thousands of years'.[4] Clark said that Brambuk 'would rename important features in the Grampians area with traditional Aboriginal names', regardless of any government initiatives.

In December 1990, without Steve Crabb's knowledge, signs carrying Koori names were erected at certain features to coincide with the opening of the Brambuk Living Cultural Centre.[5] Crabb objected; the community, he said, 'would be entitled to criticise any cost involved in erecting the signs bearing Aboriginal names before an official decision was made'. But Clark insisted that, as 'rightful custodians' of the region, Kooris 'had the authority to erect the signs'. Clark asked: 'Will Mr Crabb, with his paternalistic attitude, expect those Aborigines among us with dark faces to be selling trinkets/beads and performing

---

3 *Stawell Times-News*, 31 March 1989.
4 Press release by Geoff Clark, Chairperson Brambuk Incorporated, 29 March 1989, Koori Tourism Unit file 9/7/76/3.
5 Melbourne *Herald-Sun*, 11 December 1990.

corroborees for his tourist industry?'[6] Brambuk was not opposed to involvement with tourism, but this had to be achieved 'without exploiting, and without becoming like the exploited'.[7]

The name change had been proposed in February 1985 by archaeologist Ben Gunn, who prepared a document for the Tourism Commission on 'Recommended Changes to Aboriginal Site Names in the Grampians'.[8] The region contains 80 per cent of Victoria's identified Koori rock-art sites, and Gunn suggested that these be given more appropriate names in line with the 'planned promotion of certain sites as public attractions'. He noted that the existing 'euro-centric descriptive names' (such as 'Cave of Ghosts') could produce 'inappropriate expectations in visitors … disappointment or worse, ridicule'. Gunn proposed that Koori names be given to the sites in consultation with 'the local Aboriginal Communities'.

In 1988 an Aboriginal Tourism Survey alerted the Tourism Commission to the possibility of exploiting the region's Koori culture and history: 'Guided tours of Koori sites have the potential to be very successful. The opportunity is there to bring together the product and the potential customers.'[9] Immediately before Crabb's public announcement in March 1989, Ben Gunn conducted further research into alternative names for the rock-art sites, and for natural features of the region, He did not feel that it was necessary to consult with the local Koori community, as he regarded his research as 'an academic exercise, at this stage'.[10] The minister's announcement two weeks later, however, was not an 'academic exercise', but a highly publicised media event.

6 Melbourne *Herald-Sun*, 11 December 1990; *Standard* (Warrnambool), 12 December 1990.
7 Geoff Clark, *Land Rights News*, October 1990.
8 Koori Tourism Unit file 12/2/6/3
9 Koori Tourism Unit file 12/2/6/2: *Tourism and the Grampians Region* (Victorian Tourism Commission, 1990), p. 18.
10 R. G. Gunn, 'Alternative names for rock art sites and natural features in the Grampians National Park. A Report to the Victorian Tourism Commission', March 1989.

Crabb demonstrated a typical European disregard for the indigenous people of the area. To display 'art' was good for business, and to tag the sites with indigenous names confirmed their legitimacy as artefaces of an 'ancient' culture. But it was not seen as necessary to consult the Kooris of the Western District about the marketing of the heritage that they had managed to retain through 150 years of oppression.

Soon after Crabb's announcement, the Tourism Commission appointed Ian Clark, a geographer from Monash University, to prepare a submission to the Victorian Place Names Committee. In his consultations with the groups that form Brambuk, he found that the Koori community regarded the absence of prior consultation as indicating 'a lack of respect and recognition of traditional ownership of the National Park'.[11] As a result, a representative of Brambuk, Lionel Harradine, was appointed to prepare the submission with Clark. The submission made four sets of recommendations:

> i) that 21 incorrectly spelt Aboriginal place names currently in use be corrected, and that a further 10 Aboriginal names be retained;
> ii) that the use of 44 known Aboriginal names of features more recently given European names be restored;
> iii) that the traditional names of 11 places that do not carry European names be adopted;
> iv) that the more appropriate names conferred on nine Rock Art Sites … be formally adopted.[12]

The name restoration met opposition from a variety of groups. The Stawell Shire Council wrote to all local governments in Victoria, and gained wide support from both rural and urban shires. The Victorian

---

11 Koori Tourism Unit file 9/7/76/3.
12 'A Submission to the Victorian Place Names Committee—The restoration of Jardwadjali and Djab wurrung names for Rock Art Sites and Landscape Features in and around the Grampians National Park' (Victorian Tourism Commission, 1990), p. 5.

Place Names Committee received petitions of protest with 60,000 signatures.[13] The Council of Clans regarded the proposal as a threat to 'Scottish heritage and pioneers'.[14] The Wimmera branch of the National Council of Women claimed that 'Aboriginals' did not 'know anything about the significance' of the rock art. The Balmoral Golf Club was concerned with the effect that the name restoration would have on its greens: 'Our Club is close to the Glenelg River & uses the water for irrigating the course.' A Horsham shire councillor, Don Johns, expressed similar concerns about Horsham's water supply.[15] Bruce Ruxton of the RSL stated the League's position in his inimitable style:

> In no way would we want the name of the Grampians changed to any other name whether it be an aboriginal name or what … There is a real feeling of ill-wind prevailing over this proposal. [sic][16]

In a submission supporting the restoration, the Friends of the Grampians claimed that the League of Rights had manipulated opposition to the proposal, resulting in widespread 'racist hysteria'.[17]

The aesthetic and tourist value of the rock-art sites was also questioned. Many of the sites require protection behind cyclone-wire fencing, as they have been repeatedly desecrated by vandals.[18] Pat Reid of Bellellen Rise Host Farm, Stawell, claimed that visitors to her farm had 'little or no interest in our aboriginal pre-history', and whatever there was 'dissipates completely upon inspecting Bunjil's cave (the most significant aboriginal art site in Victoria)'.[19] E.R. of Mt Waverley wrote directly to Steve Crabb, informing him that in twenty years of visiting the Grampians she had seen 'not one aboriginal person' and

---

13 *Wimmera Mail-Times*, 16 October 1991.
14 This and the following letters are from Koori Tourism Unit file 9/7/76/3.
15 *Wimmera Mail-Times*, 20 June 1990.
16 Koori Tourism Unit file 9/7/76/3, 2 November and 28 July 1989.
17 A copy of this submission is in Koori Tourism Unit file 12/2/6/3.
18 Koori Oral History Program, Grampians Visit, 1 June 1989. Tape 46.
19 *Portland Observer*, 9 July 1990.

only 'a few miserable rock paintings'.[20] C.S. of Stawell wrote to 'point out some facts associated with Aboriginal myths of Dream time'. He denied a Koori presence in the region ('no Aboriginals ever entered the Grampians due to evil spirits') and claimed that the rock art was painted by 'a French artist who had a great appreciation of Aboriginal art of central Australia'.[21]

Steve Crabb apparently wants to promote the region as 'Victoria's Kakadu',[22] but he will have difficulty achieving this if people expect a replication of Kakadu 'art', ignorant of the regionally specific indigenous culture and history of the Gariwerd area. An officer of the Victorian Archaeological Survey informed visitors to one of the shelters in 1989 that in the past 'people were disappointed in the art itself. They were expecting something like Northern Territory art.'[23] People not only expected to view the 'ancient', but also to see its readily identifiable signifiers, the art of 'real' Aborigines.

For visitors to appreciate the art, they must come to respect and appreciate indigenous culture, both past and present, here in Victoria. An exploitative tourist industry will not achieve this. Denis Rose, a Koori cultural officer from Brambuk, feels that this will occur when the 'significance of the sites as places of occupation' is interpreted and understood.[24] The Centre has attempted to do this by erecting signs that explain the spiritual significance of the art, and the Koori history of the area. The signs also inform visitors that 'If you wish to obtain more information about this site, its art or Aboriginal culture in general, please call at Brambuk in Budja Budja (Halls Gap).'[25]

20 Koori Tourism Unit file 12/2/6/3, 10 October 1990.
21 Koori Tourism Unit file 9/7/76/3, 10 May 1989.
22 Interview with Ian Clark, 21 October 1991.
23 Koori Oral History Program, Grampians Visit, 1 June 1989. Tape 46.
24 Ibid.
25 *Stawell Times-News*, 18 December 1991. Pat Reid incorrectly blamed Crabb's 'sheer arrogance' for the erection of the signs.

Some opponents of the name restoration also ridiculed Koori languages. Old racist slurs resurfaced: 'Aboriginal names all … sound the same, and in most cases, the spelling looks the same.'[26] The *Western District Farmer* claimed that the proposal pandered to 'pony-tailed basket weavers and banjo players', and the chosen names were 'totally unpronounceable to modern day black and white alike'.[27] Les Carlyon, in *Business Review Weekly*, complained that he could not 'pronounce let alone spell' the chosen names, and was concerned that the proposal was being considered when Victoria was 'paralysed by billions of dollars of debt'.[28]

The Grampians District Tourist Association strongly opposed the restoration proposal. The Association identified 'Aboriginal cultural tourism' as a 'niche market' and therefore supported the upgrading of the rock-art sites.[29] Initially the Association claimed that it wished to promote 'aboriginal culture' in the Grampians, and 'supported appropriate names for Rock Art sites and any unnamed features'. Yet it rejected an overwhelming majority of the proposed names. This included the proposed names for rock-art sites and previously unnamed features, which would not be acceptable unless they were altered (that is, anglicised) to something 'easily recognised and pronounced'.[30]

This cultural appropriation illustrates the attitude of many tourist operators, who regard Koori culture as a product that can be altered and re-presented in an acceptable form, as a commodity, but has little or no intrinsic value. The Tourist Association objected to the removal of names such as Mr Lubra and The Piccaninny. It felt that although such terms were 'possibly racist' they were 'not truly offensive as they

26 *Wimmera Mail-Times*, 22 June 1990.
27 *Western District Farmer*, June 1990.
28 *Business Review Weekly*, 1 June 1990.
29 Koori Tourism Unit file 12/2/6/3
30 Grampians District Tourist Association, submission to the Victorian Place Names Committee, 26 September 1990. By anglicised I mean corrupted, as was the case with some existing names, such as Cherrypool for Djarabul.

are in common usage throughout Australia'. Bob Stone agreed: 'Piccaninny is a tribute to little Aboriginals,' he said.[31]

Some names were also rejected on aesthetic grounds. Ararat City Councillor Peter Wright stated that names that translated as 'pig face', 'base of spine' and 'phlegm' were 'not terribly good for a tourist area'.[32] Others related to excrement (such as Gunigalg), and 'would be more suitable for a sewerage treatment works'.

This European aesthetic ignores the relationship between naming and traditional Koori lifestyle. To reject such names is to reject their cultural significance, and to promote corrupt versions of Koori culture is not only appropriation but deception. Brambuk is disappointed that the Place Names Committee rejected some of the names on these grounds, denying the Koori community the opportunity to present and interpret the relationship to land identified in names that narrate spatial organisation.[33]

If white Australia is to move beyond a superficial appropriation of the indigenous culture of this country, those in positions of influence—be they government departments, statutory bodies or tourist promoters—have to stop re-presenting indigenous cultures in this way. If they are motivated by imperial possession, changes will not occur, as the motivation behind possession is the subjugation and control of the 'other'.

II

Piper carries a pair of handcuffs slung round him as one [black-fellow] must be taken prisoner for the sake of obtaining native names of the places.[34]

---

31 Melbourne *Sunday Herald*, 3 June 1990.

32 *Ararat Advertiser*, 31 May 1990.

33 Interview with Ian Clark. Clark stated that the Place Names Committee also rejected Bugara, not because of any distasteful translation, but because it sounds 'too much like bugger'.

34 'The Journal of Granville William Chetwynd Stapylton', in L. O'Brien and M. H. Douglas (eds), *The Natural History of Western Victoria* (Australian Institute of Agricultural Science, 1974), p. 95 (28 July 1836).

In his spatial history of Australia, *The Road to Botany Bay*, Paul Carter has written of 'how little value our culture attaches to names'.[35] This is because 'we', feeling imperially secure, and ignorant of the presence of another culture and history, see 'not a historical space' that may be contested, and may contain multiple histories, but a 'historical fact … as if it was always there'. The cultures of indigenous people are relegated to 'prehistory' and the 'ancient', allowing only for metahistorical myths, located outside the boundaries of 'historical facts', which support imperial domination. As Chris Healy put it, 'true knowledge of the past was knowledge of white Australia and reserved for white Australians'.[36]

To name spaces is to 'name histories',[37] and also to create them. The process is accepted as natural, representing a 'given', that this country belongs to and is a white Australia. But this sense of security evaporates when the hidden history of colonial domination and indigenous subordination is challenged by an attempt to alter the names of spaces.

Attaching names to landscapes legitimises the ownership of the culturally dominant group that 'owns' the names. Indigenous names themselves do not constitute a threat to white Australia. Houses, streets, suburbs and whole cities have indigenous names. This is an exercise in cultural appropriation, which represents imperial possession and the quaintness of the 'native'. For the colonisers to attach a 'native' name to a place does not represent or recognise an indigenous history, and therefore possible indigenous ownership.

It is when names are restored to recognise earlier histories and cultures that the threat to ownership occurs. Imperial history cannot recognise the existence of indigenous histories. A history of dominance is seen as the history of a 'nation'. An attempt to recognise the history of indigenous people creates insecurity, paranoia, even hysteria. It 'wipes out over one hundred and fifty years of [British] history' and 'takes away

---

35 Paul Carter, *The Road to Botany Bay* (Faber, London, 1987), p. 2.
36 Chris Healy, '"We Know Your Mob Now"—Histories and their Cultures', *Meanjin* 3/1990, p. 512.
37 Paul Carter, 'Travelling Blind: A Sound Geography', *Meanjin* 2/1992, pp. 423–47.

that heritage'.[38] Existing names are 'recommended for consignment to the scrapheap of history'.[39] The features themselves can actually vanish: 'Ayers Rock is no longer'; 'GRAMPIANS, ARE THEY GONE?'; 'Familiar places or landmarks … would disappear from the map'.[40]

Many people of the Western District of Victoria cannot accept a Koori presence in the area, either in the past or present. If they do recognise an indigenous presence, it is one that is long dead. They cannot accept a reality that makes a mockery of the racial theories and racist practices promoted for 150 years. In protest against the name restoration, B.C., 'a former Halls Gap resident', dedicated a poem to Sir Thomas Mitchell:

> He battled through the heathery scrub and scaled the
>   frowning wall
> To stand at last triumphant, on the topmost peak of all
> He named the range the Grampians.
> Why should we change it then?
> That traveller made our history, he and his stalwart men.

Of Mitchell's feats, and his place in history, she was certain. This was not so of Koori people:

> What the Coorie people called the hills we cannot ever know
> For they have gone like yesterday, with little left to show.[41]

Many opponents of the name restoration eulogised the nineteenth-century 'pioneers' who had 'developed the land using nothing but their bare hands and crude farm implements'.[42] Peter Wrigglesworth

---

38 R.S. of Stawell, 7 April 1989, in Koori Tourism Unit file 9/7/76/3.
39 *Hamilton Spectator*, 22 December 1990.
40 B.G. of Horsham, 28 March 1989, in Koori Tourism Unit file 12/2/6/3; *Boort and Quambatook Standard-Times*, 29 May 1990; *Portland Observer*, 4 July 1990.
41 Koori Tourism Unit file 9/7/76/3, 31 January 1990.
42 P. N. Griffin, in *Stawell Mail-Times* (undated cutting).

of Blackburn posed a question regarding the indigenous peoples' relationship to the land: 'Did they strive to explore, to overcome danger, to improve their lot?' His answer: 'I don't know. There's no record. Who cares?'[43]

Even when their presence was recognised, the present Koori community in the district was often regarded as a 'cultureless remnant'. J.R. of Murtoa rejected the suggestion that the Kooris had 'some sort of culture', adding 'It's too late for all this nonsense.'[44] M. W. of Phillip Island asked:

> How many Western District Aborigines are there anyway? And what have they contributed to the progress of the area over the last fifty years or so? I'd guess, not many and not much.[45]

Philip Lienert of Horsham, in a letter to the *Wimmera Mail-Times*, argued for the need to put a contact history of 'murder, theft, rape, cruelty and ignorance' into its proper perspective: 'At what time in the world's history has one group of people not done that to another group?' He claimed that the indigenous people of Australia were fortunate that they had been colonised by a civilised race: 'If Great Britain had not colonised Australia then someone else would have— and what would have been the fate of the Aborigines then?'[46]

Lienert is not the first to ask such a rhetorical question. Academic John Mulvaney has also asked 'a theoretical question but one which must be faced ... one wonders what French treatment would have been if France had been the occupying power'.[47]

The *Hamilton Spectator* urged Steve Crabb to 'leave history as it stands'.[48] By this the newspaper meant a dominant history that not

---

43 Melbourne *Sun*, 19 April 1989.
44 Koori Tourism Unit file 9/7/76/3, to April 1989.
45 Ibid., 18 December 1990.
46 *Wimmera Mail-Times*, 22 June 1990.
47 *Overland*, 114, 1989, p. 8.
48 *Hamilton Spectator*, 13 May 1990.

only ignored the Koori history of the region, but was also selectively amnesiac concerning the 'pioneer' history of the area. It was not a history of a civilised race, but one of ignorance, racism, greed, brutality and dispossession. Those who want to 'leave history as it stands' need to examine their own history with honesty.

III

Australia is owned and run by white people not black. We took it and have fought several wars to keep it and our freedom.[49]

Popular Australian history has often been written about 'winners', who fought battles with the land before conquering it. Control of the Australian landscape is vital to the settler psyche. The victors' histories falsely parade as the history of Australia. These histories are those of absence: of *terra nullius*. In order to uphold the lie of an 'empty land', Europeans have either denied the indigenous people's presence, or have completely devalued our cultures. These hegemonic histories take possession of others' histories and silence them, or manipulate and 'deform' them.[50]

This misrepresentation is now being challenged as indigenous people confront the imperialist fictions that support political domination and racism. This upsets and displaces what Chris Healy has termed 'the seamless normality [of] a triumphal national history'.

Many Australian histories authenticate themselves by drawing on 'the available myths and discourses of national character and identity'.[51] These histories often speak of Australia's 'pioneer spirit', where the 'settles' toiled in a harsh and empty land. They celebrate a hybridised Australian male: fiercely independent, but imbued

---

49 Clive Johnson, *Wimmera Mail-Times*, 8 June 1990.
50 Janet Abu-Lughod, 'On the remaking of history: How to reinvent the past', in B. Kruger and P. Mariani (eds), *Remaking History* (Bay Press, Seattle, 1989), p. 118.
51 Graeme Turner, *National Fictions* (Allen & Unwin, Sydney, 1986).

with just enough British heritage to remain above the 'natives', who hover around the fringe of such histories, or are disposed of in the 'prehistory' of the text.

Within academia, it is true, the debate has moved on. But outside the walls of the universities, where indigenous people are fighting for land rights, cultural identity and the right to present and interpret our own histories, we are constantly forced to contend with an imperialist history that is really nothing more than 'a crude apologia for the status quo of the day'.[52] It is a history motivated by cultural and political domination. It disguises its own violence and oppression by presenting sanitised 'nationalist themes, grown cosy and thoroughly naturalised by repetition, [that] disguise or celebrate the actual history of imperial and colonial domination'.[53]

These histories may not be presented in the pages of a conventional text (although they often are). They parade themselves in the media and on film. They are evoked in political discussion of 'Aboriginal issues'. It is not surprising that many of these debates centre on the relationship to land.

In Perth, the Swan River Fringe Dwellers, Nyoongar people, have waged a struggle against developers and the state Labor government over the Old Brewery site on the Swan River.[54] They are attempting to protect a sacred dreaming track formed by Waugal, a serpent that created many of the landscape features in the area, including the river. The authenticity of their claim and their culture has been challenged by those who wish to build a recreation and cultural centre on the land. Although both the developers and government had difficulty accepting the Nyoongar belief in a 'giant snake', it did not stop them from trying to appropriate this creation story for their own purposes. The original design for the redevelopment incorporated a

---

52 Rae Frances and Bruce Scates, 'Honouring the Aboriginal Dead', *Arena*, 86, 1989, p. 72.
53 Popular Memory Group, 'Popular memory: theory, politics, method', in R. Johnson et al. (eds), *Making Histories* (Hutchinson, London, 1982), p. 213.
54 *Age*, 27 May 1991.

100-metre-long 'polychrome brick Waugal path'. The Nyoongars' right to protect their sacred land is being rejected by a government that attempts to deny their cultural identity. Steve Mickler has called this 'a colonialist disdain for the fallen "noble savage", the urban "half-caste"'.[55]

The simplest way to deny groups such as the Swan River Fringe Dwellers a right to their land is to deny their existence as indigenous people. If such a denial of identity fails, some opponents revert to the *terra nullius* myth. In a recent newspaper article, a Victorian journalist opposed the Uluru name restoration, claiming that the area had been unoccupied by 'tribes of the desert … for centuries', with the exception of 'nomadic hunters' who visited the area 'in prolonged wet seasons'.[56]

At Echuca in Victoria, the local Yorta Yorta people had remains of their ancestors returned to them by the Museum of Victoria in 1990. The remains had been excavated at Kow Swamp between 1969 and 1972 by archaeologist Dr Alan Thorne. Professor John Mulvaney, a supporter of Dr Thorne, repeatedly claimed that the attempts to have the remains returned to the Koori community for reburial were 'the actions of a handful of radicals',[57] although the campaign to have the remains returned to the community was supported by the nine Aboriginal Land Councils of the Murray River Region, as well as Colin Walker, senior Aboriginal sites officer in the area and representative of the Yorta Yorta people.[58] Mulvaney and Thorne recognised the scientific value of studying the remains, but denied the historical and cultural relationship that present Koori people have with their ancestors. The remains were no longer a part of Koori history: they had become 'ancient bones [that] belong to the world—not us'.[59]

---

55 Steve Mickler, 'The Battle for Goonininup', *Arena*, 96, 1991. The Western Australian Government purchased the land in 1985.

56 'ROCK ROBBERY', Don Petersen, Melbourne *Sun*, 15 October 1991.

57 See for example *Australian*, 21 August 1990.

58 Media Release, Murray River Region Aboriginal Land Council, 22 August 1990; Age, 3 August 1990. At the time Colin Walker had recorded 160 protected sites, and 'knew of many more'.

59 *Australian*, 28 July 1990, 6 August 1990.

Thorne dismissed any ancestral link between Kooris living today and the bodies that he removed from their burial place, on the grounds that there were differences in anatomical features, while Mulvaney was concerned that 'we could face refusal to excavate any more Aboriginal sites'.[60]

Europeans continue to 'make' and 'unmake' indigenous people. When we attempt to claim rights to land, or to the bodies of our ancestors, we are separated from an 'ancient past'. Steve Mickler believes that, as the appreciation (and possession) of Aboriginal art has increased, so too has 'the intensity of the denigration of practised or "lived" Aboriginal culture'.

This form of racism relates to what Renato Rosaldo has termed 'imperialist nostalgia', which makes racial domination appear 'innocent and pure'.[61] Having altered or destroyed the culture of the 'other', the colonisers then appropriate it for their own gain, or even mourn its passing, while at the same time concealing their 'own complicity with often brutal domination'.

Historically, Europeans expected to witness the eradication of the indigenous people of this country, and Australian governments have attempted to erase the identity of indigenous people by physical or cultural genocide, the latter often parading under the title of 'assimilation'. Despite their failure, 'imperialist nostalgia' is everywhere. The passing of an ancient culture is both mourned and celebrated. The collection of art, for example, can serve as evidence of the superiority of the imperialist culture, while allowing its owners the gratification of appreciating the 'beauty' in objects from a past time. James Clifford has noted the Western preference for collectables that are from an 'ancient (preferably vanished) civilisation'.[62] This is so for art and bodies. For mourning to occur 'innocently and purely',

60 *Australian*, 28 July 1990, 6 August 1990.
61 Renato Rosaldo, 'Imperialist Nostalgia', *Representations*, 26, Spring 1989, pp. 107–22
62 James Clifford, *The Predicament of Culture* (Harvard University Press, Cambridge, Mass., 1988), p. 222.

without opposition, the possessed and commodified culture must be certified dead.

IV

As much as guns and warships, maps have been the weapons of imperialism.[63]

We should fully recognise what nineteenth-century explorers and 'pioneers' accomplished in the Western District. In 1836 Major Thomas Mitchell passed through the land of the Jardwadjali clans in and around the mountain range that he named the Grampians. During this search for exploitable land Mitchell claimed that he was exploring a *terra nullius*—a no man's land—despite his having contact with local indigenous people, some of whom his party murdered. Mitchell wrote:

> It was evident that the reign of solitude in these beautiful vales was near a close; a reflection which, in my mind, often sweetened the toils ... of travelling through such houseless regions.[64]

He described these houseless regions as an 'Eden' awaiting 'the immediate reception of civilised man'. His second-in-command, Granville William Chetwynd Stapylton, had a fine understanding of the value of their speculative exercise. The area was an 'El Dorado' which would be 'at present worth sixty millions to the Exchequer of England', and hopefully result in 'a good fat grant' for the 'discoverers'.[65]

Mitchell was a surveyor, taking control of the land by charting it on a map. By naming features, he placed a symbolic British flag on

---

63 J. B. Hartley 'Maps, knowledge, and power', in D. Cosgrove and S. Daniels (eds), *The Iconography of Landscape* (Cambridge University Press, Cambridge, 1988), p. 282.

64 Major T. L. Mitchell, *Three Expeditions into the interior of Eastern Australia* (Australiana Facsimile Editions, 18, Libraries Board of South Australia, Adelaide, 1965, 2 vols), vol. 1, p. 174.

65 Stapylton, op. cit., p. 99.

each of them. The land was charted, ordered and labelled, becoming a colonial possesion. Mitchell eulogised his own feats: 'Of this Eden I was the first European to explore its mountains and streams.' His cartography and favourable reports to the British government resulted in an immediate grab for land. He anticipated that his expedition would lead to the exploitation of 'those natural advantages [of the land], certain to become at no distant date, of vast importance to new people'. Such is the power of cartography.

Mitchell was able to map a 'socially empty space'.[66] Although the land had been occupied for thousands of years, by making a map Mitchell took possession of it for Britain. Elizabeth Ferrier has written that 'mapping determines the way landscape has been conceived'; it is described as an 'unfolded map'.[67] This is a powerful metaphor. The land that was possessed could literally be held in the hands of the invading colonisers. When Mitchell mapped his 'Australia Felix', a land without a recognised people or history was given a history—a British history. His maps conceal the presence and histories of the indigenous people.

Opponents of the Gariwerd name restoration regarded it as an insult to Mitchell's 'memory and tenacity'.[68] And although the Koori Tourism Unit's submission highlighted the fact that Mitchell had only conferred ten of the forty-four European names at issue, it also said that 'Mitchell should be credited with advocating the retention of Aboriginal place-names', and had often done so: 'I have always gladly adopted aboriginal names.' Steve Crabb, quoting the same passage from Mitchell's diary, said 'the explorer went to great lengths to use Koori words when he named landscape features'.[69]

Although the indigenous groups of the Gariwerd area followed Mitchell's party as it moved across the mountain range, they made

---

66 On which see Hartley, op. cit.
67 Elizabeth Ferrier, 'Mapping Power and Contemporary Cultural Theory', in *antithesis*, 4, 1, 1990, p. 41.
68 For example, D.S. of Bentleigh, 30 March 1989, in Koori Tourism Unit file 9/7/76/3.
69 Warrnambool *Standard*, 1 December 1990.

little contact with him. Mitchell sometimes left the main party and 'explored' ahead with a smaller group, leaving Stapylton in charge. When visited by those from whom Mitchell wished to gain both knowledge and names, Stapylton recorded: 'I wish to detain them if possible until the Surveyor General returns, for by them we may obtain a great deal of knowledge of the intervening country.' Piper, a 'black' from New South Wales who accompanied the party, carried the handcuffs that would capture the indigenous names. But Stapylton did not exactly put out the welcome mat:

> Blackfellows shot at and wounded today by one of the men in the bush. The native shipped his spear and was accord-ingly very properly fired at. Now to war with these gentry I suppose. They are encamped around us tonight. Tomorrow we will give them a benefit if they don't keep off.

Stapylton entered comments in his diary in reference to the indige-nous peoples: 'Their hollow resembles precisely the cry of some wild beast, which in fact it is.' On one occasion he disturbed a family who appear to have been hunting. He took great pleasure in the fear that he apparently instilled in them: 'these devils will always run if you give them the time'.

This is the man after whom Mitchell named Mt Stapylton. It was this feature that the Victorian Place Names Committee refused to restore to Gunigalg, apparently on aesthetic grounds.

In May 1836, north of what is now the Murray River, Mitchell's party had clashed with indigenous groups. On 27 May Mitchell decided to take action 'in a war which not my party. but these savages had virtually commenced'. Mitchell set up an 'ambuscade' in order to surprise 'the vast body of blacks' that had been tracking the party. Realising that Mitchell's men were waiting for them, the group ran toward 'their citadel, the river'. Without waiting for an order from Mitchell, his men ran after the 'blacks'. shooting them as they attempted to escape across the river. Mitchell later reported that seven had been shot. He accepted fully the decision of his men to chase and kill, 'for the result was the permanent deliverance of the party from imminent danger'. Mitchell commemorated the killings by conferring a name upon the site:

> I gave to the little hill which witnessed this overthrow of our enemies, and was to us the harbinger of peace and tranquillity, the name of Mt. Dispersion.

The massacre created enough 'ripples' to delay Mitchell's knighthood.[70]

To ensure that Mitchell's place in history is remembered, there are some fifty memorial cairns dotted along a commemorative track bearing his name.[71] This celebration of a 'great explorer' buries the dead and their histories. As Chilla Bulbeck has shown, 'most monuments avoid the sore spot of race relations'.[72]

Mitchell's exploration of the Western District had been pre-empted by the land-hungry Henty brothers, who occupied land at Portland Bay in 1834.[73] The way to gain free title to land was to exploit it vigorously. A claim was established by 'occupying it with sheep grazed in flocks from 500 to 1,000 head, each flock in the care of a shepherd'.[74] This had a devastating effect on the indigenous population. When

---

70 Manning Clark, 'Major Mitchell and Australia Felix', in Manning Clark et al., *Australia Felix* (Dunkeld and District Historical Museum, 1987), p. 79.
71 Ibid., p. 76.
72 Chilla Bulbeck, 'Aborigines, Memorials and the History of the Frontier', in J. Rickard and P. Spearritt (eds), *Packaging the Past—Public Histories* (Melbourne University Press, 1991), p. 170. See also Frances and Scates, op. cit.
73 M. F. Christie, *Aborigines in Colonial Victoria 1835–86* (Melbourne University Press, 1979), p. 24.
74 L. P. Peel, 'The First Hundred Years of Agricultural Development in Western Victoria', in *The Natural History of Victoria*, op. cit.

the Chief Protector of Aborigines, G. A. Robinson, arrived in Portland in May 1841, he discovered that only '2 of the tribe who once inhabited the country of the Convincing Ground are still alive'.[75]

Robinson's tour of the Western District uncovered large-scale murder by the European squatters, as well as Koori resistance. At Portland the Police Magistrate, Mr Blair, stated that the 'natives' of a 'tribe' that had killed a squatter and his shepherd 'should be exterminated'. He would 'shoot the whole tribe' if the murderer was not 'delivered up'. Two days later, one of the Henty brothers informed Robinson that 'the settlers were dropping them'. Blair, who was present, 'replied he hoped so', and added that 'he had no power to restrain the settlers from shooting the women and children'. At the Fitzroy River near Portland, a Mr Pilleau informed Robinson that 'the settlers encouraged their men to shoot the natives', and 'that for every white man killed 20 blacks were shot'. Robinson recorded that the settlers spoke of

> dropping the natives as if they were speaking of dropping cows. Indeed, the doctrine is being promulgated that they are not human, or hardly so and thereby inculcating the principle that killing them is no murder.

He received information of the murder of two Koori women and a boy, who had been lured to their death with the promise of food. Other women were abducted, raped and beaten. On 26 June 1840 he was informed that 'an old woman' named 'Nar.rer.burnin' had been murdered at John Henty's outstation. She had been 'shot, kicked, and stabbed with a bayonet several times ... and then buried in the ground'.

At the Tulloh property near the Grampians, Robinson 'saw the corpse of a native on 4 sticks', apparently used as bait to lure and kill emus. Robinson despaired at 'the heartless manner in which Charles

---

75 'Journals of G. A. Robinson—May to August 1841', *Records of the Victorian Archaeological Survey*, 11, October 1980, p. 15.

Winter and his ruffians [reacted to] the barbarous murder of this man'. Tulloh told Robinson that he and eight other men had previously gone to the Grampians 'in quest of blacks'. They found a child, laid it near the fire 'and roasted it or, to use his qualified expression, burnt it'. They also found a 'fine little boy', who bit one of the men who had abducted him. 'The ruffian then kicked the child to death.' A week later, following yet another attack on a native camp near Mt Sturgeon, Robinson could only state the obvious: '[this] would not be allowed in civilised society'.

In denying a Koori history, the people of the Western District have also conveniently denied their own history. This is a form of radical conservatism: the history is not unknown, but is repressed by building monuments to murderers. When this kind of façadism is threatened with exposure, the response is hostility and hysteria.

On 15 October 1991 Steve Crabb announced the Place Names Committee's decision on the name restoration. Forty-nine place-name restorations were accepted, fifteen were rejected and four required further investigation.[76] Most of the accepted names were given dual Koori/English names. The Koori Tourism Unit had publicly accepted this position during negotiations at least a year earlier: 'We have no objection so long as the Koori name goes first.'[77] But this did not happen. The National Park will be officially known as The Grampians (Gariwerd). The Koori name is therefore linguistically subordinated, 'handcuffed' in parentheses.

The local member for Lowan, Bill McGrath, promised that the names would be 'thrown out ... as soon as the Opposition was returned to Government'.[78] Bob Stone, now Stawell's mayor, said that 'you won't have anyone around here using the names'. He believed that the signs would most likely be torn down, adding 'I wouldn't do it

---

76 *Wimmera Mail-Times*, 16 October 1991.
77 *Courier*, Ballarat, 20 October 1990.
78 *Ararat Advertiser*, 17 October 1991.

myself, as much as I'd like to.'[79] Geoff Clark of Brambuk, on the other hand, felt that on its own the name restoration was 'a poor attempt at some form of social justice', and would only amount to something of substance when 'the concept of land ownership [and] recognition of our cultural heritage within this particular area is recognised'.[80]

The name restoration may be a beginning or an end. The tourist dollar chases the 'niche market'. The marketers may one day target a Western District town as a 'Sovereign Hill'—perhaps Stawell, which has a gold-mining history. Its citizens may become artefacts, performing behind colonial façades, stuck in a local version of 'American Dreams'.[81] But if the market moves away from 'Dreamtime legends', the money may as well.

Koori culture is not a commodity. It must be interpreted in an educative fashion by those who live it—Koori people. To assist in this process the Koori names of landscapes in the region should be fully restored, not presented in a tokenistic fashion, or as a 'dead tongue'.[82]

The first publication to promote the newly named Grampians (Gariwerd) National Park informs us that 'There's a place in Victoria where time seems to have stood still. A place of Dreamtime legends.' The booklet tells of the Kooris, who 'roamed' the area, the coming of Mitchell, then the squatters, 'the farmers, the foresters, and the miners'.[83] It asks tourists to visit Brambuk Living Cultural Centre, or possibly the 'Grand Canyon … Fallen Giant … Whale's Mouth … Jaws of Death'. Visitors to the park can experience 'the same panoramic views Major Mitchell marvelled at in 1836. Nothing has changed.'

---

79 *Vox Populi*, SBS Television, 28 October 1991. This had occurred earlier in 1991 when a sign was erected at the newly named Yanga Nyawi National Park in the Mallee (*Wimmera Mail-Times*, 14 October 1991). It has since occurred in the newly named national park (*Age*, 14 December 1991).

80 Ibid.

81 See Peter Carey, 'American Dreams' in *The Fat Man in History* (University of Queensland Press, 1988).

82 Melbourne *Herald*, 31 May 1990: 'DEAD TONGUE SPARKS HOT WORDS IN THE GRAMPIANS'.

83 *The Grampians Gariwerd* (Victorian Tourism Commission, 1991), p. 3.

In the Time of the Dinosaur (1995)

Elliot Perlman

Nicholas doesn't remember anything. He was still a baby really. There's no point even asking him. I have to remember it all myself. Nicholas had just stopped wetting his bed. We were living in the flats near the chocolate factory. Standing in the street at night, you could smell the chocolate cooking. Dad and I would go for a walk while Mum was getting Nicholas ready for bed. Sometimes the wind would take the chocolate into the flats and I could smell it from our room. When I went to bed Dad would read me a story and turn the light out. I'd close my eyes and, with dinosaurs in my head, I would sniff in the chocolate till I was asleep. (I always breathe through my nose so that nothing gets into my mouth without my knowing about it. Bill Economou from upstairs once swallowed a fly in his sleep. He said his window was open. He was dreaming about chocolate.)

The books Dad and I read were always about dinosaurs. I couldn't get enough of them. At that time I wanted to be a dinosaur scientist when I grew up. Dad said he thought it wasn't a bad idea and that I was well on my way already. He said it beat making shoes in a shoe factory, which is what he did. I think he had a fair amount of respect for dinosaurs too.

The first dinosaurs lived on earth more than 200 million years ago and so you can't even imagine how things were for them. I tried to imagine them in Australia, because there were dinosaurs here before Captain Cook and the Aborigines or anything you can see around now. They weren't stupid either like a lot of people think. Bill Economou said they had to be stupid because they became extinct but he couldn't come up with another group of backboned animals that lived on earth for more than 140 million years. The facts stared him in the face.

Dad calls me Luke but my full name is Lucas. Once I told Bill Economou that I was named after a dinosaur, the *Lukosaurus*. I think that shut him up for a while. The *Lukosaurus* lived in southern China and was two metres long not counting his horns. A couple of weeks later Bill Economou came downstairs to our flat all of a sudden, knocked on the door and announced to Mum, Nicholas and me that he was named after a dinosaur too, the *Billosaurus*. I told him there was no such dinosaur but he said there was. Mum shirked it the way mums do. She said she hadn't heard of the *Billosaurus* but that there might be a dinosaur called that. I went to Nicholas' and my room to get the books. There was no such dinosaur. I would've known about it if there was.

Bill Economou said it was a Greek dinosaur and that I wouldn't know about it. That's when Mum laughed. Nicholas doesn't remember this of course. Then she said that maybe it was a Greek name for a dinosaur and would he like some cordial. Bill Economou never says 'no' if you offer him something. Mum should've known that. It was probably his sister who told him to say that about a *Billosaurus*. It didn't sound like something he'd think of on his own.

Bill Economou has two sisters, two brothers and his mum and dad. One sister, Mary, is the oldest and the other is almost too young to talk. His brothers, Con and Nick, are older than him too. Nick used to play cricket with us for a while but then he stopped. I usually keep away from Con. I think Bill Economou does too. Mr Economou likes to get you in a headlock. It's not so bad sometimes. The Economous live directly above us and we hear them. Mum says we don't need to watch TV on one of their good nights. They don't sound like TV. I don't know why she says that.

Mary Economou fights with Mr Economou. Sometimes Bill Economou invites me up if it's a good one. She's seventeen and still cries. She yells at him in English and he yells back in Greek. I hear a lot of Greek words from Mr and Mrs Economou, nearly every day. Never heard *Billosaurus* though. Bill Economou says Mary's boyfriend always makes Mr Economou shout in Greek even when he's not there.

He can often predict when it will start. The best ones were when Mary wanted to leave school and when the police came asking for Mary to talk about her boyfriend. Bill Economou rang me up as soon as he saw the police car pull up in front of our block. He did the right thing.

Bill Economou was in the same class as me at school. He always copied me in lots of things but tried not to let me know. I always knew sooner or later. Earlier in the year we did a couple of projects together but Mrs Nesbitt knew that I'd done most of the work. Bill Economou was even a bad colourer. Lines meant nothing to him. I was actually pleased when Mrs Nesbitt said Bill Economou and I had to do one project each. I don't think he should've asked her why. Later he agreed with me about this.

Of course I chose dinosaurs. I had big plans. I knew my project would take days and days, some days just for thinking. There were more than 340 types of dinosaurs. I knew I couldn't include them all. I didn't actually like them all. As well as the *Lukosaurus*, I liked the *Tyrannosaurus*, the *Brachiosaurus* and the *Stegosaurus* best. My favourite period was the *Cretaceous* period. This was the 'heyday' for dinosaurs. There must have been hundreds of different kinds of dinosaurs just roaming around chomping on things during the *Cretaceous* period. Mum said this was my *Cretaceous* period. I asked Dad when his was. He said it was before he was married. He must've eaten a lot then. Dad's a big man and when he's hungry there's no stopping him. Mum says before they were married there was no stopping him.

I had figured out that some kids would just do lots of drawings of something and call that their project. Others would copy out slabs from a book and call that their project. These projects would be all right, they might even get two or three red ticks or even a silver star. But I wanted gold for my dinosaurs. One gold star was my personal best. I wanted to beat it. It had got to where red ticks meant nothing to me. Mrs Nesbitt was giving them to sucks for 'behaviour' and to milky girls for A Chart of the Fruits We Eat. Dad said that dinosaurs would be hard because there were no pictures of them in magazines to cut out. Mum tried to get me to swap to dairy products but I just couldn't. You don't get the gold for pictures of milk. It had to be dinosaurs. Dad said he admired me, which was good I thought. He said, 'Luke, I admire you.'

I had decided to write out my own theory of why dinosaurs became extinct and to do a drawing of a *Lukosaurus*. Then Dad gave me a great idea. He suggested making cardboard cut-outs of different types of dinosaurs. He said I could fit the dinosaur cut-outs into slits in the bottom of an upside-down box. Then I could move each dinosaur in a different slit to show how slowly they must've moved and which ones came first after the beginning of the earth. This was a great idea. It could get me the gold. It probably would. Mrs Nesbitt would never have seen anything like this in her life. Dad said he would bring some shoe boxes and cardboard off-cuts for me from work. I asked him not to say anything about it in front of Bill Economou.

Dad gave me the idea on one of our chocolate walks. I was pleased he hadn't tried to talk me out of dinosaurs and into dairy products. He didn't like milk much. I'd never seen him drink it. He said he'd drink it if it was on tap. Then he laughed and lifted me high up in the air. I was way above his head in those hands at the end of his thick arms, sort of near the moon. He held me up there for a good while in the chocolate wind and we didn't speak. His arms didn't waver so I was perfectly still in the air. Only the sky moved, just enough to give tiny shakes to the stars. That was the last chocolate walk we had. I don't remember a chocolate wind much after that either.

Nicholas doesn't remember the chocolate winds. But I remember them. I remember that one too. We came back to our block and before we got to the front hall we heard shouting and a door slamming. Mary Economou ran down the stairs. She shouted 'I hate you' in a new voice that sounded like someone scraping a tin roof. She didn't mean me though. She didn't mean Dad either. She hated someone upstairs. I knew Bill Economou would tell me everything tomorrow so we let her run out into the street and I went to bed really happy and sleepy in one.

I don't think anyone really knows for sure exactly why dino-saurs disappeared. I know I don't. The books shirk it a bit really. It seems that about 65 million years ago they just disappeared. I was thinking of maybe being the first dinosaur scientist to know for sure what happened.

It's hard to know where to start trying to figure out something like that. You would probably have to work out a whole new code or way of thinking, maybe combining maths and the dictionary. Between maths and the dictionary you've pretty much got it all covered. I was thinking about the dictionary a fair bit. I think there's a trick to it that no-one ever tells you. When you look up a word, like dinosaur, you get: 'Reptile (freq. huge) of mesozoic era'. Where does that get you? More words. So you look *them* up and you get *more* words. Well, sooner or later you have to be lucky enough to *already* know at least one of the words you've looked up or you'll never understand anything. No-one ever says anything about this.

One theory says the dinosaurs disappeared because of a great catastrophe which affected the whole world. Perhaps they all choked from dust in their throats as the earth passed through a swarm of comets or from bits of rock and sand from an exploding star. Some people think the earth might have been hit by a giant meteorite. Sometimes I think that might've happened. It's hard to explain these things. A great catastrophe.

I had nearly finished the writing part of my project. Even though it was his idea, Dad kept forgetting to bring home the shoe boxes he'd promised me. I asked him every day and every day he forgot. I had to change my plans. Dad wasn't co-operating. It was at about this time that Mrs Nesbitt and I started having discipline problems. I told her that she was really going to like my dinosaur project and that she might even think of gold stars when she saw it. (She keeps them in a tin in her desk drawer.) But I also told her that it was going to be a bit late. She asked me why. I didn't want to tell her. I told her that I couldn't say because it would spoil the surprise. I didn't want to tell her about Dad's box idea. She said that she was *already* surprised that my project was late. I asked her if she would hang on. She gave me three days. (Bill Economou asked for three more days too and he'd already handed his in. It was on Fish of the Sea.)

I knew I would have to change my plan. I tried to explain it all to Dad but I could tell he wasn't listening. He was all silent. He'd been that way for a while. Mum was silent too. She only said what she had to say, about things like washing or peas. On the third day, I came to school with my project but it was different now. I had two sheets of paper with writing about dinosaurs from the books and a big model of a *Megalosaurus* (a two-legged meat-eater). Since the writing was just *stuff*, all my hope for the gold pretty much rested on the model *Megalosaurus*. I had taken two wire coathangers and threaded them through 17 beer cans Dad had. (They were empty so I didn't even ask for them.) The can at the head was flattened for a snout and the whole thing could bend so I could show how dinosaurs had walked. (I kept the movement part of the first plan.)

Bill Economou loved it. Mrs Nesbitt was angry. I was surprised. She was angry in front of the whole class. She asked if I had needed the extra three days to get enough beer cans. The class laughed when she said that. She looked at them and said that she was very disappointed with my project. Then she went down the aisles between the desks asking to see other projects. She'd already seen all of them three days before. She was just doing this to make me feel bad. It worked and I felt bad, really sick. I thought maybe I'd caught an epidemic, a throat one.

At lunchtime I went home without asking. I just wanted to get away from school for a while. Mum had given me a pear in my lunch. I'd told her not to but she didn't listen and put it in my bag anyway. When I got to the front door I felt inside my bag for the door key. I felt the pear all squashed up. The *Megalosaurus* must have done it. I really wanted to be home with a peanut butter sandwich, some milk and maybe some TV. I opened the door and Dad was there. This was my third surprise in half a day if you count the pear. He was watching TV on the couch.

Dad stayed home in the days now and looked after Nicholas. It's what his work had told him to do. He hadn't told me but they'd asked him if he could stay home with Nicholas for a while and not to make shoes. That's all he said and then he went back to a TV show about hospitals. I wanted to know who was making the shoes now but I didn't ask. I had my sandwich and milk. Then I started to scrape the pear off the inside of my bag. Dad forgot to ask why I was home at lunchtime.

After that everything seemed different. Mum and Dad would be all quiet when I was in the room with them, but they'd shout when I'd gone. I couldn't hear the Economous. Dad made plenty of cans but I didn't need them. Things were different at school too. It was like Mrs Nesbitt was always thinking about my *Megalosaurus*. I just couldn't get back in her good books and I got sick of trying. Bill Economou got a silver star for Fish of the Sea. He kept showing it to me.

I suppose that's why I did it. It all happened so fast like it wasn't really me and I got caught. Mrs Nesbitt caught me at her desk, in her gold star tin. She shouted. It hung in the air and made my sweat jump. Everyone looked. She held my fingers out and showed the class. There were gold stars on my fingers. My face got very hot. She started writing a note to Mum. It was about me. I didn't let her finish it. I left. I ran all the way home again. It still wasn't me though, not really. My bag was still on the pegs.

The front door wasn't locked and I pushed it open. Dad was in the lounge room. His shirt was off and he was puffed like I was, out of breath. He said he'd just been for a run. Mary Economou was there too. Her face was red and her hair was messy. I was confused. I stood there looking at them. Then I cried, first in yelps. I felt really strange. She'd never seen me cry before.

Dad took my face and pressed it into his chest. He put his fingers in my hair. He told me that nothing was wrong and that he and Mary Economou had just been for a run. He kept telling me not to be upset. He asked me to tell him that nothing was wrong. He told me there was nothing wrong with going for a run. Then he squeezed me so hard it hurt. He smelled of sweat. Then he cried, and told me nothing was wrong. His chest moved up and down. It slapped me. I couldn't see anything in his chest. He told me he was sorry.

Two days later I came home from school and Mum was there, not Dad. He had gone. He wasn't coming back for a while. They'd swapped again. Mum would be home with Nicholas and Dad had gone to look for another shoe factory where he could make shoes again. I asked her where he was. She said he was looking for work in a Level Playing Field. I asked her where that was and if I could go there. She said I would never find it. Bill Economou had borrowed an atlas from the library for Fish of the Sea and we went to the map of Australia to look for Level Playing Field. We couldn't find it. Bill Economou said she must have meant the Southern Tablelands. When I asked her she said, 'yes', that was it. I tried to imagine Dad living on a huge flat table, making shoes and writing me letters. She said we would get letters.

If the earth was hit by a giant meteorite it would've made so much dust that the sunlight wouldn't have been able to get through and the dinosaur food chain would've been wrecked. Without any sunlight they would've frozen too. Even the biggest of them would've needed protection from the cold. Everyone does. It's just a theory. No-one knows for sure about the meteorite. If you don't know something for sure you might as well dream it.

Bill Economou dreams all the time. He dreamed Dad was outside one night, outside our flats in the wind doing nothing; leaning against the wall of the empty chocolate factory, staring at our flats. At first, he tried to tell me he actually *saw* it. Mum said there aren't many letter boxes at the Southern Playing Fields.

Nicholas dreams but he doesn't remember. When we shared the same room I could hear some of his dreams. I told him I heard them all. I've got our room to myself now. He's been sleeping in Mum's bed since he started wetting his bed again. He says he doesn't wet the bed. He says it's Mum. I wanted to check this out because he lies much more than me now. I went in and checked one night when they were both asleep. I wasn't sure about *him*, but Mum's side of the bed was wet. Her pillow. Nothing surprises me much any more, not really. Its because I'm growing up, I suppose. That's *my* theory.

Requiem for Ivy (1996)

Alexis Wright

The biggest tree on St Dominic's Mission for Aborigines grew next to the girls' dormitory. It was the only tree that had survived from the twenty-one seeds contained in a seed pod brought by the first missionary on the long and arduous trek to the claypans expanding across the northern gulf country. The pod was a parting gift from his niece; it served a useful purpose on the journey as a rattling prod to strike a stubborn mule on the rump in the heat of the day, or to slap monotonously across the hand at night by the campfire, whenever the boredom or loneliness became unbearable. It was also a useful game to guess how many seeds were in the pod and keep a record, without resorting to opening it. Abstinence in praise of the Lord, until the time of celebration was right—when the destination for the work of God was reached.

So God's celebratory poinciana tree came into being, surviving the claypans, the droughts and the wets to grow large and graceful in the presence of three generations of black girls laughing in their innocence as if nothing mattered at all. Its roots clung tighter to the earth when the girls cried out for their mothers or wept into its branches when they were lonely or hurt, enduring the frustration and cruelty of their times. The tree grew in spite of all this. Healthy and unexploited, unaffected when illness fell on all sides, witnessing the frequent occurrence of premature deaths, none of which affected the growth of God's tree.

Now a black crow sat in its branches, its beady eyes on the wait. Yes, someone else was going to die here. The branches swayed and creaked at night under the Milky Way, while all night long crickets screamed and frogs croaked back. Scarlet petals loosened their hold to fall on the carpet they were forming on the dirt below.

The crow would still be there in the morning. Several weeks the bird stayed. People looked the other way as they passed by. Everyone knew the crow was still there. It would stay until someone died. The precaution was always taken of looking the other way rather than taking the risk of checking if the crow was there. Unwanted bird. But no-one was game enough to chase it away. The Aboriginal inmates thought the tree should not have been allowed to grow there on their ancestral country. It was wrong. Their spiritual ancestors grew more and more disturbed by the thirsty, greedy foreign tree intruding into the bowels of their world. The uprising fluid carried away precious nutrients; in the middle of the night they woke up gasping for air, thought they were dying, raced up through the trunk into the limbs and branches, through the tiny veins of the minute leaves and into the flowers themselves. There, they invited cousin Crow to sit along the branches and draw the cards of death.

Every year when the flowers came the crow came too. Throughout the night the black shadow flew around the community to search for food. The girls in the dormitory prayed long and hard for salvation and tried to ignore the crow like everyone else—except the missionaries, who refused to be spooked by the devil's work. The girls lay there at night on the brink of two beliefs, one offering the wicked eternal salvation, the other no more than the chance to be saved after the price of death was paid.

'Someone awake?' The girls' whispering starts.

'Watch that window now.' Silence. 'Over there.'

They watched throughout the night until exhaustion finally took over, the whites of some two dozen pairs of eyes moving from side to side, from window to open window, on guard.

The corrugated-iron windows, held out with long sticks, always stayed open before the wet. If they were closed the heat of the humid tropical night would make it pitch-black and airless, impossible to sleep with them closed. Impossible to sleep anyway with that crow outside. But sleep they must to face each day of missionary zeal. But the door was left closed at night in case snakes came inside.

'Someone awake?'

'Watch out it don't creep up on you.'

'Might creep up on you and get you.'

'Choose now. Which girl going to die here tonight?'

Singsong: 'Which giiiirrrl going to die heeere? Might be you.'

'Might be going to choose YOOOOUUUUU.'

'Stop it. Stop it.' Younger girls start crying.

'Well, stay awake then.'

'Yep, you lot. Don't just leave it to some of us here to look after you.'

It was already hot by seven in the morning and everyone was up and about. Errol Jipp, the missionary in charge of St Dominic's, with full powers for the protection of its eight hundred or so Aboriginal inmates under state laws, stood caught in the light of the sun streaming through the girls' dormitory window. He stood directly in front of Ivy 'Koopundi' Andrews, aged about seven. She had just acquired the name Andrews. Andrews, Dominic, Patrick, Chapel, Mission—all good Christian surnames given by the missionaries for civilised living. 'Koopundi' and the like would be endured with slight tolerance as long as they did not expect to use such names when they left to live in the civilised world, whenever they acquired the necessary skills.

'Your mother died this morning, Ivy,' Jipp announced, looking around the dormitory. 'We are all very sorry.' He used his high-pitched, sermonising voice, staring down at the bowed head with its brown curls and sun-bleached ends.

Ivy did not move but gave a sidelong glance to see if the other girls were looking. She saw they were pretending not to notice. Her glance shot across to the open window. The bird could not be seen. 'It's probably gone now,' she told herself. She thought of her mother— that was about all she had done since being put into the dormitory a few days earlier. How her mother screamed, and she herself had felt abandoned, alone for the first time in her life. She could hear her mother crying, following and being dragged away, still crying. She did not know what had happened to her but she had not come back again to the fence that barricaded the dormitory after she was dragged away.

'Ah well, dear, we will give her a proper service in the chapel later on today.' As Jipp spoke he formed the funeral arrangements in his mind. Things needed to be planned down to the last detail: that was his habit, his way of doing things. It will be necessary to find some-one to dig the hole. Could he count on one of the men to bring over a plywood coffin, if there was one already made up, or should he get someone to knock one up quickly? No good keeping bodies around too long in this heat. Another thing, these people were far too super-stitious. They might all try to take off in the middle of the night, as they did last time. Better secure the gates and make sure the children are locked in tonight. But maybe not. Old Ben, who died recently, was an important man. Law man, they called him. (Heaven forbid! These people never learn.) But the woman was not from around here. A loner. A real hopeless loser.

'When you hear the bell ring after class, come over to the mission house, child. Mrs Jipp will take you to the chapel.' Best to make the day as normal as possible, Jipp thought as he gave the child a slight pat on the shoulder then turned and walked out. Ivy stood where she was, proud of the fact that Jipp had been so kind to her, hoping the other girls had noticed. She watched the middle-aged white man, the father figure, shaking out his handkerchief to wipe his hand, walking away into the distance.

'He's kind, that Mr Jipp,' she said. Life isn't too bad here, she thought to herself, while the other girls said nothing but moved away from their eavesdropping positions to finish their chores quickly then race out of the door and down the road over the tracks fat Jipp had made to tell their families what had happened.

Everyone was talking about the crazy woman from another country that had killed herself during the night. The movers and shakers of the mission had a lot to say about her.

'If you knew so much, what was her name then?' No-one knew for sure. No-one would have minded if she had settled down at St Dominic's, even though she did not belong here—so long as she went about her business and didn't interfere with others. What could be the harm in that? Nothing.

But someone said she had 'that look' in her eye. 'Down at the store that day, remember? When you went down there for bread on ration day. You said you saw it. You told me that. Told all of us. Don't muck around looking like you know nothing now. You told us yourself—that one not right.'

Another sister adds to the story: 'Crazy. Crazy. Crazy one.'

'Then you threw your hands up in the air. Then when we asked you said, look for yourself.'

'Well, I say anyway she looked all right. Nothing wrong. But then I must have made a mistake. Seein' she goes and kills herself.'

Another voice: 'Just like that. You must have known that was goin' to happen. If you could see something wrong with her. You should have done something to stop it. Poor woman might still be with us now. Instead of waiting to die. Waitin' for spirits to come and get her. You should have made someone stay with her at night when she was by herself. And that poor little girl. She didn't even have that little girl for company any more. No good that. Woman being alone at night. She had nobody. Nobody at all. And you women didn't even lift a finger to help her. Poor little thing left up there now. No mummy or daddy for that one any more. All because of jealous women.'

'Look, man. Don't you go around saying anything. Husband or no husband. Mind your lip, what I say.'

'Yep, I know poor little thing all right. Kids here say she not too upset when Jipp told her this morning. 'Nother thing. You think I can be going around looking after every Tom, Dick or Harry here? How'm I to know she wants to set about killing herself like that? How'd I know anyone want to do that to themselves? I only *thought* she was like that. Yep, crazy that's what. Lot of people around here like that. Can you blame anyone, hey? I'm asking you that. Well, don't go around with your big tongue hanging out blaming me. I'm crazy myself—got kids of mine there too in the dormitory. That don't make me happy either. But what can I do? What can anyone do to stop old Jipp and his mob? They run everything here. They in charge. Not me, that's for sure. Do that make me go around wanting to kill myself or telling other people to kill themselves too? Hey? So shutup your big mouth then. You got too much to say about things you know nothing about.'

At that moment Old Donny St Dominic walked into the main camp where the argument was boiling hot about the death of the dead woman. A lot more people were drawn to the action by mid-morning. The main camp was where some of the most influential families lived. The families who truly belonged to this particular piece of country, the traditional elders where the real law of the mission was preserved in strength, in spite of white domination and attempts to destroy it, or to understand what really happens under their white missionary eyes.

The argument progressed into a lot of wrongs floating around the place which for some time had been left unsaid. There were facts to be aired, mostly to do with the inmates' attitudes towards each other. Somehow or other it all became interlinked with the woman's death.

Old Donny St Dominic, about the oldest surviving inmate of those last 'wild ones' rounded up and herded like a pack of dingoes into the holding pen, now long pacified, sat unnoticed because of the developing commotion and looked on without speaking.

'You all know nothing!' one old *waragu* or madwoman yells in excitement, racing about excitedly and trying to hit people with her long hunting stick. She laughs hysterically at the top of her voice over the mass argument.

People weave and duck and dogs bark but the debate goes on.

'You the one now who sees things that not even there. Since when you cared about anything around here anyway? No wonder that woman gone now. Praise the good Jesus for taking her what I say.'

'Praise nothing. You church people think nothing. Woman goes and kills herself and no-good Jesus got nothing to do with it. Bloody crawl up fat Jipp's bum—lot of good it will do you.'

'Youse know nothing!' the old madwoman yells solidly into faces, and is told by at least a dozen people to well and truly shut up.

'At least we went to see her and talk to her—tried to settle her down.'

'Sure you did. What did you tell her? "God is going to look after you," did you? God's people take her child away and leave her there crying out like an animal for days afterwards. Only us here had to listen to her all day and half the night. Did whiteman's God hear that?'

'God heard. He heard her. And *you* can't say nothing. I see you down there after Jipp's God when it suits you.'

At that moment Old Donny lifts his ancient frame clad in mission rags onto the tip of his walking stick that one of his nephews recently made to support his bulk. Slowly he draws himself into the centre of his balance, then moves one stiff leg after another into the centre of trouble. People watch him approach and stop saying whatever they were saying or about to say about the matter. Silence has fallen all around by the time he reaches the shade of the surrounding young mango trees.

'A woman killed herself here last night,' he says quietly, then pauses for a few moments. 'Down near old Maudie's—under the mango tree there.'

He stands leaning on his stick and waits before proceeding any further. 'Maudie told me early this morning … said she been crying again for the child. The one Ivy … put in the dormitory with the others. Last night … she come and took Maudie's lighting kerosene … went and set herself alight.'

Someone at that moment put a stool behind the old man and sat him down on it. No-one up to this moment had known how the woman had achieved her aim of killing herself. That question had become enmeshed and lost in other issues—the reasons why and who was to take a share of the blame. The method was simply a secondary matter until Old Donny mentioned it: now everyone was dumbfounded, realising how bad the woman must have felt to go and douse herself with Maudie's kerosene then set herself alight.

The old man looked down and waited, thinking someone might want to say something. But the people gathered there either looked at him or down at the ground where the bull ants marched on regardless in their processions from one nest to another, and said nothing.

'I went back with Jipp to see Maudie this morning. She's pretty upset, you know. You women here, better look after that old woman.'

Maudie was old all right; she looked as old as the land itself. The kids thought she was an evil spirit and would only go near her place to taunt her when their parents weren't around to rouse them. She lived alone, away from the main compound in an old corrugated-iron hut and gum-tree-bower shelter, built by her last husband years ago before he died of smallpox along with several dozen others who fell at that time. Old Maudie never really recovered from his death and preferred to stay in the place alone, too old, or too previously loved and contented to want to share the rest of her life with another man.

The woman who had killed herself had chosen to move into the small abandoned shed beside Maudie's a week after she arrived at the mission. She was not eligible for a mission hut—corrugated-iron one-room huts that looked like slight enlargements of outdoor dunnies. They were lined up in rows, with a single tap at the end of every second row. One tap for every two hundred people. They housed what mission authorities referred to as 'nuclear families'. That is, husband and wife with children, no matter how many. If the children had been forcibly removed to the segregated dormitories the couples made room for grandparents, or other extra relatives these people insisted should live with them.

At first Ivy's mother had been placed in the compound of large corrugated-iron sheds which housed several families tightly packed together, as well as women alone, with or without children. This was where Ivy had been taken from her. The child was termed a 'half-caste' by the mission bosses and therefore could not be left with the others. Their reasoning: 'It would be a bad influence on these children. We should be able to save them from their kind. If we succeed we will be able to place them in the outside world to make something of themselves. And they will of course then choose to marry white. Thank goodness. For their children will be whiter and more redeemable in the likeness of God the Father Almighty.'

But Ivy was all the woman had left. The child she gave birth to when she was little more than a child herself. The child of a child and the man who said he loved her during the long, hot nights on the sheep station where she had grown up. She had not seen the likes of a mission before. That was a place where bad Aborigines were sent—as she was frequently warned by the station owners who separated her from her family, to be an older playmate-cum-general-help for their own children. So she was always certain she made sure to be good. Even to the man who seduced her by night she was good. She believed in love and he loved her just like her bosses did. With kindness.

At the end of the shearing season she was left to give birth alone, as despised as any other 'general gin' who disgraced herself by confusing lust for kindness and kindness for love.

Years later, when the child Ivy was half-grown, the woman had to be got rid of. In the eyes of her bosses she was not a bad cook for the shearers. 'Now she's had enough practice … since the time we had to put her out of the house to have her bastard child with her own kind.' But the woman was often abusive to everyone. It was said that none of her own people wanted anything to do with her. She was too different, having grown up away from the native compound in the whitefellas' household. And having slept with white men … 'That makes black women like that really uppity,' they said.

'Now she wants to take her kid with her all the time. Even out in the shearers' camp. Won't leave her even with her own family—after all, she is one of them, isn't she? And the men don't like her either. You know what she went and did? She went and chucked hot fat over one of the fellas when he was just trying to be nice to that child. Caused a right old emergency.' A shrug of the shoulders.

'Yes, might have been the father of the child … who knows. Anyway, she's got to go—this sort of thing only gives the others bad habits … if you don't deal with it properly.'

A magistrate handled the assault matter and handed the finalisation of the woman's affairs over to the Regional Protector of Aborigines, and she was promptly removed. Under ample protection mother and child were delivered into their new world—an Aboriginal world similar to that occupied by thousands of Aboriginal people at the time. In this case, the destination was St Dominic's Mission in the far north.

When Ivy was taken away, her mother had nothing left. The bad Aborigine became morose. A lost number amongst the lost and condemned, 'bad' by the outside world's standards for blacks. Sentenced to rot for the rest of her days. Even her child taken from her so that the badness of black skin wouldn't rub off.

Her heart stopped dead when they spoke to her just before taking the child, after they had shown her a spot to camp in the squalid stench of the communal shed. It was described as being 'for the good of the child'. Perhaps they were right—but how could she let Ivy go? Her whole body had gone numb. Vanished was any sense of the arrogance of the old days now for Number 976 805 on the state's tally books. Her arms and legs felt as though they had been strapped down with weights.

'No, don't,' was all she could think of to say, but the words never passed her lips. Over and over after they left, she thought if only she had said the words out loud, if she had only tried harder, then maybe they would not have taken Ivy away. She had screamed and run after them and tried to drag Ivy away until she was overcome and locked up for a day in the black hole, a place for troublesome blacks. Her release came with a warning of no further interference.

'It is best for you not to be a nuisance. People like you don't make the laws.' She was told that next time she would spend a long time inside the lock-up if she still wanted to cause trouble. 'And then we will be forced to have you removed to another reserve especially for the likes of people like you. Remember that.'

Alone she saw the blackness of the night and the men who came, small and faceless creatures. They slid down the ropes from the stormy skies, lowering their dirty wet bodies until they reached the ground outside the hut when she slept. There in silence they went after her, pulling at her skin, trying to rip her apart. Taunting her as she tried to escape, to get out of the door of the hut. All the while pulling and jabbing her skin wherever they could with their sharp nails. Satisfied with their 'bad woman's weakened state' they returned to the skies, beckoning her to come with them. Again and again they came back through the nights to enjoy another attack. Again and again they made her theirs nightly. But her final nightmare was to come.

Alone she can see the black bird fly in the night. See it hover, flap its wings faster to stay in one spot, swoop almost to touch the ground, then shoot up again to its hovering position. The process is repeated several times while the woman slinks into the darkness of the tree shadows. Frightened, on guard, she watches. Now the black bird has time for torment. It attacks in the darkness in the perfect moment— the moment of loss. Its attack is unrelenting. Face, back of head, shielding arms—the pecking persists as she crawls on her stomach into the shack which offers entrapment but no escape.

Hearing the screams, old Maudie grabs her stick and hits the ground, over and over to frighten what she thinks must be a snake, while she finds her way through the darkness. She hears the flapping of the bird's wings and waves her stick frantically this way and that, striking air, twigs, branches, but the bird escapes. The frightened old woman finds only the terrified, incoherent victim bleeding and shaking, huddled on the ground.

Maudie told Jipp and Old Donny the woman knew she was being punished and would die soon. If anyone could believe Maudie. She knew a lot of stories like that. She said she told the woman not to go on like that, she was young, she should be thinking of finding a husband for herself and having more children. Only old people like Maudie herself thought about dying. But the woman kept saying: 'I sick … I sick … sick.' That's all she could say. She thought someone wanted her dead. She was a bad woman. Bad mother. Might be someone from her own country wanted her dead and came here secretly in the night to do bad business on her.

That's why Maudie said she did it. Poured the kerosene over herself before anyone could stop her. Before the clouds broke she threw herself in the fire. All the screaming when it finally came, and, by the time old Maudie could get to the human fireball, it was over. Maudie said she tried to limp over to the mission house to get help for the woman, with only her lamp to see by in the moonless night. Then the rain came. But no-one would answer the door there. Seems that as usual, whiteman's law did not want to know what happens in the middle of the night. Such are the spirits that haunt the night in Aboriginal places.

'Maudie came and got me to go with her in the night then ... nobody else to do it,' Donny said, picking up the story. 'Old Maudie and me sat all night long with her ... all night ... you savvy ... in the rain. But it did no good ...'

He looked up and waited for the silence to be broken. But all eyes looked at his and said nothing. Then he said: 'That's all.' Meaning end of story. The people left and went home.

Ivy ran to the mission house when the bell rang. Excited by the attention. And sure she would be told of a terrible mistake. It wasn't her mother dead after all. It was someone else. She was even sure her mother would be there to tell her they were going to leave this place for ever and go back home.

Jipp's wife, Beverly, sat in the shade of her front garden amongst the prettiness of the hard-won purples and pinks of petunias and button dahlias. An oasis inside a white picket fence that separated her from the bulldust outside. This was their eighteenth year at St Dominic's and it was home, even though she wished long and often they could get away for an extended holiday. But she could not conceive of their ever leaving the place. What would the people do if they left? These were their people: to serve God by saving these black souls from themselves, from paganism, was the highest calling for men like Errol. 'Yes, of course such souls can be saved,' she heard herself saying, as she often did to her churchwomen's meetings down south, on the rare occasions when they were down that way.

Proof was there already. One only had to look at the full congregation on Sunday and the devout faces of the little children. Strict rules set the guiding principles for these people to live by. Once you established that then you had no trouble at all. She recalled trying to explain life here to the churchwomen's meetings. It was breath-taking—how those women imagined life up here, Beverly thought. She smiled at the thought of how they followed Errol around, astounded by his stories of pacifying the natives, the troublemakers. Hanging onto his every word. 'Are they really as black as you see them in books!'—and to her, in mock admiration: 'How do you manage, dear, with only black people for company? It must be so hard on you up there, so far away.'

And so it was. So it was. But to work and live in the grace of God is not meant to be easy. In time, just rewards will come to those who manage. It was worth the effort. Praise be to God Almighty for those who see His guiding light.

God's light sometimes becomes dimmed, however, Beverly Jipp thought as she watched in pity the child approaching under the stormy afternoon sky. The devil's work still persisted here even after so much diligence on poor Errol's part. Still, the dead woman had been new to St Dominic's. That was the trouble. If only they could refuse to take in the strays the authorities kept wanting to send here. If only they could concentrate simply on the ones they already had, then their efforts might bear the proper fruits.

'Here child, eat this mango'—she hands the fruit to Ivy, who looks around in vain for her mother; but she is happy for the treat. Beverly is certain the gates of salvation will not open for the dead woman, but perhaps their prayers will be answered, and he will give absolution to the poor thing. She hands Ivy a white cotton dress to wear. It was a favourite of her own daughter, now grown up. Dot, now living down south, surely would not mind giving the poor child her old dress.

Ivy is forced to drop her sack dress in front of the white woman in broad daylight for anyone to see, and struggle with the white dress. She doesn't want to dirty it, although it will be impossible to keep it clean in the living conditions she is fast becoming used to.

'There! You look lovely,' Beverly announces, scarcely believing her eyes, as she looks at the brown curly-haired child with her large, strange-looking brown-green eyes. Yes, she thinks. Quite beautiful.

'Put this around your neck and wear it all the time, child.' The bead necklace is a gift which Errol would disapprove of. 'Don't spoil the children, Bev, they are our only chance'—she can hear the familiar words of disapproval. The necklace is now in place over the white dress. Ivy, looking like God's own angel, dressed more for a party than a funeral, is ready to bid her mother a last farewell. There is no sign of her mother at the mission house: is it true, then, that she has died?

The electrical storm, typical of the tropics this time of year, suddenly broke, lashing out with all its violence at the lowering of the coffin into the freshly dug hole. Ivy stood with the Jipps, next to the elders, who were secretly partaking in their own rituals but looking as though they were converts to Christendom. The others who came to save the face of the so-called community spirit on apocalyptic occasions such as this were a few of the church-going groupers who hedged their bets both ways.

Ivy could not move her eyes from the wooden box, knowing now that her mother was inside it. The rain poured down on the box and Ivy could see the hole it was making—and soon she could see her mother's face smiling at her, a careful, peaceful smile that made her cry for the first time that day. At this moment lightning forked across the sky, and thunder shook the ground beneath their feet. Near by a prickly bush was struck, so the funeral rites were hastily brought to an end by jipp, with the coffin left to lie in the deep hole fast filling with water. After the storm ended some black souls would be sent around later on to shovel in the claggy clay.

Ivy was led away, back to the 'redemption' dormitory, shamed that the sodden white dress now revealed every inch of her body, feeling the dirtiness of her brownness beside the middle-aged cleanliness of the white missionaries; feeling, above all, her loneliness.

How to Love Bats (1996)

Judith Beveridge

Begin in a cave.
Listen to the floor boil with rodents, insects.
Weep for the pups that have fallen. Later,
you'll fly the narrow passages of those bones,
                    but for now—

open your mouth, out will fly names
like *Pipistrelle, Desmodus, Tadarida*. Then,
listen for a frequency
lower than the seep of water, higher
than an ice planet hibernating
beyond a glacier of Time.

Visit op shops. Hide in their closets.
Breathe in the scales and dust
of clothes left hanging. To the underwear
and to the crumpled black silks—well,
give them your imagination
and plenty of line, also a night of gentle wind.

By now your fingers should have
touched petals open. You should have been dreaming
each night of anthers and of giving
to their furred beauty
your nectar-loving tongue. But also,
your tongue should have been practising the cold
of a slippery, frog-filled pond.

Go down on your elbows and knees.
You'll need a speleologist's desire for rebirth
and a miner's paranoia of gases—
but try to find within yourself
the scent of a bat-loving flower.

Read books on pogroms. Never trust an owl.
Its face is the biography of propaganda.
Never trust a hawk. See its solutions
in the fur and bones of regurgitated pellets.

And have you considered the smoke
yet from a moving train? You can start
half an hour before sunset,
but make sure the journey is long, uninterrupted
and that you never discover
the faces of those trans-Siberian exiles.

Spend time in the folds of curtains.
Seek out boarding-school cloakrooms.
Practise the gymnastics of wet umbrellas.

                    Are you
floating yet, thought-light,
without a keel on your breastbone?
Then, meditate on your bones as piccolos,
on mastering the thermals
beyond the tremolo; reverberations
beyond the lexical.

                    Become adept
at describing the spectacles of the echo—
but don't watch dark clouds
passing across the moon. This may lead you

to fetishes and cults that worship false gods
by lapping up bowls of blood from a tomb.

Practise echo-locating aerodromes,
stamens. Send out rippling octaves
into the fossils of dank caves—

then edit these soundtracks
with a metronome of dripping rocks, heartbeats
and with a continuous, high-scaled wondering
about the evolution of your own mind.

But look, I must tell you—these instructions
are no manual. Months of practice
may still only win you appreciation
of the acoustical moth,
hatred of the hawk and owl. You may need

to observe further the floating black host
through the hills.

Green Target (1997)

Gig Ryan

When media fizz, silence expands
back to the clamped grass and china leaves
I scramble through my tax
to find I've eaten rent and paid with thought
I mean I'm happy that he's happy
his ornate voices mash and ripple
It went like the jeopardising stars
His husband attentiveness
amidst the democratic gossip
Unregarded catalogues pile up
Cars squeal and ring
Favoured love falls through dreams
You cry until they go, yank happiness
back to life's clocked cell
vaguely listening to the sliding ocean's
                    soft detergent foam

Membranes (1998)

Kevin Hart

1
A voice, almost a voice, in the wee hours
When no-one else is home: a body turns
And feels its comprehension of the bed,
An ear affirms the silence of its house

And only then admits a pounding heart.
Heat sits in judgement over everyone,
O Lord, this summer night whose rising up
And going down give cruel sleep at best:

Each louvre set to catch the storm's cracked air
And old verandahs slung out round the back
All drenched with moonlight and mosquito nets.
Tough kids are fucking in the high school yard

While traffic whispers on the Ipswich Road;
A train bears empty carriages out west,
The river sighs while passing Mandalay.
There was no voice. That girl from years ago

Was not about to speak before you woke.
Ah, let her go. And let those other souls
With cold, fixed eyes of dolls left under beds
Go home, o let them slip into the dark ...

A voice, almost a voice, though not a voice:
Something between the mind and night, perhaps,
Something that tries to speak but always fails
And leaves a memory with nothing there.

2
To walk all day beside the lazy river,
Beginning from its loop at Blackheath Road
And vaguely heading down to Cockatoo,
A full canteen of ice slung round my neck,

Then cutting back at four down bolted paths
That open, suddenly, onto thick bush
Or spiky fences running fast for miles
At Wacol Prison or the 'Private Road':

It was somewhere round there I lost my way,
Some Sunday when the mercury went mad,
And found a factory defunct for years
With grass that grew right through the broken glass,

And I remember climbing up and down
And gulping thick warm water with a taste
Of tin and leather from my father's war,
And I recall a sign that said 'CONDEMNED'

Through cobwebs, swastikas and clumsy hearts,
And red brick dust that ran beneath my nails
And loud mosquitoes ripping up my arms,
The walls all going wavy in the heat,

And none of it adds up to anything,
Only a nameless fear that sometimes leaps
From nowhere on these summer evenings:
Just coming to; no stars; a drip of blood;

The sweat already cold upon my back,
And drunken voices flapping in the wind,
And someone, me, now smashing through the bush
And leaving someone, me, still sleeping there.

3

Half-dreaming of desire, or solitude,
I thought, Apollo Bay: arriving there
One winter evening while driving west
And drinking dirty water from a hose

Then clambering around the breakwater
With a kind girl I didn't love enough:
The fishing ships at ease, a massive hill
Intent on brooding over all the bay

And moving closer, so it seemed, as night
Came home at last, but slowly, wave on wave.
Nowhere more beautiful than here, I thought
(A sorrow old as all the stars was out

And roaming round the bay, as though it knew
Our bodies were both made of stars). No time
More radiant than now: her fingertips
Just touching near her mouth, and ocean waves

Returning once again in their good time
While I was nearly breathing her warm breath.
A moment that unfolds and makes a life,
A moment surely reaching out to—no,

Not that, I thought, not that, and then stepped back.
An icy breeze was on the loose, and so
'As Goethe said,' I said, and she agreed,
And there was somewhere else we had to go.

4
(*i.m.* G.H.)

The train is skimming Maryland at night
When you are called back home. But who? And where?

You look outside, and someone there looks back.
It's you, thank God, well almost—yes, it is,

And sleep belongs to someone else's life
And that was you as well, or nearly. No:
Old questions breathe beside you as you wake
And bring old answers slowly to their knees.

Snow falls on roads where you will never walk,
On trees that you will never sit beneath;
It was her face you saw out in the night
And she was whispering a word. Lost, lost,

Forever lost, and waves pass over you:
A mountain, and a wine glass being filled,
A long embrace and then a sudden look
That cancels years and years. Well it was her,

And so her dying enters into you;
After a year or more of clenching hard
At last it happens, all that void at once,
Its full enormous rush against the heart

With people all around awake, asleep,
Some counting minutes till they open doors
And others reading Bibles with a pen,
And no one here can take the truth away,

Not the conductor in his uniform,
Not the dark face that looks at you outside.
O let her go the train wheels start to chant
But to the dark you whisper *No no no*—

Living Death: An Online Elegy (1999)

Hannah Fink

I was wearing a pale blue seersucker hospital gown that joined at the nape of the neck with velcro—I had taken my nightie off as it was soaked with blood and amniotic fluid—sitting on the very edge of the bed standing on the points of my toes, neither standing up nor sitting down, saying to the anaesthetist in a tiny voice, 'Help me.'

Then it was quiet. I had stopped vomiting and trembling, and the pain was gone. It was just Tessa and me and Andrew in the big pink room. Dr Grey had gone home. Tess said to Andrew, 'There's a little red button next to the bed. Push it if I tell you to.' And then, gently, slowly, he came. I could feel the contractions through the anaesthetic. It was the most perfect stillness. Tess turned his head around, and delivered his body. 'It's a beautiful little boy,' said Tessa. Andrew burst into inconsolable sobs. Tessa cleaned him, measured him, wrapped him, then brought him to me. I was so happy holding him—I was so happy to see him. He was exactly who I thought he was when I was carrying him. Tessa took some photos of us together and I look just as a mother does, gazing with love at her infant.

We buried him at Rookwood the next day. Cantor Deutsch sang a brief prayer; Andrew wrapped his coat around the little coffin. It was painted tar black; I thought it would be pine like Papa's coffin. I put a photo of Andrew and me in the grave, smiling to the brim on our wedding day. We passed the shovel between us—me, Andrew, Dad, Mum, John, Ben, Aunty Bev, Phil, Sole, Anne, Aunty Jenny, Tessa. The gravedigger put a Letraset sign on top of the little mound: BABY SHAPIRO. He has a name but it is not spoken.

When we buried Papa two months earlier, the marker on his grave was handwritten in spiky capitals. JACK FINK, it read, and it was impossible to believe someone of such great will and wit could be contained in that small mound of earth. His death to me was as appalling, as outrageous as that of a young person. 'It's your grrrandt-fader here', Papa would say in his Bialystocker accent when he telephoned, and implicit in the magnitude of my love for him is my failure to capture him beyond the grave, to make his peasant brilliance live.

I spent the seven days of Shiva staying at Grandma's. I looked for something, a talisman, that would keep Papa with me. *Dancing Rebecca*, his favourite record? Grandma wouldn't part with it. A tie? A siddur? He was not a man of objects, of things. In the kitchen I found a shopping list next to the telephone, written in his beautiful, curlicued migrant's hand. Cheese, Tamatos, Milk, Eggs, Apples, Salman. Papa could speak five languages and he was a self-made millionaire, but he never quite mastered written English. Nothing is more dear to me than this piece of paper. I fancy that a tiny part of his spirit is caught in the flourish of the T.

It was the day Jason came to connect my modem that I found out my baby was dead.

I had been tired, dreadfully tired, all weekend. By the time Jason came, on Monday, I could barely stand up and I had lost my voice. I tried to sit beside him as he fiddled with my password—HANDBAG 1—but had to lie down. I rang the doctor, and said, without even having thought it, I haven't felt the baby move today. I had already rung once that day and been dealt the usual sedative platitudes fed pregnant women—it's *perfectly normal*—but the receptionist didn't say that, she said come in straight away. So I went in to Jason, who was tip-tapping away on my keyboard, and said 'I have to go out for a minute. There's something wrong with my baby.'

Sitting in the waiting room of the ultrasound clinic, I put my hand on my mother's arm and said, gently as one might to a child, 'You know that the baby might be dead.' I still don't know how I could have said that, because I hadn't thought it. My baby's dead. My baby died. I had a baby that died. The words were as unbelievable then as now.

I knew it could happen. My second cousin Naomi died of pre-eclampsia with her baby still in her womb. She was seven months

281

pregnant and she had had an ideal pregnancy until that day. I knew unnatural death, too. My first boyfriend, Blake, was killed in a car accident when he was just twenty-two. His preternatural beauty and brilliance lent a false logic to his death—we sang 'Vincent' by Don Maclean at his funeral—but I learnt then, after two years of crying, that things didn't make sense.

It was when the radiologist said 'Are you going back to see Dr Grey?' that the silence weighing on me buckled, and I knew.

I rang my friend Tessa and told her my baby was dead. Tessa is a midwife. I met her ten years ago in the Evening Star Hotel in Surry Hills when I was in a band called Pressed Meat and the Smallgoods. I went to hospital the next day. Tessa came in an hour or so after I was admitted. I knew if I kept looking at her beautiful smiling face I would be OK. She showed me how to make the bed head move. 'Bed goes up, bed goes down,' she said, quoting Homer Simpson. I thanked Tessa for coming in when she wasn't working. 'I would do anything for you, Hannah,' she said.

It wasn't until six weeks later that I actually went online, my first venture into the Net. I typed in STILLBORN, and was asked to provide a subsidiary term. STILLBORN + INFAMY, one of the offerings, got me ORDER FROM CHAOS: Stillbirth Machine/Chrushed Infamy. On www.hannah.org/loss.html I found Hannah's Prayer E-Mail Pal and Prayer Support Connection, which has its own quarterly publication, 'Hannah to Hannah (H2H)'. STILLBORN + INTRAUTERINE revealed SANDS Australia, but the link didn't work.

Then I found my group. It is a board where mothers of stillborn babies write letters to one another. It was the first site I found and I've never gone anywhere else since.

Over the next year I spent countless hours weeping and laughing into the green glare of my computer screen as I read missives from Karen and Carrie and Shannon and Sharon, from Myrna, Nina, Rebekah, Cindy, Mindy, Jodi, Julie, Jan and Justina. I loved these women fiercely, wholly, and we poured the love we could not give our dead children on one another. We were all in the sorrowing no-man's-land between having had our babies and trying to conceive again, a nowhere in which time is measured by ovulatory cycles and trimesters, birth days and death days. So while we obsessively talked about temperature charting, mittelschmerz, and the quality of menstrual blood, we also talked about our babies, our husbands (there were no single or gay mothers) and our grief. Our intimacy was forged in words, tears and endless descriptions of cervical mucus.

Months went by before I realised that what I was doing was participating in a self-help group. And as a Net naif, everything would strike me as novel, ingenious. 'Just lurking', a casual visitor would announce, and I would be struck by the wit of the phrase, little realising that this was everyday Net speak. Being slow-witted myself, the delays of letter-writing suited me better than live chat; it also promoted the kind of thoughtfulness necessary in a group where everyone was still sharp with pain.

Except for me, Padma from Singapore, Sarah from Warwick and Debbie from Darwin, all the women were American. I was at once charmed and nauseated by their Americanness. There was so much that was galling—calling each others 'ladies', for a start. 'Hey ladies how about a rollcall. I'll go first. ++++ vibes!!!!!!!!' The cheerleading. The exclamation marks. The miles of bad poetry (which always contained the words 'angel', 'tears', 'Mommy', 'heaven', 'Jesus', 'love' and 'rosebud'). Some women degenerated into writing wretched, rambling letters to their babies. Others posted memorial web pages, as though the Internet were heaven itself, index of God's mind.

My correspondents were simultaneously unabashed and puritan: mawkish, effusive, bubbly, *sincere*. Yet I admired their openness, their confidence, their sense of play. They shared a freewheeling cultural freemasonry of which they were unaware and in which I longed to participate. Being American was evidently great fun. And there was a generosity, a womanly good-humouredness. Soon any ambivalence I'd had was lost. More than anything I longed to be able to say 'YOU GO GIRL!'

It took me a while to learn the protocols of the group. There were rituals of welcome and condolence, cheer squads (GO SPERMIES GO!!), and even an eccentric system of acronyms for things to do with fertility (so AF stood, inexplicably, for Aunt Flo—a menstrual period—whose unwelcome visit would often be preceded by her dog Spot). The advent of a period was received with commiseration, and the announcement of a pregnancy with jubilance. There were set pieces; the birth (or in the case of a caesarean, operation), the funeral, the gravestone, the empty cot, on first seeing a living baby or hearing that a friend was pregnant, and the anniversaries of conception, birth and death. Together we trawled over the things that haunted and punished us: the test we forgot to take, the party we should have skipped, the work we should have refused.

When I discovered the site I didn't realise that it was new and still in the process of invention—I assumed everyone was an Internet habitué and knew the rules of the game—and so I delivered my first post with some trepidation:

My baby was delivered at 33 weeks on 29 October last year. He was my first child. He had died in utero some days before. I was put on drugs for two days to induce labour then the doctor broke my waters. Very swiftly I went into full labour. I was incredibly fortunate to have a very dear friend who is a midwife who delivered him.

His birth was beautiful (after the pain, when I was on the epidural, that is)—strangely, it was still the most wonderful thing, even though I knew he was dead—and he was a beautiful baby. He looked just like his father and half-sister.

I had a million tests done and the doctor said that the cause of death was fetal-maternal transfusion—that is, the baby haemorrhaged into my blood stream through an imperceptible fault in the placenta. He had only heard of this once in his career 15 years ago. They don't know how or why it happened. My pregnancy was a healthy one. There was nothing wrong with my baby or with me. Although the doctor has spoken to me twice about it I don't understand what actually happened.

I then went on with a lengthy catalogue of my every anxiety: about my menstrual cycles, my teeth falling out, my grandfather's death, my grandmother's grief, etcetera, etcetera, etcetera. Not the way to post, I realised, when I got only three responses, compared with Angie, who posted a single paragraph immediately after me and who got no less than eight replies. 'Thank you', it was titled:

> I can't thank you enough for having this site. I have spent the majority of my day here reading, re-reading, crying and laughing. I lost my son Tyler last Wednesday, at 20 weeks. All my feelings and thoughts were posted here as I read through your messages. It is truly a comfort to know that there are people who understand, and it helps to know that it will get better with time. How did people make it through those first weeks? I have another son who is two and a half and I am having trouble coping with him and this loss. Any suggestions?

At first I was terribly hurt that only three people had responded— I had cried so hard reading their stories—but then realised it was because I hadn't pitched my post right. In contrast, Angie's message had all the hallmarks of the perfect post: brevity, a direct emotional response, a clear question and, above all, immediacy. Immediacy is the marrow of electronic meaning; its effect is cumulative yet very much located in space and time. There is no point in printing posts, as by the time the ink is dry any meaning will have expired: like a shiny black river rock that glints underwater, once collected it loses its sheen.

For months I did it all wrong. I would read all the posts, then mull over which ones if any I would respond to. Then I would cut and paste the post into my word processor, compose my reply, then paste it back onto the bulletin board. Being part of a community network, I had only two hours a day online, and I needed to spend them carefully.

Yet when I'd finished writing down how I felt, and fiddling a little with it—fixing commas, changing the odd word, deleting things that might make me sound too brainy, too much like a writer—somehow I couldn't feel it any more. I'd read back what I'd written and it would seem false, ornate—writerish. The way I wrote and how I read was perverted by my relationship with words. Where words to me were magic tokens, beautiful ornaments, vessels of truth, to my correspondents they were things you use in order to speak.

Writing, I realised, was something I had to get over. I'd find myself extemporising into cul-de-sacs where I knew my meaning would be lost by my readers because there was none. Or at least any meaning that mattered. I learnt to write only when I had to, when I was desperate; the pleasure in writing was not in the writing itself but in knowing that I had said what I meant. Gradually, eventually, I lost the little person sitting in my brain who evaluated people according to their syntax or their spelling or vocabulary, the fear that prompts irony and distrust: finally, writing and reading became purely subjective—a language of love.

The grief of a mother may be inexpressible but it is also encyclopedic, and our project was the communal articulation of our experience. 'I feel like I am deaf and dumb,' said Myma, and as we moved our hands over our keyboards we began, painstakingly, to decipher the unwritten world in which we had found ourselves. Writing was very much about the articulation of pain, as though in capturing it in words it would remain captive, be staunched, and from the mire of feeling, words became oracular, astonishing. Yet our writing was as much an articulation as a transubstantiation. The meaning of the percussive AAARGHs, OOOOOs, GRRRRs and YAAAAYs that punctuated our letters was gutteral, visceral: when we pressed 'Post your message' we sent little shots of pure emotion coursing through the electronic currents that linked us. There is perhaps no word more poignant, more replete, than *Oh*—more a sound or a breath, a sigh, than a word—and it is through these sounds, the invisible capillaries of chatter, that feeling travels.

We came to share one another's language, to speak a common tongue. Our letters were threaded one to the next, stitched together with a borrowed phrase, a common word, a caught sentiment. Reading my later posts I barely recognise myself: I lost the I of writing and could only write in the corporate voice that we had become. 'Sometimes when I read your posts I think you must be able to see inside my mind,' says Nina; or, 'Reading your response was like talking to myself,' a common refrain. Soon there was no I: we had become one person.

Well, almost. Insincerity, I discovered, is a vital component of female friendship, and the capacity of women for becoming one another—for empathy—often arrives at a loss of self. I developed irrational dislikes for certain members, and equally irrational fondness for others. I was astonished to find myself feeling pangs of envy—that Sharon did not reply as warmly to me as she did to Shannon, that everyone fussed over Jennifer as though she were a child, that Maureen all of a sudden stopped replying to my posts—and, worse, to find myself competing for the affections of the other women. As much as I wanted to be understood, I wanted to be liked, I wanted to be *popular*. I would stare aghast at the screen in these realisations, appalled by my petty schoolyard jealousy, my vanity. The screen may be a window but it is also a mirror.

I loved Karen best, and I loved her straight away. She always managed to say exactly the right thing, and her voice to me was one of pure reason and pure love. I wrote for Karen and read for her responses; I had made her my ideal correspondent. But I loved Karen as much for her perfect punctuation as for her kindness and wisdom: I had fallen in love with her literacy. Because our relationships were comprised entirely of words, I made the mistake of confusing articulateness with goodness, literacy with eloquence. It was often the less literate writers who were able to speak the most clearly. 'I am so depressed all the time I feel like a dead person inside a living body,' wrote Shannon, and I was riveted by the rightness of her phrase—it hit me with all the force of a cliché realised. I had written reams trying to articulate how I felt and there it all was in eight words.

Darlene has gone into premature labour on *Roseanne*. She is in hospital, and her baby is going to die. The whole episode is about the family, mainly the women, coming to terms with the fact of the baby's impending death. I sat with Andrew and Anna through its 24 minutes crying, a continuous stream of water falling from my wide eyes, transfixed by the flickering colours in the little box, thankful, released. I couldn't believe what I was seeing and hearing. I was so grateful to Roseanne for representing us, at last. My heart was opened. This is what is meant by catharsis.

But then the baby lived. It was a miracle—a sitcom miracle. What bitter salt for my wound. 'Wouldn't it be good if shows didn't always have the right ending?' said Anna.

'But can I ask you,' said my psychiatrist in her Indian accent, 'who *is* Roseanne?'

I went to a shrink so she could tell me that what I felt was normal. I spent most of the time entertaining or shocking her with all the stupid things people say. Like 'Don't you want to know what's *really* wrong with you? I mean, the *psychological* reason you can't have children?' Or the standards, 'You weren't ready to have a child', 'Are you over it yet?', or 'Have you thought of adopting?' 'Well, you know,' said Andrew's brother, one, I was to learn, who was incapable of dealing with death, 'infant mortality was commonplace before this century'. Did women in the nineteenth century love their children less because they were more likely to die?

Losing a baby is very different from other kinds of deaths. It is a physical mourning, a bodily grief. One carries about oneself a constant, palpable absence, like wearing an empty knapsack. It is a diminishing experience. It makes you weak, depressive and slightly agoraphobic. And it is terribly lonely. You are ostracised from the world of pregnancy and of motherhood—pregnant women and new mothers are the first to shun you—and you fast learn that it is unwise to discuss your baby or your body with anyone. To do so is to invite them to say the wrong thing. What has happened to you is unimaginable, and so unwittingly people say the most grievous things.

'I'm convinced it's just ignorance,' says Mom09, writing to Shantele,

> I remember when I had no problem getting pregnant and carrying a baby to term. I just assumed that it was just as easy for everyone else. And I admit that I was guilty of saying some pretty ignorant things to people who had a problem pregnancy or couldn't get pregnant. If I had all of their numbers or addresses now, I would call each one of them and apologise for being so insensitive. So I will apologise to you, for them, to try to start making up for all of the times that I was ignorant.

I was so shocked the first time I walked down a street not pregnant and someone bumped into me. Pregnant women are hallowed beings for whom crowds part, cars stop, strangers smile. But just as a pregnant woman is a sacred object, so a mother of a dead child becomes an object of fear, a pariah. She is the embodiment of every pregnant woman's worst phantasms; she is a living death.

Last summer Tessa and I often met to go swimming at the Icebergs. We sat in the sun chatting and looking at all the different shapes of women—the stubby middle-aged Russians, the rake-thin teenagers, the jelly-thighed new mothers—and among everything else we talked about, Tess would tell me about the deliveries she'd done that week and I would tell her about what was happening with the women in my group.

One noon as we were sitting looking out to sea I felt two small hands on my shoulders and heard a little boy say, beseechingly,

Mummy. He had mistaken me for his mother, who also had short dark hair and a black swimming costume. I could feel his wet lips on my ear, and I didn't so much hear as feel the absolute trust and intimacy of his small voice, deep in my body as though from inside a sea shell. For one second I knew what it felt like to be the mother of a living child, to live in the world of motherhood.

RE: The Late SHAPIRO; BABY who passed away on Wed 29/10/1997 (29thTishri 5758).

To erect a single memorial stone as follows:

> Grey granolite [cement composite mixture] headstone/ desk lying flat on the ground and inclined at the back with a FLUSH BELFAST black South African granite panel 14" x 22" x 1" polished face only, edges sawn [unpolished] finish. Including ALL the raised-polished, natural, everlasting letters, the sum of $690.00.

There is a line to be crossed and at a certain point the highly unnatural activity of spending all day writing to people you've never met becomes ordinary. But after spending four or five hours thinking and writing to all the day's correspondents, realising that the day had in fact gone, and that I was quite spent for it, the evanescence of my friends, of our link, would strike me, and I would fend off the thought that our bond was as fragile as the lives of our children, and as random as their deaths. I knew it couldn't last, that our friendships were ephemeral and, quite literally, insubstantial. That which bound us would pass, and we would be drawn back into the cycle of life, some of us with children, some without.

I rarely post nowadays. I don't know anyone in the group any more, as almost all my friends have moved on. Last month Kate gave birth to Krystal Rose, LeeAnn to Trevor and Angie to Tanner Christian. Karen and Carrie are pregnant, Karen courtesy of IVF, Carrie of

Clomid. Shannon has disappeared. I lurk occasionally, but the tone is not so thoughtful, the women seem more cavalier. It took hundreds of thousands of words to get to know my friends, and I don't seem to have the heart to invest in the new crowd. Disconcertingly, a couple of months ago the site hub crashed, and all our archives are now irretrievable.

On the anniversary of my baby's death I went with Tessa to Rookwood. It is such a long drive there that arriving always comes as a small shock. A dog had shat on his grave. I didn't mind; at least it was compostible. The grave is near the curb of a road and the earth in which he is buried is unnatural, full of asphalt and bitumen. Tess had brought some white roses, which she placed over the dog shit.

The day before, Tessa had asked if I wanted her to come with me to the cemetery and I had dallied, not wanting to prevail on her kindness. But then I realised that she wanted to go—he was her baby too.

The only answer to radical loss, said Rabbi Fox at our baby's consecration, is radical love. And there I think of Tess. I stop, stilled by the thought of her great grace and beauty—I can still feel her gentle midwife's hands pressing my abdomen, still see her dear face as she brought my son from me. Out of love, from friendship, Tessa made the worst day of my life the most miraculous thing.

There is a grease-stained fingerprint on the top right-hand corner of page 199 of my Urtext Mozart Sonatas. It is Blake's fingerprint; he had turned the page for me while I was playing and he was eating fish and chips. I think of him sitting beside me every time I play Köchel 333, and I remember how I snapped at him for blemishing the page.

Blake is dead now—he has been dead for fifteen years—and apart from that fingerprint I have an old pyjama top and a gingham shirt he loved. They have not smelled of him for years. I have a few photographs. But I also have a small suitcase of his letters, letters to me. His mother burnt my letters to him, thinking that I didn't want them, that she would preserve our intimacy by destroying them. He died all over again the day she told me she had burnt my letters: it was the end of our conversation.

My baby did write to me, a long black line down the middle of my torso. It has faded now, my linea nigra, been rubbed off; there are crumbly remnants in my belly button. How proud I was of this tattoo—it was his message to me, his love letter. My memorial, my love poem to my dear little baby, is thousands of words floating in cyberspace, everlasting words inaccessible in links that are now lost.

2000s

Suttee (2001)

Alison Croggon

I was the sick one in a forest of icicles
I looked out windows and the stone looked back
eating the morning sun as if it were emeralds
everywhere windows and everywhere flowers burning
everywhere viruses sweating out of the earth

I had no time for their careful measurements
already busy with the swift decays
how brittle these arms reach towards the end of things
talking it so comfortable it's frightening
and these glass screens glaring and a music
strange and intimate like the hum of cars
or jets screaming so high you cannot see them
imagining the sky itself is screaming

no might I say to the demon it is spring
and a child leap from my vulva like a coal
flaming and alive and consuming itself
no I might say it is the afternoon of me
these endless flanks of sand and a single
silhouette where once unsalted
an oakapple wove itself to itself
no I might say it was a wound reopening
like the night which deepens in a locked roc m
a deadly rose seductive and odorous
the red pulse of rain in an empty house
the ghost in the mirror like a cut hand
o lovely lovely violence

whispers the demon the locks are mute
in the planet's hollow children are screaming
they are not my children their lips bleed in my skull
my skin a lace of burns the soft air hurts
yes I would sleep in thy mild arms o black f ower I would
sleep and never wake again

I (2002)

Helen Garner

Last winter I had an unexpected visitor: the man I called Javo in my first novel, *Monkey Grip*, turned up at my front door. He looked fabulous, like a crazy Red Indian, healthy as can be, the father of two kids, and talking like a Buddhist. We stood in my back yard looking at the vegetables and he said, 'Listen, Hels. I used to think *Monkey Grip* was the worst thing that ever happened to me. But now I love it. My only criticism of it is that you should have left in all our real names.'

Shouldn't a *real* writer be writing about something other than herself and her immediate circle? I've been haunted by this question since 1977 when a reviewer of *Monkey Grip* asked irritably what the fuss was about: as far as he could see, all I'd done was publish my diaries. I went round for years after that in a lather of defensiveness: 'it's a *novel*, thank you very much'. But I'm too old to bother with that crap any more. I might as well come clean. I *did* publish my diary. That's *exactly* what I did. I left out what I thought were the boring bits, wrote bridging passages, and changed all the names. It was the best fun I ever had, down there in the domed Reading Room of the State Library of Victoria in 1976, working with a pencil and an exercise book on one of those squeaking silky oak swivel chairs. I'll never be that innocent again.

Why the sneer in 'All she's done is publish her diaries'? It's as if this were cheating. As if it were lazy. As if there were no *work* involved in keeping a diary in the first place: no thinking, no discipline, no creative energy, no focusing or directing of creative energy; no intelligent or artful ordering of material; no choosing of material, for God's sake; no shaping of narrative; no ear for the music of human speech; no portrayal of the physical world; no free movement back and forth in time; no leaping between inner and outer; no examination of motive; no imaginative use of language.

It's as if a diary wrote itself, as if it poured out in a sludgy, involuntary, self-indulgent stream—and also, even more annoyingly, as if the writer of a diary were so entirely *narcissistic*, and in some absurd and untenable fashion believed herself to be so entirely unique, so hermetically enclosed in a bubble of self, that a rigorous account of her own experience could have no possible relevance to, or usefulness for, or offer any pleasure to any other living person on the planet.

What is the 'I' in a diary? There can be no writing without the creation of a persona. In order to write intimately—in order to write *at all*—one has to invent an 'I'. Only a very naive reader would suppose that the 'I' in, for example, the essays and journalism collected in my book *The Feel of Steel* is exactly, precisely and totally identical with the Helen Garner you might see before you, in her purple stockings and sensible shoes.

The word 'invent' here is probably not the right one. It seems to imply something rational, purposeful, clear-headed, conscious. What about 'choose', then? How about this: 'I choose, in the act of writing, aspects of myself that will suit the tale that is wanting me to tell it'?

No. That sounds as if one were confronted with a clear array of possibilities, leaning in a row against a wall all oiled and primed, like rifles.

Choose, like 'invent', is in this context as hubristic as the grandiose political fantasy that one *chooses* one's sexuality. There's something organic in the development, the crystallisation of a persona. I don't understand this process—how I 'do' it, or how it's done to me, or in me, by the demands of my story.

There must be a connection here with the experience that most writers would recognise—that of having to learn to write again for each new book. Between books one passes—or *I* do, at least—through a phase of having *no accumulated competence*, of being once again a complete beginner, helpless, frustrated and dumb. The term 'writer's block' hardly touches the sides. It's a painful state, and it can continue for years. I've been stuck in it since December 1999. Many false dawns have announced themselves in the meantime. Despair is not too strong a word.

But it occurs to me that what I'm doing in this state, perhaps, is waiting for the new persona to crystallise—the one that suits the story, the material, the particular area of darkness I want to go stumbling and fumbling into. I need to find a new 'I' that feels right. I can't rush this process. I can't force it. It's organic, instinctive. If I launch out by force with the wrong persona, I start after about three pages to feel phoney. I get lost. And I waste the freshness of the material.

I'm always surprised when people I know express appalled amazement to me about what they see as my 'self-exposure'. One of my sisters, a nurse, told me that when she read my story 'A Spy in the House of Excrement', about the Thai health spa where one fasted and took enemas twice a day, she wanted to 'pull the screen around me'. But I don't feel exposed—because in this mysterious way I'm trying to describe, the 'I' in the story is never completely *me*.

I'm aware that the persona I create—or that crystallises between me and my story—may not strike the reader quite as I imagine or hope it will. In a piece called 'Regions of Thick-Ribbed Ice', about a trip I took to Antarctica, the 'I' who tells the story is a bruised, aching, unsociable, crabby, purse-lipped, middle-aged, pedantic, recently deceived wife on whom, against all her efforts to remain unmoved, the glory of her surroundings breaks in to bring a sort of redemption.

The piece is republished in *The Feel of Steel*. The reviewer of that book in the Melbourne *Age* (29 September 2001) sees the narrator of this piece as a woman who is 'vain, contemptuous, snobbish, gratingly school-marmish'. (I smile as I report this, but as Bob Dylan sings on his latest album *Love and Theft*: 'I'm not quite as cool or forgiving as I sound.') Be that as it may, such a critique, however galling, calls attention in its clunky way to a deal I have always one-sidedly struck, ever since I started writing helplessly about the intimate—and when I say 'helplessly', I'm thinking of a perceptive remark made by the painter Georges Braque: 'One's style is one's inability to do otherwise.'

The deal is this: if I'm rough on myself, it frees me to be rough on others as well. I stress the unappealing, mean, aggressive, unglamorous aspects of myself as a way of lessening my anxiety about portraying other people as they strike me.

I have learnt, to my cost, that this will not always stand up in court. The intimate involves other people. But where do I end and other people begin? I once went on holiday to Vanuatu. There I saw a row of tall trees across the tops of which a creeper had grown so hungrily and aggressively that it had formed a thick, strangling mat: the trees were no longer individuals, but had become part of a common mass. I found this spectacle strangely repellent. It filled me with horror. But the older I get, and paradoxically the more *hermit-like* I become in the wake of my spectacular failures to be a wife, the more I am obliged by experience to recognise the interdependence of people.

How inextricably we are intertwined! We form each other. We form ourselves in response to each other. It's impossible to write intimately about your own life without revealing something of the people who are close to you. This has always been an ethical problem for me, and it always will be. Scour and scourge my motives as I may, consciousness always lags behind action—sometimes by years. Self-awareness is studded with blind spots. Writing, it seems, like the bringing up of children, can't be done without causing damage.

But I hope that if I can write well enough, rigorously and imaginatively enough, readers will be carried through the superficial levels of perviness and urged into the depths of themselves. I hope that we can meet and know each other there, further down, where each of us connects with every other person who has ever loved or been loved, hurt and been wounded. Because at my age, pushing sixty, I know for sure that there is nothing in my way of experiencing the world, in all its pleasure and ordinariness and suffering, nothing about me as a writer or as a person, that marks me off as forever separate and unique, or disconnects me from the rest. And like everyone else, to twist a little what Yeats wrote in his poem 'The Circus Animals' Desertion': 'I must lie down where all the *stories* start / In the foul rag-and-bone shop of the heart.'

Asylum Elegy (2004)

M.J. Hyland

Depression doesn't run in my family: it crawls on all fours from the bed to the bathroom at 4 a.m.

My father—who spends his life moving between prisons, psychiatric wards and homes for alcoholic men—has been depressed for a very long time. My brother, too. I have depression in common with them, not much else. They are depressed and criminal, and I am sometimes one of these things, but never the other.

I speak to my father once or twice a year, or I speak to the people who look after him: doctors, prison warders and welfare workers. I haven't spoken to my brother—who is awaiting trial again—for eight years.

ANTIDEPRESSANTS AND BANANAS

My father has been taking the same antidepressant for about fifteen years and on this medication he can't eat certain foods, including bananas. He says he never liked them much anyway: 'a horrible fruit'.

I couldn't take Parnate, since I eat bananas every day. There were days—when my depression was at its worst—when bananas were the only food I could eat at all.

Perhaps it was something about the way bananas can be broken into small and manageable parts, the lack of preparation or chewing involved.

Perhaps it was because my mother and stepfather used to buy bananas in a bunch on Saturday and then lock them in their bedroom and ration them: one banana per day, per child.

I remember seeing my mother with a bunch of green bananas in one hand, the keys to the padlock in the other, and as I stood outside her bedroom door, I wondered if keeping bananas behind lock and key was really a sane thing to do.

During the worst of my depression, I was often unable to move, unable to get out of bed, 'too sad to live, too curious to die'.

I don't know who said that. Somebody interviewed by Michael Parkinson once. All I know is that I wrote it down in the diary I kept while I was in Larundel, for one strange night and day in 1994. It was not my first visit there.

THE BIN IN BUNDOORA

I came home from school one summer's day in 1982 and found my father lying on the kitchen floor next to the fridge. He was wearing his pyjama bottoms and a white singlet.

There was an empty packet of Serepax on the floor next to his arm, like a business card: *While you were out, Serepax called by.*

I stood over him and wondered whether he was dead yet. I made Vegemite on toast. When my mother came home from work she said, 'I'm going to call an ambulance.'

I wondered whether talking about calling an ambulance rather than just getting on with the job of calling an ambulance meant that she was thinking the same thing: that we should leave him on the floor to die.

I waited.

'O Mary mother of God,' said my mother over and over again, staring down at his still, non-violent body. My hopes were raised.

'Maybe we should just leave him,' I said, and I think by saying this I blew it. I turned what was a mutual, unexpressed desire into something criminal and premeditated.

'Oh no,' she cried. 'God forgive you! We can't just leave him.'

'Why not?'

'Because he's your father.'

'Oh,' said I. 'I thought he was a fucking hopeless alcoholic.'

The ambulance came, my father was carried away on a stretcher and his stomach was pumped at the Moorabbin Hospital.

'The specialist asked your Da to stand up,' said my mother, 'And when he stood up the specialist punched him in the liver and your Da collasped.'

'Colla*psed*,' I said. 'Not colla*sped*.'

My mother's inability to pronounce any word with more than two syllables concerned me more than my father's suicide attempt.

The specialist sent my father off to Larundel, a psychiatric hospital that has since closed down. Larundel wasn't the first bin my father had stayed in. He'd spent a while in Greswell and before that he'd spent a few nights in lock-ups in Ireland.

He didn't want to go, but since he was so sick that he couldn't eat—even a cup of milky tea went straight through him—he reluctantly packed his little brown suitcase and got into a taxi.

A MANSION WITH COKE MACHINES

By public transport, it took us two hours to travel to Larundel, but we made the journey to visit him every Saturday. I was thirteen years old and used to naught but poverty and chaos. As far as I was concerned, Larundel was a million-dollar mansion set in huge grounds, with Coke machines in the corridors and free food for everybody.

While my mother cried, and pursed her lips, and shook her head, I wandered the wards and loved every bit of what I saw. I would like to live here, I thought. A big, clean, mostly white place, with table-tennis tables.

We sat with my father in the common room, but since he wasn't in the mood for talking—he only talked when he was drunk, and since he loved to talk, he had spent most of his life drunk—we watched the big television in the corner.

'So how are you?' my mother asked my father.

'I hate this madhouse,' he said and we looked, as he did, at the packed suitcase by his feet.

An hour or so before dinnertime, a nurse wheeled a trolley into the middle of the room and the inmates, all of them men in this ward, formed a neat queue to receive their medication.

I liked this queue in the same way I liked the queues for communion in church—expectant people with tongues or hands held out for the small wafer to make them feel better—and I liked it that most of the cure was in the queuing for it.

How I wanted to stand in that line of men and how I admired that trolley! It was waist high and had four layers, and each layer housed hundreds of small white plastic cups, with the names of patients written on them. I stood up to take a closer look and my mother told me to sit.

'Why should I?' I said.

The trolley and its cargo fascinated me; its super world of organisation; its doll-house perfection; its hotel-room-like compartments; the multicoloured pills in those cups parked in neat rows like new cars in a car park.

I'd stolen and swallowed fistfuls of my mother's Valium several times before and knew all about the oblivion promised by these pills. I wanted some.

The nurse called my father's name and he waved her away. I wanted to jump forward and offer to take the pills for him. I wanted to say, 'Let *me* stay here and send him home. He doesn't deserve to be here.'

As well as cleanliness and order, Larundel represented hope and community, and above all else it signified being looked after, being cared for by doctors and nurses, people who knew what they were doing and how to do it. So I paid no attention to the fact that its inmates were mostly miserable and psychotic men with no homes, or homes that no longer welcomed them.

I liked Larundel for its friendly staff, its vending machines, its smell of disinfectant, its closed doors without signs, its chapel, and its thousands of white beds made as tight as tablets, but I couldn't have known that about ten years later I'd be back.

NOT LISTENING TO PROZAC

I was studying law at Melbourne University and for most of the decade since my first visit to Larundel I had found ways to manage, or mask, my ever-worsening depression: alcohol, sedatives, dope, and ever other kind of unhelpful self-medication.

My biggest and most obvious symptom was insomnia. I also suffered from panic attacks—a kind name for a set of symptoms that make sufferers feel like they are dying of a massive coronary. And although I thought I wanted to die, I didn't want to do it by panic attack. And so I sought the help of antidepressants.

A few months later, I was in a taxi on my way to Larundel.

There is nothing inherently wrong with the drugs I had been prescribed—Prozac and Efexor. I know many people who have been saved by them. But they were absolutely the wrong drugs for me. Instead of alleviating my symptoms (hyper-vigilance, sleeplessness, dysphoria and panic) they exacerbated every one.

I sat up through the night, every night, sweating profusely, convinced that I would die. I couldn't eat and couldn't think straight. After one particularly nasty episode of panic I took a fistful of sleeping pills, and when I could feel the approach of 'the anaesthesia from which none come round' I called myself a taxi.

The doctor at St Vincent's called Larundel and booked me a room.

THE CUPBOARD OF CLOTHES

I felt happier as soon as I walked through the doors of my ward. It was 2 a.m.

Being admitted took about an hour. Two doctors and a nurse interviewed me, and then I was shown to my room. It was small and rectangular, neat and clean, and the bed was made like a hospital bed should be.

I had nothing to wear to bed so one of the staff, a friendly fat woman with long red hair, showed me to the clothes cupboard.

'Take anything you'd like out of here,' she said, as she put her hand on my arm. How happy this made me. I loved free things and I especially loved other people's clothes. When somebody lent me a jumper or a pair of gloves on a cold night, I found it nearly impossible to return them. Other people's things were always infinitely better than mine.

I saw a pair of pyjamas I liked the look of, and a pink bra. I took them out and held them up.

'Can I have these?' I asked.

She smiled. 'If you like.'

'Yes please.'

I was, of course, still heavily sedated and slept very well in my narrow hospital bed.

THE BOY WHO STARED AT THE WALL

The next morning seemed to me one of the brightest and gentlest I had seen in a long time. All of what I had loved about Larundel the first time seemed present: its order and size, its vast grounds, free food and white rooms.

After breakfast, and after queuing up for the morning meds trolley, I took my first sober look around.

There was a beautiful boy, dark-haired and long-limbed. He was seventeen at most, perhaps as young as fifteen.

He sat in the big common room in a chair that faced the wall at the end of the room closest to the door. He was the first person I saw when I walked through, on my way outside to the courtyard. I smiled at him as I went by, and felt sure that he would smile back. But he stared at the wall and seemed not to notice me.

I went outside and had my cigarettes. I talked to some of the other patients who stood in a group around enormous ashtrays filled with sand. Most of them were schizophrenics who talked the way I imagine Munchausen's syndrome sufferers might: incessantly, and with relish, about the state of their illness, their medications, and medical procedures.

And they laughed and helped each other out.

I could see the boy who stared at the wall through the glass and I felt awful for him. I went back inside and smiled at him some more. He stared. I quit smiling and sat down by him.

'Hello,' I said.

He stared at the wall.

I felt not sorry for him then, rather, impressed by his capacity to sit so still. I was in awe of his ability to stare so long, so unblinking, so sure of his pain, so utterly unwell, so completely miserable, so out of the world, so totally sore, so far gone.

He was the real thing. He was out of this.

I stood up. 'Good luck,' I said, dumbly. I was an amateur; just passing through. I went to the desk and checked myself out. It was beginning to get dark outside.

POSTSCRIPT

My depression is under control now, and I've been seeing the same, wonderful psychiatrist for seven years. I take an antidepressant, one that treats insomnia particularly well, and I am more up than down, more happy than sad, more good than bad.

I often wonder what happened to the people who lived in Larundel. Where do they go now when they need a community of people a bit like them and some looking after? What happened to the trolleys that delivered their pills and the clothes in that cupboard?

So many babies, so little bathwater.

Transatlantic (2004)

John Tranter

Paris was not a place, it was the event,
and in that event the great writer
wrote about her grand obsession: herself.
Remember that the great writer liked
the evening telephone. The fade of age.

She said, snob strongly and snob often,
that was what she wanted.
If you go to the reading rooms
as a result of smoking the herb of contempt
nothing you read will do you any good.
Why am I talking to you?

We received at least the evening sky
which was hers to inherit; that,
and a few thousand dollars.

My friendships after all, Helene said,
were based on direct emotion.
She did not stifle the great writer,
rather the work of the great writer
stifled others, a known council of vulgarisers.
You are journalists, Helene said,
you are all mechanical men.
Helene would be more inclined to violence, and
these *femmes de ménage* stumbled into
a life filled with permanent anger.

Naturally it is a big explosion,
she yelled. You remember emotions.

The great writer had a mystic in to teach us
mysticism. He was attracted by Janet;
drop dead, Janet said. So he taught
moral tales, how ambition clogs the career.
Discretion is a kind of dilution, courtesy a limp.

O far shore, wrote the voice.

They met at the Luxembourg Gardens and
paperbark in hand, turned to rend
what was left of my love story.
O those dark intellectual comments,
later printed in those Moral Tales.

There were traces in the enormous room
of what had made them.
Just stay here. We spent hours there.
To have lain with a little book.

Oh, drink, bring peace to the flesh.

The Sorcerer's Apprentice (2005)

Stephen Edgar

The cards are dealt.
Tables are scanned in the ephemeris.
Letter by letter round the board are spelt
The promptings of possessive fingertips,
While deep analysis
Draws the invasive fear which grips
Abducted thousands. The altar candles melt.

Who are they all
Who measure magic by the Five of Cups,
Or fancy in the planets' rise and fall
A future clearer than their children's eyes?
The draught which interrupts
The séance, did they realise,
Has deeper secrets than the ghost they call.

Let the sun come
To conflagrate the river's incandescence,
Blazing at dawn like the exordium
Of *Thus Spake Zarathustra*, eponym
Of light—what alien presence,
Or host of the bright seraphim
Can add one candle to that blinding sum?

So here I stand,
Apprentice to an absent sorcerer,
As with a flourish of that wand, my hand,
Each day to conjure up another day

Which will and won't recur,
Which comes on call and gets away,
And multiplies the terms of its command:

Cushions of mist
Suffused with lemon light among the hills,
The good will of the dead who still persist
In dreams, the grass that lifts the pavement's weight,
Breaks it and overspills,
The faces of the compound fate
Around me, the hand that flowers from my fist.

What Lies Beneath (2005)

Larissa Behrendt

In her novel *The Secret River*, Kate Grenville tells the story of a family that moves from England to the new penal colony of New South Wales after the husband is convicted of stealing. At the end of the book, when the family has staked its piece of land and made a small fortune from trade, they build a colonial mansion as a testament to their wealth. Grenville, unlike her fictional family, understands that the land that has brought it such riches was also acquired through an act of stealing. We learn that the foundations upon which the house is built cover the carved stone image of a large fish that was created during ceremonies performed by Aboriginal clans, who had lived in the area for thousands of years but have been pushed away, massacred or have died of illness.

Grenville's symbolism is a striking reminder of the history that lies beneath our modern Australian state and of the ways in which that history has sometimes been deliberately suppressed to give the impression of more noble beginnings.

'Not real ones' and no community

Since the decade of the Royal Commission into Aboriginal Deaths in Custody and the *Bringing Them Home* report, it is harder to argue that Aboriginal people no longer form part of the Australian consciousness. And the predominant telling of history now acknowledges Aboriginal presence—even if we still see arguments between academics and other commentators about how many people were killed on the frontier and even whether there were massacres at all. But how to navigate that relationship has continued to be the question that has been most difficult to answer. This is further compounded by the way in which dominant Australian culture imagines Aboriginal

Australia and the vast chasm between that image and the reality of how Aboriginal people live and relate to each other.

On the eve of the 2000 Olympics hosted in Sydney, the *Sydney Morning Herald* ran the front-page headline: 'Corporate Dreamtime collides with reality' (20 March 2000). The story concerned a Qantas advertising campaign that had used a photograph of an Aboriginal girl and used the slogan 'The Spirit of Australia'. The photographed girl, Carol Green Napangardi, was eighteen years old at the time of the article and she received 20 per cent of the fees paid to the photographer. An accompanying article, 'Now the picture's not so perfect', revealed that the life of Carol Green Napangardi was far from being what the romanticised advertisement might imply. She lived in a mission dormitory at Wirrimanu that she shared with more than a dozen in-laws, her husband, two daughters and ten dogs. Although she received some royalty money from the image, this did nothing to alter the systemic poverty of her community that had suffered problems with diabetes, heart disease and obesity, and had poor access to essential services and few work opportunities.

The controversy wasn't so much that Carol Green Napangardi was being insufficiently paid for her image by corporate Australia but rather, as Linda Burney, then chairwoman of the NSW State Reconciliation Committee, noted: 'These beautiful and glamorous images about indigenous Australia often belie the reality of these people.'

When Australia hosts an international event or seeks to entice overseas visitors, consumers or corporations, it is not shy about using images of Aboriginal people or symbols derived from Aboriginal art and artifacts. One need look no further than the incorporation of a boomerang as part of the official Olympic motif. The unconsidered appropriation of Aboriginal imagery for marketing purposes was not impeded by the actions at the time of the United Nations Committee to Eliminate All Forms of Racial Discrimination, which called into question Australia's record on Indigenous rights and referred to a range of issues, including the *Native Title Amendment Act* of 1998. This highlights the extent to which white corporate Australia is able and prepared to unhook happy images of Indigenous Australia from the politicised environment in which Indigenous people actually live. This invisibility of the real because of a focus on the imagined creates a kind of psychological terra nullius, where, even though Aboriginal people are physically present, they are not seen.

And there are definitely none in the city ...

The psychological terra nullius is particularly a feature of the urban areas in Australia where Indigenous presence is pervasive. There are some tenacious stereotypes about Aboriginal people in urban areas such as Sydney. I am often asked, 'How often do you visit Aboriginal communities?' And I reply, 'Every day, when I go home.' The question reveals the popular misconception that 'real' Aboriginal communities exist only in rural and remote areas. It is a reminder of how invisible our communities are to the people who live and work side-by-side with us. I suspect that this misconception finds its genesis in the once-orthodox view that Australia was peacefully settled, with Aboriginal people simply giving way naturally to a far superior (as the story would be told) technology of British civilisation.

A further glimpse of this trend to ignore and silence Aboriginal Australia can be found in Mark Latham's diaries. Speaking of his electorate of Werriwa, Latham notes changes in its moods relating to various social issues, including reconciliation, and it's telling that his response was to move away from pushing such policies as part of the Labor platform. They weren't, to use his term, vote winners.

There is also a view that those Aboriginal people who live within a metropolis such as Sydney are displaced, and therefore do not have special ties there. This view can persist even if the Aboriginal families concerned have been living there longer than the observer's family. While it is true that an Aboriginal person's traditional land has fundamental importance, it is also true that post-invasion history and experience have created additional layers of memory and significance that relate to other parts of the country.

If I think of my traditional land, the land of the Kamillaroi, the areas of Lightening Ridge, Brewarrina and Coonamble, I think of Redbank Mission where my grandmother was born or of Dungalear station, on the road between Walgett and the Ridge, where the Aborigines Protection Board removed her from her family. I remember our elder, Granny Green (my own grandmother's cousin), taking me and my father across the paddocks and pointing out the spiritual places but also the sites of our more recent history where children were stolen or, as she would tell us in whispers, where massacres had taken place. The 'traditional' and the colonial and the present are all a fluid history connected to place and kin in our culture.

And so too, wherever we have lived in urban areas, there is a newer imprint and history, one that is meaningful and creates a sense of belonging within Aboriginal communities that have formed in urban areas. This is a cultural and political history that is implanted in the area where we now live. I live right next door to what was once Australia Hall, the place where the Aborigines Progressive Association organised the 'Day of Mourning and Protest' in 1938, a key point in political activism, marking the beginning of our civil rights movement. I also think of places such as the Redfern Medical Centre where important community meetings have taken place. Or South Sydney Leagues Club, which attracted young Aboriginal men from across the state, including my uncle, to come to the city and play football. I think of Redfern Park where I heard the then prime minister of Australia, Paul Keating, acknowledge that this is an invaded country.

Another dimension to the cohesiveness of Aboriginal communities in the Sydney area is the tight-knit kinship and family networks that exist there, reinforcing traditional ties. Once a network of clans within the Eora nation, in Sydney now there is a large Aboriginal population (second only to the Northern Territory) that consists of clusters of Aboriginal communities in La Perouse, Redfern, Marrickville, Mount Druitt, Penrith and Cabramatta. Family and kinship networks help tie these separated enclaves together.

One of the consequences of overlooking Indigenous presence and experience is to exclude us from effective participation in civic life, notably social policy-making—whether in areas specifically relating to Aboriginal people themselves or broader collective decisions in areas such as town planning and urban development.

There are some troublemakers …

I am not arguing that Sydney's dominant population thinks there are no Aboriginal people there, but media attention becomes intense only when there are socioeconomic problems or racial tensions, such as the so-called 'Redfern Riots'. It is through these images and stories of youths committing violence, engaging in criminal activity and anti-social, self-destructive behaviour that the Indigenous presence often breaks in to the consciousness of Sydney residents.

Little attention, however, is paid to the vibrant and functional Aboriginal communities throughout the metropolitan area. There is no media coverage of the successful—and rather uneventful—day-to-day lives of Aboriginal people that show participation in a broad range of community activities. We do not see stories about the success of Aboriginal women's legal services, our Indigenous radio service, Gadigal, our child care service, Murawina, or homework centres for our kids after school.

These community-building activities and organisations are hidden by images of out-of-control and violent Aboriginal people who are seen as lawless, without a sense of community responsibility. And through these images, Aboriginal people are seen as a threat to peaceful and cohesive community life within the city. People become fearful of Aboriginal people and see them as a danger to the social fabric rather than as making a contribution to it. These images also reinforce the impression that no cohesive Aboriginal community exists in urban areas, so we once again become invisible.

There does seem to be a greater interest in including Aboriginal people in broader community-building activities involving green spaces within metropolitan or urban centres. For example, in the national parks that surround our city, there are more active initiatives to engage Indigenous people in co-management arrangements, eco-tourism, educational programs about bush tucker and resource management. While not diminishing the importance of this collaboration, it is noticeable that there is a greater willingness to include Aboriginal people in the 'nature' and 'environment' aspects of planning and land management than in the planning of urban spaces and communities. It is hard to ignore the element of 'noble savage' romanticism in this preference for Indigenous involvement with plants, trees and animals over involvement with town planning, infrastructure and housing.

The challenges of recognising Aboriginal urban communities
The romanticism of stagnant stereotypes of Aboriginal people comes at the expense of the social and economic needs of those communities in urban areas. The focus on 'traditional' cultural aspects is one that ignores the interweaving of contemporary Aboriginal nations in such areas. While these newer nations, not descended from the 'traditional owners', have no right to speak for country, they do, as Aboriginal people with distinct post-invasion experiences, have particular socioeconomic problems that often require special services and targeted policies.

Poorer levels of health, shorter life expectancy and higher mortality rates, lower levels of education, higher levels of unemployment, and serious and increasing levels of overrepresentation of Aboriginal people in the criminal justice system are all dimensions of the distinctive needs and circumstances of Aboriginal people in the Sydney area. And it is not surprising that specific services, such as the Aboriginal Medical Service and the Aboriginal Legal Service, were first formed in the Redfern area to address the needs of Aboriginal people living there and as a response to the racism that many felt they were experiencing when they did try to gain access to mainstream services.

Yet under the current national arrangements for Indigenous funding, there is an increasing focus on Aboriginal communities in rural and remote areas. This has already meant a redirection of funds away from urban centres such as Sydney. This focus on remote communities has been driven by the findings of the Commonwealth Grants Commission's 2001 *Report on Indigenous Funding*. The report identified places of relative need and found that they were predominantly in remote areas. No-one would quibble about the needs of people in remote communities, especially those who have seen the level of disadvantage and the social problems up close, but there is just as much need in other Aboriginal communities. Current official estimates of the Aboriginal and Torres Strait Islander population indicate that remote communities make up almost a quarter of the total Indigenous population, but how can those other Indigenous communities in places such as Walgett, Framlingham, Brisbane, Melbourne and Sydney be left out of the account, especially when we consider the poverty in areas such as Mount Druitt and the Redfern Block? It seems an abandonment of responsibility when a government fails to provide adequate resources to address the needs in one type of community because it has a preference for another.

Some of the commissioners themselves were unhappy with the report as a measure of 'need' and thought that it would have been better to analyse disadvantage in terms of absolute need rather than relative need. While the report focused on where the greatest need existed, so that limited resources could be shifted there, some believed that the correct process would have been to assess the needs of everyone in rural and urban communities across Australia. It is perhaps easier, politically, to gather support from the broader Australian community for dealing with problems in Aboriginal communities where the population looks more like 'real' Aborigines, but it is irresponsible—and in the end, bad policy—to ignore the other 76 per cent of the Aboriginal community.

The policy of diverting resources to remote rural communities is also underpinned by the ideology of 'mainstreaming'—the belief that communities in urban areas in particular should be serviced by mainstream organisations. But policies of 'mainstreaming' have generally failed to make any significant difference to lower levels of wealth, health and education, higher levels of unemployment and the poorer standard of housing that Aboriginal communities have experienced. They have also failed to protect Aboriginal cultural heritage, interest in land, and language. And to date they have not enabled Aboriginal people to play the central role in making decisions that have an impact on their families and communities.

The failure of mainstreaming has stemmed from its inability to respond to specific issues that arise in Aboriginal communities in relation to health, education, housing and employment. Mainstream services need to develop special mechanisms and strategies for Aboriginal clients and present resources are insufficient for this. In addition to these challenges, Aboriginal people claim that they are often subjected to racism when dealing with mainstream services. Those claims of racism, particularly in relation to the delivery of health services, were well documented in the Royal Commission into Aboriginal Deaths in Custody and highlighted by the case of Arthur Moffitt, who was found on a train and taken to the police lock-up because he was assumed to be drunk; a diabetic, he was actually suffering from a hyperglycaemic episode and died in custody.

In current mainstreaming policy the focus on projects rather than programs means that policy-makers are primarily engaged with the delivery of project funding rather than developmental programs that invest in people—they focus on short-term outcomes, not long-term need, and they address symptoms, not causes. The focus on projects fits easily within budget cycles, whereas longer-term structural programs require funding commitments over a longer period. The focus on project funding means that organisations are unsure about their future viability. Such policies focus on achievements within the political cycle that will create good news stories and do not look beyond the immediate future. They equate accountability with accounting, progress with funds disbursement. The focus is on money without a complementary focus on social consequences.

This policy environment generates anxiety within community organisations, which become focused on ensuring continued funding (which means activity reporting, accounting, submissions) at the expense of a focus on their core function. Funding of organisations frequently occurs at the level deemed to be required at that particular moment, and while this is understandable when resources are limited and demand is great, it means in effect that organisations are expected to achieve their stated goals with no guarantee of adequate and ongoing funding.

Despite the way parts of the electorate have been seduced by the notions of 'shared responsibility' and 'mutual obligation' in relation to welfare recipients generally and Aboriginal people in particular, there are certain responsibilities that government cannot abrogate. One of those is basic health services. In a report commissioned by the Australian Medical Association, Access Economics estimated that basic Indigenous health care was underfunded by $750 million, despite budget surpluses that have run to the billions. With such fundamental levels of underfunding, it is not surprising that socio-economic problems fail to be alleviated and cycles of poverty persist.

Under the current federal arrangements and policy directions, urban Aboriginal communities can anticipate decreases in funding and a push towards the use of mainstream services. There are, however, two mechanisms that could be employed to redress this socio-economic disparity.

The first involves home-ownership schemes. These have been mooted for communal land but there are questions about their viability and effectiveness in places where there is no competitive housing market. The Sydney property market does not have these limitations and could be used as a means to create intergenerational wealth.

The second mechanism involves claims under the NSW Aboriginal Land Rights Act. This legislation provides for claims over certain areas of crown land, and successful claims can generate wealth for Aboriginal communities.

An imagined future

How would things be different if Aboriginal people were included in the planning process in a more meaningful way? Such 'cultural' recognition involves acknowledging coexistence. This recognition manifests itself in acknowledgement of country, respecting the knowledge of elders, using Aboriginal placenames and erecting monuments that acknowledge the post-invasion history of Aboriginal people. Progress on reconciliation has taken place most actively at the local level and many local governments have been exploring these kinds of initiatives as part of an attempt to rethink sharing the country. The flying of Aboriginal flags on municipal buildings represents another attempt to acknowledge this presence and history. Public spaces and art have also been used as ways of recognising shared history and coexistence.

In addition to this, it would be important to include Aboriginal cultural values, values that permeate our contemporary communities, in urban planning processes. At present, plans tend to focus on infrastructure, particularly roads and transport. There are references to public spaces and the environment, the importance of gaining access to employment opportunities and the recognition of diverse modes of housing. But the emphasis tends to be on the bureaucratic rhetoric of economic rationalism rather than on the importance of strengthening community ties and facilitating community obligations, especially to children and to elders.

The values of social responsibility, reciprocity and interaction, of community, kinship and the importance of place, are inherent in Aboriginal culture, while not unique to Aborigines. (Many other demographic groups within Sydney would claim that the importance of family and community was at the heart of their cultural practices.) What increased Aboriginal participation in social policy-making can do is to underline and reinforce the importance of those principles in building a future for all Australians. Such principles are also an abiding reminder of the deeper foundations of our past—the layers beneath the colonial mansion.

Before the Big Bang (2006)

Clinton Walker

One of the great conceits of the rock generation is that, as John Lennon once put it, 'Before Elvis, there was nothing.' But it was never as simple as that. American cultural historians now recognise that rock'n'roll was a form that evolved after the Second World War in an explosive confluence of technology with economic and social imperatives. Even in isolated Australia, rock'n'roll didn't emerge from a vacuum. Like the rest of the world, we had been copping American music long before rock'n'roll came along, and Australian rock'n'roll began in much the same way the Beatles did in Liverpool, picking up on American records and putting them through a local cipher. But how may we identify the first Australian rock'n'roll record?

Pre-rock'n'roll popular music in Australia after the Second World War is a historical no-man's land. Both our jazz and country music histories take a fairly purist view of their genres, disregarding the edges where they may stray or cross over into the dreaded shallow waters of commercialisation. Again, that's why, with postmodern disdain for 'authenticity', I'm trying to find out how a transition was made, to plot the way existing local traditions fed into the birth of rock'n'roll in this country, to locate the 'tipping point'.

There's no doubt that Johnny O'Keefe was the Big Bang of Australian rock'n'roll. After Bill Haley's huge hit with 'Rock around the Clock' in 1955–56, JOK was the first local act capable of shar- ing a stage with such American invaders. In January 1958, when he recorded 'The Wild One', the claim could reasonably be made that he'd cut the first truly great and certainly the first hit Australian rock'n'roll record. 'The Wild One' is one of the few Australian tracks of its era that has survived as a classic, despite or perhaps because of the fact it was one of the few local compositions of the era. But the road that led to 'The Wild One' is dotted with proto-rock'n'roll records.

By 1956, when rock'n'roll had the name—by which time it was also already widely tipped to die—Australian record companies were jumping on the fad. A couple of records, 78-rpm singles, released in late 1955–early 1956, have vied for the title of Australia's first rock'n'roll waxing: Vic Sabrino's single, a version of 'Rock around the Clock' coupled with 'Magic of Love', and Richard Gray's versions of Chuck Berry's 'Mabellene' (sic) and Fats Domino's 'Ain't that a Shame'.

Yet Les Welch had been releasing records since the 1940s that mark him out as Australia's great anticipator of rock'n'roll. Might it not be reasonable to posit some of his last great records as our first rock'n'roll records? Or even some of his early R&B records? Welch is the Invisible Man of Australian music history. A once-huge star and industry innovator, the virtual godfather of the entire modern Australian record business, Welch is still alive and living in Sydney but remains a frustrating enigma.

Before and after the war, EMI had a virtual monopoly on the recording industry in Australia. But with the influx of even more things American during the war—including, especially, music and fashion—and with the economic and baby booms after the war, everything began to change. In the wake of prewar stars such as Tex Morton, EMI recorded more hillbillies, notably Slim Dusty. It even started recording 'hot' jazz.

But in the 1950s, just as Holden's monopoly of the car market would be broken in the 1960s, EMI's music monopoly was broken. The company's complacency allowed new operators an opening. After EMI let its local US Decca option on 'Rock around the Clock' lapse in 1955, Festival Records' co-founder and musical director, none other than Les Welch, pounced on the record. In the fifteen years from the end of the war to 1960, Australia was colonised by foreign majors such as Philips (later PolyGram, now Universal), CBS (now

Sony) and RCA (later BMG, now merged with Sony); and also it spawned several regional independent labels, such as the Australian Record Company (ARC), Festival, Astor and W&G. And it was these labels—everybody but EMI!—that fostered early rock'n'roll.

Off the back of local rock'n'roll, Festival would become 'the Australian major' (acquired by Rupert Murdoch in 1960 and only recently, following his purchase of Michael Gudinski's Mushroom, sold to Warners). Festival was formed at the end of 1952 after Les Welch left the Australian Record Company looking for new opportunities. ARC had been founded by George Aitken in Sydney in 1948, after the model of successful new US independent Capitol, home to Nat King Cole and Frank Sinatra. ARC divided to conquer with two distinct labels, Rodeo for country music and Pacific, under the direction of Les Welch, for pop and jazz.

Like other, mostly modern, Sydney jazzmen such as Charlie Munro, Don Burrows and Wally Norman, Welch began by playing (underage) for US servicemen during the war, largely as a solo boogie-woogie pianist. Welch's first formal release under his own name was 'Elevator Boogie Blues/Cigareets and Whusky and Wild Wild Women', which he recorded with a full band for the short-lived Tempo label in 1949. Recognised at the time (October 1949) by *Music Maker* as an 'exceptionally interesting disc', *Elevator Boogie Blues* was a landmark recording that broke all Australian sales records. It was a cover of Mabel Scott's US R&B hit on one side and a Sons of the Pioneers country and western hit on the other. Although he was still billed as our 'King of Swing' as late as 1948, Welch was taking Australian music somewhere new with *Elevator Boogie Blues*. If one thing hadn't changed since the war, it was that people still wanted to dance. That's why trad jazz enjoyed such a boom in Australia in the late forties and early fifties—because it was all about dancing. *Elevator Boogie Blues* catered to that need, but with a much more modern, urban edge than, say, the trad jazz of the period. This was the new 'rhythm' style as it was then called, jump blues/R&B basically, and it was music for a new, young audience.

In 1950, Welch was effectively head-hunted by the newly formed ARC. There, with the Pacific label, he set up a virtual hit factory turning out Australian cover versions of American hits that were unavailable in this country, owing to EMI's failure to take up its local licence options. With the help of house arranger Wally Norman and often in league with singer–drummer Larry Stellar, Welch recorded smooth commercial sides such as 'Mona Lisa', 'Rosetta', 'My Foolish Heart' and 'Lucky Old Sun', novelty songs ('I've Got a Lovely Bunch of Coconuts'), even modern jazz ('Caravan'). He also supervised the sessions of singers such as Edwin Duff, who was a teen idol in his own right and who, like Johnnie Ray, with his great flamboyance, helped build the bridge between Sinatra and rock'n'roll. But best were the rhythm records Welch released under his own name: 'A Little Further Down the Road Apiece', 'Jungle Jive', 'Saturday Night Fish Fry', 'Dupree Blues', 'Castle Rock' and 'Hambone'. 'Then on the B-side', recalled Wally Norman, 'they'd put a jam or a local composition that let them blow off'—something like 'Kings Cross Boogie', 'Pacific Boogie Woogie' or 'Rockin' Boogie'.

In 1952, when ARC picked up Capitol's local licence (thus a source of the *original* hits), Welch left the company to help form Festival Records; he was replaced at ARC by public relations man, French bandleader Red Perksey. The first Festival release was Welch's version of the US hit 'Meet Mr. Callaghan', a 78 on the Manhattan label. More pertinent perhaps was a subsequent release, Welch's *Tempos de Barrelhouse*, the first 10-inch 33-rpm album made in Australia. Released at the end of 1952, the album had a foot in both the trad and rhythm camps, with tracks such as 'St Louis Blues' and 'Snatch and Grab It.'

Until 1954, Welch continued to churn out hits for Festival. Early in 1955 he released an EP called *Saturday Night Fish Fry* that included his second version of the title track (a Louis Jordan jump blues original), plus his second version of trad standard 'Darktown Strutters Ball', this time with the legendary Norm Erskine on vocals. With his Dixie Six, he even cut a trad version of Hank Williams' proto-rockabilly 'Jambalaya', which goes to show how blurred the genre boundaries could become.

Alan Dale, a young band singer who would switch over to rock'n'roll about the same time as his friend Johnny O'Keefe, recalls:

> Les Welch had a record out called 'Saturday Night Fish Fry', which was actually a twelve bar blues song, which was a forerunner of rock'n'roll. You could play that now and say it was a rock'n'roll record, it was blues and let's face it, that's what rock'n'roll was.

In similar vein, Wally Norman has observed:

> When rock'n'roll hit, of course not many people realised it is based mainly on old blues chords. The first rock'n'roll musicians were people who'd heard the jazz and blues and R&B and they would improvise on these chords. The kids of the time—I'm talking about the early fifties now—they appreciated the strong beat in rock'n'roll, which is a similar type of beat to the old traditional jazz. Dixieland jazz had a very, very strong beat.

The year 1955 began with a Lee Gordon–promoted Australian tour by Frank Sinatra, the biggest singing star in the known universe. But by the end of the year Sinatra was old hat, and the worldwide musical landscape irrevocably different.

In July, premiere Australian screenings of 'juvenile delinquent movie' *Blackboard Jungle*, which sported Bill Haley's 'Rock around the Clock' as its theme song, caused near-riots. The song itself had been out in the United States for more than a year on Decca Records, but EMI Australia, which held the local licence option, had passed on it. After Les Welch left, Festival released it as one of its first singles in the new 7-inch 45-rpm vinyl format. The 10-inch 78 single-play would soon be dead.

The following month, around the time promoter Bill MacColl put on a rock'n'roll show at Leichardt Stadium featuring Welch, Monte Richardson, the Four Brothers and Norm Erskine, the *Sun-Herald* in Sydney ran a story headlined 'Rock and roll is here now'. The story quoted Welch, who asserted that rock'n'roll was 'the purest form of jazz—the real jazz. Here in Australia it will be the young person's music. It is something new to them. Actually it is nothing new—we have been recording and playing rock and roll for the past twelve years. For me, it is the only music'

The newly arrived multinationals and even EMI dabbled in rock'n'roll, but were soon discouraged. ARC had by now been bought out by US company CBS, and its new label Coronet wouldn't touch rock'n'roll. Les Welch's glory days were numbered too. Festival had taken on a new sales manager, Ken Taylor, who would soon replace Welch as the company's A&R manager.

Dutch major Philips, under the musical direction of Englishman Gaby Rogers, started recording local, mainly country artists in 1954. It was probably the first label to try to cash in on rock'n'roll with a waxing by Richard Gray, 'Mabellene/Ain't That a Shame'. Backed by Rogers' band with the Four Brothers' vocal backing, Gray was a ballad singer unsuited to Chuck Berry and/or Fats Domino, and even *Tempo* magazine could see, 'as both sides are slanted towards R&B style, the orchestra lacks the exuberance and impetus that this type of music needs to be convincing'.

Much more convincing were a single called 'End of the Affair' by Nellie Small and Vic Sabrino's version of 'Rock around the Clock'. Small was fittingly pintsized, an Australian-born Jamaican whose schtick was that she dressed and generally presented as a man, off-stage as well as on. She sang with trad jazz outfits such as the Port Jackson Jazz Band and Graeme Bell's band. Ken Taylor, before he joined Festival and was still working freelance, could see some potential. He co-wrote 'End of the Affair' with a moonlighting Red Perksey and produced the session with Trevor Jones' orchestra. Released on the Mercury label through Astor, it became, at least according to

Taylor in his memoir *Rock Generation*, 'a minor rhythm-and-blues hit with a heavy rock'n'roll accent'.

Vic Sabrino is yet another elusive figure. 'Sabrino' in the first place, was merely a stage name for George Assang, a Torres Strait Islander who was regarded by many as the only man in Australia in the 1950s who could really sing the blues, which he did with bands such as Graeme Bell's. Assang was taken under the wing of Red Perksey, at Pacific Records, and Perksey straight away changed his name, presumably because it was felt a mixed-blood Asian blackfella had less chance of making it than some would-be Italian stallion à la Dean Martin. Perksey's arrangement of Sabrino's debut version of 'Rock around the Clock' is better than stiff, and even features a fairly honking sax solo, but it's Sabrino's deeply hued vocals that lift the track.

Probably the best of all these 1955 recordings were the four tracks Les Welch cut with Mabel Scott when she was on tour in Australia. It was a sort of full circle for Welch, since his 1949 debut 'Elevator Boogie Blues' was a Mabel Scott cover—and the two Festival singles that resulted stand as his virtual swan song.

Ever the opportunist, when he appeared at Bill MacColl's Leichardt show in August 1955, Welch was by now Australia's king of rock'n'roll: the five numbers he performed that night were 'Rock around the Clock', 'Mabel's Blues', 'Elevator Boogie Blues', 'Rain or Shine' and 'Bucket's Got a Hole in It'.

When Mabel Scott was in Sydney the following month as part of the Harlem Blackbirds all-Negro revue, Welch went down to the Palladium Theatre to record with her. They waxed four tracks: I Wanna Be Loved, Loved, Loved', 'Just the Way You Are', 'Boogie Woogie Santa Claus' and 'Mabel's Blues'. In a way these tracks were a throwback to unabashed pre-rock'n'roll R&B, and as such, with great performances by both band and vocalist, they are lost treasures—raucous, joyful and reverberant. 'Boogie Woogie Santa Claus' still rates as one of the best Christmas songs of all.

But for Les Welch, these tracks were the beginning of the end, and rock'n'roll in Australia, which Welch had done so much to pave the way for, would grow without him.

By 1956, with Elvis having hit now too, the rush was really on. Vic Sabrino released a second single; Frankie Davidson and the Schneider Sisters entered the fray with creditable efforts; while other acts such as Frank Crisarfi, Ray Melton and Peter McLean, even Jimmy Little and Ned Kelly, all pushed the boundaries.

Rock'n'roll was so entrenched, despite continuing predictions of its imminent demise, that it was already being co-opted. No less than three local versions of the Patti Page hit 'Rock'n'Roll Waltz' were released in 1956: one of which was by Les Welch, somewhat fittingly his last release for Festival.

Vic Sabrino's second Pacific release was probably better than his first, he and Perksey getting more into the rock groove. But an Elvis twofer—'Blue Suede Shoes/Heartbreak Hotel'—was a bit too obvious for real rock'n'roll, and Sabrino a bit smooth.

Aboriginal country crooner Jimmy Little merits a mention because his earliest releases for EMI label Regal-Zonophone, songs such as 'Sweet Mama', had a rockabilly lilt to them. Similarly, Ned Kelly was a would-be rockabilly rebel, although he remains almost a phantom compared to Jimmy Little, who today is the grand patriarch of black Australian music. Kelly was much more an American-style honky tonk singer than a bush balladeer, and it was this plus his volatility that saw him almost run out of the business. Arriving in Sydney from Parkes, the former shearer and Hank Williams acolyte released four tracks through Prestophone in 1956: 'I Can't Help It/Everybody's Lonesome' and 'They'll Never Take Her Love from Me/Moanin' the Blues'. This sort of hillbilly boogie was but one step short of rock'n'roll.

The record that really saw country take the obvious leap was the Schneider Sisters' Magnasound EP *Rock'n'Roll with the Schneider*

Sisters. Mary and Rita Schneider were a hillbilly duo who had specialised in comedy and yodelling. 'Country music with a backbeat' was how Col Joye described their new exuberant brand of rockabilly, 'which became rock'n'roll, which was an extension of jive, which was an extension of the Black Bottom, all the way back to the Charleston and so forth'.

The 1956 recording that is at least as good as any other is Frankie Davidson's version of Freddie Bell and the Bellboys' 'Rock A-Beatin' Boogie'. Davidson, like Vic Sabrino or Edwin Duff or Alan Dale, was a band singer, whose regular gig in Melbourne was at the Ziegfield Palais, where the house band was led by Max Bostock. In early 1956, he went into the studio with Bostock: 'They put down three tracks,' he recalled, 'and they said, "Why don't we try a rock'n'roll track?" and we weren't allowed to do "Rock around the Clock", so we got a copy of "Rock A-Beatin' Boogie"'. The track was included on an EP on the Danceland label called *Dancing at the Ziegfield Palais, Volume Two*. 'It wasn't done with a rock'n'roll band, it was done with a ballroom orchestra as such, but it still had the rock beat.' Davidson followed this up later in the year with a version of Bill Haley's 'See You Later, Alligator', which was included on the Danceland EP *Rock and Roll with Frank Davidson*; Bostock's band was here billed as the Rockets.

By 1957, the challenge was on to find or create Australia's first fair dinkum rock star. Les Welch cut a few tracks for the Prestige label, but before long, with television now in the offing, he would join Channel 7 as its musical director, not to release another record till the early 1970s. Ken Taylor lured Vic Sabrino over to Festival from Pacific before he was virtually blackmailed into giving Johnny O'Keefe a contract, and after that, nothing was the same again. Sabrino recorded a number of singles for Festival but wouldn't have a hit, nor come very close to real rock'n'roll.

The lasting breakthrough of 1957 belonged to O'Keefe, of course. When in October Bill MacColl staged a show at Manly called Jazzorama, featuring O'Keefe, Les Welch, Col Joye and trad jazz outfit the Ray Price Trio, it marked a changing of the guard: O'Keefe would lead the way for all the other first-generation Australian rockers, including Col Joye.

Like Vic Sabrino or Alan Dale, or Edwin Duff, O'Keefe started out as a band singer, essentially a Johnnie Ray impersonator, in which role he was making such headway that in November 1955 he played the support spot on an Australian tour by Mel Tormé. But even as he was taken under the wing of prominent bandleader Gus Merzi, he was already torn, because by then he had heard Bill Haley and been blown away.

During 1956 O'Keefe wrestled with trying to move in this new direction, to shake off the Johnnie Ray songs, and this he did when he hooked up with US émigré sax-man Dave Owens and formed the Dee Jays. It proved to be the key: O'Keefe was the first with a *band*. If you wanna rock, you gotta get with the beat.

Dave Owens was already assembling a jazz band with an R&B edge in Sydney before O'Keefe came along. Owens had arrived in Sydney from the US after meeting Jack Brokensha and his Australian Jazz Quintet in Detroit. As the Blue Boys, Owens led some sessions with Vic Sabrino. But Sabrino was a shrinking violet next to O'Keefe.

When Bill Haley toured in January 1957, O'Keefe managed to get backstage at the Sydney Stadium and even obtained a song from Haley. It was this song, 'Hit the Wrong Note, Billy Goat', that convinced Festival to sign O'Keefe and would become his first single. In February 1957, after his debut at the Trocadero, JOK and the Dee Jays launched their own regular dance at Stone's in Coogee. When JOK appeared at Brisbane Town Hall with the band, he was now billed as 'Australia's King of Rock'n'Roll'. The Dee Jays opened their sets with 'Blues by Five', by Miles Davis.

John Greenan, who left Ricky Miller's Brothers to join the Dee Jays, recalls:

> Dave was the brains behind the band because he knew black music; he was a great jazz soloist. Dave could really get in and play the R&B–rock'n'roll sound that was really convincing, and we hadn't had that here. Johnny really took to that; he was sort of into jazz but he knew rock was going to do it, and so Dave was a great help to him. There was this marriage of convenience.

In June 1957 O'Keefe and the Dee Jays went into the Prestophone studios with producer Robert Iredale and recorded 'Billy Goat', with a Dave Owens composition ('The Chicken Song') for the B-side. It wasn't great, or a hit, but still O'Keefe, with his usual larrikin front, managed to convince Lee Gordon to put him on the bottom of the bill of October's Little Richard tour. O'Keefe's second single, 'Am I Blue?/Love Letters in the Sand', was a stiff he quickly disowned. The kids didn't want to hear ballads. O'Keefe knew that they wanted to rock, R-O-C-K: the search was on for the Song.

Greenan observes:

> One night we played a dance in Newtown, a place called Mawson's. We were playing upstairs, not a big hall and it had a balcony which overlooked the square where all the trams used to run in Newtown. There was an Italian wedding going on downstairs. Halfway through the night, all of a sudden, our dance clears out, the kids are all gone, and I'm saying, 'What's wrong? Our music's not that bad!' So we went to the balcony and looked out and there's this huge brawl. Naval police, civil police and they're all biffing up and we found out what went on: Somebody upset one of the Italian people at the wedding and then the kids all got involved and there was this massive brawl. They cleaned

it up. The dance ended, we didn't finish it, and Dave and I went back to listen to some Miles Davis and we had a couple of bourbon and cokes to sort ourselves out and Dave was very sardonic, he had this sense of humour, and he said, 'Hey man, what are we doing with all these kids? You know, we're corrupting them!' So after a couple more bourbon and cokes and a bit more Miles Davis and John Coltrane, we started writing these words down. It was as simple as that. It was quick. We both contributed and had all this stuff in another two hours, about four o'clock in the morning. We had a recording session I think two days later with Johnny at Festival down at Pyrmont. We took it in and ... John said, 'Gee I like this Wild One stuff, you know—what's the chord progression?' I don't think Dave and I had even discussed it. Oh, it's 12-bar blues, we said. So we there and then did a head arrangement. We used to do a lot of head arrangements on the spot. O'Keefe loved it and we recorded it on the spot. Festival released it and it was his first hit.

'The Wild One' wasn't released as a single, but rather as one of four tracks on the EP *Shakin' at the Stadium* (studio recordings with applause grafted on so as to sound live)—though it soon stood out, not least as an original composition alongside covers 'Ain't That a Shame', 'Silhouettes' and 'Little Bitty Pretty One'. The song was given a boost when O'Keefe appeared on Lee Gordon's Buddy Holly–Jerry Lee Lewis Big Show tour of January 1958, and by March it had hit a high of number 26 on the newly formed Australian charts.

O'Keefe was now poised to become a star of a magnitude and type never before seen in Australia. EMI inexplicably let Johnny Rebb go after one single—the classic original 'Rebel Rock'—and he went on to significant success (if no more great records) on Lee Gordon's boutique label at Festival, Leedon Records. Col Joye didn't hit till 1959 either, with 'Bye Bye Baby', written by local DJ John Burles. The Joys Boys' sound was a soft, gentle rockabilly one, like Digby

Richards' to follow. After O'Keefe, early Australian rock'n'roll tended to be much more Nashville than New Orleans.

Still, jazz continued to enrich emerging Australian rock: pianist Mike Nock would do a stint in the Dee Jays; John Sangster, Graeme Lyall and Stewie Spears all played rock in Melbourne; drummer Spears and former Dee Jay Bob Bertles would ultimately unite to make Max Merritt's late sixties–early seventies Meteors one of the world's great white soul bands.

As for Alan Dale, he was the ultimate bridesmaid. After getting the brush-off from Ken Taylor, he was called in, too late, by EMI. EMI let him debut, in 1959, with an original composition, 'Kangaroo Hop', but Australia would have to wait a few years yet for its own dance craze, the Stomp. For his second single Dale covered two titles from the Chess Records catalogue that EMI itself refused to release in Australia—Chuck Berry's 'Back in the USA' and Bo Diddley's 'Crackin' Up'. But by then even Slim Dusty was jumping on the 'Pub Rock' bandwagon. Barry Crocker was making his vinyl debut as a 'rocker'. Elvis was in the army and Buddy Holly was dead.

O'Keefe died in 1978, a year after Elvis. Nothing else he did, or that any other Australian rocker of the first wave did, has lasted or travelled quite like 'The Wild One'. Both Buddy Holly and Jerry Lee Lewis recorded versions of the song almost immediately upon their return to the United States in February 1958, although both would trail O'Keefe's own US release of it, in May of that year. The song was retitled 'Real Wild Child' in the United States to avoid confusion with the Marlon Brando movie and at that time wasn't a hit for anyone there. But it wouldn't die, and has since become a signature and a standard. It's been about the only real hit single Iggy Pop has ever had.

At the Olympics: Handball (2007)

Martin Langford

Overweight and bony-jawed, she cowers,
one step at a time, up the tiers of the Dome. Someone
has got her to come here—her mother perhaps:
They won't come again in your time! The teams flex,
and pepper the goalies in warm-up: high fives,
and clatter, and edge. But what draws your gaze
is the way that her whole body pleads,
in its twisted withdrawal, for the seat she can't find.
She clutches the handrail for comfort. She searches
without looking up. Such hopeful gestures:
the Def Leppard T-shirt, the limp knot of lace in her hair.
She is maybe nineteen, maybe more. But you know
when the first chance arises—some drunkard,
some brother's mad mate—she will pray to hold on:
her bed like a plain in the dark
where there are no kind choices.
                    What horror
have we laid down here: when a girl's need
first leans like a bud towards sun—and the one thing
that happens is judgement—the great stone
that lies on our kind like the distance to God?
                    How did we get to the point
where it's cruel and absurd to imagine a lover:
someone whose hand turns her head in delight
and in awe at her presence here too:
smoothing aside all she's learnt of the old prohibitions—
wonder, attentiveness, bubbling, upwelling—
like the pooling of permission, of forgiveness?

Italics Mine (2007)

Peter Rose

Go down to her now, the one who is calling you.
Go down and bury her in air.
The voyage must be solitary and ashed,
the road blatant as a song.
By fiat they open it for you
despite the wrongness of the hour.
Note the frank and unavailing lines,
sinuous as an athlete, a syllogism.
Speak to no-one on the way
lest you linger or succumb—
though what is there to entertain but frost?
It's over now: the lullaby, the filial song.
Acute and more terrible is the mortuary of self,
communing with one long graphic
and shambolic, a ruin of herself, a travesty,
darting plaints at the ticking world—
yet proud and weirdly tenable,
the folds of self that constitute and call.
Or that other, that married past.
Let him be the one to solace and recall—
those amplitudes, those everythings.
Going down to her now, going down to bury her.

Caesarea (2007–08)

Dorothy Porter

The Mediterranean lifts
its barnacled blue arm
and throws you
a Roman coin.

It isn't beautiful.
Neither are you.
But you pray
its sea-roughed emperor
will somehow benignly
see you through.

The gold-melt moon.
The aroma of gritty six a.m.
Turkish coffee.
Harsh warm Hebrew
pounding the air
like a confounding family
squabble.
The marooned marble column
on which you dry
your shabby old towel.

This glittering port city.
A sophisticated paradise.
Where Pontius Pilate thirsted
for the humanity
of face-saving lies.

You are only eighteen.
But thousands of years
of brackish biblical history
sweep into you
and catch
like a thousand sharp
glass beads.

Sometimes a new place
has the ferocity of a gale
ripping the calm
off a safe harbour
making the drowned bells peel
Hallelujah
for all your future
false prophets
and glorious. glorious.
lost gods.

Chagall's Wife (2008)

Abigail Ulman

I had never before bumped into a teacher on the weekend. But there he was, sitting at the counter in the window, and I slowed down to take it all in: the face that looked more relaxed than it usually did, the late breakfast in front of him, the hardcover book in his hand with the library tag on its spine. Through the glass I saw him slide something off his fork with his mouth. I felt his eyes land on me the second I took mine off him. I drew in a breath and sauntered in.

I took a seat next to the wall and sipped my juice through a straw, flipping through every page of a magazine without taking my eyes off his back. Dressed down for the weekend, he was wearing a pair of faded black jeans and a khaki jacket, and his dark hair, usually as neat and orderly as the jars that lined his desk, was ruffled on one side as though he hadn't even checked it before heading out that morning.

When the waitress came to collect his plate, I saw her brush her arm against his as she reached over him, and he looked up and smiled and said something before going back to his book.

Under the fluorescent lights in the toilets I rubbed some gloss into my lips. I yanked my hair out of its ponytail, ran my fingers through it, and arranged it over my shoulders. it was dirty blonde, and dirty. I tied it back up. My jeans were good and new and tight but the grey hoody that showed a stripe of stomach kept going from daggy to sexy and back again. I narrowed my eyes at my reflection. Whatever you do, I told myself, don't mention tampons.

'Mr Ackerman.'

'Sascha, hello.'

'I saw you earlier, when I walked in.'

'Ah, yes.'

'You saw me, too. Why didn't you say hi?'

'I don't know. I suppose I thought you might have better things to do on a Saturday than chat to your daggy old science teacher.'

'You're not daggy.' I lap-danced my eyes over his weekend stubble, the grey T-shirt, his right hand, which was tugging at the leather band of his wristwatch. 'What's that you're drinking?'

'An affogato.'

'What? Like the vegetable?'

'It's a coffee drink. Kind of like a spider for grown-ups.'

'I see.' I leaned one hand on my hip and sucked my bottom lip under the top one until it disappeared. Mr Ackerman looked down to the floor, where one of my runners was standing firmly on top of the other. Then he blinked around the room, at the smattering of people reading newspapers or quietly chatting to each other, and back at me.

'Would you like to try one?'

I perched on the stool next to his and leaned my elbows in front of me. We kept our eyes on the street. It was early afternoon in the middle of autumn, and the sun was bright but stingy with its warmth. A woman walked past pushing an empty baby pram; she was talking on her mobile phone. Our silence was long and expectant, like the minutes between the snooze button and the return of the alarm.

'So,' I spat out. 'Sorry about the tampons.'

'Oh, don't worry about that,' he said. 'You've done your time.'

Every year, since year seven, a nurse had come to science class to talk about periods and menstruation. We were never warned beforehand; it was always sprung on us at the beginning of the lesson. They'd schedule it for first term so the weather was still warm enough for the boys to go play sport with Mr Ackerman on the oval, while the girls were forced to sit again through the same embarrassing question time; the same video with the same girls wearing eighties hairstyles and wardrobes, back when it was really the eighties and before it was cool again.

This year when the boys returned after the talk, Sam Kinley and Sam Stewart had snatched my box of complimentary Tampax off my desk, and I was too embarrassed to ask for it back. While Mr Ackerman was out saying goodbye to the period lady, the boys had taken the tampons out and wet them under the tap, and then thrown them up at the ceiling where they'd stuck; hanging down above us for the rest of the lesson like the stalactites we'd learnt about the year before.

Later that afternoon, the tampons had dried up and started dropping one by one onto the heads and desks of Mr Ackerman and his year seven students. I wished I could have seen it. We were halfway through English class, and the boys were excused and the girls told to produce their tampon boxes right then and there. Of course, I was the only one who didn't have mine so I got dragged to Mr Ackerman's office, where I stood in front of him and told him with a straight face that I had got my period that day and had used them all up already.

'All of them?' he'd asked.

'Two at a time,' I'd said.

Unfortunately for me, Miss Varnish, the swimming teacher, had been keeping track of our cycles so we couldn't use the same excuse every week and, when consulted, she had divulged that I wasn't due for another fortnight. I wasn't about to dob on the Sams, so I'd sat through detention every Thursday night for a month.

When my drink came, I started eating the ice-cream out of it with a baby spoon. Mr Ackerman told me in his class voice to stir it in so it would sweeten the coffee. I left it to melt and reached for the sunglasses sitting next to his book and keys.

'Are these yours?' I asked, putting them on. They were too big for me. The arms reached way beyond my ears and I had to press the lenses to my face with my fingers to stop them falling off. The world looked blue from beneath those glasses, like science fiction. 'They're so bling.'

'I don't know about that.' He smiled for the first time, his face stubbly and blue now, too. 'I've had those since I was in high school. They're probably as old as you are.'

I kept them on while I tasted my coffee. It was still bitter and black and it made me cough so hard my throat stung. I pushed it aside. By the time we stood up to go, the ice-cream had floated to the top and was sitting on the surface, solidifying.

Mr Ackerman was shoving his wallet into his pocket when he came outside to where I waited on the kerb. 'Well, thanks for the company.'

'Thanks for the coffee.' I took a step closer. His eyes veered past me to the traffic in the street. 'You don't have to worry about being spotted by someone. I don't know anyone who lives on this side of town.'

He looked down at me with a small smile. 'I live on this side of town.'

'Oh, really? With your wife?'

'No, with my parents. I'm just here temporarily. On Charles Street.'

'Is that where you're going now then? To your mum and dad's?'

'No, actually, I was planning to go over to the NG—'

'I could come,' I cut in, lowering my voice, my eyes still on his. 'I've got nowhere else to be.'

On the tram, I sat down while he went to buy himself a ticket. When he came back, he stood across the aisle from me, and tilted his head to look out the opposite window. I looked too.

'Think it'll rain?' I asked without caring, and he shook his head.

'Nah,' he said. At a tram shelter outside, a group of girls were laughing and backing away from another girl, who was sitting on the bench, pulling off her jumper. She was red-faced, and laughing, too. A bird probably shat on her, I thought.

'Where are your friends today?' Mr Ackerman looked over at me.

'Uh, Amy's at drama lessons. Nat's babysitting. Courtney's at home, she's still got glandular.'

'And your family? How come you're out by yourself?'

'My parents are in Sorrento. We've got a place down there.'

'Ah, yes,' he said, as though he'd known that already. He had his sunglasses on his face now so I couldn't see his eyes. More than half the seats around me were empty but he stood the whole way there, his arm reaching above his head, past the swaying handles, to hold onto the rail.

The security guard and I played the game: he pretended not to be checking me out while I pretended not to notice. My teacher went to the cloakroom and I stopped at the first picture and checked my reflection in the gold frame. Why, I wondered, couldn't I have just drunk the stupid coffee?

'A monogamist.' Mr Ackerman had come up behind me.

'A pardon?'

'Chagall. He loved his wife very much.' He leaned in close to the painting. 'That's her up there, see? She's flying. And there he is, on the ground below, waiting for her to come down. Hoping to catch her. He put her in all his work.'

He walked on to look at the next one and I watched him go. For a science teacher he seemed to know a lot about art. I, on the other hand, didn't feel like learning school-ish things on the weekend. I dragged myself from painting to painting, ignoring the essay-long inscription next to each one, staring at the colours till they blurred before my eyes. I made inkblot tests of them all. Instead of a tableful of angels I saw a close-up of a mouth with teeth falling out; I turned a juggling bird into a woman belly dancing; a bunch of doves in a tree became soggy tampons just hanging there.

But it was true what Mr Ackerman had said, about the guy's wife. She was all over the place. First she lay draped naked over a tree of roses. Then she was dressed as a bride with a long veil and holding a baby. And later she wore a housedress and the two of them floated together above the orange floor of their kitchen.

I finished the room quickly and wandered back out to the foyer. That's where Mr Ackerman found me fifteen minutes later, sitting on a cushioned bench with my legs tucked under me, staring at the floor and pressing the pad of my thumb up onto the roof of my open mouth. He sat down beside me.

'I don't get what he saw in her,' I said. 'I mean, she was nothing special, as far as I could see. She had no fashion sense whatsoever and I'm sorry but her arse was gigantic.'

'Maybe Chagall liked substantially sized women,' Mr Ackerman offered. He laughed when I rolled my eyes at him. 'You've had enough, Miss Davies. You want to go home.'

'I want to eat.' I dragged myself to my feet. 'I haven't had anything all day.'

He knew a place in Southbank that was nice and quiet, with white tablecloths and waiters in half-aprons. He furrowed his brow over his menu like he did in class when someone gave a wrong answer, and he chose my meal for me because I couldn't decide. Then he asked me what had brought me to the 'wrong side of town'. So I told him about the formal dress, and the sewing lady at my dad's factory who had put straps on a strapless gown and how I wished I'd just gone to Chapel Street and bought something off the rack like all the other girls had because now I didn't even think I should go to the formal because I'd probably be the only one in straps. He was silent through all this, looking around the room at the empty tables, the waiters chatting near the kitchen, then out the window at the river.

'What's wrong?' I asked him.

'Oh. Nothing. It's just a little strange, I suppose, sitting here.'

'Do you want to go to the food court?'

'No. I just—I haven't eaten out in a restaurant for a long time. But this is nice. This is fine.' He looked at me. 'You're hungry.'

'I'm ravished,' I said, and he smiled and nodded down into his bread plate.

Halfway through our risottos, I finally got up the nerve to ask him if he was married. He had been, he told me, for three years, but it was over now and he didn't say why.

For a while after the divorce, he told me, he had stopped reading books. He couldn't sleep properly any more either. For the longest time, he said, he would go to see movies, dramatic movies, and keep his eyes closed the whole way through. Just so he could be moved by the music. I asked him why he didn't just stay home and listen to CDs in the dark, and he said he liked the ritual of buying the ticket, smiling at the popcorn sellers in their vests, and sitting among the couples and groups of kids who didn't bother turning off their phones before the main feature. He said he liked the way the score kept up throughout the whole film, dipping and rising, like someone's chest as they lay sleeping. It was cathartic, he said.

'What, like churchy?' I asked him.

'No,' he said. 'Like healing.'

'So now you read books again?'

'Yes, I've started to. And I guess I'm becoming more social.'

I had waited through the last few hours for him to tell me something about himself, something personal like this, but now that it had happened, I didn't know how to respond properly to any of it.

As he talked I found myself imagining the scene at home when I got back. The quiet that would greet me once I'd shut the big door behind me. The laughter of my sisters coming from somewhere in the back of the house. I saw myself going to the pantry and standing there, surveying the shelves full of lunchbox food: Le Snaks, fruit leathers, apple purees, and twelve-packs of Twisties. Leaving the kitchen without taking anything, I would sneak upstairs to my room unnoticed and lie on my bed in the dark, fully clothed, with my school books open on the desk, Natalie Portman grinning down off the wall, and the duct on the ceiling slowly exhaling its heat into the room.

'Excuse me, Sir, this card's been declined. Did you want me to try it again or use an alternative method of payment?' The waitress stood beside him with her hands behind her body. The two of them looked down at the insolent card that lay on the tablecloth, silent.

'Uh, give me a second.'

'Certainly, Sir.' She unclasped her hands but stayed where she was. Mr Ackerman fumbled through all his pockets.

'Shit,' he murmured, and I bit down on the inside of my lip. I shouldn't have eaten a main course, should have insisted on a soup or salad. I shouldn't have said I was hungry in the first place.

'I have some money,' I said. I took out thirty dollars and handed it to him.

'Thanks, Sascha, I'll pay you back. I have the money, it's just in a different account and I haven't transferred it yet.'

When the waitress came with the change, neither of us touched the five-dollar note lying on its plastic tray. The kitchen staff were loitering near their window, looking out at us. What are they thinking? I wondered. She's too old to be his daughter, probably, and too young to be his sister. I wondered what conclusion they'd reach.

Outside, a chilly afternoon wind had started blowing, and the clouds over the city were threatening something worse. We walked among the Saturday shoppers, all searching the sky for a sign of what next. By the time we reached Collins Street it had started to spit and I tried to lead him into a shoe shop.

'Don't worry,' he told me. 'It'll clear up any second.' But a few blocks later it was aiming at downpour status and the wind was so furious it was sucking people's umbrellas up into tulip shapes. 'Here.' He pulled me into a building and we stood inside the door, staring out at the water thrashing onto the road. We looked at each other, the rain streaming down our faces, and laughed.

We had walked into the foyer of an old school theatre. There were a few people sitting along the wall, reading or staring out at the rain, paying us no attention. There were posters behind them advertising films I'd never heard of, and the candy bar consisted of a basket of mixed-lolly bags selling, the handwritten sign told us, for $1.50 each.

The woman at the box office was glaring at us as though we should be paying for the privilege of taking refuge in her dingy little foyer. As though he agreed with her, Mr Ackerman wandered over and asked her when the next session started.

'There's one just started at four,' she growled at him. 'Or the next one's at half past.'

'Should we hide out 'til the rain stops?' he asked me and they both watched me nodding.

'One adult and one child?' She coolly met his eyes.

'Student.' We both reached for our wallets. 'One adult and one student.'

The movie was a foreign one, old and black and white, and as we sneaked in he whispered that he'd seen it before. The plot was non-existent and there were no effects or celebrities; it was just people talking. I ignored the subtitles and studied the main girl, who had cropped hair and sold newspapers on the street. I wondered if he found her attractive. Probably, but why? I was yet to work out exactly what it was that guys found sexy in women but I knew whatever it was, I had it. My body was still boyish and small and straight up and down, but I knew that it was interesting to men, not necessarily the guys from school, but other men. I'd known this fact for two years now since the day on the train.

I had felt them before I saw them, the man's eyes on me. I had been sitting across from him and his family and looking out the window behind them at the back fences and side streets and the lights being turned on in small office buildings. Then, with a snap like a rubber band, I felt the heat of his gaze and shifted mine until we met.

It had been a Tuesday evening and I was twelve years old and heading home from school with my mind on homework and netball and *Big Brother* and then suddenly this man had found me, my reflection in the window, and held me there. His arm was thrown around his wife's shoulders and she fussed with the two small kids beside her.

'Don't do that!' She slapped the toddler's hand from its nose and the man smirked at me in the window and raised his eyebrows.

I don't know how long we sat like that for. My house was pretty close to school so it couldn't have been longer than five minutes but I knew as I sat there in my uniform, my nipples growing hard, my cheeks hot, the terrible secret passing between me and the stranger, that I was being admitted into a new world, that I was growing old or dying or changing or something. A sensation passed over me then, like insects crawling around on my back.

That was the first time. Since then I had started a list in a note-book in my room of other things that gave me that sensation. Like 50 Cent clips on MTV. A car crash I saw happen on Glenferrie Road. An article I read about peacekeepers and refugees in Africa. Being on a tram without a ticket when the inspectors climbed on. The faces of people waiting outside nightclubs on weekends. A porn site I'd found open on my dad's computer when I was checking my e-mail in his study one night. And standing in front of Mr Ackerman in his office and lying to his stern face that I had been shoving tampons up into my vagina, two at a time.

And so today, walking down Smith Street, when I'd glanced up from the footpath and seen him sitting there in the window, looking both strange and familiar, like photos of my parents when they were young, I had felt it—the heat, the hardness, the insects. I had turned into the café without missing a beat, as though this were a movie and I was only just now being shown the script. I had had the sudden and full knowledge that there was a reason I had been admitted into this new world, that here, today, later today, sometime, Mr Ackerman was going to take this feeling to its real and necessary ending.

In the flicker and dark of the movie, I closed my eyes. There was no soundtrack but I listened to the up-and-down lilts of the language as though it was music. I leaned my head onto his shoulder. His jacket still held the cold of the rain and it smelled like outside when I breathed into it. Mr Ackerman put his hand on my hair and stroked it. I felt dizzy and humid, like I was flying above myself in the dark. I imagined him standing below me like that painter guy, getting ready to catch me before I hit the ground.

'Mr Ackerman,' I whispered, my teeth against his jacket.

'Are you tired, Sascha?' His mouth found my ear and he took his eyes off the screen. 'Or do you want to go somewhere else?'

Graphology 808: Beetopic or Beetopia? (2009)

John Kinsella

Indifferent to imagery and choreography,
the bee colony intense with the sparseness
of pollen—only wattles and some eucalypts
are in blossom. Near the hamlet, in the hollow
of a York gum—fruits of dead core,
living tree eaten out, dead bone within
living bone, all trace of age digested like ritual—
a message from Rumi, master of the whirling
dervishes, implanted like compassion shaped
as 'hive' amid 'nature', God's exotica,
we are annihilated, forgetting consequences,
disciples threaten, letting the 'wild' be 'wild'
and the farmed be farmed, a cartoon gimmick
in the age of cinematography: Australian
cinematographers famous for their clarity,
preciseness of imagery exported across
the world stage, elevation of local
to a universal chatter, blasphemy
holy and healthy, desirable.
Within the hive, within the nest,
admire warily, as politics
is proximity cross-pollinating
to make food an essential alibi,
performing to be heard, to gain
right of entry, see in and out
of the dark heart
where the queen works
the crisp cold of a valley winter.

Timid Minds (2010)

Hilary McPhee

'Cringe', wrote A.A. Phillips, is 'a disease of the Australian mind.' This was an unpleasant enough notion in the Australia of the 1950s, then a remnant colonial monoculture with no separate language to hide behind. Now, with our cosmopolitan aspirations and liberal assumptions, it seems unthinkable.

Arthur 'Angell' Phillips, critic and schoolmaster, had been commissioned by Clem Christesen to write 'The Cultural Cringe' for *Meanjin* in 1950. Clem did not much like the essay when it came in but ran it anyway, and eventually conceded that the reader response had been gratifying. Alliteration always helps and the phrase soon entered the language. Though some, like the member of the Commonwealth Literary Fund when asked to support publication of *The Australian Tradition*, a collection of A.A. Phillips's essays, wanted 'The Cultural Cringe' dropped. Australian culture, they argued, needed bolstering not admonishing.[1]

But A.A. Phillips was no reprimander. His assessment was affectionate but very much to the point. Menzies' Australia was an insecure, often sycophantic nation, its cultural baggage a complex mix of adulation and hostility. Intellectuals headed to Oxford or Cambridge almost as a matter of course. The centrifugal pull of the great British metropolis was irresistible and the anticipation of rejection must have guaranteed it. Phillips's recognition of the tendency to tag along dutifully behind England instead of doing our own thing may have been a bit too close to the bone and the psychological insight uncomfortable. He knew what Australian intellectuals were up against, not only

---

1 I am indebted to Jim Davidson's forthcoming entry on A.A. Phillips for the *Australian Dictionary of Biography*, and his *Sideways from the Page*, Fontana Books, Sydney, 1983, p. 34.

within the institutions of the day but also inside their own heads, and he named the crippling lack of self-esteem, which yearned for Australia's meaty individualism to be appreciated. But by the early 1950s there were signs of real change. Returned soldiers and artists and writers among the refugees and 'New Australians' were making intellectual life here more complex. Debates in the pubs and at the university seem to have been increasingly about our place in our region and the distinctive shape of Australian culture.[2]

Phillips did not fit the mould. He was an Australian Jew whose bookish family had been here since the 1820s, after a short time spent in London's Whitechapel. His father had been a president of the Australian Natives' Association; his mother wrote pieces for the weekly papers and a novel. Except for a pre-war stint at Oxford, Phillips spent very little time in Britain and did not enjoy it much. His tastes were European, his reading wide and his eye on an emerging Australian culture perceptive and acerbic. His critical writings about the *Bulletin* School of the 1890s as the beginnings of an Australian tradition meant that he was typecast, somewhat reluctantly, for the rest of his life as one of Australian literature's foremost advocates and interpreters through his regular reviews and critical essays. But first and foremost he was a schoolmaster, and over forty-five years at Wesley College generations of schoolboys were taught to comprehend that 'finely responsive reading is primarily an act of surrender, and only secondarily an act of judgement'.

Australian poetry and fiction were always part of his curriculum, and the anthologies he produced with Ian Maxwell, from as early as 1932, meant that some Australian writing was included in the syllabus of the English Department at Melbourne University. *The Australian Tradition*, published by Cheshire in 1958, was an attempt to counterbalance *The Great Tradition* by F.R. Leavis, which had already defined the ground for the canon, and English departments around the world had fallen into line.

---

2 Tim Burstall, *The Burstall Diaries 1953–56*, forthcoming.

From this distance, Phillips's diagnosis of the postcolonial Australian psyche probably prepared the ground for those swingeing works of history and culture of the next couple of decades, works the scale and confidence of which have rarely been attempted again, intellectual fashion and increasing cultural complexity mitigating against them—books sweeping in their scope, short on introspection, utterly sure of their ground. Fine writers, all of them, and men for whom the Cringe was unimaginable. If any of them suffered from self-doubt, the point was to conceal it.

Russel Ward's *The Australian Legend* appeared in 1958, then in 1960 came Bernard Smith's *European Vision and the South Pacific* and Robin Boyd's *The Australian Ugliness*. The first of Manning Clark's six-volume *A History of Australia* appeared in 1962, and Donald Horne's *The Lucky Country* in 1964. Australian painters and composers were not cringing either. In 1961 Arthur Boyd, Charles Blackman, Sidney Nolan and others successfully showed at the Whitechapel Gallery in London to largely good notices. Peter Sculthorpe returned from Oxford in 1961 with 'a sharpened awareness of things Australian' and his great *Sun Music* series was composed and premiered between 1965 and 1969. In 1970 the first history of Australian culture appeared, Geoffrey Serle's *From Deserts the Prophets Come*, an iconic Fred Williams desert landscape on the jacket.

Each in its own way was a statement of cultural confidence written with that 'fine edge of Australian responsiveness', to use Phillips's phrase, and the 'security and distinction' that doing so gave its interpreters. Their perspective was from here, from within the damaged past and the transplanted class divides of a settler nation, recording the melancholy and the dire mistakes of displaced people. None was written with an international readership in mind, none would create a ripple anywhere else. Even when *The Lucky Country* was renamed *Australia in the Sixties* for Penguin UK, only the Australian branch office noticed. The English-speaking world wasn't much interested and few of the books would ever be translated. But the great project of cultural self-definition had begun.

Cringe still had deep roots at Melbourne University by the time I arrived in the early sixties. I did not know enough to argue with those who ranked Australian literature 'second rate' or to challenge the dean who discouraged me from taking Australian history because it was 'rather thin'. Instead, I steeped myself in the Renaissance and the Reformation and in Anglo-Saxon and Old Norse Literature. By the end of my second year I was in a student household where we swapped the latest Patrick White and Randolph Stow and stayed up all night writing scripts and making costumes for revues and plays. But it was not until my fourth year when I stumbled into a new subject called Australian Prehistory that I began to comprehend where I was. Led by a considerable Hungarian scholar of the Central European Paleolithic, whose qualifications were not recognised here, I joined a group heading for the Nullabor in the long vacations. Alexander Gallus showed us how to read the land and signs of human occupation. He introduced us to Jung, and around the campfire at night, encouraged us to imagine the people who had inhabited the sinkholes we were excavating by day, people who had left their quartz axes in the fine white sand and their intricate fingerlines on the smoke-stained walls deep in the labyrinth of the caves.

Cringe didn't come into it.

I went to Arthur Phillips's funeral in 1985 with its schoolboy guard of honour and its throng of elderly actors and writers, not because I knew him well but to pay homage to the man who had contributed so much to what we now took for granted. The 'upright carriage' of cultural confidence that he advocated was by then the norm, unstoppable, a given, or so we liked to think.

This was an era of much activism and feminism, of doing your own thing. There were dozens of us, starting little theatres and film companies and publishing houses in crumbling warehouses, all of us with minute resources but galvanised by a sense of possibilities and collective ideals. We were having ideas and commissioning them, interviewing politicians about where they stood on equal pay and abortion and holding them to account in the press. We backed our own judgement about the new writers and thinkers who came with their portraits of the place, supporting and reassuring, all learning as we went. Publishers then paid tiny advances, films and plays were low budget, marketing was largely word of mouth and parties not yet about networking. But the print and broadcast media were hungry for stories of the phenomenon of it all. (Television was mostly oblivious, of course, and author profiles and 'Australian stories' were still years away.) We shared information across art forms and companies and saw ourselves as being in the larger cultural project, whatever it was, together.

The Cringe in its original form sometimes surfaced at Writers Week in Adelaide where overseas writers were still being given preferential treatment and better accommodation, and in occasional outbursts of paranoia in the pub, but it did not run very deep. Australia was where it was all happening. British publishers made overtures to our authors for British Commonwealth rights and were astonished to be turned down. The tone of the annual survey of Australian literature in the *TLS* made us cross, with reviewers inclined to whack writers for sounding 'too Antipodean', but we saw it as their problem not ours. Selling rights to the English was never easy but American agents and publishers behaved for a heady while as if they had discovered a new frontier of books waiting to be born. We sourced novels and stories for translation from our region and produced kids books in Turkish, Greek and Vietnamese for here. As I write this, it all sounds too good to be true, and of course, in the end, it was. From the mid eighties on, our rapid growth and expensive distribution were starting to give us sleepless nights.

We made our own creative spaces in the culture, although 'creativity' was not yet a buzzword and 'spaces' meant simply places where new work could flourish. The conditions needed for cultural production—which in the case of books seemed to us to be quite simple—writing time involved editorial support and lots of discussion face-to-face. The ghosts were not, to quote A.A. Phillips again, 'sitting in on the tête-à-tête between the Australian reader and writer, interrupting in the wrong accent'. We used to joke that our books talked to each other through their threads of ideas. It still seems a better way to work.

Australian writing, if we ever bothered to define it, meant writing that was original, challenging, fully imagined and unfettered by worn-out scholarly protocols. It was writing that was argued about, sought after, set on school syllabuses, even for a few short years taught in Australian universities until the new cringe to the French set in. But in our little bubble at the edge of the world we were becoming far too big for our boots, and meanwhile economic rationalism, like the cane toad, was spreading south.

This was still a time when Australian cultural activity and a political climate of big possibilities and 'punching above our weight' were aligned. Policy-makers listened to experts on the ground; practising artists and writers were in positions to make decisions about arts policy and funding. The corporates were not yet running the place. But the election of the neo-conservative Howard government in 1996 ensured that the dominance of the marketplace was complete and quite rapidly an insular hard-heartedness prevailed.

The 'minatory ghost' has been at the levers of the global market machine for decades and we have all been snagged in the workings. The corporatisation of the universities and cultural institutions meant larger salaries and career paths for some but, for many, short-term contracts meant insecurity. People inevitably took fewer risks. Research corralled in profit centres encourages the promotion of the complicit not the brave and cannot suit the slow build needed for creative and intellectual work. The sums don't work, nor do the spaces. The business model with its emphasis on predictable outcomes and competition encourages over-claiming and is a dead weight for individual artists and companies competing for public funding. It almost always guarantees that the work, whatever it is, will be undercooked.

Political correctness, once a source of jokes, had now become a straitjacket, used by both sides of politics—by conservatives as a way of short-circuiting discussion of injustice and inequity, and by ideologues on the left and those seeking the security of high-minded ethical processes. It is more than fifteen years since it all unravelled. First there was the self-righteous uproar over Helen Garner's *The First Stone*. Then there was eagerness to find a new young multicultural writer, which produced and rewarded a 'Demidenko'. A series of identity witch-hunts followed, and so too then the inevitable and understandable 'new generationalism' crying discrimination against youth and popular culture. The blaming left its scars: for those who woke up one day and found themselves in the firing line for saying the unacceptable or just for being in the way, the vehemence was divisive and dismaying. And despite the books that poured forth and the frequent debates, many of the so-called gatekeepers are still with us.

A long period of cultural navel-gazing followed—the endless, sometimes myopic Culture Wars, the polarising History Wars, and the ever-widening gulf between public policy and cultural concerns. We, the 'enlightened liberal elites', were seen to be talking only to ourselves about our own concerns. Only rarely were the divides that separated the affluent, Howard's battlers and the rural poor fearlessly examined. The increasingly frequent local outbreaks of xenophobia and racism were deplored and the government blamed, but there were few attempts to comprehend them as symptoms of a growing global malaise—and in any case neither side of politics was listening.

A.A. Phillips identified a species he called 'the denaturalised intellectual' as the Cringe's unhappiest victim—and cursed him down to 'his indifferent eyebrows'. The eyebrows may not be indifferent, but nearly twelve years of the Howard government, followed by three years of Rudd and Gillard, have ensured that the old Cringe, which Phillips saw as a form of estrangement of the intellectual, has morphed into a kind of stylish but timid conformity. The timid intellectual holds politicians in contempt and feels free to lecture them occasionally, but fails to hold them to account or imagine new mechanisms that might start them listening again.

We are the only Western democracy with no bill of rights; there has been no equivalent here of the Hutton Inquiry in the United Kingdom, no serious public investigation into the increase of corruption in our globalised economy, no exploration of the likely impact of climate change in our region and our responsibility to peoples displaced. It is a long time between books of fearless reportage by writers with time and resources to dig as deep as they must dig into Australia's relationship with the rest of the world. Journalists who can write fast, tell a good story, sniff out a scandal and do a professional interview now write almost all the local works of social and political commentary and we import the rest. Some of them are great reads but only rarely are they works that will change anything. Despite more hard-hitting essays being published, more forums for debate existing than ever before, more think-tanks probing the issues that define us and will shape the future, the capacity for intellectuals with expertise to influence public policy is at an all-time low.[3]

There are many impediments to those intellectuals re-entering the public debate and contributing to policy-making in the way they once did. Much needs to be confronted—including self-censorship. Australia doesn't score well on freedom-of-speech indices. Our print media are contracting. Newspapers and journals here are more tightly controlled for content than those of most other Western countries. Owners call the shots and are rarely challenged. One of our best magazines that promotes itself as a journal of ideas does not provide any coverage of Middle East politics or Afghanistan or the aftermath of the war in Iraq—but its silence may well be preferable to the misinformation peddled elsewhere.

---

3 Let us hope that Hugh White's recent Quarterly Essay 39, *Power Shift: Australia's Future between Washington and Beijing*, Black Inc, Melbourne, 2010, is the exception, coming at a time when the new government must be redefining its foreign policy.

Our commentators and politicians seem to suggest that global-isation will save us in our island continent. How similar we are in outlook to each other, how confidently we can appeal to a homoge-nous liberal readership and Western state of mind. There's comfort in waiting for others to act and being interminably 'in conversation' on panels at festivals all over the world. Since 9/11 the big questions have been turned into global questions and, inevitably, we cannot find answers to these questions alone.

We welcome international speakers—the celebrity intellectuals—who tell us what we want to hear: that Islam is all evil, that the rise of China can only be malevolent, that a military presence in Afghanistan is the best we can do, that the rest of the world is clamouring to come here, that our form of democracy and economy is the only benign and enlightened model. Only rarely do we challenge or contextualise what these speakers say, and journalists leave the audience to do the research in order to 'make up their own mind'—as an ABC spokes-person said recently about what passes for the new balanced report-ing. While the issues needing informed analysis and humane and lateral solutions proliferate, we are often exposed to something rather close to propaganda, or so it seems to me.

Festivals of Big Ideas and Big Ideas for the Next Generation (which, wisely, stays away) have proliferated around the English-speaking world as if in response to the fear that grips us all in the dead of night—a security blanket of like minds. International intel-lectuals join local experts mocking those who seek the consolation of religion, bemoaning the absence of social democracy and feeding our prejudices. We bask in a semblance of cosmopolitanism and being in the club.

Talking is not doing: a talkfest-dominated culture cannot be a courageous one, or one that can effectively inform public policy. Crucial debates packaged as entertainment don't create change. Audiences are consumers rather than citizens, booking the sessions out, asking their questions, getting their books signed and going away until next year. The emphasis is all wrong, the effort misplaced.

The times don't suit those who want to produce the kind of work that needs time and deep thought and courage. They suit best those who have the stamina and personality to perform. Those whose work needs the freedom to take risks and speak truth to power have much to lose—and the culture is the poorer for it. Despite our cultural confidence and easy gait through the festivals and airports of the world, we still rely on many of the same filters that A.A. Phillips would recognise.

The great British metropolis, as it always has, sieves for us the world's writing in languages other than English. The selection of books for translation into English is largely made in the United Kingdom. Most of them are works of fiction. Few are works of cultural, philosophical, political analysis or cross-cultural theory that might better reflect our particular concerns and help us to understand the divides we must learn to straddle—between the West where we still belong and our region of India, the Middle East and Asia. The number of books read in translation in Australia, as in the United States, is low and the amount of translation done in this country infinitesimal despite our having, as we always have, fine translators and scholars in our midst.

Imagine encouraging communities here who produce their own intellectuals and poets to participate in our thinking through our 'big ideas', to help select works for translation. Many have come from countries where local publishing is damaged or censored or is in a similar emerging state not unlike this country's publishing was thirty years ago but publication on the internet is leaping ahead. Stories of the recent past are being written. Issues of modernity and the rise of fundamentalisms are being widely debated—and lived out—in Europe and the Middle East in ways we rarely hear about. Dissemination of ideas from non-Western parts of the world is not encouraged. Language barriers and 'security concerns' mean that the wider public's awareness of them is negligible and their response to both the international propagandists and well-meaning cultural relativists is ignored. Contemporary writing in Farsi or Arabic or any of the other languages in our region is rare in public libraries, which, if anything, confine themselves to the classics. Are there any book groups and creative writing courses in languages other than English? Instead immigrants are encouraged to study Business English while keeping their poets and their perceptions to themselves.

There is a great deal we can and must do in this country in our own name. 'Australia' does have a point of view and a mix of peoples that is unique. Self-definition is still the great unfinished cultural project and always will be—but without contributions from our changing population we are talking only to those who share the same perspective and who are invited into our privileged and privatised cultural spaces. Collective purpose has to be rediscovered and celebrated as an opportunity rather than a threat. The safety of like minds is a delusion.

Australian culture has not been monolithic for a long time. Writers and intellectuals who are wrestling consciously or unconsciously with identity, authenticity, compassion and cultural difference know this. The times demand deep thinking and deep writing and places to do it.

There are reasons for optimism; there always are. In 2009 the estate of the former minister for industry John Button created a most significant prize for the best piece of writing on politics or public policy. This year it was awarded to anthropologist and linguist Peter Sutton for *The Politics of Suffering: Indigenous Australia and the End of the Liberal Consensus*, a scathing and despairing account of the failure of progressivist Aboriginal politics since the 1970s. Sutton writes out of a lifetime's experience in the field and directly into the sphere of public policy.

Then, in the last couple of years, the remarkable Renew Newcastle project has taken off, with its basis in DIY and its emphasis on physical space and dynamic experimentation rather than capital, making defunct industrial buildings available to local artists, musicians and craftspeople linked into the rest of the world on the web. The tired old newspaper model is being challenged by several new magazines using a mix of print and online formats, and the Emerging Writers Festival is often more of a lift to the spirits than the mainstream versions.

And then there is the next generation of students—young nomads skilled with keyboards and rapid responses and their own relaxed way of cross-cultural engagement with each other and the world. A few months before he died in August 2010, intellectual and historian Tony Judt dictated a book for this generation, who will inherit the whirlwind. *U Fares the Land* comes closest to what I construct in my head as essential reading—a book of great lucidity and urgency about posing the questions that frighten us and to which we, like Judt, do not have the answers.[4] Finding ways to help frame them is the crucial next step and the very least we can do.

---

4 Tony Judt, *U Fares the Land*, Penguin, New York, 2010.

Aubade (2010)

Peter Coghill

In the half-light, before the workday stir,
three strips contour her body, cross the bed
and this dull morning seems a watershed
with me indifferent to the sight of her

as, with her sleeping eyes, she is to me.
Once I had rockclimber's hands: worn thin,
one layer more naked, they'd sense her skin
aware an inch away, like witchery,

yet over years hands callous with the wear
of touching her, and fierceness seems absurd
as does delusion when the fever's cured,
and the strong arch our marriage made won't bear

a tower to our passion, or a child's home.
Instead there's empty stairs and controlled climate,
too many books, too much reason for quiet
where something squalling with life might have grown.

I stand in the door, neither there nor gone;
through blinds the sun insinuates its way,
casting a chart of the approaching day
where I should lie, and where her arm is thrown.

The Office of Icebergs (2011)

Rebecca Giggs

Here, we are accustomed to slippery immigrants, to changeable states and submerged anatomies. So at first, when we met Isca, we did not feel threatened. Regrettably there were looks—reactions of alarm and repulsion—because it was only later and in confidence that she filled us in on the deal with her face. But after the double-take we realised, *it's a woman!* and we swivelled around in our chairs, raising our brows at one another as if to ask: *but how did she get in?* There had been no call forewarning us of her arrival, no intra-office memo, or email from our truant Director.

The woman put down her knapsack and introduced herself. Isca, the glaciologist. *Isca*, we thought, taking her hand in ours, is that Jewish? Do we know any Jewish glaciologists? 'We're all glaciologists!' we exclaimed jumping up, because by now we wanted her to join with us in whatever game was being played, and, also, we felt really bad about her face. When we had been standing for a minute she said, 'I'm from the Polar Ombudsman's,' and to make it clear that she was on our side she produced a business card. 'Oh yes!' we said, like it was no big thing, this tiny card. 'Oh *that* Ombudsman, we know about him and his powers.' We hung out our healthiest smiles. 'So ...' Isca folded her hands into her armpits.

'So where do you want me?'

The truth of the situation at the Office of Icebergs was that we had been spiralling out of control for months. The brakes were totally off. Back when we got started only a handful of bergs exited the polar sea nurseries every summer and we geotagged them so easily, using our glaciologist know-how. We even had betting pools—wagers on how long the bergs would survive on the high seas—with zany penal-ties for the loser. It was not so disappointing to see something the size of architecture thaw down to a glass fist, then wink and disappear, if you stood to make some money behind it! Occasionally someone would even be made to take the lift *without pants*. Yes, those were the salad days.

Now everything was very far away from those days, but we still had the illusion.

'Here,' we said, 'this one is definitely the best one,' and we shuffled Isca across to a console that had begun to glitch whenever anyone breathed on the screen. Somebody (and we all knew who) had knocked an energy drink into the top drawer and now a multicoloured mould spread a broad stain like a star map behind the monitor, crocheting soft, disgusting sleeves over the cables. It might have been art, if it were not putrid. 'This seat raises,' we demonstrated, up and down, up again. We suspected Isca was short but we couldn't bring ourselves to look her straight in the face to be sure. Or: we could do that, but that would not be the friendly thing because of our rebounding looks. Instead, we kept our eyes downcast. There were some charts that we rolled up quickly because they were lying. 'We'll get you fresh ones,' we said, 'crispy fresh charts. For now you should get yourself acquainted, spend a few days. And coffee! There's coffee.'

In the kitchen we sank to our knees like professional athletes or priests defrocked. The bright ran right off us. We had been wondering when someone like Isca would appear—bringing credentials and two faces, come to change our ways— but we were expecting that person would be a man in bullet-proof clothes. Probably more than one man! We were psyched for the wretchedness—it was what we deserved. Confess, and next: the leg irons. What was she doing out there? Isca and her oversight authority. She was wearing cork sandals and a rain-jacket that rustled when she tapped on the monitor—that type of fabric would easily tear.

'You shouldn't do that,' we called through the doorway, 'it works best when you only look. Belt-tightening!' She frowned and shook her head. Her hair shimmered like wet shale.

We would not be afraid of her. She was just another glaciologist, a small glaciologist, working the iceberg system like all of us, impeded by malfunctioning resources. Oh no, we confirmed it with nods, she could not bring us down! We poured the kettle and returned to our desks with resolve, and steaming drinks.

On Thursday the *Limits of All Known Ice Report* went out as usual, and we were on tenterhooks for the afternoon. Every time the phone rang we expected it to be the Maimed Sailors' League calling to report a sunken fleet—listing the names of their dead and injured men. But as the day went by we loosened up a little. Our forgeries were very convincing! Besides, how were we supposed to explain that the Antarctic ice had stopped behaving like ice used to? That ice didn't even seem to be ice any more? These were problems that were too complex for our computers. We called those machines 'The Grunters' because they were so overloaded and noisy. Did it really matter that there were more icebergs in the sea than there were in the report?

At five o'clock we exhaled. We brought out beers and the switchboard held our incoming messages. Even though it was only Thursday, we harboured some victorious sentiments.

'Isca,' we asked with sociable beckoning. 'Hey Isca, where are you from?'

'Not as in, "the Ombudsman's", from *in the world*?'

Well, Isca was born on a boat! She was Australian, but her mother had been some kind of pioneer for science and Isca was delivered on a research vessel in the Pacific. Isca was two months old before she was put down and rolled in the sand.

'Huh,' we said. 'Does that also make you a type of sea-nationality?'

'It's my nose you want to know about, right?' said Isca, turning around from her console. 'And why I don't have eyebrows?' We each stared into the skylight above us or the brewery logos in our palms. Isca wasn't *hideous*, but we all agreed: she had one face on top of another face. Her expressions stayed underneath like objects covered by a cloth. She made us think of the taut heads of those bog-men that are sometimes unearthed when glaciers melt. All Iron Age nasal cavity and sinew.

'Frostbite,' she said, tearing a bottle from our six-pack. 'I was an idiot. My eyebrows are probably still out on that ice-shelf, two cryogenic caterpillars.' Was that humour or was that horrific? We experimented with laughing, with goading digs in the ribs. She told us how, after a time with lasers and creams, her face had healed scald-smooth—except that the new skin dragged her nose to the west and her eyebrows would never grow back. She didn't tell that story to people straightaway, she said, because she was embarrassed at having been so feckless. And she would appreciate if we didn't make a big deal out of it.

We had some new respect for Isca then. Not for being able to use the word 'feckless', but because none of us had actually been on an ice-shelf since university days. Some of us hadn't even done Antarctic fieldwork back then. She pulled her hair over one shoulder like a pet. Everything we knew, we knew by satellites, but Isca's hands knew real ice.

'I've considered having them tattooed back on,' Isca said after a moment of reflection, up-ending her beer. 'The eyebrows. But I'd look like an alien, right?' *No, Isca*, we thought, *not right. You'd look like a pre-historic bog-man. With tattoos.* But of course we didn't say it out loud.

Frankly—and perhaps it was the beers, but all the same—the closer we got to her the more we wanted to press our fingers into her face. She had strange creases brinking her eye sockets, like punc-tuation marks from a language we couldn't speak, while the sweeps of her cheekbones looked hard and cold. Would there be ticking undertows there, we wondered, little swells pushing up? Isca wasn't so unattractive. Maybe she wouldn't mind that. In fact, maybe she *longed* to have her face stroked. Slowly, with calm precision. It could be collegiate and team-building. We thought about folding in around her with our palms held out flat.

Isca threw her bottle into the wastepaper bin and checked in on her wristwatch. We snapped out of whatever it was we'd snapped into. What were we doing with such early alcohol in the office? This fine line was a high wire!

'You don't mind if I take my copy of the *Limits Report* home, no?' she said, unzipping her knapsack. 'You've all worked so hard.' Isca appraised the cover page. 'These graphs look impressive.'

Shock, gelid and sudden, flooded us. That *sly quisling*. Distracting us with stories of ship birth and frostbite, making us imagine the nap of her skin. She must have collected a copy of the report off the printer when we weren't watching her.

'Oh,' we grasped for it but the report had already slid with a handful of other papers into her bag. We'd been so careless. 'Oh'—in the most nonchalant tone, we told her—'the Polar Ombudsman had his copy faxed already. It's very boring,' we said. 'We'll just send you the executive summary.' Someone reached to take the report back, but she rebuffed them. Isca showed us some of her canines then and said in a sinister way: 'Don't undersell yourselves. I bet it's really interesting.' She collected her thin jacket and left before we could think of anything more to say.

Standing there in the office our frantic hearts pumped a chilly froth.

We couldn't sleep that night. In bed we kicked our wives. They told us to *just get up or lie still*. Two of us who owned dogs took those dogs out to local parks. We listened to leaf math in the wind, or cars in the distance, or breath in the bedrooms. Rain eddied high above, but it didn't fall down. Each of us wondered if the rest of us were awake too, and hearing the garden, or the highway, or some lungs.

The Ombudsman was who we were thinking of. The luminous Ombudsman. How he stood for transparency, for shining through. We had never seen him at the Office of Icebergs, but we felt sure he was foreign and back-lit with authority. Probably he was Canadian, or French-Canadian. But wasn't the Ombudsman also connected to the Queen in some familial way, too? So, aristocratic and British then.

He might own hounds for sport—dogs more fierce than our own. The Ombudsman was the light at the end of our tunnel. Coming to shackle our ankles. The baying of the pack. We were brimming with penitence.

Isca was a *very* convincing traitor. The next morning she didn't say a single word about the report or what she had conveyed to the Ombudsman about us. She came in early and brewed a plunger of coffee in the kitchen.

'TGIF,' she called out as we arrived and sat down at our consoles. 'What have you all got planned for the weekend?'

We didn't know what that was a code for. Who was she talking to? We swung on our chairs, sleep-deprived and fretful, wearing our very best business socks and pumping our fists. Was she going to say nothing about the *Limits of All Known Ice*? No-one answered her. It was too much—there needed to be some *reckoning*. Where were the dogs and the men wearing Kevlar? Didn't they know about the lives we'd put at risk? We were a public menace!

'What about you, Bill?' Isca waved a mug through the doorway. 'Are you going to the game, Bill? You're a supporter, yes?'

Supporter? We looked at one another. 'I'm a supporter,' Bill said quickly. 'Definitely, I'm a supporter.'

'We're all supporters,' we shouted. 'It's not a game! We support it all.'

It was hard to tell what Isca thought of that, but she didn't say anything else. She took her mug to her desk and stared into her screen with a scarf wound around her ghastly face to suppress the dank smell. Exactly what she knew was unclear, but until she had amassed the evidence it seemed that she was going to keep quiet. She was in league with the higher forces of the Ombudsman—they were keeping a file, building a case, planting monitoring devices. Or: Had she in fact not figured it out yet?

For most of the morning we did our best work, tagging and monitoring the sea-ices as they moved across the great blank table of the

Southern Ocean. Around eleven Bill's biggest berg broke up and sent out snarlers—bits of ice that travel in a flotilla and make a gnashing noise as they rub against each other. The snarlers entered a rubbish vortex and started to cause trouble. If we had still been gambling then, Bill might have had to ride the lift in his underpants. He was always lucking out, that Bill. He wore his superstitious boxers every day, and he was always lucking out. Of course, we were not going to gamble with Isca around.

We rang the guys in the Office of Shipping Routes and told them to warn their fishing trawlers about the snarlers. Sometimes, when the bergs went into a rubbish patch, they would take up plastic waste and refreeze it into blocks of ice-locked trash. This was becoming more frequent. Shipping Routes emailed through some photographs taken from the deck of a bulk carrier last week, of icebergs full of crisp packets and shopping bags. *It's completely normal*, we wrote back, *for this time of year. Just try not to hit those ones. Try not to disperse the rubbish.*

What was normal any more? The guys in Shipping Routes didn't know! They relied on us, and we were off the deep end, out of line, flying blind. We had stopped tagging all the bergs because there were too many for us to keep track of. Even the bergs we did follow were behaving in ways we couldn't predict. How they picked up sea trash was not the half of it! The circumpolar currents were nearly always off course now, and tomato-coloured tides had started to appear in water that was supposed to be too cold for that. We suspected that there were large blood-bergs in those tides: ice dyed haemoglobin-red by the bad plankton in the sea. But how could we pick them out from the satellite images? Who could see a red thing in a red sea?

It wasn't that we were afraid of losing our jobs. We knew that was the end that was coming to us, and we would be relieved when it arrived. We would be penitent, like bankers, then. But right then we weren't bankers, we were *glaciologists*. We were *scientists*. We couldn't just say that we didn't *understand* the things that were going on with the icebergs. There were our grant applications to think of. And Isca—the mole, our infiltrator—had begun to compile records. We didn't know how long we could wait, but the end, the end *had* to be close.

After lunch Isca suddenly stood up and her chair tipped over backwards onto the ground. She made a loud gurgling noise and pointed at her console. At first with caution, and then some shuddering anticipation, we gathered around. One huge megaberg lurched across her screen, newly splintered from the Ross Ice Shelf. The berg was flanked by a navy of inferior sea-ices, as if it had been dropped from a great height to break there. Whitescrap (wave-caps, wreckage and wakes) seethed along its perimeter, and a plume of sea-soil rose up behind it, showing where it had dragged its thick root along the ocean floor. This berg was far bigger than anything we'd ever seen at the Office—it had the dimensions of a small continent, and it was ploughing an unnaturally straight line in the sea. Isca plotted its trajectory while we watched. She amended her estimate for the curvature of the Earth, then replotted it thrice to confirm. Bill seemed crestfallen and delighted all at once, as if he'd finally won a bet that he never knew he'd made.

The megaberg was coming, the megaberg was seeking landfall. It was headed directly for the peninsula on which the Office of Icebergs, the Office of Shipping Routes and all the other Offices of the Atmospheres, Grounds and Oceans were located: as punctual as an omen.

When Isca turned her two faces to us, we understood perfectly what needed to happen next. There was a moment when everything was very still and sharp, and every one of us noticed that the rain had begun to drum its many fingers on the skylight. Then we felt something flip over to its shining side within us, and suddenly Isca's knapsack was on the ground being stamped on. Someone had her by the lapels, demanding her allegiances, the jacket sliding all around and someone else was tearing all the cables out from all the grunting machines. 'Shhhh,' we said, 'shhhh.' Sit down. Shut up.

We were all glaciologists, and we knew exactly how things should end.

The Higher, the Fewer (2011)

Mal McKimmie

I
Yes, the bees are leaving.

Humans in their swarming
Have become unwavering in both belief & disbelief.
Once an antidote, the bee-sting is now
A used hypodermic signifying a corpse.
Where once the flower grew is built
A funeral parlour or tautological high-rise.
The child is lost in the crowd like doubt,
The lover clamours for processed sugar.

The category of super-morbid obesity is a bell tolling the departure
    of bees …

II
Poetry is now the only difference between
Those who write poetry & those who do not.
Fear of this is why poets read to poets and are happy.
She said of her 500 Facebook friends:
'They are not a swarm, they're a print run.'

The anonymous reader is the true apiarist, humming
From page to page, cramming his pockets with pollen until he's
Jodhpur-thighed, trailing legs shaped like hams & has become a bee.

He might be living in a house on fire, smoke might have
Pulled a grey Salvo Army blanket up to his chin & tucked him in,

But in his sleep, one by one or two by two, like the zzzzzzz of a
Gentle snoring, bees slip from his mouth, his dream
& swarm into the shape of tomorrow.

III
Everything seemed like an accident:
All I did was keep bees & sleep, bees & read, sleep & bees.
Writing was only to stay awake in the smoke. Now what am I?
(Somehow saw the bloom in slow motion,
Caught a glimpse of the locksmith opening the flower.)

IV
It seems I disagree with almost everyone.
Yes, I have been nostalgic since I was born,
But it does not follow that the events I remember did not happen:
A bee's compound eye pardons certain shades of romanticism.

So what if I remember the Queen's rare, once-upon-a-time lover?
That his heart was on a sleeve tailored too short for his desire.
That he was an ill-suited man with always ten secrets but only nine
        pockets.
That he could not hide his love—from himself, from others
& the agony caused by this—to him, to others.

I don't know why I can't remember the happiness.

V
If there is no such lover in this one-ball circus where anybody can
        be a juggler,
Where we briskly pace from known to known
Opening door after door on the expected
As if we think this is how love is found in the final days,
Then we may be right—these may be the final days.

Perhaps the Queen is tired of being the engine at the heart of the
    labyrinth,
Tired of every moment's necessary egg,
Tired of the sting of the mob that sacrifices, one by one, her subjects
    & consorts.
(Who am I when compared to them?)

Perhaps from this darkness she is preparing to sing out
The blue & gold chariot of her origins,
Just as Elijah sang his from the ash of his own cremation
Leaving his lover, Elisha,
To watch the skies with vigilance until
He was broken open & did not matter.

VI
Yes, it is not that the bees are leaving.
Pardon my euphemism.
I cannot look directly at the absence of the sun.

Acknowledgements

Meanjin is Australia's second oldest literary journal. Founded by Clem Christesen in 1940, it has documented both the changing concerns of Australians and the achievements of many of the nation's writers and poets.

A fiftieth anniversary *Meanjin* anthology was published in 1990 that included historical commentary and a seventieth anniversary journal in 2010 comprised new and past articles.

This collection offers a broad sweep of essays, fiction and poetry, sampling from the entire palette of writings published in *Meanjin* since the magazine began. Readers will get a sense of the debates waged in print over those seven decades and the growing confidence of the Australian written voice. They are presented chronologically, leaving the different forms and focuses to rub shoulders.

It's a collection that will interest the general reader, the literary enthusiast, those interested in Australian culture and the many other students of creative writing and journalism.

It was a great honour that Gerald Murnane agreed to write the fore-word. The anthology has been compiled by current *Meanjin* editor Sally Heath, associate editor Zora Sanders, poetry editor Judith Beveridge, eagle-eyed proofreader Richard McGregor and intern Emma Fajgenbaum. Many thanks go to the previous editors whose advice assisted in the compilation: Jim Davidson, Judith Brett, Jenny Lee, Christina Thompson, Stephanie Holt, Ian Britain and Sophie Cunningham.

Additional thanks goes to Chris McAuliffe, Professor Kevin Brophy, Chris Wallace-Crabbe, Jenny Grigg, Michael McGirr, Rosanna Areiuli, Jessica Barlow, Paul Bugeja, Penelope White, Tahlia Anderson and Sarah Hollingsworth.

The publication was made possible by grants from the University of Melbourne's Cultural and Community Relations Advisory Group and the Australia Council.

Contributors

Adamson, Robert
Robert Adamson has published fifteen volumes of poetry and has organised and produced poetry readings, papers, lectures and readings at literary festivals throughout Australia and abroad.

Astley, Thea
Thea Astley was one of Australia's most renowned authors. She won the first of her four Miles Franklin literary awards for *The Well Dressed Explorer* in 1962, followed by *The Slow Natives* in 1965, *The Acolyte* in 1972 and *Drylands* in 2000.
Published by arrangement with the Licensor, *The Thea Astley Estate*, c/- Curtis Brown (Aust) Pty Ltd.

Banning, Lex
Although he was affected by cerebral palsy, which left him unable to talk clearly or write with a pen, Lex Banning produced influential poetry and wrote for print, radio, TV and film. Three volumes of his poetry were published in his lifetime and the volume *There Was a Crooked Man: The Poems of Lex Banning* was published in 1984.

Behrendt, Larissa
Larissa Behrendt is a writer, barrister and professor of law. Her debut novel, *Home*, won the Queensland Premier's Literary Award and the David Unaipon Award in 2002, and her second novel, *Legacy*, won a Victorian Premier's Literary Award in 2010.

Beveridge, Judith
Judith Beveridge is the author of four books of poetry: *The Domesticity of Giraffes, Accidental Grace, Wolf Notes* and *Storm and Honey*. She teaches poetry writing at the University of Sydney.

Birch, Tony
Tony Birch writes short fiction, novels and essays. His 2011 novel *Blood* was shortlisted for the 2012 Miles Franklin literary award. Tony teaches at the University of Melbourne.

Brett, Judith

Judith Brett is Professor of Politics at La Trobe University. She has written extensively on Australian politics, including *Robert Menzies' Forgotten People, Australian Liberals and the Moral Middle Class* and Quarterly Essay 42, *Fair Share: Country and City in Australia.*

Carey, Peter

Peter Carey's first novel, *Bliss,* won the Miles Franklin Award and the NSW Premier's Award. Since then he has published twelve novels and won many other awards such as the Man Booker Prize (twice) and the Commonwealth Writers' Prize.

Clark, Manning

Manning Clark published his six-volume *A History of Australia* between 1962 and 1987. He was Australian of the Year in 1981.

Coghill, Peter

Peter Coghill is a physicist based in Sydney. His first published poem was in *Meanjin* and since then he has published poems in many volumes. Peter's first published book, *Rockclimber's Hands* (2010), was commended in the Anne Elder Award.

Croggon, Alison

Alison Croggon is a Melbourne writer. She has published collections of poetry, novels, critical works and several works for theatre. Her most recent collection of poems is *Theatre*, from Salt Publishing.

During, Simon

Simon During has held positions at the University of Melbourne and Johns Hopkins University, and is a research professor at the University of Queensland. His latest work, *Against Democracy: Literary Experience in the Era of Emancipations*, is due out in 2012.

Edgar, Stephen

Stephen Edgar is the subeditor of the literary quarterly *Island* and has published several collections of poetry including, most recently, *Eldershaw* and, in the United States, *The Red Sea: New and Selected Poems.*

CONTRIBUTORS

Farmer, Beverley
Beverley Farmer is a novelist, poet and critic. Her first book, *Alone,* was published in 1980. Several of the stories in the collections *Milk* (1983) and *Home Time* (1985) draw on her experience of living in Greece, as does her novel *The House in the Light* (1995).

Fink, Hannah
Hannah Fink is an author and editor from Sydney, and is writing a book about the Australian artist Rosalie Gascoigne.

Fitzgerald, Robert D.
Robert Fitzgerald's poetry had a modernist influence on Australian literature in the early twentieth century, and was strongly influenced by his experiences as a surveyor in Fiji. He won many awards for his work, including the Grace Leven Prize for Poetry three times.

Garner, Helen
Helen Garner has published novels, short stories, essays and nonfiction books, and has won many awards. Her latest novel is *The Spare Room*.

Giggs, Rebecca
Rebecca Giggs is a Western Australian writer working in fiction and creative non-fiction. Rebecca is most passionate about grass-roots arts collectives.

Gilmore, Mary
Dame Mary Gilmore was a prominent Australian poet and journalist. She long campaigned for better working conditions for women, children's welfare and indigenous Australian rights.

Hampton, Susan
Susan Hampton published her first collection of poems and short stories in 1981. More recent publications include her poetry collections *A Latin Primer, The Kindly Ones* (winner of the ACT Judith Wright award) and *News of the Insect World*.

Hart, Kevin
Kevin Hart teaches at the University of Virginia and the Australian Catholic University. His poetry collections include *Flame*

Tree, Young Rain and, most recently, *Morning Knowledge* (Notre Dame UP).

'Membranes' by Kevin Hart, from *Flame Tree: Selected Poems*, Paperbark Press, Sydney, 2002, p. 147. Reprinted with permission from Golvan Arts Management.

Harwood, Gwen

Gwen Harwood was regarded as one of Australia's finest poets and librettists. Her work won many awards and prizes, including the Grace Leven Prize for Poetry, the Patrick White Award and the Victorian Premier's Literary Award.

Hope, A.D.

Alec Derwent Hope was a professor of literature. He published several collections of poetry and criticism.

Published by arrangement with the Licensor, *The AD Hope Estate*, c/-Curtis Brown (Aust) Pty Ltd.

Hyland, M.J.

M.J. Hyland is a lecturer in Creative Writing at the University of Manchester. She has written three novels, including *Carry Me Down* and *This Is How*.

Keneally, Thomas

Thomas Keneally is an Australian novelist, playwright and author of non-fiction. He is best known for *Schindler's Ark*, the Booker Prize winning novel of 1982.

Kinsella, John

John Kinsella is a Professorial Research Fellow at the University of Western Australia and a Fellow of Churchill College, Cambridge. He has published numerous volumes of poetry, fiction, criticism and plays.

Kirsner, Douglas

Douglas Kirsner holds a Personal Chair in Philosophy and Psychoanalytic Studies at Deakin University. His publications include *The Schizoid*

World of Jean-Paul Sartre and R.D. Laing (2003) and *Unfree Associations: Inside Psychoanalytic Institutes* (2009).

Langenberg, Carolyn van

Carolyn van Langenberg's books reflect her background in Australian and English literature, Asian history and creative writing.

Langford, Martin

Martin Langford has published six books of poetry, most recently *The Human Project* (2009). He is the author of *Microtexts* (2005), a book of poetics, and the editor of *Harbour City Poems: Sydney in Verse 1788–2008* (2009).

McAuley, James

James McAuley was an academic, poet, journalist and literary critic. McAuley co-founded the *Quadrant* in 1956 and was chief editor there until 1963. From 1961 he was professor of English at the University of Tasmania.

Published by arrangement with the Licensor, *The James McAuley Estate*, c/- Curtis Brown (Aust) Pty Ltd.

McGregor, Craig

Craig McGregor has published twenty-three books, including two novels, a collection of short stories, four books of essays and several books on Australian society. A memoir of his life and times, *Left Hand Drive*, is to be published in 2013.

McKimmie, Mal

Mal McKimmie has published two collections of poetry: *Poetileptic* (2005) and *The Brokenness Sonnets I–III* (2011), both with Five Islands Press. He lives in Melbourne.

McPhee, Hilary

Hilary McPhee co-founded McPhee Gribble Publishers. She was a chair of the Australia Council for the Arts. In recent years she lived in the Middle East and Italy. She has since returned to Melbourne and her selection of new Australian writing, *Wordlines*, was published in 2011.

McQueen, Humphrey

Humphrey McQueen is an author, historian and cultural commentator. He has written many books, appears on radio and is regularly asked to speak at public lectures and conferences.

Malouf, David

Writer and poet David Malouf is a winner of the Australia–Asia Literary Award and the International IMPAC Dublin Literary Award, among others. His works include *Remembering Babylon*, *An Imaginary Life* and *The Conversations at Curlow Creek*.

Morrison, John

English-born John Morrison published two novels, four collections of stories, a book of essays, book reviews and journalistic works. He won a number of awards, including the Patrick White Award in 1986.

Murnane, Gerald

Gerald Murnane is the author of eight books of fiction. His novel *Velvet Waters* won the Fellowship of Australian Writers Barbara Ramsden Award. Along with Christopher Koch, he won the 2008 Writers' Emeritus Award from the Australia Council.

Palmer, Vance

Edward Vivian 'Vance' Palmer was a writer, essayist, critic and dramatist. Along with his wife Nettie, he was credited with promoting Australian literature unlike any other of his generation. The Victorian Premier's Literary Award for fiction is named for Palmer.

Perlman, Elliot

An author and a barrister, Elliot Perlman has written the novels *Three Dollars*, *Seven Types of Ambiguity* (shortlisted for the Miles Franklin Award) and *The Street Sweeper*, and a short-story collection, *The Reasons I Won't Be Coming*.

Phillips, Arthur

A.A. (Arthur) Phillips was a writer, critic and teacher. He taught at Wesley College in Melbourne. His essay 'The Cultural Cringe' set early terms for postcolonial theory in Australia and was the focus of his book *The Australian Tradition: Essays in Colonial Culture*.

Porter, Dorothy

Dorothy Porter's first verse novel was the award-winning *The Monkey's Mask* and was followed by others including *Akhenaten*, *Wild Surmise* and *El Dorado*. She published several collections of poetry and wrote lyrics and libretti.

Porter, Peter

Peter Porter wrote more than fifteen collections of poetry. He received a number of awards for his work, including the 1990 Gold Medal of the Australian Literary Society.
Poetry published Copyright ©Peter Porter 1987. Reproduced by permission of the Estate of Peter Porter c/o Rogers, Coleridge & White Ltd., 20 Powis Mews, London, W11 1JN.

Pybus, Cassandra

Cassandra Pybus is a historian and author of eleven books, including *The Devil and James McAuley* and *Epic Journeys of Freedom*, which was shortlisted for the prestigious Frederick Douglass Award in the United States in 2006.

Rhode, Robert

Robert Rhode was published in *Meanjin* in 1962.

Rose, Peter

Peter Rose is editor of *Australian Book Review*. His poetry collections include *The House of Vitriol* (1990) and *Crimson Crop*, his fifth. He has published two novels and his family memoir, *Rose Boys*, won the National Biography Award.

Ryan, Gig

Gig Ryan has published six collections of poetry, including *Pure and Applied*, which won the 1999 Victorian Premier's Prize for Poetry, and *Heroic Money*. She is a poetry critic and is poetry editor for *The Age*.

Shapcott, Thomas

Thomas Shapcott has published many poetry collections and novels, his most recent work being *Parts of Us* in 2010. He was emeritus professor of Creative Writing at the University of Adelaide.

Steele, Peter

Peter Steele was a Jesuit priest and emeritus professor at the University of Melbourne. He wrote seven books of poetry and several books of essays and criticism. His last work was *Braiding the Voices: Essays in Poetry* (2012).

Stivens, Dal

Dal Stivens won the Miles Franklin Award in 1970 for his novel *A Horse of Air*. He helped create Public Lending Rights and won the Patrick White Award in 1981 for his short stories and novels.

Tranter, John

John Tranter worked as an editor and a producer for the Australian Broadcasting Commission. He was one of a generation of poets during the late 1960s whose aim was to introduce modernism into Australian poetics.

Ulman, Abigail

Abigail Ulman is now based in San Francisco. A former Wallace Stegner Fellow at Stanford University, her debut short-story collection, *Hot Little Hands*, is forthcoming from Penguin Books.

Walker, Clinton

Clinton Walker is best known for his works on popular music. He published his first book, *Inner City Sound*, in 1981. He worked as a freelance journalist for newspapers and magazines, including *Rock Australia Magazine* and Australian *Rolling Stone*.

Wallace-Crabbe, Chris

Chris Wallace-Crabbe's first book of poetry, *No Glass Houses*, appeared in 1955. He went on to publish many volumes and won a number of prizes, including the Grace Leven Poetry Prize in 1985 for *The Amorous Cannibal*.

Webb, Francis

After being diagnosed with schizophrenia in the late 1950s, Francis Webb spent most of his life in and out of psychiatric hospitals. He wrote and published a good deal of poetry against these odds, and is widely regarded as one of Australia's most prodigious poets.

White, Patrick

After serving in the Second World War, Patrick White settled in Australia and wrote twelve novels, collections of short stories, plays and a self-portrait. He won the Nobel Prize for Literature in 1973.

Wright, Alexis

Alexis Wright is a member of the Waanyi Nation of the southern highlands of the Gulf of Carpentaria. Her writings include the novels *Plains of Promise*, *Carpentaria*, *The Swan Book*, and her non-fiction book *Grog War*.

Wright, Judith

Judith Wright came to prominence with the publication of her poetry collections *The Moving Image* in 1946 and *Woman to Man* in 1949. Her life in Queensland engendered a strong political edge to her later writings on conservation, the value of Australian wildlife and Aboriginal rights.

Judith Wright: 'Dust' from *A Human Pattern; Selected Poems* (ETT Imprint, Sydney 2010).